The Dead Horseman

by Freida Kilmari

Content Guidance

Violence

This book contains scenes of graphic violence and deals with this both emotionally and physically.

Profanity

This book contains excess profanity from all characters.

Sexual Situations

This book contains explicit sex, including MM, FF, and MMF scenarios. Kink List: DP, mild bondage, mild s/D, and vampirism.

Dark Themes

This book deals with war, anxiety, loss, and gender identity issues. This book also contains a death scene.

MIND THE MOTHER OF ALL CLIFFHANGERS!

For those who know who they are but are still processing. You're beautiful at every stage of life.

Chapter One

New Orleans Still Locked Down

My brother? I have a brother. Had? Is it still a relation if you're technically the walking dead? Shaking my head, I take a few steps backward, away from the boy across the room, from the lying douche canoe of a godfather, Nigel, and from the team.

I have a brother. A twin brother.

An actual relation.

I'm not alone.

"Now, Taylor," Nigel begins. "Don't be mad—"

"Magic," I whisper without lifting my gaze from the floor. "My name is Magic."

But if he's my brother, then why didn't he come find me when we announced ourselves to the world? We must not have been close then. Just another person who abandoned me.

The team have all shut their complaints up for now, all

staring at me with those same pitying eyes; everyone, that is, except Arrie, who just stands with his arms crossed over his chest with not a care in the world. As usual.

Will he ever care?

He does care. That's the point.

I ignore Nine's cryptic nonsense with a headshake and walk up to Nigel. "How?"

The boy, Aki—my brother—has grown silent in the face of all these revelations, but his look of bewilderment whenever he faces me says it all.

"You didn't know, did you?" I ask him.

He shakes his head. He opens his mouth to speak, but nothing comes out, so he closes it again.

I turn back toward Nigel and repeat my earlier question. "How?" My fists clench, my control slipping, and I quickly change into my male form lest I burn my library to the ground. And I guess I don't really want to hurt anyone. Well, many of them anyway. Nigel might be the exception right now.

He shakes his head and sighs. "It's a bit . . . complicated."

Aki stands beside me and says, "Then explain it," through clenched teeth.

Nigel looks from me to Aki, then back at me, and then back at Aki, until he sighs and runs a hand through his hair. "This is insane." He shakes his head. "Seeing you two together is . . . Wow."

"Here," Nine says, "take a seat." He asks the house for a chair beneath Nigel.

Nigel plonks himself down with a look of bewilderment and utter exhaustion.

He did just help me break into a Supernatural Council HQ building. Maybe I should cut him some slack? That's the reasonable thing to do, right? "We can chat about this tomorrow, if you'd like?" See, I can make adult decisions.

Nigel goes to nod, but Aki cuts him off. "No fucking way. This asshole is gonna explain how I have a twin sister when I didn't even know my own parents because they abandoned me when I was born." His face slackens. "They kept her? But gave me away?" Grief chokes him. "Why?"

I place a hand on his shoulder, trying to comfort my . . . brother. Jesus. That's ridiculous.

"Because two Angel-descended Witches growing up with little-to-no control over their death magic in the same place would have put an even larger target on your heads." Nigel shakes his head. "There was no rhyme or reason why it was you, Aki. It just was."

"But," I interrupt, "I thought it took time for the Angel-descended powers to manifest into death magic? How did they know?"

Nigel looks to Aki with pity, his usually cheerful eyes turning solemn. "Because Aki killed the delivery nurse upon arrival. His powers manifested the second he was born." He looks at me. "You took the usual number of years."

I look to Aki, surprise etched onto my face, no doubt. He's strong. Really strong.

"I see," Aki whispers. "So, what happened then?"

Nigel looks to Aki and says, "They placed you with me, until I found you a suitable home in Japan, where you grew up with Witches who knew of your powers and could help train you." He looks at me. "And they left you in the care of your parents."

"Who died when I was six," I finish. "Then you placed me with Witches in the US." My eyes widen. "That's why, isn't it? Because the Witch Coven in Japan was already looking after Aki. And there are so few Witches in the world."

Nigel nods. "The next best place was with the Witches near me."

I spin to face Aki. So this guy, who nearly arrested me and took me to the enemy, is my twin brother? And then he hijacked my teleporting crystal—which I didn't even know was possible—and stumbled upon an unknown-to-most realm? I turn to Nine in befuddlement. "Well now what the fuck do I do?"

Nine rests two hands on my shoulders, looks me in the eyes, and says, "I have no idea." He smirks. "But this was your plan, so you deal with the fallout, Sweetie." He gives me an I-told-you-so smile and winks.

"Seriously?" I ask. "Fucking seriously?"

"Well, Angel," Dea starts, and I sigh, "you did sneak into a secure building, steal all their data, nearly get Nigel in a lot of trouble, and then had a fight in a server room with your twin brother." He shrugs. "This is very much your mess."

"What were you even thinking?" Arrie grumbles.

I swear, I'm gonna throw a fireball at that stupid asshole's face one of these days. He's such a fucking deku. "Well"—I turn to him with a big stupid grin on my face—"I was thinking that if I know what the SC are planning to do next, I can intercept or reduce the damage to the supernatural communities at risk."

"So you're taking a side?" Aki asks.

I spin to face him. "What?"

"By standing against the SC, you're taking a side." He shrugs, as though that's obvious.

"Well . . ." It is, isn't it? "How am I supposed to protect humans and supernaturals if I can't actually protect them?" I groan. "And maybe the SC needs to be taken down a peg or two? They are kind of a bunch of controlling a-holes."

Connie shrugs. "They're just trying to protect their people."

I spin to face her—I'm getting dizzy with all this spinning—in shock. "By threatening the lives of other species? Are you fucking serious?"

She walks up to me and wraps me in a hug. "I know." She breathes me in as I wrap my arms around her waist. "But they believe supernaturals are a threat to humankind. They're trying to separate them so that humans can go back to normal."

"But supernaturals were always around." I gesture around us. "This is normal. Now everyone can see it."

"Angel is correct," Dea says, looking at me. "This is how it has always been."

I ponder for a moment, hand scratching my chin in thought. "Maybe we just need to reduce the risk to humans and get them to see the benefits of supernaturals . . ."

There is so much going on right now that I have to think to myself for a moment about my top priorities. I look to my brother, who is still in a realm he doesn't understand talking about shit he knows nothing about. "Right, Aki."

He snaps his face toward me.

"You're staying in a guest room until I know what to do with you."

"What?" he squeaks. "What do you mean 'do with me'?"

"Hey," I say, poking him in the chest, "you're the one who hijacked my teleporting crystal and came here without permission. I don't know what to do about that right now." I ask the house for a room besides Nigel's and am greeted by a quiet grumble. "Nigel, please take Aki to the room next to yours."

Nigel nods while Aki protests, but Nigel grabs him by the

upper arm and steers him out of my library, saying, "You're the damn idiot who came here illegally. Be thankful you still have your head attached to your damn body, kid."

A sigh escapes my lips. "Fuck me." That was exhausting. "I need a list, or maybe a mega board."

Connie snickers. "What for?"

"All the fucking issues I have to solve."

She places a gentle hand on my chest. "We have to solve."

"Right." I smile. "We."

Chapter Two

THE SC CUT OFF NEW ORLEANS BLOOD SUPPLY FOR TRAPPED
VAMPIRES

The next morning, I wake up with Dea and Nine snuggling into me and Connie hovering above me, where she stands on my bed, handing me a piece of paper.

"The list you asked for." She climbs off the bed and walks back into my library.

Are they all gonna hang out here forever now?

Not if you don't want us to.

Eh, it's fine. I'm just feeling a bit overworked and crowded. I wince.

Sorry.

You're allowed to need alone time, Sweetie. He places a sweet kiss on my temple and gets out of bed.

"Where is mine?" Dea asks, a lazy morning smirk on his face aimed at Nine.

Nine blushes and crawls over me to get to Dea, who grabs both sides of his face and plunges his tongue past his lips, drinking him in as though he's the last drop of water left.

I'm just enjoying the show.

Perv.

Dea runs his hands under Nine's sleep tee and sticks out a bare wrist for me. And I dig in for breakfast, just slightly weirded out that this has become my normal. The piece of paper in my hand crumples as Dea moans into Nine's kiss.

Fuck. Bro, you're hard as steel, Nine sends to us both.

I take one last pull, and Dea grinds into Nine, who's straddling his waist with lust filling his gaze, before I pull away with a smile. "Thank you."

Dea snaps his gaze to me, heat filling those now-golden irises. "You are most welcome." Nine tries to get off, but Dea's firm hand on his waist keeps him in place. A beautiful hand wanders down Nine's waist to his underwear, and my breath hitches.

A good morning threesome sounds like a great way to wake up.

Nine groans. I knew you'd be hot as fuck after we snapped that restrictive band you placed around yourself.

Dea chuckles. "If that is what you want, Angel."

He's offering me two dicks on a silver platter and asking if I want that? Who the fuck doesn't want that? I couldn't be happier about the direction my relationship has gone in.

But the bedroom door slams open as Arrie grumbles his way in, takes one look at us, and storms into the library.

Right. Everything isn't quite perfect yet.

"It will be," Nine says. "I promise." He kisses my forehead and gets out of bed, the lust spell broken.

I straighten the piece of paper and read Connie's list:

- App advertisement
- Nigel and Aki
- New Orleans
- Rogue Vampire faction
- Fae Queen
- Blood supply
- Embassy creation
- SC data

"Wow. That's a lot."

Nine snatches the paper out of my hands and glances over it. "Divide and conquer, Sweetie."

Dea reads over Nine's shoulder and agrees, his eyes lancing mine, saying we'll definitely be coming back to that threesome conversation later. "Well, let us make some plans over breakfast."

I bring my clenched fist up to the white door and hold my breath. Terrified.

Knock, knock, knock

A soft shuffle on the other side of the door sounds, and then the click of the lock, before a Japanese man who looks similar to my reflection stands before me. Bewilderment on his face, surprise in his eyes. "Please don't arrest me. Or kill me."

"I . . ." Wait a minute. "You think I'm here to kill you?"

His brows shoot to his hairline as he gasps. "You're not?"

I shake my head. "Jesus Christ, no. What kind of monster do you think I am?"

He shrugs, clearly not wanting to answer the question. "Well, I saw the viral video, so . . ."

Ugh. Of course he has.

Couldn't I have gotten a long-lost twin brother who is

anti-social media?

But alas, my karma meter is still running on empty.

"I'm not going to kill you. Or have you arrested. I'm actually here to offer you breakfast. And maybe a chat?"

"Oh." He freezes for a moment, not sure what to do with himself, before he opens the door all the way and gestures me inside. "Then come in, I guess."

I walk into the room with some trepidation. "Wow. A twin brother." My head spins as the realization hits me like a freight train. "This is insane."

He gestures to a round armchair that swivels. "Maybe you should sit down. You kinda look like you're gonna pass out."

"I feel like it."

"It's been a rough couple of days." His hand rubs the back of his back. "So I know how you feel." Aki sits next to me, perching on the edge of the large armchair. "I . . . I'm sorry I hijacked your teleporting crystal. I-I-I didn't know."

I smile. His face is so cute when it's flushed. "It's okay. I mean, it's not, but since you're my brother, I guess you get family privileges."

"Family privileges, huh?" His worry turns to a smile. "Does that also mean I get to use this magical house?" He looks around, awe-stricken. "Because it's sooo cool."

"She is pretty cool. And yes, feel free to ask her for whatever you like."

"Really?"

"Yeah. Really." I ask the house for a cupcake and a glass of water, then settle in to devour both. "These are great cupcakes."

After a moment of us eating cupcakes together, I swallow my last mouthful and sigh. "So, I guess my question is: what now?" He doesn't answer, so I make an offer. "If you wanna stay here, you can. If you wanna grab a place nearby, I can help. If you wanna walk away and pretend this isn't a thing, return to your normal life, you can do that too. I'm happy to support any decision you make." My voice trails off, fear seeping through the cracks. "But I'd love for you to stay."

I don't have much family. And yeah, I was pissed yesterday, but today I realize he was doing his job. "Though, only if you don't report me." I jab a finger at him. "I was doing something important yesterday. Illegal, but important."

"Yeah, I was thinking about that. And I get it."

"You do?" Wow. That was easy. I thought I was going to have to use facts and figures and seven-point slides to persuade him. "Really?"

"I've been researching more about you and the Horsemen last night, and what the SC have done to New Orleans. I guess before, I just didn't really think about it, you know. I was just following orders. But I get it. You're trying to help." He grabs my hand and smiles. "I'm your brother. It's my job to keep you safe."

"That might be a tall order. We're at war. I'm gonna be fighting armies sooner or later."

"Then I'll be there to cheer you on. Or bandage your wounds. Or whatever it is a brother does for an immortal sister at war."

We all sit around the breakfast table an hour later, including Nigel and Aki, and discuss how we're going to conquer all the items on Connie's list.

"We should divide things by priority," Nine says. "That way we can focus more energy on important things and less energy on things that can wait."

Dea chimes in with, "Right. And I think the embassies

should be in the top three, since that will help us tick off other things as we will ask for assistance."

"And you," Connie says with a smile, "will have more troops to order around."

"Therefore," Nine says, "making you less stressed."

I'm uncomfortable talking about our plans in front of Aki. I want to trust him, but I don't really know him all that well. Most of my adult memories have come back by this point, and my nightmares ended weeks ago, but I still don't have most of my childhood memories, other than flashes, and I don't want to trust anyone in vain.

What if he betrays us?

"Well, the blood supply, the embassies, and New Orleans should be our key priorities, right?" I ask the team. "That way we're helping as many people as possible. I'd include the app stuff in that, but it's all working itself out."

Connie nods over a bite of egg. "I'm hiring a manager for that, so they can deal with all the advertisement, running, and managing of it all." She looks at me. "That okay?"

"Absolutely. But we still own it, right?"

"Of course."

"Good." I don't want someone else owning something so important when I don't even know who is on our side.

I look at Aki and sigh. What do I do about him?

"Err," Aki says, "I'm thinking about finding a place in town. Sticking around a little?" He scratches the back of his neck while avoiding my eyes.

He phrased it like a question, but is he actually asking permission?

I look to Dea, who shrugs and nods.

"Sure," I say. "That would be . . . nice."

He looks at me with shy, hopeful eyes. "Maybe I could

help you out?"

"Yeah," I mumble. "Maybe."

"C'mon," Nine says to Aki, "I'll take you to the housing office to see what's available. Or I can take you to a few hotels?"

Aki smiles and nods. "Thank you." He bows his head. "That would be wonderful."

Nine offers him a hand up and guides him toward the front door with a smile, his arm around his shoulder.

When did they get all buddy-buddy?

"Hon?"

"Huh?" I spin back toward Connie. "Sorry, what?"

"I asked, what did you want us to do?" She gestures to herself, Arrie, and Dea. "And," she leans in and whispers, "don't worry, he's crazy about you."

I shake off the paranoia. "Right." I look at Dea while I attempt a smile. "Can you please handle the embassy? If possible, I'd love everything set up in a couple of weeks. Possible?"

"Absolutely, Angel."

He gets up to leave, but I jump to my feet and spin him around at the last minute and yank him into my arms. "I love you," I whisper up at him.

He smiles down at me and tucks my hair behind my ear. "I love you, too." Dea then leans down and places a light kiss to my lips, but nips my lower lip hard before pulling away. "Do not overwork yourself today."

"Yes, sir."

He shakes his head and turns to leave.

Turning back to Connie, Nigel, and Arrie, I blush a little before shaking it out. No need to be embarrassed in front my girlfriend and . . . Arrie. But looking around, I notice Arrie isn't there anymore. Where'd he go?

Sighing, Connie gets up and wraps me in a hug. "Just ignore him." She smiles and asks, "What about me?"

Right. "I need you to hire someone for the app, see the advertisement through, and make sure everything goes perfectly." I peck her on the cheek and smile. "You are the team's official manager."

Her face lights up. "Really?"

I nod. "Yup. You're great at it, Connie."

She blushes. "But that's a . . . normal job." She can't stop smiling, and it's adorable.

"It is. Is that okay?"

She picks me up by the waist and circles me around the room. "It's more than okay. It's . . . awesome!" She squeals in my ear. "I have to go!" She runs out of the kitchen with a spare piece of toast hanging out of her mouth. "Got shit to do."

"See you later," I say as she sprints up the stairs.

Nigel sits at the kitchen table still, having stayed silent throughout the entire breakfast ordeal, but he gets out of his chair and looks at me. "So," he starts, "you and the Horsemen?" He gives me that fatherly 'is everything okay with your boyfriend?' look.

I groan. "I'm . . . happy." I look to the back door, where I assume Arrie went. "Nearly."

Nigel sighs. "Well, it's not exactly what I had planned for you, but if you're happy . . . then . . ." He wraps me in a hug. "Who am I to argue?"

"You'd have to fight me, old man."

"Old man?" He laughs. "I'm not old."

I shrug. "Not yet."

He laughs, and I release a breath. I'm still mad. He should

have told me about Aki. But he was only trying his best. We're all only human. Well, most of us anyway.

"Wanna help?" I ask as I raise the flash drive that holds all the gathered data from the SC into the light.

He flinches. "Are you sure the rest of the team will be okay with that?"

I shrug. "The damage has already been done, right? What harm will looking do?"

"Okay. If you're sure?"

"Nothing to lose." I hope.

Chapter Three

MEET THE FIVE HORSEMEN: A FIVE-PART EXPOSÉ

Nine is out with Aki, Dea is dealing with the embassy and the Sheruta Council, Connie is off dealing with press stuff and the app, and Arrie is somewhere being his moody self; all the while, Nigel and I are sitting behind my desk, about to plug in the flash drive.

It's time to see what the SC is planning.

"I really hope we gain something useful from this." I sigh. "It'll suck if this was for nothing."

"Yup." Nigel put a hand on my shoulder. "There'll be something we can use. I'm sure of it."

Taking a deep breath, I open the folder and take a quick browse through.

There's a lot on here. And I mean a lot. Hundreds, possibly thousands, of files. Some are labeled—things like financial, taxation, and importation and exportation records—but other things are numbered, lettered, or use some other nonsense system.

"Ugh," I groan, "it'll take ages to trawl through all this."

"Maybe search for keywords, like blood, Vampires, Fae, pixie dust, or something?"

"Not a terrible suggestion, old man." I smirk while trying to find something—anything—on the Vampire blood supply and New Orleans lockdown.

A file pops up labeled AREA 50 PLANS.

Well, that sounds ominous, at best.

Opening up various maps, plans, and details, Nigel and I gasp in unison.

"Is that . . .?" he asks.

"I think so . . ." I hiccup as I scroll through. "But that's so . . ."

"Evil?"

"Yeah."

He sulks back into his chair and rakes a hand through his hair and slams a fist on the desk. "That's it."

"Huh?"

"I can't do it anymore." He looks haggard, his eyes worn out from years of hardship. "Taylor . . . I mean, Magic, they're planning on locking down every Vampire city in the world! I can't stand by and silently work for a company who does that shit!"

I watch with sympathy as he struggles with the idea of his employer being so evil. "Move here." I look to him with a serious expression. "If you'd like, you can move here to Sheruta." I shrug. "You don't have to, but it would be nice to have you around, I guess."

He looks to me with a smile, curious. "Any werepanther packs around?"

"The were packs here in Sheruta are mixed, and then they have their own individual families. But it shouldn't be too hard to find a nice place in the pack."

He sighs. "I guess I'll hand in my resignation then."

Wait. Do we need him? Like, if he were a part of the SC, does that help us in any way? No. I can't ask that of him. He's risked too much already. It wouldn't be fair.

"What is it?" he looks at me and asks.

"Well . . ." I sigh. "I was just thinking that if you leave the SC, we can't use that connection anymore. But it's okay. I don't want you to have to do something you're uncomfortable with."

He looks to me from his seat. "What kind of things?"

I shrug. "No clue. But we wouldn't have that for the future, just in case." I place a hand on his shoulder. "But it's okay, Nigel. Honestly."

He nods, and I turn back to the screen, scrolling through the paperwork, maps, and more that detail the plan. I need to put a stop to this. It's not okay to single out an entire species like this. And, if anything, the Fae are the most trouble to humans, so why pick on the Vampires? It doesn't make sense.

"I'm going for a walk," Nigel mutters.

I watch him leave with a heavy heart, genuine concern flooding my face for a moment, before I continue reading the files. I'll need help. There are five cities in the world, after New Orleans, that are the biggest Vampire hotspots, and they're all home to feeding clubs, light-protected housing for turned Vampires, and are a general safe space for them to be. It isn't fair to take that away from them.

There's only one person who can help strategize a solution to something this complicated, and it's the one person I don't want to deal with. Arrie.

CHAPTER FOUR

THE SC: GOVERNORS OR DICTATORS?

I find Arrie outside in the horse paddock, giving their unused steeds a bit of attention. I wonder why I don't have one? Eh. I guess I don't really need one. Arrie's is the biggest, with black coat, a long flowing mane, and strong legs; but the others are also huge, much bigger than regular horses, with Dea's being spindly and a weird translucent white color.

I don't really want to disturb his peace, given that he's actually not frowning right now, with his hair tied back and his jaw relaxed, not a frown line in sight, but I don't have a choice. I need him. The world needs him. And I know how pissed I'd be if someone waited, like Dea did with the New Orleans thing, to tell me I was needed.

Clearing my throat, I yell, "Arrie!"

He looks over his shoulder and sighs, a frown now marring his beautiful face.

"Please," I say, hearing the whimper in my voice and wincing. Goddess, I sound so pathetic. "I need your help."

"What do you need me for?" he grumbles. He's still stroking the horses, one hand on Dea's and his own. "You have three slaves all ready."

I wince. Again. "Well, I need your strategy ability."

"Sure you do."

"Arrie!" My anger slips through, and I snap. "I don't have time for your sulking. The Vampires need your help. The Supernatural Council are planning their first big move: they're going to shut down the five major Vampire cities."

Arrie spins around with a concerned look on his face, his ice blue eyes piercing mine, trying to see if I'm being serious. "Really?" He walks closer, his voice now easier to hear. "You're being serious?"

"Would I fucking be here talking to you if I wasn't?"

He smiles at me for the first time in days, and my heart feels like it's about to burst. That smile . . . It's beautiful. Full of wonder and magic and hope. Like I can breathe again just at the sight of his lips curling and his laughter bubbling. Maybe I can save whatever we have?

"Fine," he grumbles. "I'll help."

"Thank you." Relief washes over me. "C'mon, I need you to help me with this now."

He nods and follows me back to the study, where I print a physical copy of the main map out and lay it on the desk.

"This"—I point to the five marked areas—"is where they'll shut the cities down: New York City, Delhi, Shang Hai, Cairo, and Dhaka."

"That's a lot of ground," Arrie grumbles. "Across large expanses of Earth." He rakes a hand through his hair. "This won't be easy."

"I know." I place a comforting hand on his arm and smile. "But we have Earth-Earth teleporting crystals now, so that'll make the travel easier, right?"

He looks relieved by that fact. "Right. If you make enough of them, we can just hop back and forth between each other."

I look at him questioningly.

"Oh, the best way to deal with this is to divide and conquer, like Nine said this morning. Each take a different city and defend it."

That's a good plan. "But we'd be alone . . ."

"Not if Dea can get the embassy up and running in time."

"Then we'll have help from at least two pillar communities!" Maybe more . . . "But there are other species," I mumble to myself.

"Huh?"

"Nothing." I spin around and head into the middle of the library to do some deep research. "Just come up with the best strategy for me, okay?"

"But what if it's not enough?" I hear him whisper to himself.

Pretty sure I wasn't supposed to hear that.

I turn back around to face him with a smile. "I believe in your powers, Arrie. Even if you don't."

He nods and takes a deep breath before delving into the files open on my computer.

Meanwhile, I head into the section of my library that holds the books on magical species. See, there are lots of different species in the world—not just the main four and humans—so what if I asked for help from them, too? They might be small, but together, they could be powerful.

Really powerful.

But I know little about them. I know Fae farm dust from

pixies, so maybe we can help there. And I know fairies are in danger from deforestation and losing green spaces and gardens. And Nine mentioned something about a few Demon species still existing? Argh! I need a lesser supernatural expert.

Well, Nine answers, all you had to do was ask. He turns the corner from where I'm sat and smiles.

"Did you find somewhere for Aki to stay?" I inquire, trying not to seem too interested. "You know, that he likes?"

Nine chuckles. "Yes. He's renting a small apartment near to here. He'll be close by when you're ready." Nine settles on the floor next to me and rests his head on my shoulder.

"There's so much to do."

"There's five of us." He entwines his fingers through mine, and I smile.

"You're right." I am not doing this alone. I have an entire team to help.

You have an entire family to help you. "Now how about we start crossing things off that list?"

Chapter Five

Twelve Porcupine Shifters Turn Up Dead in San Francisco

By the time I'm done chatting with Nine, Arrie comes to join us with a smile on his face. "I did it," he says. "I know the best strategy in each city and who to use for each one's defense based on the information I found on the flash drive."

"Good job."

But at the sight of my proud smile, he frowns and huffs to the floor.

Seriously? Can I do nothing right anymore?

Sighing, I growl. "Just write it all up for me."

He rolls his eyes at me but nods.

At least he can follow instructions, which is an improvement from earlier.

"Then we're going to take back New Orleans for the Vampire Royal Council."

Nine and Arrie swivel their heads my way with equal shocked expression on their faces.

"Seriously?" Nine asks. "That's your plan?"

"Yes." They still look shocked, so I flop to the floor on my back and explain. "The Vampires need their hometown. New Orleans is their capital. It would be like France without Paris."

Connie runs down the library out of nowhere and spins toward me. "I've had the best day!"

"Yeah?" I grab her arms to steady her. "Wanna tell me all about it?"

"Hell yeah I do." She turns to Nine and Arrie and smiles. "She made me Team Manager. And in doing so"—she spins back around to me—"I am going to help you plan all of this workload and suggest who you should use for what tasks. Helpful?"

"Fuck yes." I sigh in relief. It's all so daunting to me. Like a pile of rocks I have to somehow turn into a mountain but with no plans, no knowledge of how, and no skills to do so with. "That sounds great."

"Good. Because the first thing on my list is to stop us training you."

Wait. "Huh? But—"

She holds a finger to interrupt my interrupting. "I know. But you need us elsewhere. And we can't do our jobs if we're too busy training you. So I'm going to look for other people to help. Maybe a Fae magic expert to help you delve into your spellwork better. And there's bound to be a bo staff fighter around somewhere, right?" Her thoughts trail off for a moment before she shakes her head and comes back to us. "So for now, the only training you'll have is with me and Arrie in the mornings for combat."

I internally grown. Of fucking course the only bit to stay is the bit with the grouchy asshole who'd rather punch me than train me.

"Dea is handling the embassies with the Sheruta Council, so all of that will have to wait until he's done. We're guaranteed the Shifters and Vampires, which just leaves the Witches and Fae."

Connie's hand rests in her hair, and I can't help but stare in wonder at her for a moment while she goes to work. She's amazing when she's being herself.

"And the lesser species," Nine chimes in.

"Huh?" Arrie and Connie ask at the same time.

Nine fills them in on my plan to get as many species involved as possible, and Connie breathes a sigh of audible relief at the plan.

"That helps."

"It does?" I ask.

"Well, yeah," she replies, as though it's the most obvious thing in the world. But at my confused expression, she explains, "Because now it won't be two against two. It'll be hundreds against two."

"And who knows where the humans will side," Nine says. "Not all of them are going to blindly follow the SC. They're not known for their unity."

I listen to them chat about the state of the world for a bit while I mentally check out. It's been a tiring day, and it isn't even lunch yet. This leadership thing is harder than I thought it would be.

All we need now is the date of the SC's Area 50 Plans. The plans make it look like it'll all be simultaneous, so as to dissuade the Vampires from rallying against them, but the actual date is a mystery.

Dea's still out dealing with the embassy by the time my training session with Connie comes around, but the rest of us have had a successful afternoon: Nine and I researched as many lower supes as possible, Connie handled the app advertising and hired a management company, Arrie continued with plans for stopping Area 50, while Nigel continued looking through the data we got from the SC.

All in all, it's looking successful.

"So," I ask Connie for a second time, "everything with the app management is handled?"

"Yup." She dodges my fire attack and rolls back. "And the interviews and press releases from our PR stunt went okay, too." She shoots an arrow at me from across the room. "You can search it all up if you like."

Right. The PR guy. "The guy from the SC?" I stop fighting for a moment and take a deep breath. "That went well?" I guess I just thought the SC would do anything to smudge our name. "Really?"

"I know," she breathes. "I'm shocked too." She lunges at me from across the room and tries swinging her sword toward my face. "But we do have one or two more things to be released."

"I don't understand." I pin her to the floor with a foot swipe that knocks her off balance. "If they don't like us, then why are they helping us?"

Connie shrugs from her place on the floor before grabbing a fistful of my sports bra and yanking me on top of her. "No clue." Her lips part as her eyes gaze at me with a familiar glint to them. "But your official manager is ordering you to stop worrying and kiss me."

"I could get used to these orders." I lean down to drag my

lips against hers in a teasing whisper of a kiss.

She groans in impatience beneath me while trying to yank me closer.

But I just laugh under my breath and kiss her again—hard. Without holding back, I press my body against hers and tangle our lips together in a growing need I find myself struggling to satiate with a single kiss.

Just as I'm undoing the first button on Connie's gym shirt, the door opens and someone coughs to announce themselves. "Maybe, Angel, you should take that upstairs?"

"Pfft." Connie raises her head from the floor. "As if you'd have a problem walking in on us . . ."

"I would not, no, but others might. And I might remind you we have a guest."

Nigel, right.

Sighing, I stand up and move to help Connie to her feet. "Dea's right."

"Guess so." She leans in and kisses me gently, leaving a trail of fire everywhere she touches. "But we will return to this." With a wink, she exits the gym and leaves me alone with Dea.

"Soooo . . ." Dea smirks. "You and Con have been getting pretty serious recently?"

"Yeah." I cough. "Ummm . . . We, you know, have made things more official."

Dea smiles down at me. "I am happy for you, Angel." He places a gentle kiss to my forehead. "And very proud of how far you have come."

"I feel like there's a but coming."

"But—"

"Why is there always a but?"

He places a finger to my lips, silencing me, and whispers,

"Remember what we talked about in Tokyo?"

I look at him in confusion, my brows furrowing.

"I suggested you spend more time in your male form so that you can get used to it." He wraps me in his arms as I freeze, not wanting to have this conversation. "I know you are scared, I know you have been staying in your female form to avoid the issue, and I know you do not want to talk about it, but both forms are an important part of who you are." He pulls back and holds me at arm's length. "Even if you decide that your female form is your go-to, that you identify as a woman, you should not feel uncomfortable using your male form." He brushes a hair from my face. "You are going to need it, after all."

The scary thing is, I don't think of my male form as strange, weird, or not a part of me. It's become an important part of who I am, like the second side of myself I never knew I needed. And that terrifies me. I know it's weird. I know it doesn't fit in. And I know by now that I should be used to feeling like a freak, but I'm not. And I don't think I ever will be.

CHAPTER SIX

PROTESTS OUTSIDE SC HQ BUILDINGS ALL AROUND THE
WORLD TODAY AS ALL SPECIES CALL FOR VAMPIRE AID

I spend the following day mostly alone with my thoughts; I do
my best thinking alone, so I ask everyone to leave me be while
I mull things over. Because sometimes, the best plans come
from isolated thinking. And this plan is definitely a winner.

But I'll need a big brainiac to pull it off.

Luckily, I know just the guy.

"Nine?" I yell in the middle of my library. I swear he's
around here somewhere.

Yeah?

I could use some of your sexy brains over here, if you're
free?

I'm always free for you.

Then get your ass over to the comfy teal-blue couch by
the window in the northwest corner of my library.

After a few minutes, Nine rounds the corner with a big smile and wraps himself up in my arms and between my legs for a giant cuddle. "What kind of fancy thinking you been doing, then, Sweetie?"

"Well, I was just thinking that fixing the blood supply problem would go a long way right now."

"It would."

I hand Nine a mini chocolate cupcake I asked the house for earlier and watch him eat with glee.

"So, would it be possible to create a synthetic type of blood that could sustain a Vampire, even temporarily?" I sigh, knowing how stupid my thoughts are. "It's just, if we could take the pressure off the blood supply, make sure the cities are protected, and win back New Orleans, then the Vampires should be able to live happily without the SC controlling the blood supply."

"It's a lovely thought, but I've tried a few times over the centuries to create synthetic blood that could sustain a Vampire, but with no good results."

Poo. That sucks.

Nine shoots up and jumps to his feet. "Wait . . . what did you say?"

"Say what when?"

"Earlier . . ." He runs a hand through his hair as his eyes glaze over and that perky smile crosses his face. "You said it didn't have to sustain them permanently, just enough to remove some of the pressure off the blood supplies."

"Well, yeah, permanently would be great, but it's not realistic, and the primary goal is to get the Vampires of New Orleans up and running again."

"Right, right, right." He paces in front of the couch, mumbling words I barely understand to form sentences I can't follow. "So if I were to reduce the number of white blood cells and remove that problem from the equation, then I might be able to solve Armen's Gap."

"Armen's Gap?"

Nine turns to me with a smile and says, "The problem with creating a blood supply for Vampires is that creating so many moving components to a living cell is difficult. One of the more difficult parts to make is the white blood cell. It's tricky, and its function is vital. I can't just miss it." He flicks his eyes to mine with a grin wider than the ocean. "But what if I could?"

"If you're not creating a type of blood as a permanent form of sustenance, then it's okay if something is lacking."

"Yes!" Nine yells and drags me into a tight hug. "Because they'll still be getting that from the other part of their diet." He puts me on the floor and runs away, off to some lab somewhere, I assume. Just before he leaves my line of sight, he says, Thank you. I love you.

I love you too.

I don't think I'll ever get used to saying I love you.

One day, it'll be the first and last thing you say every day.

After a quick search of the house at Vampire speed, I find Connie and Dea doing lengths in the pool.

"Hey guys!" I run over to the edge. "Mind if I join you?"

Connie swims up to me and says, "Not in that form." She leans up and kisses my cheek. "You'd out-swim us in a heartbeat."

Right. Fair enough.

Dea gives me a look of concerned warmth, but I shake my head. It's okay. He's right. I need to start being more me. No more being afraid of the world's judgement. No more stupid freak outs over the littlest things. And no more fear of being myself. So, with an instance of magic, I change forms, and then I put some swim shorts on.

Doing lengths in my male form is hard. Like, seriously hard. Shifters are supposed to be naturally fit, but it's like swimming up a mountain against an ocean current. And Connie is making the effort look easy, as usual, but even Dea is having an easier time of it than me.

Connie swims up behind me as I gasp for breath at the edge of the pool. "We need to get this form fitter." She wraps her hands around my waist and curls around my back, her hot skin pressing against the warmth of the water. "You rely too much on your female form."

"Is everyone going to have an opinion about that? Am I seriously going to have to listen to that four times over?"

"Who . . .?" She looks over to Dea with her famous stink eye, and he shrivels. "Stop making Magic feel bad." She whispers in my ear, "I can cheer you up, hon, if you like?" She edges her hands to the rim of my shorts, her nails teasing along the sensitive skin there.

I tense, not really sure what to do or how I feel.

"It's okay," she whispers. "We don't have to do anything you're uncomfortable with."

She spins to swim away, but I grab her hand last minute and twirl her back to me. Her lips are so soft beneath mine, I take a moment to simply breathe her in and watch her shudder beneath my touch as I skim a hand beneath the material of her bikini top. When we part, momentarily breathless, I whisper, "I just need some time to get used to this form." I grab both her hands in mine and trace kisses across her knuckles. "Go slow with me?"

She nods, her gaze more than a little hazy. But she eventually snaps out of it and swims away with a small smile on her face.

"We are all more than a little taken with you, Angel," Dea says from behind me, making me jump.

"Christ, Dea!" My hand jumps to my chest and rubs soothing circles over my frantically beating heart. "You scared the shit outta me."

He chuckles and places a warming hand on my shoulder. "Sorry. It was not intended."

Spinning around to face him, I hover in place as I take in the glowing galaxies that are his eyes. "So beautiful," I whisper. I shake my head when I realize I said that out loud. "Err . . . Your e-eyes, I mean."

Those golden irises glow brighter as he laughs at my fumbling. "Oh, Angel, you are a delight."

"Aaaaaand now your head won't fit through the door."

"Anything you want to do now?"

"I'd like to know how the embassies are doing, but Connie forbids me from talking work in the evenings, so that'll have to wait." I swim closer and let his arms fold around me as I take in his tattoo up close. "I . . . I'm scared," I admit.

"Of what?"

"Of not being good enough. Of being too weird. Of never fitting in. Of failing." Taking a deep breath, I whisper, "Of everything."

Dea lifts my chin with a single finger, forcing me to meet his steely gaze. "It is okay to be afraid, but you must never let that fear defeat you, or scared is all you will be." He smiles, his lip piercings glinting in the gym lights. "How about we start with afraid and happy? And go from there."

"I think I can manage that."

Chapter Seven

DRAGONS OF THE WEST: THE EAST PREPARE FOR WAR AS THE
WEST BATTLE WITH SC RESTRICTIONS

Everyone sits at the table the following morning, and I take charge with ease. For a change. "Nine, you're still working on our idea?"

He nods with a mouthful of eggs, which he swallows before saying, "Gonna have to call some friends and colleagues and work on it together, though. It's a big job."

"What is Nine working on?" Dea asks.

"A blood supplement for Vampires."

All four heads snap Nine's way—with Nigel looking more impressed than the others—and everyone speaks at once.

I cut them off with a wave of my hand. "Yes, we think it can work, but no, we're nowhere near ready to talk about it." I look back toward Nine. "ETA?"

"A few months?"

"Dea, where are we with the embassies?"

"A few days out, at most."

"Wow," I breathe. "That was quick. How?"

He shrugs. "A friend on the Sheruta Council owed me a favor, and with Nine's new communication technology, I contacted all the councils, covens, and whatnot with ease. They are sending their chosen representatives in three days' time. They are just waiting on ours." He looks at me expectantly.

Thinking about it, I do have a preference. "Prince Lucien. But you guys can pick everyone else. I don't know enough about the other pillar communities to make a choice."

"I think Pansy would make an excellent choice for the Shifter seat," Connie chimes in. "Having a smaller, respected Shifter within the community would help balance out all that testosterone-driven power in the endless meetings." Connie looks to me with a smile. "She's a rabbit Shifter, but she's fearless."

"And maybe one of the Coven's relatives for the Witches?" Arrie suggested. "Might help us win back some of their favor."

I look to Dea. "The Witches actually agreed to send a representative?" I expected them to tell us to go to hell.

He grins in that devilish way of his. "I persuaded them to put it to a vote among their people. Seems lots of Witches agree with you, Angel."

"Good." I pour myself some OJ. "That should shake them up a bit."

"The Fae, on the other hand," Dea says, "are refusing to send anyone, wanting no part in our world."

Connie snorts. "There's a surprise." When everyone looks to her, she continues, "Well, what did you expect?"

"She's right," I chime in. "They'll hopefully play ball one day. But right now, we need to do the best we can."

Nigel coughs to get our attention and looks at me with a serious expression. "On top of moving in with Aki this afternoon, I've decided to stay on with the Supernatural Council for now. You're right, Magic. We might need an inside pair of eyes."

Anguish tears through me. "You don't have to—"

"I know," he interrupts. "But I want to." He gestures to all of us. "You're putting everything on the line for this war that I've helped create." His eyes sweep to his lap. "The least I can do is help fix it. Plus, maybe I can get you a meeting with the SC."

"If you're sure?"

He nods.

"Then, I have a task for you."

He looks up at me with pure determination.

"I need to know the date for their Area 50 plans." He looks concerned for a moment, but I shake my head. "Nothing that will get you into trouble. Do not risk your life over this. You hear me?"

He nods, but I get the feeling his heart isn't in the agreement. He'll risk everything if it comes down to it, I just know it.

"I will not come break you out of prison." I stab a fork in his general direction. "No matter how much you plead and beg."

Everyone laughs, knowing I'm joking. I'd move Earth itself to keep Nigel safe. He's the only family I have left after all. Well, not anymore.

Connie gets my attention. "No more news about us for now, the app is doing well with over a thousand jobs being posted and accepted every day, and I've arranged for a Fae to help you with your spellwork. She lives here in Sheruta so should be free from any influence from the Fae Queen. I've also found a bo specialist in Tokyo. She's actually on the Shifter Council, so it wouldn't hurt for you to strengthen our ties there."

"Good. I'm happy to start training again."

"One more thing," she says with a wince.

I'm not going to like this, am I?

"I've asked Aki to help you with your death magic."

Silence grounds me as no one speaks.

"I know you're going to be mad, but it'll help you learn to control it."

"Since you nearly killed me the other day," Arrie grumbles.

My hands clench into fists seconds before reaching the table. "Would you shut the fuck up for once in your damn immortal life?" Tears brim my eyes. I snap my attention to Connie. "Why?" I try to ask, but it comes out as more of a whine. I will not cry right now. I will not cry. Nope. Not happening.

Connie's expression softens as she reaches a hand to me and squeezes my arm. "Because I get the feeling you'll need it."

Dea moves to stand behind me and rests his hands on my shoulders. "There is someone out there pulling the strings, Angel. Someone cloaked in shadow."

"They'll come out," Arrie says. "Eventually." He shrugs when I look at him confused. "They'll want their moment in the spotlight. Their big hurrah."

"I know I would." Connie laughs, but it doesn't eviscerate the tense silence permeating the air.

Someone pulling the strings, huh?

Someone with a death wish, clearly.

Chapter Eight

THE FAE QUEEN HAD NOTHING TO SAY WHEN ASKED FOR HER STANCE ON THE SC's RECENT ACTIONS AGAINST THE VAMPIRES

Connie arranged for me to meet my new Fae spellwork trainer this morning, so I sit in my favorite little café, eat cake (it's never too early for cake), and drink coffee until eleven am comes around and a tall, blue-haired, green-skinned Fae woman walks through the door, her hips swaying beneath a small ruffled skirt and a scowl crossing her otherwise beautiful face.

She scans the small number of people in various seats and settles on me with a smirk.

I jump to my feet and smile. "You must be my new trainer." I bow deep. "Magic. It's lovely to meet you."

I haven't spent a lot of time in my male form, so I'm surprised when that smirk turns into a smile. "Yeah, I know."

She rolls her eyes. "Come on." Her head nods toward the door beyond before she spins on her heel and exits.

Eyeing my half a cup of coffee with disappointment, I sigh. Great. Another bossy trainer. Can I not just for once get a kind-hearted trainer who wants to joke and gently guide me in the right direction?

Just once?

The Fae lady leads me out of town, past all the shops and nice buildings, across a few fields filled with various produce (from wheat to cotton to potatoes), over a rickety bridge passing over a stream that hops and jumps around jagged rocks, and down a small path through a copse of trees. She stops, waves a hand through the air, touches a magical rune, and reveals a hidden village of Fae.

"Wow!" My eyes don't know where to look; from the modern cottages to the small rainbow gardens outside each, and from the magic barrier that turns the sun purple to the green-skinned Fae children playing in the stream running through the village center, my eyes drink everything in. "This is . . . beautiful."

I trudge through the barrier, running my hand along its spellwork and marveling at the complexity with a jaw-dropping mark of surprise. I didn't know Fae spells could be this amazing.

I creep around the edges of the village, observing. The sun shines down on the Fae, who watch me curiously but continue with their tasks. Everyone is doing something, from looking after children to harvesting vegetables to tending gardens to fixing holes in various houses. It's like a little self-contained community.

The Fae who led me here grabs my hand and pulls me to the edge of the village, where a small cottage sits away from the others. "This is where you'll be training every other afternoon."

I think I whisper an acknowledgement, but my breath catches and my eyes can't stop wandering. I think I'm in some form of beauty shock. Is that a thing? It absolutely should be.

"Are you going to just stare all day, or would you like to get to work?"

"Oh, right." I shake my head out of its glow and face her. "May I ask your name?"

"No." She sits cross-legged in the center of the garden that surrounds the small cottage and closes her eyes. "Sit in front of me."

I follow her instructions.

How does Connie know this Fae? Where did all these people come from? Why do they live separate to the rest of Sheruta? Why is she my trainer?

The Fae sighs and opens her eyes. "Fine. I will answer three of your questions if we can begin straight after."

"Deal."

She looks at me expectantly and waves her hand, indicating I can ask away.

"Who are you and your people?"

"We are Fae. Nothing more. Nothing less. But we live in our own world, of sorts. We prefer to remain unconnected to others, where can thrive in peace."

"I see." So they're like the Witches, then? Here's to hoping our relationship doesn't end the same way. "Why do you all live separately to the rest of Sheruta?"

"It has always been that way. When our first found her way here, she preferred the company of nature and decided to live in the forest. Eventually a few people joined her, and our numbers have grown since. We just want our own piece of peace. We live off the land."

I look to this strange lady with the green skin, blue hair, and purple tattoos inked down her arms and frown. "Who are you?"

"I do not take kindly to people nosing their way into my business. But if you must know, I joined my people thirty years ago, where I have been ever since. I prefer solitude over the company of others. But I also happen to be one of the strongest spellcasters in Sheruta, so Connie asked for my help."

I bow my head. "And I thank you for it." Taking a deep breath, I relax my shoulders. "If I'm being honest, Fae spellwork concerns me because it takes time to learn. It's one of the least intuitive forms of magic. But I don't have forever."

"Yes, Connie explained the time-sensitive nature. But you must be patient or you will not master Fae magic. You are right to be concerned regarding its complexity, for Fae magic contains many aspects and moving parts that create a whole."

"Right," I reply. "There're runes, ingredients, incantations, and other things that make up Fae magic, right?"

She nods.

"And getting a handle on all of them just seems so . . . daunting."

She purses her lips and frowns. "Look, Magic, I'm here because Connie asked me to be, and I owe her. But if you're not in this with both feet on the ground running, then feel free to leave."

Shock plasters me to the spot. She thinks I should leave? Fuck that. "To hell with that. I have Fae magic to learn and a world to save, so stop being a mysterious piece of shit and start teaching me."

For the first time since I've met her, she smiles. A genuine, heartfelt smile. "Well then, I guess I'll train you." She coughs to clear her throat and then forms a ball of plasma between her two hands in mid-air. "This is a form of energy known as plasma. It is Fae created. It is the substance our spells are made from. And what we use to create plasmascreens and other such technologies. It's easiest to see when in the form of a barrier spell, like the one surrounding our village."

She throws it at me, and I catch it between my hands.

"You should be able to feel it, latch onto it, and shape it in any way you see fit." She watches me create shapes with the already-created spell with a harsh scowl on her face. "If you explore the plasma enough, you'll start to feel the spellwork that makes it and keeps it steady."

I've done this already when in the Andes Mountains, when I took down that cloaking spell, so I easily find the runes, incantations, and ingredients that make up this one. But it's different. I've never seen a more complicated piece of spellwork. It's like she's taken an emotion and crafted it into a spell. "Incredible," I whisper. "It's like you've woven the incantations into the runes."

She looks at me a little impressed for a moment before saying, "It is a small piece of what makes up our barrier." She stands, hands on hips, and orders, "Your task for today is to get out of the barrier."

"Wait. What?"

"Must I repeat myself?"

"Err . . . yes."

She sighs and walks up to me. (Will she ever stop sighing?) "Today's exercise is to break through the barrier. If you can do that, I'll continue training you." She walks into what I assume is her own cottage and slams the door.

The barrier? I have to get myself through the barrier.

Somehow.
 Okay.
 Deep breath.
 I can do this.

Chapter Nine

WorldXpo App, Designed by Horsemen, Wins Alliance Peace Award

I sooooo can't do this. I've been standing beside the barrier that sits a few meters from my new trainer's cottage with a frustrated frown on my face for the last few hours. No matter what way I rewrite the runes or what incantations I use, nothing is working. The stubborn barrier remains in place.

"Ugh. Couldn't we have started simpler?" I complain to myself under my breath.

"No," she says from behind me. Making me jump. "If you want to go home today, you'll have to break through the barrier."

"Wait. You're kidnapping me?"

She scoffs. "I'm training you." She places a hand on my shoulder and whispers, "Break through the barrier."

My fists clench as my breath comes out in ragged, uneven

huffs. "Any further instructions you wanna give, or are you going to stand there repeating yourself all afternoon?"

"You know the incantations are tied up in the runes, but what about the ingredients?"

"The ingredients?" Right. This spell uses more than just runes and words. "I don't know much about spell ingredients," I admit sheepishly.

"You've been relying on runes and incantations until now?"

I nod. "I've only really used Fae magic when needed, so it's all been on-the-go kind of spells, which don't tend to use ingredients."

"You're correct." She places a hand on either shoulder and squeezes. "But Fae magic can be useful for multiple purposes, including defense, which many believe to be its primary and original purpose. Learning complex spellwork will help you overall, even if you mostly use your magic for fighting."

I don't want to use my magic just to hurt people. I want to use my magic to make people's lives better. "Okay." I turn my attention to the spellwork at hand and analyze what effects are being placed upon the runes and incantations. "Well," I say, "there's something stabilizing this flower-looking rune here and something else kind of . . . gluing this incantation to this spirally rune over here."

"Well done," she says. "That's a stergi root stabilizing a compulsion rune, otherwise it wouldn't wear off and people who come near the barrier would simply be under our thrall forever, since the barrier spell never deactivates." She moves to stand next to me and grabs a tendril of the barrier and pulls. "And that glue you spoke of is a combination of mint, volcanic earth, and blessed flowers that have been spelled to form a rune adhesive that helps some incantations bind themselves around more repellent runes. That rune creates the barrier's shape, so it tends to not like being stable. The incantation helps the rune stay in the shape we want, which is a sphere."

Wow. It's so complex. A lot of work has gone into this. "I'm impressed. Most spells I see are just simple runes and words, sometimes with an ingredient in or two. But nothing that winds and weaves together like this." I stop to take a breath and wipe the sweat from my brow. "Whoever designed it is a truly skilled Fae."

"Thank you."

"Wait a minute." I spin on my heel to face her. "You designed this barrier spell?" I try to hide my surprise, but I ultimately fail. "Really?"

She nods, her pastel green skin tinting a vague shade of pink under the afternoon sun. "They had something else before, a weaker spell. So I offered to replace it in exchange for a place among their village."

She must be hiding from someone; otherwise, why would she live here and not among other people? And why fight to create something so complex that clearly took her some time and effort if the needs of doing so weren't dire?

I wonder what her story is.

"So," she continues, snapping us out of our moment, "you should be able to see a few ways around this spell now I've basically spoon-fed you the answers."

I cough and splutter. "I should?"

She smiles for a moment—I'm pretty sure it's the first time I've ever seen her do so—and walks away. Again.

"Great," I mumble.

Okay, so we have a rune adhesive, but that would be impossible to remove since it's a form of glue. There must be an easier way to break the barrier. The stergi root would be easy to remove, but that wouldn't help me; it would just destabilize the compulsion rune—which would have no effect on me anyway, I don't think.

Think, Magic, think.

I need to get out of here, dammit!

That's it!

I need to get out of here. I need to be on the other side of the barrier. But that doesn't mean I need to break the barrier. That would take ages and probably more knowledge than I currently possess about its makeup. But maybe I could create a hole or write myself into the spell. After all, these Fae can come and go as they please. All my new trainer did was put her handprint on the barrier.

Maybe there's a rune or an incantation that creates a kind of ID chip in the spell? And if I find out what that is and how it works, maybe I can magically hot-wire myself into the spell.

I weave through incantation after rune after effect for a full hour before I come across the little bundle of spellwork at the center of the barrier's alignment runes that allows for the people of the village to pass through with ease.

But I've seen nothing look like this in any textbook or spell before.

"What are you?" I whisper to myself.

It seems to be a joining of four different runes—a storage rune used to store their identities, a detection rune used to identify their magical signature, a separation rune that creates a ripple in the barrier, and a time rune that shuts the entire process off after thirty seconds—but there's also an ingredient here that links the separation rune to the detection rune, otherwise it would just separate the barrier anytime it wanted.

"What is that ingredient?"

Taking a step back, I look around me. It looks like there's nothing where the barrier should be, but that's not the case. There's a circle of weeds every few feet going all the way around, if I'm not mistaken.

"Wow."

They look just like forest foliage. Completely camouflaged.

I bend down to take a peek and a sniff, then it hits me. I recognize this plant. It's the gugi plant. The same one I use for directional intent when making the teleporting crystals. I would know its green, heart-shaped leaves anywhere.

But how is a weed, used for directional intent, helping link the detection and separation runes?

Oh, I get it.

Direction isn't just one-dimensional; it's all over the place. The weed is telling the separation rune how big to be and what shape to be and where to situate itself in relation to the habitant's data stored in the storage rune detected by the detection rune.

"That's truly brilliant."

I might have a hard-on for this Fae's mind.

That's a bit weird, isn't it? Oh well.

But how do I write myself into the spell?

I sit in a huff on the forest floor for a while, thinking around everything I've learned and experienced while pulling apart the barrier spell and seeing how it has been created.

I could just add my magical signature to the storage rune. Could it really be that simple? That easy?

It's like how the magical signatures on my library doors work—not that we shut my library door.

I stand against the barrier and bring up the storage rune, where I place my magical essence inside, watch it get added to the few dozen already there, and step back.

"That should do it."

Holding my breath, I place my hand against the barrier, watch it glow like it did for my trainer earlier, and step through.

"I did it!" My fist pumps into the air and jump up and down. "I did it."

"That you did, Magic." My trainer stands on the other side of the barrier with a wide smile. "Well done."

"How long were you watching me?"

She shrugs. "The entire time." She walks back to her cottage and shuts the door. "It wasn't a hard task, but finding the solution was challenging. You navigated a complex spell and pieced everything together. I would be happy to train you, Magic."

Guess it's time to go home.

CHAPTER TEN

THE FIVE HORSEMEN: WHAT ARE THEIR POWERS?

Night falls by the time I get home, and I'm exhausted. All that puzzling everything out was hard work. But the magic itself was simple to accomplish. Guess that's the difficulty with Fae magic—it's more of a science than a magic. Once you know all the moving parts, it's easy, but learning those parts well enough to recognize them on the fly . . .

A lifetime of work.

Everyone's doing their own thing when I get in, so I grab a book and head to my bathroom for some me time to unwind. I love Connie and the guys, but sometimes I just need a conversationless moment so I can breathe again.

By the time I'm clean, my legs are like warm Jell-O, my skin is wrinkly, and my mind is a relaxed mush, Nine, Dea, and Connie are already in my bed—which I swear gets larger every time I see it—and I smile to myself for a moment.

"I could get used to this."

"You already have." I hear a familiar grumbling voice echo from the doorway.

I spin to face Arrie with a sour look on my face, but he seems calm tonight. Less agitated. Maybe some mental space away from me helped him think? He did once tell me he struggles to communicate with people and that he talks best when driving.

"Yeah, I guess I have."

"I've been working on the plan, if you wanted—"

I walk up to him and place my finger on his lips. "Not right now," I whisper. "I'm exhausted. That Fae Connie has teaching me magic is grueling, at best."

His face lights up with a smile for the briefest of seconds, and for a moment, I remember what it's like being happy with this man. He's unique, and I miss him. And it hurts that he wants to label us as friends after we've spent so much time together.

But I don't push for answers.

Instead, I turn around and head to bed. "There's always a free space to join us, if you wish," I whisper over my shoulder.

He moves a foot over the threshold to my rooms, but he scowls and steps back. "I don't think that's a good idea."

Oh. "The offer's always open, in case you change your mind." I shrug and clamber into the pile of heat under my duvet.

The next morning, I find myself being escorted to Tokyo by Connie and Nine to meet my bo staff trainer. After yesterday, though, I'm a bit nervous. My Fae magic trainer is . . . hard. Is that how this is going to go, too?

Chin up, Sweetie. I don't think this'll be the same as

yesterday.

How do you know?

Because unlike yesterday, you're with the Shifters. And they're pretty cool and chilled.

Promise?

I promise.

Nine rubs his thumb over mine, where our hands are entwined, and looks at me. "You're going to be fine."

"Of course you are, hon." Connie, holding my other hand, yanks me into her for a quick, reassuring hug. "This'll be great. But if you're really nervous, I can stay?"

I think about it for a moment but shake my head. "Thanks, but I think this is something I have to do on my own."

"If you're sure?" Connie asks, mother-henning me, as usual. "If she gives you a hard time, though, just come get me." She punches a fist into her other hand and smirks. "I'll defend you."

"But not against my Fae trainer?"

Connie shivers. "I like you, Magic. I really do. But that woman terrifies me."

Nine laughs. "Only cos she put you on your ass when you first met."

Connie sulks, but I drag us along to the nearest entrance to the Shifter Underground. "C'mon," I whine. "I might be nervous, but I don't wanna be late."

"Right," Nine says. "My appointment is five minutes after yours. I can't be late for that."

Nine's only tagging along to meet with a fellow scientist who wants to help on the blood supplement project. And if Nine needs help, then it's clearly some serious juju.

The Shifter Underground is a series of networking tunnels, hideouts, rooms, and underground houses that permeate the beneath of Tokyo, just underneath the subway network. It's just as large as Tokyo and just as impressive. There's space for every Shifter possible, from large open parks for wolf packs to small networks of hidey-holes for hibernating Shifters. It's one of my favorite places on Earth.

Connie leads us down a series of tunnels and into a gym arena, where a woman sits with two bo staffs in the middle of a cordoned off area.

"Right," Nine says and grabs my hand, "I'm off, Sweetie." He places a gentle kiss to my knuckles and spins me into his arms. Try not to worry too much. I promise I'll come pick you up in a few hours.

I nod and watch him leave, his red hair remaining in my vision until he turns the corner and is out of sight.

"Hon, over here!" Connie yells.

I run over as fast as possible, not able to manage Vampire speed in my male form, and smile as politely as possible at the lady beside Connie. "Hey! I'm Magic." I offer her my hand.

She shakes with a firm grip and smiles. "Korby."

Connie smiles at me and nods reassuringly. "I'm not staying, Korby, but I'm sure you two will get along just fine. Basically cut from the same cloth." She waves me off as she leaves, leaving me to my fate.

"So, you wanna know how to use the bo staff, right?"

I nod. "Yeah. We're stretched a bit thin right now, so we thought some outside expertise might be useful."

"What drew you to the bo staff in the first place?" she asks as she hands me one of the bo staffs from the floor.

"Well, it was Connie's idea at first, but I wanted something less brutal." I shrug. "Something more me."

"Bo staffs are pretty brutal when used right, you know. But I get what you're saying."

"Plus," I add, "we can really utilize this with my magic when the time comes."

Her eyes glow bright for a moment, as all Shifters do when they get emotional, but she settles back down and faces me. "You can't use magic while training with me. Just your Shifter side. Otherwise I can't help."

Sounds fair. "Sure. No problem."

"Besides, that way you can master the bo properly before getting all fancy and tailoring your style to you." She eyes my body up and down, and her eyes glow a bright gold color.

I suddenly realize the problem. "I know this form can be difficult for some, but I need this to be professional. Besides, I'm already involved." I just wanted to get that out in the air. "Sorry. Awkward, I know."

Her cheeks blister a bright red color, and I'm floored by the stuttering and stumbling and flailing she does for a moment. "It's . . . err . . . n-no problem. S-Sorry."

"Hey, stop that." I wave a hand in her direction. "I get it." I think back to Dea and how I can still barely look at him without getting my panties in a twist. "Trust me."

"Sure." She gets into a stance ready to fight me. "Sorry, again."

"Don't mention it." I mimic her stance and try my best to parry her oncoming blow, but it's like all my usual natural talent with this weapon has flown out the damn window. "Ah!"

"Thought Connie said you had some basic skills?" she taunts.

"I do!" I yell as I parry another blow to the head. "Usually."

"Well"—she stops—"you're holding the bo wrong." She puts her bo down and comes to help me. "You want to place your hands so you're dividing the bo into thirds, like this." She places one hand one third of the way down the bo, and the next another third of the way down. "Your left hand should face down while your right hand should face up. That way you have maximum control."

"Right."

"Your stance is good."

I look down to my feet and smile. Yes, go feet!

"I'll go through some basic bo staff maneuvers with you, and then we'll put them into practise. Okay?" She smiles at me, and it feels good to be smiled at after yesterday.

"Okay. Let's do this!"

Korby takes me through ten different maneuvers and then has me put them into practise in all kinds of combinations, defending her attacks and defending myself. And I can already see the possibilities of how to use my magic. My elemental Witch magic in particular will go well with this type of weapon. And if I carve some runes into the wood and maybe add some charms, I can really vary it up.

After three hours of the most grueling workout possible, I'm done. My body is about to collapse in on itself, and I can't lift my arms above my head. But it doesn't look like Korby is doing any better.

"You alright?" she asks as she slumps beside me.

I nod, barely able to move. "Think . . . so."

"That was intense."

"Yeah . . ." I chuckle. "I've had more chilled workouts with Connie."

"Sooo . . ." Korby starts, and I internally cringe. "You and Connie?" She coughs to clear her throat. "Is that a thing?"

"Uh-huh." I sit up and look over at Korby, who's still flush-faced and struggling to sit up. "I'm kinda in a relationship with Nine and Dea too."

Once she sits up, her eyes go wide. "Like, all of them?"

I nod, my eyes shooting to the ground in embarrassment.

"Hey, no." Korby grabs my hand and helps me to my feet. "Sorry, I didn't mean to embarrass you. It's cool you've found your family." She smiles up at me. "Genuinely."

Looking around, I don't spot Nine, so I turn to Korby and ask, "Wanna hang out for a bit?" I shrug when she looks at me in surprise. "I've got time to kill before Nine picks me up."

"Sure." Her eyes brighten at the suggestion. "That'd be great."

"Well, the where is on you. I barely know my way back up top." I point to the ceiling and laugh. "But," I start, "would you be more comfortable if I were in my female form?"

She looks to me and frowns. "I don't want you to be uncomfortable on my account." She looks to the floor. "It's okay, honestly."

I shrug and switch to my female form. "Then I'll go like this."

Korby looks up to me and smiles with relief. "Thank you."

She takes me to a bar a few tunnels down, and it's drowning in Shifters.

"Maybe I should have stayed in my male form . . ."

"Why?" she asks, genuinely perplexed. I flash my fangs, but she laughs. "Don't be stupid. We used to war with Vampires, but that was a long time ago. We've coexisted in peace for hundreds of years now. There're even some living down here in the Shifter Underground."

"Oh, I thought there was still some . . . tension."

Korby shakes her head. "Even the councils are friendly with each other. The Vampire King is an amazing ruler. He really helped bring us all together."

"Really?" I ask as we sit at two stools up at the bar and order some cocktails. "How so?"

She sips her bright blue cocktail and turns to me with a smile. "Well, for starters, he pulled all of his forces back to Vampire-controlled states the day after he took his place on the throne. His decision to do so pretty much ended the war. They signed a peace treaty soon after, and the rest is history."

"Wow," I exclaim. "That's amazing."

"Uh-huh."

Looking Korby over, I'm surprised someone so young is on the Shifter Council. Her dark brown eyes smile every time she looks at me while her flawless skin glows under every light. She couldn't be older than twenty, surely?

"Magic?"

I shake my head out of my thoughts. "Sorry. What were you saying?"

Korby laughs but shakes her head. "It's okay. I get that a lot." She takes another sip of her drink. "I'm older than I look."

"Really?"

She raises her eyebrows. "Asking for my age, Magic?"

"Maybe." I gesture with my fingers. "Just a little."

Korby laughs. "I'm thirty-two."

"No fucking way!"

A few people near us scowl at my loud exclamation, but that just makes us laugh louder.

Korby places a warm hand on my shoulder. "Sorry. Didn't mean to embarrass you further."

"It's okay." I wave her off. "I do a good enough job on my own usually, anyway."

Ready to go?

Sure. I'm in the bar a few tunnels down from where you left me.

I know.

My head snaps up and looks around, landing on a familiar red-head standing in the doorway. "Nine!" I run over to him and wrap my arms around his neck. "I missed you."

He giggles at my antics. "I missed you too, Sweetie."

Korby walks from behind us. "Hello, Famine."

He waves a dismissing hand at her and says, "Call me Nine. No need for formalities."

"If you're sure."

"Positive." He smiles at her, and I watch her blush in that cute way of hers. "So," Nine asks, "when's the next training session?"

I look to Korby in question.

"Oh, I was thinking three times a week? If that's good?"

"Sounds perfect," I say as I wrap my arm through hers. "Don't think I could do that every day, anyway."

Chapter Eleven

Twenty-Two Confirmed Dead in Hate Crime Spree.
Species Unknown

"Soooo," Nine asks on the way home, "how'd it go? You seemed to like Korby . . ."

"She's great." I change into my male form, stretch my arms, and wince. "But seriously, though . . . That was a workout from hell!"

Nine wraps an arm around my waist and yanks me closer. "Connie went home earlier, so it's just us. Wanna grab something to eat before we head back?"

Just the two of us?

Yup.

Sounds great. I've missed everyone over the last few days. I'm so used to having you all around so much, I guess.

He rubs circles on my waist, where his hand sits, and says, Yeah, it's been tough on everyone. Dea the most, I think.

Really?

Yeah, he's been a bit . . . depressed.

"Maybe we should all go out tomorrow? Like a date?" I hesitate a moment. "But won't that upset Arrie?" Ugh. Why am I even thinking about that asshole?

Have you talked to him yet?

I shake my head.

You should.

Maybe Nine's right. Maybe I need to be a little more proactive with Arrie, rather than wait for him to be ready and come to me. I just don't wanna force his hand or make him uncomfortable or anything.

Maybe he needs a little uncomfortable nudge in the right direction.

I look into Nine's brown eyes and smile. "Maybe."

"C'mon"—Nine drags me down the next turning—"I know a great izakaya near here."

"Really?"

Yeah, you'll love it.

Nine guides me down the street and into an izakaya, which is like a tavern or pub, and we sit at a small table in the corner. It must be a good place because it's packed. But then, it is straight after Tokyo's work day.

"Ohhhh, look, Nine! They serve umaki here." Nine looks at me like I'm crazy, but the eel wrapped in omelet is sooooo good. Goddess, I'm drooling just thinking about it. "Oh, and look at that sushi platter!" I point to the menu and smile.

"How about we get the sushi platter to share, and then we'll each have our own sides?" Nine suggests.

"Sounds perfect!"

We order, and when Nine looks at me like I'm his whole world, I stop and ask, "How has your day been?"

"Mine?" He chuffs. "Not nearly as exciting as yours, Sweetie. I met with some scientists here, and some specialists and contacts thanks to Alpha Cal. I think I got them all onboard."

"That's great."

Nine's face splits into a grin as he spins into an excited stream of nerd talk I can barely follow. But watching his eyes light up will always be worth it. "And when I told them about the idea to forgo the white blood cell creation altogether, they balked. But I talked some reason into them."

I can imagine Nine standing in front of some lecture theater full of people just like him—though, maybe not as hot—talking their ears off about this brilliant new idea he needs help with. In fact, I kinda wish I skipped out on Korby and went with him. Maybe one day I can persuade him into some lecture theater sex.

I might even wear some glasses.

I nearly spill my drink.

You'd do that for me?

I'd do anything for you. Especially if it turns you on.

He brushes his foot up against my leg and sears me with a heated gaze as I lean in for a kiss.

Our food arrives, and we both drink Hoppys and chat shit until it gets dark and we decide to head home.

"Thank you," I whisper.

What for?

"For taking me out and forcing me to relax. I'm not very good at it on my own."

Nine laughs, his smile lighting up insides until I'm a gooey pile of mush. "No, you're not. But that's okay." He grabs my hand. "You've got us."

We walk through the front door just as Connie and Dea

spring on me, yanking me away from Nine.

"We missed you, Angel," Dea whispers in my ear, his voice a little more sullen than usual.

"Wanna snuggle and watch a movie?" Connie asks. "All of us?" She gestures to Dea and Nine as well as me and herself.

"That sounds perfect."

We all snuggle under blankets on one of the corner sofas in the cinema room, and even Arrie joins us, though he sits apart from our snuggle huggle.

And for the first time in a really long time, things are looking up. Two nights in a row I fall asleep peacefully in the arms of the people I love. And I feel loved too.

Chapter Twelve

Do the Horsemen Have the Power to Destroy the World?

Nine cuddles into my side the next morning and nuzzles my neck. I told Dea that we're taking you on a date today. All four of us.

You did?

Uh-huh. Figured we could go on that holiday to Paris you mentioned, but then I thought maybe not, since that's Fae central.

Yeah. Maybe it's best we don't antagonize them further. Before we go, I want an update from everybody. Make sure there's nothing we need to do.

Nine puts his finger on my lips. Shhhh. Everything is fine, Sweetie. Promise. But yeah, okay. If it'll make you feel better.

It will.

Dea mumbles something as he stirs on my other side.

"Wha are you two talking about?"

"I didn't think our mental chat would wake you." I wince when I realize how tired he looks. "Sorry."

"No problem, Angel. I was waking up anyway."

You look exhausted, bro. We can lie in if you like?

"Yeah, it's cool to lounge for a bit. I don't mind what we do."

"Mmmmm . . ." Dea mumbles before closing his eyes and rolling into my side for another hug. "But then we will have less time together."

But it'll be time better spent.

"Maybe just another hour." He snuggles further into my arm, and I can't help but lean down and press a kiss to his head.

He's so adorable like this. All peaceful and not in control.

He is, isn't he?

I look to my left to find Nine staring lovingly at Dea and sighing in that loved-up puppy dog way of his, and I smile. "You're both amazing," I whisper.

Dea grumbles something that sounds like shut the fuck up, but I can't be sure.

He said he's an Angel of Death, not adorable.

"Well, our Angel of Death is definitely adorable."

Yup. Definitely.

Dea rolls back over. "Ugh." He smiles. "How does this Angel of Death go back to sleep with all of this audible loving going on?"

Nine and I get up after that, not wanting to wake Dea—again—who has been working immensely hard on the embassies over the past couple of days. Just the thought of all that politics makes me shudder.

Breakfast is a grand affair this morning: French toast,

strawberries, something called crumpets, and croissants.

We wanted to start your day off with a foodie bang.

It's gorgeous, thank you.

I take a bite out of my French toast that I topped with strawberries and groan.

And delicious, too.

"So, Arrie," I start with a wince. Those piercing ice blue eyes still hurt to look at when he stares at me with that much animosity. "Where are we with the war plans?"

He rolls his eyes. "This isn't a fantasy movie." He takes a deep breath. "I can't do much else until the ambassadors arrive, which isn't until tomorrow." He shrugs. "Anything else you need?"

I do not miss the sarcasm in his voice. "If you're going to a bitch about everything, then yes, I'm sure I can find something for you to do." I look to Connie. "What about you?"

Connie looks sheepishly to the floor. "Well, I . . ." She looks to Nine and then back to me, a small blush forming on her cheeks. "I can't come today. I'm sorry."

"Why not?" I ask, trying my best to hide the disappointment but failing miserably.

She grabs my hand and rubs circles over space between my thumb and forefinger. "Because there's still loads to do. I haven't picked a manager for the app, I need to get hold of the SC's PR manager to ask when the rest of the interviews and stuff are going live, I need to somehow get a meeting with the SC for you, which we're still working on by the way, there's still a ton of data to trawl through on the flash drive . . ." She takes a deep breath and then makes an annoyed face. "And shit, I haven't sorted out temporary accommodation for the ambassadors yet." A string of less-than-lady-like curses leaves her mouth. "I'm sorry, I'm really busy doing all the backend work here."

I get up off my chair and go to stand behind her, massaging the stress out of her shoulders. "It's okay." I place a light kiss on the top of her head. "How about we do something just the two of us on Earth this Friday? Our usual dates, but more . . ."

"Date like?" she offers.

"Yeah."

She jumps to her feet and beams at me. "I'd love that!"

Maybe she prefers dating me alone, rather than making it a group thing? I'll ask on Friday. "Then it's a date."

She slams her lips against mine suddenly, causing me to stumble into the wall, but she holds us both up with a powerful arm around my waist. At first, we don't move, just smile against each other as we stifle our laughs, but eventually she moves our lips in a rhythm I pick up with ease, and the world melts away.

Warm hands snake up my top and settle on my chest, as though she can't kiss me without touching my skin, caressing some intimate part of me that burns with her every touch. A delicious sizzle of need that sets my body alight and makes me gasp into her mouth.

I go to pull away, diving left, but she pins me to the wall and captures my lips again. My eyes snap open and see the need in her closed-eye gaze, the lines of want highlighting her brows as her hair flies behind her.

Fuck.

Seeing the need on her face and feeling the desperation in the way her hips move against mine causes a low growl in the back of my throat to slip free.

I need her, too.

My mouth trails kisses down her jawline, past her neck

and onto her collarbone, and her giggles send a thrill through me. I want to delve below her top and pepper kisses across her chest, play with her nipples until she is no longer holding back, and see where it takes us.

But she takes a deep breath and places a solid hand on my chest, pushing me away. She looks at me with swollen lips and a gleam in her eye. "You have a date with your boyfriends."

"Pretty sure they won't mind me starting my day off with a piece of my girlfriend."

She groans into my mouth once more for a small, deep kiss, but she pulls away. "Friday we'll have all the time in the world. I promise."

"Friday."

She walks away, and I watch her ass sway across the kitchen in that seductive rhythm of hers.

When I turn back to the table, both Nine and Arrie have disappeared. Arrie probably left in a huff. But where's Nine?

In my bedroom with Dea.

Oh, cool.

Dea's voice echoes into my mind. We have been arranging our date. We will come and get you in half an hour. Wear something for hot weather.

Hot weather. Got it.

Chapter Thirteen

Hot sun blasts my skin as a gentle breeze breathes life back into my sweat-soaked nape. I shoved my hair up this morning in expectation of the hot weather, and I'm thankful I did.

Mid-October in Borneo is hot.

But beautiful.

"This morning," Dea starts, "we will be checking in to our private villa. Then we will go snorkeling with the turtles and have a beach lunch before going . . ." Dea's dramatic pause is of note this morning. "Orangutan trekking."

"Orangutans? Wow. Really?"

Dea nods but looks a little nervous, while Nine smiles at me and loops his arm through mine.

"That's amazing!"

"Then," Nine adds, "we'll be having an amazing dinner

and then spending the night here in the villa."

"But," Dea adds, looping his arm through my free one, "we do not have to do anything sexual this evening if you do not want to. We can just spend time together."

I giggle. "Yeaaaah, cos I'm going to be able to keep my hands off the pair of you in nothing but shorts." I roll my eyes.

Seriously, are these two mental?

They both chuckle.

You packed a bikini, right? Cos I'm okay with going nude. He winks at me.

Dea chuckles beside me. "You are terrible, bro."

As if you're really complaining.

"No. Never." Dea leans over and places a quick kiss to Nine's lips, but he pulls back in a red-flushed haze of embarrassment.

Seems they're still not really used to public displays of affection.

"You know, you guys can do things without me. I'm okay with you both having time to yourselves." I shrug.

They don't answer but drag me forward, hopefully toward somewhere I can sit down—I'm sweating like a pig. Which, now that I think about it, is actually ridiculous because pigs don't sweat. Who even made up that phrase? What a moron. I'm sweating like a . . . horse. They sweat a lot, right?

Yeah, they do.

I look to Nine in a flourish of embarrassment that he heard my ridiculous inner monologue. Oh well, he's probably used to it.

Trust me, your mind is awesome.

Really?

Yup.

We continue up the road for a little while, until I pause in a breathless huff. "Can I not just fucking fly us there?"

Dea sighs. "Fine. If you must."

"I must." I change into my female form and gather us all into the air.

For a moment, I chuckle to myself that I'm making Dea fly when he has wings, but I mention nothing. He probably doesn't want to flare up our angel connection so soon after that night in the hotel.

"Ready?" I ask, not waiting for a proper answer as I shoot us forward. And in less than thirty seconds, I see a sprawling house that looks beautiful. All straw roofs, infinity pools, tiki bars, and loungers. "Is that it?"

"Yes," Dea answers and grabs hold of my hand. "Take us down to the gates. We should ask for entrance before terrifying the security team."

Right.

I set us down a few feet from the main gates.

The two security guards let us in with a few gasps and murmurs, one of them even pointing at me with a shaking hand. They weren't speaking English, but I'm not sure of the local language.

Bahasa Malaysian.

Ah. Okay. Nothing I can speak.

Shame.

The security guards continue to whisper to each other in feared, hushed tones, but there is nothing I can do about it.

Nine rips his arm away from mine and steps toward them, hands held above his head. I don't know what he says, but after a few minutes, they calm down and stop giving me weird looks. Instead, they just avoid eye contact and step away from us entirely.

"What did you say to them?"

Nine shrugs. "Just explained you weren't an enemy and we want to be left alone for the day."

"And they just agreed?" Dea asks.

"Sure." He looks at Dea as though it shouldn't surprise him. "I am the Horseman of Famine. A large part of dealing with food and resource scarcity is sharing it among people equally and creating decent economies, which requires talking and negotiating."

"Remind me again why you can't just deal with the Witches for me?" I sigh in exasperation. "Or why you didn't tell me the whole New Orleans thing would blow up in my face? Or why—"

"Okay, first, I'm not a fortune teller. I'm just me." He stops us in the middle of the driveway and turns me to face him with a hand on each shoulder. "Second, the Witches are annoying, and I've tried dealing with them before, but what they want is what they already have. They gain nothing from coming out of the supernatural closet."

"And third," Dea says from behind me, pressing his front up to my back, "Nine is good but not foolproof." His hands skate up my top and land in a firm position on my stomach as he blows kisses against my ear and down my neck.

A small moan escapes me, and then Nine captures my lips in a searing kiss that blows away any doubt in my mind that I'm not ready for these two.

"We . . . have . . . an . . . itinerary," I say between gasps and clashing lips. "I really do want to see the turtles and orangutans."

"I know," Dea whispers in my ear. "I was just reminding you that I love you."

"I was just looking for an excuse you kiss you," Nine chimes in.

"You never need an excuse." I run a hand down his face and cup his jaw. "You can kiss me anytime you wish."

Dea pulls us both away and turns us to the front door. "The world's perfect date awaits, Angel."

"I'll be the judge of that." I glare at him. "Besides, I have another date with Connie on Friday. Really gonna compete with her?"

Dea visibly shudders. "Not worth the pain of winning." He smirks at me to let me know he's joking, and then swings the door open.

Nine gives the grand tour: three bedrooms, two bathrooms, four reception rooms, two pools, and a minibar. "We could have gone grander," Nine says, "but we wanted intimate."

"I think it's perfect," I whisper as I hug them both. "Now, when do I get to see the turtles?"

Dea looks at his watch with wide eyes. "In twenty minutes. You might need to fly us there."

"No problem." I quickly change into my bathing suit in both forms, then run back out and grab both their hands, lift us into the air, through the front door, and up above the house. "Where to?"

"Over there." Nine points to a bit of coastline with some people dotted every few meters. "We're hiring the equipment from a shop near the beach."

"Pfft," I spit. "You're hiring equipment. I can shift into any animal I want, and I don't need to breathe under water in my female form."

Dea laughs. "I said she would laugh at the idea of using equipment, did I not?"

Nine scowls at him and throws a middle finger in his direction. "Know it all," he mutters under his breath.

I laugh. "Says the nerd."

We land a few minutes later on the sandy shores of the whitest beach I've ever seen, and the feel of it between my toes is like vacation running up my body in waves of relaxation. No world war on magic here. No sex-changing body issues confusing my gender here. No stupid boyfriend/not boyfriend pissing me off here. Nope. Not at all.

Nine grabs my hand and then Dea's—who has turned visible—and leads us to a small hut-like store renting out all kinds of equipment: surfboards, beach stuff, and more importantly, snorkel equipment. For them.

No way am I not swimming with the fishes.

The straw hut shop blends seamlessly with the beach, weather, and endless ocean waves in the distance as I take a deep breath and inhale the salty sea air, the sunshine, and the warmth crackling against my skin. My bikini is a deep red that matches my skin tone against the kissed sun and my tattoos.

But the guys are the real show.

Dea steps out in black shorts, his swirling golden tattoo glowing and his pale skin almost as white as the sand beneath my toes. Nine holds his hand, his red and white shorts falling longer than Dea's but suiting his slicked-back red hair and flirty smirk. With both their bodies on display, it's definitely shaping up to be a good day.

"You two are totally going to mess your hair up and freak out about it, aren't you?"

They both chuckle, but it's Dea who says, "We brought hair gel with us, do not worry."

Of course they have.

The water moves around me in ripples of coolness, washing away the sweat, rinsing off the stress, and invigorating me with something akin to peace—though not quite, since it's impossible to be at peace with so much on my shoulders.

I've stayed in my female form, letting the water trickle over my skin, drawing the guys' gazes more often than I thought it would. And it feels good to have their attention. So I let it roll around me, soak it in like a good breath of fresh air.

Turtles move beneath me as small fish swim between them, darting from one spot to another. Some of the larger fish swim more slowly, like a mountain against the breeze, but they're full of bright colors and sunshine nonetheless.

Focusing on the turtle beneath my face, I shift into my male form and then into a sea turtle, and I watch the world change before me. Colors and ripples on the water all blare across my vision, but the sounds of everything around me dull and flatten to a low vibration I can barely perceive.

Nine? Can you still hear my thoughts like this?

Yup.

Can you see through my eyes like this, too?

Yeah. It's pretty cool.

It is, isn't it . . .

I shift into something small and bright yellow so I can dart around everyone—much to Dea and Nine's amusement. I brush up against their torsos and arms, letting Dea tickle my dorsal fin. Next, I shift into a dolphin so I can jump around and act like a child in the ocean for the first time. And after lots more shifting and exerting most of my energy, we swim ashore and dry off under the sun while lying on the beach.

"That was so much fun," I say on an exhale.

It was amazing to watch everything through your eyes.

Dea rests a warm hand on my thigh, inches from my cock—and judging by the smug smirk on his face, he knows it—and asks, "Do fish see in color?"

"Yup. They—"

"The composition of the color is different; brighter in some places and duller in others," Nine interrupts.

The know-it-all.

"Sorry."

"Sooooo," I start, "what are we doing for lunch?" I don't want to be picky, but I'm starving after that much shifting. Maybe I should have gone a little lighter?

Oh well.

"Oh," Dea says, "it is behind us."

I drag my head up off the beach floor and peer toward the treeline behind us, where a table with three chairs are set up. And on top of that table sits a spread of so much food my stomach grumbles loud enough for Nine to laugh.

"Stop laughing and help me . . . I'm dying," I dramatically groan.

"You're fine, you drama queen."

"But what if I never gain enough strength to move? Then how will I ever continue living?" I giggle under my breath and hold a hand out for either of them to help me up off the sand.

Dea's the one who obliges my drama and yanks me to my feet, but he spins me into his arms and places a gentle kiss to my cheek.

My cheeks burn a deep crimson as my brows rocket to my hairline on a sigh. "Mmmmm . . ."

C'mon, you two. Unless you want this food to go to waste. We've only got an hour before we need to be at the meeting point for the orangutan spotting.

Right. Food.

The only thing better than kissing. Maybe.

Chapter Fourteen

Are the SC Behind the Recent String of Shifter Attacks?

An hour later, Nine and I are trekking through an endless forest, with Dea invisibly walking behind us. He used up his visibility earlier, but we're alone with the guide anyway, so it isn't a problem.

"The forest is 140 million years old, making it the oldest forest in the world," the guide says. "And wild orangutans are only found here."

I'm glad I ate myself stupid earlier. I definitely needed the energy for this. Nine, remind me again why I can't just do this part in my female form? I'm getting used to my male form just fine, but this is torture.

Because Shifters are strong too, and you need a good workout in this form as well.

Between Korby and this, I'm sure I'll be ripped in no time.

"Sarcasm, huh?" Dea asks.

Yup.

Nine's gotten into the habit of projecting all internal conversations to everyone when it's the three of us, so no one misses out. Could he get any sweeter? Seriously, what did either of us do to deserve Nine?

Nine runs his finger between mine and grabs my hand, then strokes circles between my thumb and forefinger, sending shivers up my arm and down my spine. Dea, being invisible, wraps an arm around my hips and rests a thumb in my shorts.

The dense jungle around me sways with the barely there breeze, a cool stream on the nape of my neck that sends more shivers down my spine and air rushing out of my mouth in a relaxed gasp.

The guide treks us through various worn paths until we stop just off the side of a small trail and look up. Spots of dark orange leaping from tree to tree catch my eye, and I gaze in wonder at the strange animals living above us.

I look to the guide, then to Dea and Nine, and back at the orangutans. Yup. I'm gonna do it.

I study a still one for a moment, and then focus on its shape and features until I'm half the size I was and standing on Dea's feet.

"Wow," the guide gasps, "you're a . . . orangutan Shifter?"

Nine chuckles and Dea smiles. "Not quite," Nine says. "They're the Horseman of Magic."

His eyes widen as he takes a step back. "The . . . the one from the video?"

Ugh. That stupid viral video. What was I thinking? We need to take back New Orleans or do something. Something to pacify humans and the supe communities. Connie said the interviews are going well, but they're not as viral as that stupid video. Maybe we can do something else? Something more showy?

Stop spiraling. It's weird to watch in orangutan form.

Sorry. I am in Borneo with the orangutans, and I'm going to play with them. I will not be distracted by work right now. I'll fix all that when we get back.

But now, I need to figure out how to climb a tree.

After the third time of falling on my ass, I harrumph and crawl back to Dea's leg like a grumpy child.

Harder than it looks?

Yes.

Have you considered flying up as a bird and then changing when up there?

My eyes widen as I ooh my excitement.

You're a genius, Nine.

It's been known to happen.

Hardy-ha.

I shift into a crow and then fly up the trees until I'm a few feet away from the edges of the group. Then, balancing on a sturdy trunk I think will take my orangutan's weight, I shift. The tree creaks beneath me, and I use my arms to steady myself, but I end up whacking a thorny plant in the process and howling in pain.

Why are orangutans so hard to maneuver?

Nine and Dea are wetting themselves with laughter on the trail below me. I swear, when I get down there, I'm going to fly myself back to the villa and leave them behind.

No, you won't.

Oh, won't I?

No. How else will you get that delicious threesome you've been imagining all day?

Dea's voice echoes in my mind. What kind of things do

you imagine, Angel?

Nope. Not right now. Trying to figure out how to be an orangutan without killing myself.

There's a tree branch I can swing from, and then I'll be closer to them. But I don't want to scare them. So I wait where I am situated until one notices me. And luck is favoring me today because a young orangutan looks my way and walks over, curiosity lingering in its eyes.

I hold out my hand, hoping it'll be okay if I touch it. I don't really know much about orangutan behavior. But how hard can it be?

Hard. Apparently.

When the youngster notices I'm not anything familiar, it immediately alerts mom, and then the entire group makes these guttural sounds and thrashes around until I'm so scared I fall to the floor and crash onto the path beneath me.

Shifting back into my male form, I groan, "Okay, never let me do that again." I wipe the jungle floor from my ass while Dea and Nine huddle over laughing, trying to catch their breaths.

"Oh god," Nine says, "that was hilarious."

"Yeah, yeah, yeah." I stalk myself and my bruised ego back down the trail and toward home.

"It's this way," the guide says as he corrects my direction.

Which only serves to crack Dea and Nine up again.

Fucking boyfriends.

We trek all the way back with the guide, and by the time I walk through that front door and let the AC suck all the hot air from my body, I'm exhausted. Bone tired.

"Wanna chill by the pool for a while?" Nine asks.

"It is cold," Dea adds.

They both offer their hands, and I take them, letting them lead me outside. Since I'm in my bikini in my female form, I shift and then cannonball into the deep end.

Fuck me, this water is kept cold somehow. But I am not complaining.

Nine and Dea jump in after me, and we bathe and fool around as the sun sets behind us, a perfect backdrop to a perfect date.

"You really think this has been perfect?" Nine asks as he floats next to me.

"Uh-huh. I got to be a fish, I ate great food, we all laughed and had fun, and I've not thought much about work the entire time."

"Or Arrie," Dea adds, then winces at Nine's accusatory glare.

I laugh at them both. "It's okay. I'm sure Arrie and I will be fine. Eventually." But there's something in the hesitation he showed the other night that has me doubting that. I'm not sure Arrie is ready for a serious relationship. Has he even had one since becoming a Horseman? Aside from his friends-with-benefits things with Connie. Which doesn't really count.

Now is not the time, Magic.

I shake my head, trying to shake the thoughts from my mind. I can always ask Arrie when I get home. Somehow.

Should go on a drive somewhere.

Right! Arrie talks more when he's driving.

You are a genius, Nine. And sorry, I'll stop thinking about Arrie while we're on a date.

Dea floats silently next to Nine, and part of me wonders if he's asleep, but then he flutters those beautiful eyes open and the question dies on my lips. He swims underneath Nine and comes up between us, settling me with a dark look, his pupils glowing gold. I've only ever seen that look that intensely once. In the hotel bedroom.

Fuck me sideways.

This man is going to kill me.

But you'll enjoy it.

If hell is a platter of Death, I'll happily spend the rest of eternity trying to die to get there.

"No need to die to taste this platter, Angel." He winks and grabs my chin in one hand before sweeping his lips against mine. Once. Twice. And on the third brush of a kiss so delicate I'm worried he'll break beneath me, his tongue delves into my mouth and tackles mine.

One point seven seconds.

That's how long it takes for my panties to soak through, Nine to grab my hips from behind, and Dea to groan as he leans into the kiss.

"Angel," he says between breaths. "You are perfect."

Exquisite.

Nine trails fiery kisses down my neck that leaves my skin tingling against the water and my arms shaking in Dea's hold. A nip here and a sucking lick there. And my legs wrap around Dea's waist, bringing us closer. So close I can feel the tremble in his hands as he strokes delicate fingers along my collarbones and down my shoulders. So close his cock is nudging my clit, and I can't breathe for how tense this atmosphere has gotten.

Like it'll swallow me whole one orgasm at a time.

But it turns out, I do not have a problem with that.

Nine delves his hands under the water and skims teasing fingers along the underneath of my bikini bra and up.

"Nine," I gasp.

"Yes?" he asks, fake innocence lacing his voice.

"Don't stop."

Dea groans in front of me, his eyes squeezing closed as he rolls his hips against me. "You two will be . . . the death of me." His voice a soft, husky whisper that sends delicious pleasure dancing down my spine. "Do you have anything you would like to do, Angel?"

"Or try?" Nine adds. He resumes his kisses, like his very existence relies on touching my skin. "You never know, we might play out one of your many fantasies."

I try for an indignant sort of sound, but Dea dips a hand into my bikini bra and flicks a harsh thumb over my nipple. "Do not play games with us, Angel," he warns, that familiar dominant edge returning to his voice. "Nine shares all kinds of things with me."

I go rigid for a moment, concern lacing my body, but then I relax. Who am I kidding? I love that they talk about me. Wonder if they compare notes?

Yup.

Dea snorts. "Nine told me all about how you love to beg, and I nearly orgasmed on the spot."

"It was hilarious."

"Did he do that thing like in the kitchen, where he pouted and screwed his eyes tight shut while trying not to go all dominant bear on you?"

Nine laughs, his hands gripping my hips. Yup.

Dea, on the other hand, swoops in with a dominating kiss that must take Nine by surprise, because his grip tightens on my hips as he rolls his cock into my ass.

And I think I just might know what I want.

I send the fantasy image to Nine, who breaks his kiss with Dea to give me a look of surprise, his eyebrows shooting to his hairline. "Really?"

"What? I can't be adventurous?"

He holds up his hands in defense. "Just assumed it would take longer to persuade you to lose those inhibitions."

"Pfft. I've already sampled both the goods, what's the point in holding back now?" Now I want both. Together.

I notice the moment Nine sends the image to Dea, because Dea's eyes glow a brilliant gold as he yanks on my wrapped legs to grind against me. "I will always find your mind fascinating. And I will forever be jealous that Nine gets to spend every second he can in that gorgeous head of yours."

Chapter Fifteen

The Five Horsemen: Are They Safe or Are They Dangerous?

We decide that to fulfill this particular fantasy, we really need Dea's bed and his box of goodies. I mean, how else will he tie us both up together?

I transport us straight into Dea's room, and Nine asks the house immediately for some refreshments while running his still-wet hands down my arms and nipping at my bottom lip until I grant him entry and he wraps his tongue around mine to distract me. Meanwhile, Dea steps up behind me and pulls me to the bed, yanking my thighs apart to straddle him as I face Nine, who stands between our legs and continues kissing the ever loving fuck out of me.

Dea's hands roam up my sides before he leans back and unties my bikini top with skilled hands and a sigh of relief when he has free access to my nipples.

Nine wastes no time in breaking our kiss and sinking to his knees, where he lavishes the nipple Dea leaves free for him.

And fuck if two pairs of hands and two mouths don't feel like I'm in some kind of heaven. A really good heaven. Filled with dick. And tongue. Maybe some boobs, too. Oh, and some chains and rope.

Yup. That's heaven.

Dea wiggles out from beneath me and pulls my hands together in a clasp behind my back, then yanks me backward. "Are you going to let me tie you up like a good sub, or are you going to be a brat?"

I wish I was the kind of person who could backchat and talk shit, but I just want to get fucked, so I say nothing and just let him tie my hands to each metal loop of the bed while I rest on bent knees.

Dea strokes gentle fingers down my arms as he goes, whispering, "Good girl."

His praise shoots straight up my body, setting it alight and dousing me in oil to fan the flames higher.

"Damn, bro. Magic looks good like that."

Dea takes a step back to admire his work and nods. "My Angel will always look good in restraints." He turns to watch Nine's eyes sparkle as he looks me up and down. "Just like you."

Nine turns to face him and wraps his arms around his neck. "I don't think I look quite as tasty as our little prize over there." He nods toward me. "But I can put on a show for you whenever you want."

"Do not sell yourself short, Famine." Dea grabs his chin and forces him to meet his gaze. "You look beautiful in restraints with that perfect scrunched-up look on your face just before I shove your dick down my throat."

A small whimper escapes my lips before I can catch it, and they both smirk in my direction. A predatory look in their eyes that sets my nipples on edge and reminds me I'm at their mercy tonight.

Totally at our mercy.

Nine creeps along the bed toward me and grabs my bikini bottoms in both hands before running them down my legs and throwing them off the bed. "And I want you screaming both our names before this evening is out."

Dea leans over and ties Nine's hands to the same loops as mine, smirking at us both the entire time. Then he kneels behind me before palming both ass cheeks and biting the sweet spot between my neck and my shoulder that always makes me shiver.

My head thrown back and my eyes closed, the guys revel me in warm kisses, nips and bites, firm hands, and gentle strokes. And just as I'm about to ask them to touch me somewhere better—anywhere with more nerve endings—Nine bends down, stretches his restraints as far as possible, and places a warm kiss to my clit.

My breath rushes out on a whisper as Dea rubs harsh thumbs over my nipples. "Yes. More, please." My hips rock into Nine's mouth of their own accord, and I can't help but moan as he takes me between his lips and sucks, flicking a quick tongue over the top.

"Harder, Nine," Dea orders.

And Nine submits to his demands and sucks harder, nipping his teeth with just the right amount of pressure to shoot stars across the backs of my eyelids as his tongue flicks quick, tense laps.

Dea delves a hand between my thighs and runs a finger up my slit. "Fuck. She is soaking wet."

Nine pops his head up in interest, and Dea pops his fingers into his mouth for him to lick clean. Nine's eyes close as a small moan escapes. "Fuck, Sweetie," he says once Dea returns his fingers to my teasing my slit. "You taste so good."

As Dea pumps one finger inside me, Nine secures his lips back to my clit and sucks hard enough to have me crying out and bucking into their hands and mouth. Nine's tongue travels farther south and tangles itself with Dea's fingers as they pump in and out of me.

I can feel the tension building just from their foreplay, and I briefly wonder if I'll survive this night with them teasing and dominating me in equal measure. But I still want them both inside me, so I can't put out just yet.

"She's holding on for later," Nine groans. "For when we're both inside of her."

Dea leans down and whispers in my ear, "You really want both our dicks at the same time, don't you?"

I nod, not trusting my words as Dea pushes another finger inside to match the first and Nine returns his attentions to my clit and nipples, his arms stretching wide behind him.

"Get undressed, Famine." Dea unties his restraints.

When Nine lets me go and steps off the bed, I groan as the ache for his tongue and teeth pound at me, causing my body to buck into nothing but Dea's fingers.

Nine strips his swim shorts off and sets his hard cock free with a swipe of his hand.

Dea leans around me and gets off the bed, joining Nine, then removes Nine's hand from his cock and replaces it with his own. "This is mine this evening. You will do with it as I say. Understand?"

Nine nods and looks at me.

"Yes," Dea confirms. "Stick that delicious cock of yours

inside my sweet little Angel's pussy and make her moan so I can watch."

His words spin through me, searing through the lust haze they've both webbed over my mind that's left me speechless and right to the searing throb between my thighs making them shake.

Nine kneels in front of me, a playful smirk on Nine's face I wipe off with a kiss and a nip at his bottom lip. "Fuck me already. Please." I can't keep the whimper out of my voice.

But Nine seems to hear me because he lifts one leg over his hip and lines his cock up before easing himself home.

"Nine!" I gasp and whimper and moan as he stretches me, the friction shaking my thighs and throwing my head back. When he begins to move, I tug on my restraints and grab the rope hard. "Yes . . ."

"Harder," Dea instructs from where he's sat at the end of the bed, watching with eager eyes shining like gold. "And faster." His hand wraps around his shaft and tugs. "God, you two are so hot to watch like this." His breath ragged, his knuckles nearly white, and his eyes staring holes in our bodies.

Nine shuffles backward and leans me at an angle so he can bend his head to capture my nipple in his mouth, and I gasp.

"Dea . . ."

His gaze snaps to mine as his hand stops moving. "Yes, Angel?"

"I . . . help."

Nine snickers around my nipple as he pinches the other.

"Fuck!" A scream leaves my throat as my pussy convulses around Nine's dick, making him snap his hips and pound me harder.

My eyes still locked onto Dea's, I watch the moment that

control snaps. The moment his desire wins out. "Fuck this." Dea crawls up the bed and kneels behind me. "Grab me the lube."

Nine gently pulls out of me—much to my disappointment— and reaches into the nightstand drawer. He throws a tube of it Dea's way.

"Good. Now get back inside of her."

Nine wraps my leg back around his hip and fills me tight, sending jolts of white-hot pleasure through me, while Dea runs his hands down my back. But he doesn't stop when he reaches the bottom, he continues, trailing gentle fingers down my ass, running tight circles around my ring, and continues down until he reaches the connection between me and Nine.

Nine suddenly moans, his eyes rolling and his lips parting. Yes, that . . . Seems words are lost on him, too.

I look down and see two of Dea's fingers and a thumb wrapped around the base of Nine's cock while he pistons into me. Just imagining myself in Nine's shoes has a different rage of desire infernoing around me.

Dea's hand on my cock . . .

Nine's mouth wrapping around the head . . .

Fuck, that's hot, Sweetie.

So hot.

Dea growls in my ear. "Is that what you want in the future?"

Nine must have sent the image his way.

I nod and thrust my ass backward, reminding him of what I want right now.

"Such a demanding little thing." Dea takes a moment, but then returns to my ass and runs a finger around the rim, pulsing gentle waves of pleasure through me every cycle.

"Dea, please . . . stop teasing."

He chuckles in my ear and presses a kiss to my neck. "Just making sure you are ready and relaxed enough, Angel. Trust me."

I nod. "I do trust you."

Just as Nine picks up his pace and slams into me at a new angle, Dea inserts one finger.

"Fuck!" Yes, I definitely want something bigger.

He doesn't move for a moment, so I thrust back and bury that finger to the hilt in eagerness, reveling in the slight sting that permeates my body. He adds a second finger, then a third, until I'm a whimpering, sobbing mess in their arms and the only thing keeping me up is the restraints and Nine's cooling hands on my ass cheeks.

Dea's hand runs up and down his shaft, spreading more lube, while his other hand remains buried in my ass. "Ready, Angel?"

My head nods of its own accord.

"She's more than ready, bro. Her pussy's been clenching for release for minutes now."

Dea grabs a fistful of my hair and turns me to face him. "Is that so?" He kisses me and pushes the head of his cock against my hole. "We will just have to do something about that."

Nine grabs my chin and forces my lips back to his as Dea slowly enters me. He's slow at first, not wanting to hurt me, but soon he's buried all the way in and they're both groaning at the tightness while I'm trying to keep it together.

But damn. I feel so full. They're touching every needy part of me, hitting every right spot, and I want—need—them to move. To—

"Shit, yes!" I scream as they both move at the same time. My head flops back onto Dea's shoulder and I'm gone. Lost in pleasure. My mouth is making all kinds of sounds I've never made before, and my desire shoots through the roof.

Dea wraps both my legs around Nine's waist and lifts me up and down onto their cocks like I'm their personal sex toy.

I can feel you, Dea. So good.

"I can feel you, too. You are so hard. Angel is so tight."

"Dea," I beg, "faster. Please."

His grip on my hips tightens as he slams me down faster, helping me chase the release that's just around the corner.

Fuck. I don't think I can hold on if Magic—

My world explodes in stars that shoot across the backs of my eyelids. "Goddess, yes!" The feral scream that escapes my throat makes it hoarse and dry, but I don't care.

Shit. Nine volleys a string of curse words into the air as his hands grab Dea's on my hips and yank me down. Fuck. He rides me through my orgasm as his crests and explodes into me.

I can't see Dea, but by the frantic pace and pounding into my ass as hard as he is, I know he's close. "You are both so . . ." He steals me from Nine's cock and buries his face into my neck as hot ropes of desire drown me.

We're all panting and heaving in silence, our breaths the only sound in the room.

"We're definitely doing that again," I whisper on a breathy exhale.

"Absolutely," Dea agrees. "That was some of the best sex of my existence."

Agreed.

Dea unties me and lays us on the bed, where he proceeds to clean me up with a fresh washcloth and warm, gentle hands.

Damn. I'm so in love with these nerds.

CHAPTER SIXTEEN

WHO IS THE FIFTH HORSEMAN?

A pile of limbs, snores, and sweaty bodies wake me the next morning, all of us having passed out in Dea's bed the night before after the best orgasm of my life ended my ability to speak.

But I seem recovered this morning, if a little sore. A delicious kind of sore, though, that reminds me how it got there with every shift of my thighs.

Today's the day.

The chosen ambassadors are coming to Sheruta this morning to officially meet us and each other. It's a momentous occasion.

A knock at the door has me yanking the duvet up across my boobs while Nine and Dea groan themselves awake.

"Yes?"

"It's just me," a bright-sounding Connie says on the other

side.

"Oh, come in." No longer concerned about my boobs being on show, I let go of the cover and smile at her. "What's up?"

Her blonde hair matches her bright smile as her brows raise in question at the pile of obviously naked bodies.

"Oh, shut up, Con," Dea groans. "It is too early to deal with your silent communication." A morning person he is not. "What do you need?"

"We only have thirty minutes before we need to be at the embassy to meet the ambassadors."

"Shit," I exclaim. "I have to get dressed." I rush to the door, give a quick kiss to Connie, and then Vampire speed to my bedroom just in time to see Arrie heading through the open door to my study.

Wonder what he's doing in there this early?

I don't have time to ask right now, though. I'll have to deal with Arrie later.

I get showered and dressed as quickly as possible. Twice. Then rush out to meet anyone else who's ready.

"Hey, hon!" Connie runs into me from behind and wraps her arms around my male form. "You okay?"

"Uh-huh. Kinda nervous about today, though." I spin to face her and am once again shocked at her beauty.

Surprise, surprise, she looks amazing. As usual. A short deep-green dress that stops mid-thigh, is clean cut, and shows off her figure perfectly. She's paired it with light makeup and long hair she left in soft waves down her back. After having cut her hair from floor-length to the bottom of her back-length, she's taken it well, but seeing it still makes me wince.

Maybe hair-growing spells are a thing?

I'll look into it.

"Don't be nervous," she whispers into my ear after leaning in. "You'll do great." Her hand brushes my chest as she steps closer and places a quick kiss to my lips. "I promise."

I nod, trying to big myself up into believing her, but I stop short of actually reaching that goal. I have no idea what I'm doing. I'm gonna mess it all up again, and then I'm gonna have to somehow fix my mistakes, and then I'll—

"Stop spiraling!" She takes a deep breath and looks me in the eye. "You're going to be fine because we'll be there with you."

My hands rest around her waist as I breathe in her mango-scented conditioner and let it fill me up. "You're right."

"There will be some press and journalists there today, but I've made it press-pass only."

"Okay, good."

We could handle some basic press, right?

Eh, I'm sure it'll be fine.

Just as we turn around to head downstairs, Arrie steps out of my room—clearly having come from the library—looking dashing in a dinner jacket, laid-back professional sort of style. And he's tied his hair up into a ponytail.

I itch to wrap my arms around him, tell him he looks hot, and sink my lips against his. To remind him he's loved. But I can't. He doesn't want that.

Arrie stares at me, those ice blue eyes drilling holes into my soul. He opens his mouth and then closes it again. And again. And again. Until eventually he grunts a hello and turns to walk away.

Damn him.

Connie sighs. "One day he'll pluck up the courage to speak to you."

"If I'm lucky."

We all stand together at the top of the winding path that leads to town, and as one, we take a deep breath.

"Everyone ready?" Dea asks.

No one answers, but we all stand united nonetheless.

"No matter what happens today," Connie starts, "no matter what drama the Vampires, Shifters, or Witches start, we stand as a united front."

Everyone nods at her, but Arrie does so with a grimace. "And who's leading this front?" he asks, sarcasm lacing his voice.

I clear my throat, and he sighs. "Dea."

The man in question looks surprised, but I shrug. "You've been dealing with this from day one. You know these people better than anyone. Usually, I'd ask Nine, but he'll be busy starting the blood replacement research tomorrow, so he can't. Connie's busy doing PR management and helping me not totally freak out. And Arrie will be busy with war plans. It's me or you, buddy."

"Okay, okay," Dea says with his hands in the air. "You are right, Angel." He places a solid, sturdy hand on my shoulder. "I will gladly lead today and tomorrow."

Arrie smirks at me.

But I ignore him. Which is my strategy for the entire day. "You're the best at politics, anyway."

Dea's head raises at the praise, and I smile. It feels good to make them feel good.

Yeah, love'll do that to you, Sweetie.

I chuckle and start walking, hoping I'll make it there without sweating too badly. No one talks on the way there, silence entering tense on the scale of atmospheric conversation. And I direly need to break it.

But for once, it's not me who does.

It's Arrie.

"So, what's the goal for today?" Everyone looks surprised he cares, and he huffs. "I'm still a part of this team, even though I'm the only one not fucking the captain." He shoots daggers at me.

Connie coughs. "I'll have you know, Magic and I are taking things slow. We have not yet slept together."

Arrie raises his brow at her. "You are going . . . slow? You?" He coughs to hide his laughter. "Sure."

Connie punches him in the arm hard enough to make him stagger, and now it's me who's hiding a laugh behind a cough.

"The plan," Dea intervenes before we all have a three-way fight. And not in a good way. "Is to welcome the new ambassadors, show them around the building, show them to their offices, and then brief everyone on the primary goals of the embassy."

"While cameras are there," Connie says. "There's a press conference after the briefing for our journalists to ask as many questions as they want."

Nine steps in. "I'll handle that."

I look him in the eyes with gratitude.

"It'll be easier, since I know what they're really thinking."

"Right," Connie says, "but I think Magic should at least open the press conference with some fancy words and explain our overall goal."

"Like a speech?" Nerves shoot through me.

"Yup," Connie says, "but I knew you'd hate that, so I prepared some words for you on key cards."

A sigh of relief escapes me. "Thank fuck."

The new building looms in front of us—seven stories

of sea-green plasma-infused polymer, with plasmacsreens imbedded along the windows, night-time technology along the Vampire floor, and an impressive number of balconies, plant walls, and witchlights.

"Wow, Dea," I whisper, "you've really outdone yourself."

He chuckles. "I . . . had help."

"From who?"

"From us," a familiar voice echoes behind me.

I spin around and notice a familiar purple-haired Fae whose cakes never fail to make me smile. "Hey!" Various Sheruta residents surround him, all wearing the council pin on their breast pockets. "You're part of the Sheruta Council?"

He shakes his head. "Not quite, Miss."

An older Shifter with an impressively long beard steps forward with arms wide. "He volunteered to help us help you create the embassy."

"There were a hundred of us, Miss, who volunteered." He looks sheepishly to the floor. "You've inspired a lot o' people since your outin'."

Really? I don't think I have.

You stood up to the Fae Queen, attacked the rogue Vampires, and are not friends with the Supernatural Council. That last one alone has made you many friends.

Yeah, and many enemies.

You won't win 'em all, Sweetie.

I can damn well try.

I bow to café owner and say thank you before turning to the Sheruta Council. "Thank you for dealing with my request so quickly. It surprised me we could make a building in such a timeframe."

A man and woman behind the older Vampire both chuckle. "We have lots of united forces here on Sheruta.

Including Witches and Fae willing to work together, Vampires willing to put in labor, and large Shifter packs. Plus, they all like you." Her dark hair and skin shine under the morning sun as she smiles.

"Well, I cannot thank your peace enough."

The older Vampire, who Nine informs me is called Derek, interrupts us. "We have new residents to greet and visitors to entertain, do we not?"

"Indeed, Councilman Derek. And again, thank you." Dea offers me his arm and swings us toward the portal building.

And for once, I'm heading there with a smile on my face, since it won't be me using that vomit contraption. Ever again.

Inside the building, we wait at the front desk for the various supernatural communities to arrive. And first to come through are the Shifters, who brought Alpha Cal, another woman from the council I just recognize, two other young men, and . . . Korby.

Korby runs at me with her arms outstretched and a smile wider than the sun plastered on her face.

"What are you doing here?" I ask, squeezing her tight.

"Well, you need to keep up your training, and Alpha Cal wanted to bring some friendly faces, so I volunteered. Figured I could stay in-realm for a few weeks to help you out."

"That's . . . Wow! Thank you so much." I shake my head. "I was happy to commute, you know."

She shrugs. "It's no big deal. Besides, now I know this place exists, I can't wait to explore it!" She bounces up and down on the spot, her short hair bouncing with her. "It'll be so much fun!"

"That it will."

I show her, Alpha Cal, and the others outside. "We'll be reconvening at the embassy once everyone arrives. Terrance here"—I gesture to a Sheruta volunteer—"will show you to your hotel rooms and personal lodgings in the meantime."

I thank them as they leave, giving Alpha Cal a personal handshake and an extra thank you, before turning back around and waiting for the next load of guests and residents.

"You think the Witches will still be angry with me?" I ask, my voice a gruff whisper. My eyes avoiding the team's.

"Yup," Arrie confirms. "Mad as the last rose of summer."

Connie scowls at him, then turns to me. "Probably, but this'll go a long way to mending things."

Dea adds his usual wisdom. "They will probably not be helpful to our overall cause, but they might offer assistance behind closed doors. And who knows, this might strengthen ties between them and the Vampires."

Speaking of, the Vampire King, Prince Lucien, and a familiar face walk through the doors next. Prince Phillipe's wife. The Vampire King chose her? That's so . . .

Generous. An inspiring move.

She's being abused by her husband, the next Vampire king, leader of the rogue Vampire faction, but by being here, she can't be touched.

I'm so shocked by this political move that it takes me a moment to realize I'm staring at the Vampire King with an open mouth. "I . . . I'm sorry, Your Majesty." I bow low. "Your choice surprised me for a moment."

He smiles. "I hope she will be a worthy asset to your goals, Horseman of Magic." He places his frail hands on my shoulders and whispers, "Keep her safe for me, would you?"

I nod. "I'll do my best."

"Soooo . . ." Lucien begins, "you picked me?" He smirks, all devilish and charming, as usual. "Really?"

If I'm not mistaken, there's an air of nonconfidence

in that tone. He's not sure he can do this. But that's okay. Because I am.

"Yes, Prince Lucien. You are just the man for the job."

His eyebrows raise. "And how do you figure that?"

"Well, there are lots of benefits to the embassy plan, but we're pretty friendly with the Vampire Royal Council, so we don't need stronger ties there. What we need is unification. With your passion and charm, I'm hoping you can at least manage amicability with the Witch ambassadors."

He snorts and darts his gaze away. "Not bloody likely, love."

"I believe you'll be fantastic at this ordeal."

Prince Phillipe's wife walks up to me with a gentle smile and a little trepidation, which I don't blame her for. "I think that's a wonderful plan. And maybe seeing how united Witches and Vampires are here on Sheruta might give them the dose of reality they need."

"Precisely." I smile and offer my hand to shake. "I'd like to apologize for how I treated you before. I let anger get the best of me before looking at all the facts."

She waved me off. "Nonsense. I would have done the same thing in your shoes."

"Well, aren't we all peachy and making friends today," Lucien says, the sarcasm lacing his words stinging just a little.

"Don't be jealous, little prince. I'm sure we'll the best of friends before this war is over."

Mention of the war has everyone's faces sobering, the reality of why we're here sinking through the atmosphere like a stone.

"I'll try," Lucien says with more conviction than I've ever heard from his mouth. "I'll try my best."

Another volunteer shows them to their hotel rooms and

personal lodgings while we wait for the third and most nerve-wracking visitors to arrive.

The Witches.

Fifteen minutes later, and I'm pacing the reception in frustration. They're late.

They're probably doing it on purpose as a political move.

Ugh. I swear, when all this politics is over, I'm never fucking dealing with it again.

I wish I could grant that request, Sweetie.

I know, I know. I'll be doing this for the rest of my existence. Which is immortal. So I should just suck it up with a smile.

And lots of internal sassing. Sassing is key.

That serves to make me chuckle, and the others look over at us with questions on their faces, but I wave them away. "It's nothing important."

Just at that moment, the doors to the spinning vomit room open, and the full Witch Coven and several other Witches arrive, all dressed in their typical garb.

And I start to shake and sweat.

The entire Coven. Why?

This is gonna be a pain, isn't it?

Probably. Have you considered apologizing?

Me apologize? They're being ridiculous!

You did insult their way of life, their culture, and disrespected their laws. And then assaulted one of the most important people in their world.

I grumble under my breath. But he's fucking right. As always. Guess it's time to suck it up.

I stroll up to the air Coven Witch and smile. "I'm glad to see you are well. I am . . . sorry for the way I behaved last time we met." I bow my head, a red blush blossoming across my cheeks, and say, "I hope that will not cause any problems with our goals at the embassy."

The seer Witch is smiling at me when I lift my head, and I get the feeling she likes me, though I have no idea why.

The air Witch simply nods her head at me and walks past, as though I'm an unimportant fly on her pristine wallpaper.

For fuck's sake.

They're not particularly forgiving, are they?

Nope.

Chapter Seventeen

Reported Break In and Data Theft at the Supernatural Council's Chinese HQ

A couple of hours later, when all our new residents and their guests have settled in and met us back at the embassy, we settle into the meeting room with an array of cakes, pastries, and tea—curtesy of our wonderful resident baker. The heads of all three councils and the council representatives of each main species here on Sheruta sit at a large round table with us. Everyone else sits around the edges of the room.

Dea turns visible for the first time today, and everyone turns their heads his way. "I will lead today's events." He coughs to clear his throat. "As you all know, communication between us Horsemen and the various supernatural councils has strained over the last few centuries. But with a new war brewing on the horizon, we feel it best to strengthen our ties. We hope that increased communication between the supernaturals present will also be of use."

The Witches shift uncomfortably in their seats while the Vampires do their best not to look their way. You could cut the tension with a knife.

"We have the four representative heads of the Sheruta Council with us today, so you know who they are. They will be designating a single individual per community to join each of your teams." Dea sips his tea and leans back. "But you all have chosen a member. As have we."

Alpha Cal bows his head in respect to Dea. "We Shifters feel proud and welcomed by our Horsemen, and we thank them for their generosity in allowing us a free choice during this troublesome time."

The Vampire King speaks up, adding his own gratitude. "We also would like to thank the Horsemen for inviting us to such a prestigious event and political movement." He looks at me. "It's truly a work of social art."

"Thank you, Your Majesty, Alpha Cal."

Everyone looks to me, but I keep my mouth shut and look back to Dea, not wanting to make any further mistakes.

Dea picks up the hint and takes over once more. "We hope to use this embassy to work together. To better connect the various councils and covens around the world by having one communication hub."

The head seer Witch clears her throat and looks to Dea with a question.

"Please," he says, "no need for permission to speak. We're equal here."

"Will we be joined by the Fae today? And what of the humans?"

Dea looks at her with a soft smile that borders on sad. "Unfortunately, the Fae Queen denied our request and is choosing not to participate."

Derek, the Sheruta Vampire representative, clears his throat. "And as a rule, we have no humans here on Sheruta."

"But does this not alienate them further?" Alpha Cal asks. "Would it not be best to extend a peaceful hand their way?"

"I agree," Connie says, "it would at least look good, if nothing else."

The four Sheruta Council representatives shift in their seats, but it's the Shifter representative—a mousy brown-haired man with a graying beard—who says, "I guess we can bring it up with the full Sheruta Council next meeting."

The head seer Witch nods in agreement along with the rest of the table, but I'm not so sure. "Where does that leave the SC? Should they not be involved? Do we directly oppose them?"

Someone from the back seats surrounding us coughs to get our attention, and Aki stands. "If I may interrupt?"

What the hell is Aki doing here in the first place?

Dea gestures for him to continue.

"Thank you." He bows in his direction. "I think Nigel has some good news on that front, but I'm uncertain."

"What news?" I ask.

"He mentioned this morning about maybe having persuaded the SC to meet with you."

Finally.

A sigh of relief escapes my entire team as we collapse into our seats.

"We will have to reconvene to discuss this further once we have had a conversation with them to see where they stand," Dea says.

Everyone seems in agreement, so Dea switches out with Connie for a bit to allow his visibility to recharge. I swear I'll look into making a visibility charm so he can use that before using his own energy stores soon. I really need to get on that.

Ooh, it might make a good Christmas present. That's just around the corner, right?

It is indeed. I promise I won't tell anyone what you're getting them.

Shoot. How do I keep things from you again?

Not a clue. You managed it once and then haven't done it again.

Fuck.

Connie goes through who's been picked for each species, starting with the Vampires. "For the Vampires, Prince Lucien was our pick, Princess Felicity was the king's pick, and Harrow was the Sheruta Council's pick."

One by one, they add themselves to the table, taking the place of the king himself.

"For the Shifters, Pansy was our choice, Leva was Alpha Cal's choice, while our very own Roofus was the Sheruta Council's choice."

I don't know any of them, but they all seemed friendly enough. Pretty sure I've seen Roofus around from time to time.

"For the Witches, Aki was our choice, Red was the Coven's choice, and Nana was the Sheruta Council's choice," Connie announces as, again, they join the table, taking the Coven's places.

What!

Why did no one tell me Aki is going to be on the council?

He said he'd tell you.

What?

Sorry, Sweetie, I've been a little busy recently.

Oh, Nine. I'm sorry. I didn't mean to shout at you. I'm

mad at Aki. That conniving little toad.

"This is it." Connie gestures to everyone. "For now, this is the entire embassy representation. For us Horsemen, you'll likely interact with myself and Dea the most, but don't be afraid to ask any of us for assistance with anything you might need."

Everyone stands and claps, a few cheers whoop out, and the few journalists, who were making notes until now, congratulate us on this momentous occasion.

After a few hours of pleasantries, where I had to undergo more small talk than I have ever used before—and hope to ever use again—we're stood outside the embassy's front doors, with all the members standing behind us and a massive audience in front. Including many journalists with cameras, notepads, and floating microphones to be heard over the crowd.

"This is your bit, hon," Connie whispers in my ear as she shoves the key cards into my hands.

I wish I had more time to prepare, but alas, I've been busy.

Looking to Nine and Dea beside me, Nine mentally adds, Real busy.

I sigh in my head and shake myself into a more professional mental position. I can do this. It's just a dumb speech. Nine'll take over halfway through, anyway.

Opening my mouth to start, I glance at the first card and smile. "Welcome, everyone, to the opening of the first multi-species embassy since the Supernatural Council opened its doors. We are very excited to introduce you to the new faces of Shifters, Vampires, and Witches here today." I gesture to the group of politicians behind me with a grand smile. "While we have a fair way to go, I'll admit, we will be stronger for having done this together. As a team."

The crowd cheers, and I hand over the microphone to Nine, who smiles at me and places a gentle kiss to my forehead. "You did great, Sweetie."

I finally exhale after stepping back into Dea's and Connie's waiting arms.

"Well done, hon."

"Yeah, Angel, you did great."

I don't think I did much of anything, but at least Nine can take over and do some real good.

He answers questions, smiles and diverts insults, hands over some questions to the relevant ambassador, and dodges tricky inquiries we don't have answers for yet. He truly shines.

"He's made for this," Dea whispers.

"Yeah, he should really do this full time."

Yeah, but Dea looks hotter doing so. And besides, I'm busy with the blood supplement plans. We start research in my lab tomorrow.

More visitors to Sheruta?

Yup. But I rented a building in town for them to stay in so we don't impose on the residents.

Sounds like you have everything covered. If you need anything, though, Connie can help with the minor details.

She's doing well with the management side of things.

Yeah, and she's enjoying it, I think.

She loves being this busy and doing something normal that isn't fighting related. But she misses you and is still hurting over Bandio Bontanos.

Just hearing that bastard's name whispered in my mind is enough to have my fists clenching and my breath hitching.

"You okay, hon?" Connie asks as she squeezes my hand.

"Yeah, yeah. I'm fine." I place a quick kiss to her temple and return my attention to Nine, who's wrapping things up for the day, it would seem.

"Thank you," he says, "to everyone who asked questions, will report on what we have done here today, and for supporting an important movement in these troubling times." He turns around and walks back into the building, gesturing for us to follow.

"Well," I say once the door closes, "that went well."

"Better than expected," Leva adds with a smile.

For a Witch, she's been pretty polite so far.

Maybe she's not aware of my troubling past with her Coven? Or maybe she cares little for all of that and wants peace?

Eh. I have no idea. But I'm determined to find out.

Chapter Eighteen

The Five Horsemen and Their Accomplishments

Dinner tonight at the house is a simple affair: we ask the house for pizza, eat, and go straight to sleep. But not before Arrie wishes us goodnight.

He actually says goodnight to me.

And I might have a little dance party in my chest as I lie between Dea and Nine while Connie's working out in the gym.

He said goodnight. To me.

Maybe he doesn't hate me after all. Maybe he's just dealing with some shit, and I should try to talk to him about it. Yeah, I'll talk to him in the morning. If he'll let me.

In the meantime, snoozy snooze.

But by morning, Arrie is nowhere to be seen, Connie leaves early to handle some embassy setup stuff, and Nine meets his colleagues to work on a Vampire blood substitute.

Which leaves just me and Dea.

"So," I start, "I think we should give the embassy an update on what's going on. Tell them about the rogue Vampire faction and the Fae working together, and what we're going to do about it. I also think being 100% transparent will be the best course of action. Tell them about the SC's plans to take down the world's major Vampire cities."

"We should also give them hope, Angel. Tell them about Nine's blood substitute plans, about your plans to unite the lower supernatural world and ask for their help, and we will have to ask Arrie to work with them on defense plans."

"Sounds like a plan."

"Con said to meet her there at eight am."

Looking at the wall clock, I gasp and hurry. "That's fifteen minutes away!" Thank god we're already dressed. "Hurry up!"

Dea downs his fancy tea, I shove my coffee into a to-go cup, and we shoot out of the door faster than a jackrabbit. Haha. I can probably shift into a jackrabbit if I want to.

Now is not the time, Magic.

Dea grabs me around the waist and carries me in his arms, then fazes us the rest of the way. "There you go, Angel. Now we are early." He smiles a cheeky, charming grin at me.

And I can't help it. I bring my lips to his and wipe it off his face in a searing kiss. "I could have done that myself, you know."

He smiles against my lips. "I know, but then I would not have gotten to hold you."

What is with these guys? "None of you ever need to look for an excuse. You can just come right over to me, pick me up, and hug me."

"We know. But you're very busy, and you have four

partners. We just like making the most out of the time we have."

Three. I have three partners. But now isn't the time to bring that up. "Okay. Well, feel free to steal me whenever you like."

Smirking up at that beautiful face, his grin spreads wide across that sharp jawline as his eyes glow gently beneath the sun.

"Hey, guys!" Connie yells from a distance as she runs toward us. "You made it!" She grabs me into a hug and then rests my hand in hers. "I'm so glad you're here. They're all asking for updates on things, and I didn't know what to do."

The fluster on her face mars her usually calm and excited features, and I want nothing more than to smooth those lines and make her laugh again.

So I guess I'm going to update the supernatural communities about the Fae and rogue Vampire faction's bullshit.

The drama that causes oughta make her smile plenty.

The glass walls, the plasmascreen walls, the plants hanging from every ceiling, and the regular break and game rooms every few meters make me smile. They thought of everything. A universally liked space.

The double door to the main meeting room looms in front of us, all beautifully decorated in plants and woodwork that makes it look inviting. How misleading. This room is anything but inviting. In there, I have to tell the Vampires that the SC is planning to shut down their main cities. In those comfortable as fuck chairs, I have to sit and ask the Witches for help. Through those doors, I have to prepare our world for war.

And I sure as shit don't want to.

"It is okay, Angel." Dea stops beside me, a friendly hand

on my shoulder. "We will do this together."

"Yup," Connie says with a smile. "It's gonna suck, but we'll be there with you."

One deep breath later, I swing the doors open.

Lucien lounges on a sofa he's brought in while Pansy's blonde hair sits perfectly on top of her head in a neat bun as she straightens her back upon seeing us.

Dea, Connie, and I sit at random intervals around the table, trying not to sit at the head like some immortal dictators. My eyes swing to Aki, and for a brief moment, our gazes meet. He offers me a smile, and I try to return it, but something about him unrests me. Something I'm not sure I have a name for yet.

Maybe I'm just worried about having a brother?

"Do you have any updates for us?" Lera asks. She's one Shifter assigned by the Shifter Council, and her bubbly smile eases my concerns somewhat.

"Yes," Connie says, "though you'll have to forgive Magic. Uniting people is not really their strongest skill."

Prince Lucien snorts an agreement, and I would have glared at him, but Connie's use of their throws me for a loop. It's gender neutral.

I . . .

It's . . .

Fuck.

What's with these Horsemen always throwing my emotions under the bus when I need them to be on the sidewalk in step with me? Goddess dammit.

Dea coughs and looks at me expectantly.

Right. Vampires. The SC. War.

More important shit.

"A few days ago, I broke into the Supernatural Council's

Chinese headquarters to steal as much data as possible. It was an intelligence gathering mission to help us prevent further destruction like what happened in New Orleans."

Prince Lucien's head crooks up, and he joins us at the table. "Do you have a plan for New Orleans? Because the king wants me to ask for your aid."

I bow my head. "We do. But we have a more pressing matter to deal with first."

Harrow looks astounded. "What could be more important than giving the Vampires back their kingdom?"

Both Vampire ambassadors look to him with small smiles of compassion and gratitude.

I glance at Dea, who nods and takes over, "Protecting the other five Vampire capitols." He coughs and takes a deep breath. "We believe the Supernatural Council is planning an attack on all Vampire capitols around the world."

All faces at the table look horrified, even the Witches look unsettled. Red looks like she wants to say something, but then holds back.

"Did you want to say something, Red?" I try to be gentle, but I'm still struggling with the idea that the Witches won't help.

Because they won't.

They never do.

"I . . . I just . . . I cannot believe the SC would do such a thing." She turns to the three Vampires in the room and grimaces. "I'm no fan of your kind. But you are a species, and you deserve to live. There's a reason Witch Hunters are no longer decreed in our Coven, because one of the early Coven Councils outlawed the practise. We don't like you, but we won't cause war by hunting you out either." She looks at Aki with a frown. "I have to wonder why the SC are suddenly picking up the mantel."

Aki coughs. "I handed in my resignation this morning, so I can stay here and help you." He looks to me when he says it, and I can tell he's trying to make a connection. To be a brother.

But I have no idea how to be a sister. Brother? Sibling.

"And what of Nigel?"

"I'm sorry," Lucien interjects, "but who is this Nigel guy?" He shrugs. "I'm not fluent in Horsemen Who's Who. Sorry."

Sighing, I explain that Nigel is my godfather, but that he works for the SC. "He wanted to quit. To work with us full time, but I mentioned that maybe we could use his connection, and now he's working undercover with us." I look to Aki to reiterate my earlier question.

"He's been going into the office from here, using some of your teleporting crystals."

"Ohhh," Connie says, "that reminds me. Magic combined Fae and Witch magic to make Sheruta to Earth teleporting crystals, as well as Earth to Earth. We'll get you all a supply." She looks to me, silently asking if that's okay.

I shrug. "They're easy to make now I know how. I can even show you how." Then I wince. "But I guess with no Fae in the embassy, it won't matter."

Roofus, the Sheruta Shifter representative, chooses that moment to add to my list of things to think about. "That reminds me. The Sheruta Council wants us to consider adding a Sheruta Fae to the embassy. Ready for when the Earth Fae join our ranks."

"But there's no guarantee they will."

He shrugs, as if to say he has no clue either. "They're pretty certain they will. That, or they believe in you a lot more than I do." He picks lint from his nails, and I have a deep desire to rip them off one by one.

Cool it, Magic. You need to get along with these people like a grown-ass adult. Internally groaning, I just about resist the urge to slam my head against the desk. Why is adulting so hard?

In my next life, I'm living as a fucking tree.

"So," Connie interrupts, "soon, Magic will be leaving to try and ask for help from the lower supernatural world."

Gasps and natters fill the room, with some looking at me in awe and others with confusion.

"We'd like any information you can give us regarding what's out there, their whereabouts, and anything else that might be useful. We'll reconvene soon to discuss. We understand it might be a little much to ask this of you from the off."

They all nod thankfully.

"Famine," Dea says with a nod toward Nine, "is creating a synthetic blood supply for the Vampires. He has tried working on this before, but he feels we have a new lead on how to solve a critical problem in its creation. Please offer all the support you can to help us with this, because once we take back New Orleans, getting up a fresh blood supply will be top on our list of priorities."

"War," Connie starts, "will be leading the defense plans for all five cities, and you'll all be required to help with that. Are there any problems?"

"Yeah," Roofus interrupts, "are we Sherutans obligated to help with Earth problems?"

Connie grinds her teeth. "No one is obligated to do anything. If you'd rather not help with the war plans, then feel free to leave." She gestures to the door.

Roofus looks at her like she's kicked his puppy, but he

quickly recovers and smirks. "Noted."

"For now," Connie says, "we'll be meeting every day. At least me or Dea will be here in every meeting. We want to keep each other as updated as possible."

Everyone seems to understand the necessity. And surprisingly, everyone is more on board than I thought they'd be.

Chapter Nineteen

New Horseman Embassy a Political Attack on the SC or a Pathetic Attempt at Peace?

We get everyone on board: Vampires and Shifters. Both will need permission first, but they're pretty confident. But the Witches need to petition the full Coven Council first, otherwise the ambassadors will only be able to help from the sidelines.

Walking out of that meeting room is like a destressing massage.

"Hey, Magic!" Aki calls out from behind me. "Wait up!"

I spin on the spot and smile at my brother, who's running toward me. "I just wanted to say that as a Witch who isn't affiliated with the Coven Council, I'm with you." He places a steady hand on my shoulder. "To the end." His brown eyes meet mine, and for the first time, I'm glad I have a brother.

"Thank you, Aki."

"Say, d'you think maybe we could get a drink at the bar downtown?" He looks at his watch. "It is lunchtime."

The hope in his eyes is furious, burning like a flame that'll go out with even the slightest gust of wind. How can I say no? He's just offered his services—the strongest Angel-descended Witch in the world. We need him.

I need him.

"Sure. But I'm due for a Fae lesson in a couple of hours, and if I'm late, then I'll be legit worried for my life. That woman is terrifying." I shiver at the icy rage my tardiness would be met with.

"Okay, that's cool." He smiles. "I'm just glad to . . . meet you." He sighs. "You know, properly. Spend time with you and—"

I save him by laughing and shifting into my female form for lunch. "I get it. It'll be nice to get to know each other a bit better."

I say goodbye to Connie and Dea, who both look at me with proud smiles and kiss me in that deliciously possessive way of theirs that makes me flush, considering Aki is standing just a few meters away.

And then I'm off to lunch with my brother.

It's the same bar I went to with Connie that time, when we danced, got obscenely drunk, and then I flew us through the porch ceiling. The memory makes me chuckle under my breath.

"Something funny?" Aki asks, looking a little put out by my randomness.

"Just a memory of the last time I was here."

"What happened?"

We sit at a table in the corner, away from prying eyes and ears, and I regale him with the tale—leaving out the steaming hot kiss and wandering hands, of course—and when I get to the part about crashing through the ceiling, his laughs warms me.

"Right through the roof?"

"Uh-huh. Enough that Dea had to heal the shard of glass that shot straight through me."

He gasps. "You should be more careful!" His voice raises people's ears our way, and he shrinks back. "Oops. Sorry." He winces. "But you should be more careful."

"The glorious thing about being immortal is that careful means something different to us." I smile gently at him. "I can race at three hundred miles an hour and crash the car, and I'll be fine. I can get my head chopped off and it'll just grow back."

"Really? Like . . ." He gestures to his throat and lops his head to the side. "Like, clean off? Are you serious?"

"Yup." I smile, pride washing through me. Maybe it's cool that I'm immortal?

Aki beams at me just as our fries and beers arrive. "That's amazing!" He looks at the food with hungry eyes, but he turns his attention back to me. "What else can you do?"

"Well, I have two forms, each holding the different species' powers. Witch and Vampire in this form, Fae and Shifter in my male form."

"And you can shift into any animal, use all six types of Witch magic, and don't specialize in any specific form of Fae spellwork?" His eyes pierce mine with excitement.

"Yup. That's about it."

"Other than your dea—"

I throw my hand across his mouth. "Not here. But yeah, that too." I sigh. "I have no control whatsoever over it, but I'm kinda hoping that you'll help?" I meant it as a statement, but it came out as a question.

His eyes beam with pride as a smile takes over his face. "Yes. A million times yes!" He wiggles in his seat and looks like he wants to explode into rainbows.

It's cute.

"Need any help uniting the lower supe world?" Aki asks.

Do I? I'm not even sure when I'm leaving. "I need to make a plan first. See what supes we think we'd have a chance of helping in return for good favor. But yeah, maybe . . ." In truth, I'm still not sure I can trust him.

His face looks crest-fallen; his previously lit eyes now a dull shadow, his smile a frown, and a worrying crinkle in the center of his forehead.

For goddess' sake.

"Okay, okay, okay. You can help."

He looks at me like a child on Christmas morning.

Christmas! It's only two months away, and I want to get everyone a gift. A meaningful gift. Which means I need to work on Dea's invisibility charm and think about something for Connie and—

"Magic?" Aki waves a hand in front of my face, trying to get my attention.

Oops. Must have drifted off into another spiral. Damn. I've been doing so much better.

Okay, focus, Magic. Focus.

"Sorry, what were you saying?"

"I was saying how I can give you a few"—he looks around us with suspicion—"lessons before you leave, if you like." He looks to the table. "Not sure how helpful it'll be for your mission, but you know . . . Maybe it might come in useful."

Chapter Twenty

The rest of my lunch with Aki was spent chatting about the world, our lives, and how great it would have been if we knew each other sooner. When I was mortal. I dodged the subject of me being an assassin for the Hunter's Society. But it'll come out eventually. And when it does, people won't want me interfering at all.

Which means I need to leave as soon as possible.

But I need to be better at Fae magic first if I have any hope of helping the pixies. And being better at death magic and more proficient with my bo staff won't be awful either. Who knows what kind of things I'll have to do to get their help.

Hopefully, if I can help them, they'll be more inclined to help me.

Getting through the barrier to the remote village is easy this time around, since I have already written my data into the storage rune, so I just press my palm against the detection rune, and bingo, I'm in. Just like my library door.

Right on time, too.

Phew.

Fae children play in small groups, laughter flitting through the air like hummingbirds while they run around and chase goddess knows what. They are all kinds of Fae, from green-skinned summer folk to blue-skinned winter folk, to pale-skinned fall and spring folk. No one argues, there is no tension. It's more peace than I can ever hope to create.

"Magic." A familiar grumbling female voice grates my ears. "You're here. Finally." Her arms crossed over chest and a frown on her otherwise beautiful face, she stalks over to me. "I've been waiting."

"You said two." I point to my watch. "It's two. Exactly." I cross my arms over my chest and smirk. "I'm on time."

"Humph." She turns and stalks off.

This time, I don't hesitate to follow.

She leads me not to her cottage, but to a small stream peddling through the center of the village. A few small children play along its banks here and there, but it's mostly raw and untouched.

"This is our main water supply." She gestures to a well a few meters away. "We collect the water from the underground stream that runs parallel to this one. It's our only source of clean water."

Seems a little risky, if you ask me.

"Today, I'm going to contaminate that supply with something unknown to you, and then you'll need to wash the stream clean so we may drink again."

Again, she's floored me. "You're going to risk your own water supply?"

She nods. "Of course." She taps me on the back. "You need proper motivation." She stares at me in confusion. "Can you do Fae magic in your female form?"

Oh, right. I change into my male form, still in the formal clothes I wore to the embassy, and smirk. "No, just this one."

"Strange." She wrinkles her nose in confusion, her pale green marred by the action. "So long as you can learn Fae magic, I guess."

My heart shrinks inside my chest as it hammers against its cage. My fingers clench into fists. I hate how much emotion lays beneath the anger, how much I want to break. Does she really find me that strange?

She turns around and places something green, slimy, and covered in mud into the stream, and I watch it pollute the stream as it creeps toward the well.

The entire water turns a dark green color, and as I run my fingers through it, I realize the texture has changed too. It no longer runs through my palms like water, but sticks to them like slime. What did she put in here?

Is it some kind of poisonous plant?

Or is there some spellwork at play?

Did she create it just for this purpose?

Ugh.

As usual, I know nothing.

Why am I always fighting blind?

Three deep breaths later, and I finally sit on the stream's bank to analyze any and all spellwork. If I want to know what's going on, I need to know the components in play and how they interact, otherwise I'll have no hope of getting home before nightfall.

First things first, this stream is spelled to be clean, which makes sense, but the water below is not. I wonder why until the answer hits me. There's no need for it to be. It's already clean. It must be, otherwise they wouldn't all still be alive and healthy. So why is this top one unclean to begin with? Maybe it's something in the topsoil? Or the plants?

Or maybe something in the above stream gets oxidized, and that causes a reaction . . . No, there's air below ground, too. So that doesn't make sense.

The clean rune is affecting some living component in the stream, so it's probably some kind of bacteria or fungi. A damn antifungal or antibacterial product would be more efficient, but whatever floats their boat, I guess. Besides, I get the feeling they don't use outside help much. Or at all.

But I don't really know the difference between antifungal and antibacterial spells, and I would probably need to google it to find out, which I don't have access to here—damn lack of a datachip—so it can't be that.

Can it?

All these questions are making my head spin.

I keep scanning the spellwork at play and pick up something interesting in the stream. A kind of plant with a rune attached. Could this be what she contaminated the stream with?

I hope so.

Analyzing further, it looks to a be a plant. Maybe some kind of weed. Damn, I need to get better with my botany if I have a hope of proceeding in these lessons.

Sure, I'll just add that to my list of shit to do. No problem.

The rune, on the other hand, is what's making the plant spread quickly and reproduce at such a rapid rate. Otherwise it would have taken a few weeks for the whole stream to be contaminated. But getting rid of that won't help me now.

I need to know how to get rid of the plant from the stream. I need to know what she meant by washing it clean. I know a couple of water spells if I want to get rid of all the water here and replace it with fresh stuff. Could that be the answer? Would be draining, though. There has to be an easier answer.

If I knew what the plant is, I might be able to know something about contradicting it—maybe a rune that cancels its effect or kills it entirely. Wait. There probably is a rune that kills fungi. An antifungal rune? Maybe a cleanliness rune? That's what's running through the stream already, though. If that works, then it would already be working.

So why isn't that rune doing something? If it's not cleaning the fungi or bacteria out of the stream, then what the fuck is it even doing in the first place?

I analyze that rune again, but this time, I look at what properties it looks for in the first place. What kind of things does it recognize as 'unclean?' This rune is only for non-living things, like acids, urine, and minerals the Fae don't want to be consuming. It does nothing for the living biomass around the stream. They mustn't be harmful. No point in wasting your energy topping up a rune every few weeks that doesn't even get triggered.

Okay, so do I know a rune that could work against living contaminants? No. Great. Helpful. Oh, maybe I could adjust the rune already in the water to include biological contaminants. That seems relatively quick.

Runes are lines, swirls, and patterns that form various magical bonds with the Fae's magic. Each line and swirl and pattern does something different until the whole creates the desired effect.

This rune looks like two swirls that meet each other in

the middle. But how do I make that incorporate biological matter? Hmm. I really want a rune book right about now. "How am I supposed to know this off the top of my head?"

"Runes are intuitive to Fae," my trainer says. "That's how we discover new ones every few years. Reach inside yourself and see."

Reach inside myself . . .

She realizes how much 'myself' there is, right? She realizes how chaotic I am, right?

Blowing out a frustrated breath, I concentrate on the Fae part of me, ignore the Shifter stuff, and try to focus on my internal reservoir of magic I get from the leyline below the house. It's topped full, like always. But how do I get it to search for a rune pattern?

Can I make the magic reach out and touch the rune already there?

Fae magic is a bit weird; it's the only time a supernatural deals with raw magical energy. Even Witches only deal with the plasma particles given off by the leylines. But because Fae can tap into the leylines directly, they have a direct link to magic. Or energy, as some scientists prefer to use.

So maybe that means I can direct the store inside of me toward the rune. Runes are made of this same energy, after all. I channel some of my stored plasma—or energy—toward the stream, where the rune is tethered. It wraps around the rune, analyzes it, and brings up an exact copy.

Hmm. "So that's what happens when you channel plasma around a rune."

My Fae trainer huffs in amusement from wherever she sits glaring at me. I closed my eyes a while ago so I can concentrate.

But how do I add to the rune to biological matter? She said it's intuitive. But do I add my thoughts and feelings to the plasma? Can I show my plasma the problem?

Don't be stupid, Magic, it's not alive.

I have to add the intent myself.

I wonder if it works like Witch charm magic? Intent is important there, too. And they do use the same source; albeit in different ways.

Using my own intentions, I guide more energy to the rune, but this time, I mentally will it to shape into a new rune that also cleans harmful biological contaminants.

Please work, please work, please work.

I really want to get back and make some plans for mine and Connie's date. A real date this time. Not just a friends thing.

The rune copies itself, like before, but this time it adds new swirls to the pattern, so it's four joining, rather than two. Could this be it?

Oh my goddess, this is it, isn't it?

Yes, yes, yes.

I finally let go of the intent when the rune finishes forming and place it into the stream, where it quickly turns the water from green to transparent again. And, just for good measure, I shift into my female form and touch the water, hoping to get some kind of sign that it's okay.

C'mon, c'mon, c'mon . . . Make me look cool in front of my trainer. Pleeeease.

The water ripples from my fingers all the way down the stream, and I can sense it rippling through the underground stream, too. Everything is clean.

Yes. Fae magic and Witch water magic.

Woo!

Nothing can break me now.

Chapter Twenty-One

She cracked a smile. An actual smile! I got my Fae trainer to smile at me and say congratulations.

I sprint home in a flit of Vampire speed and race through the front door with a beaming smile on my face. "I did it!"

Connie rushes down the stairs to meet me at the same time Dea fazes to me from the kitchen. "Achieved what, hon?"

"Not only did I figure out her puzzle in record time, I used my Witch's water magic to send a ripple down a stream." Now I say it out loud, it sounds dumb.

I must have looked to the floor or something, because Dea grabs my chin and forces me to look at him in those beautiful galaxy eyes. "That is amazing, Angel. You are developing at a phenomenal rate."

"Yeah." Connie wraps her arms around my waist from

behind. "It took us hundreds of years to develop as fast as you've managed in a few months."

"You're right." I pridefully turn around to face her and whisper, "Tonight's date is on me." Placing a gentle kiss to her cheek while not letting Dea run away, I whisper, "Thank you," to them both.

Connie smiles while Dea nuzzles my neck and says, "You are most welcome." He smoothes circles across my hips. "If I am not mistaken, you have a date to plan." He pulls away, and this time, I let him. "Have fun."

He sounds a little depressed, so I turn back around to face him with a question on my face.

"It is nothing important. It is just that Nine is busy and you are planning your date tonight." He waves away my concern. "It is okay. Maybe Arrie would be up for sparring and a movie marathon." He smiles at me.

"While you're spending time with Arrie, could you try to casually drop that I still like him," I mumble. "You know, if you don't mind."

Dea traces a thumb down my cheek and rests it on my lips. "Of course."

"Now c'mon," Connie nearly screams. "I wanna know what my date is!"

Yeah, me too. "Let's plan it together?"

She grabs my hand and yanks me upstairs. "You bet!"

Early the following morning, we take a Sheruta-Earth teleporting crystal straight to the Bahamas. Bikini-clad, sun-lotioned skin free to breathe and smiles all around, because the date we planned together is an all-star luxurious cruise around the islands on a personal yacht. Staff, cocktails, an all-you-can-eat buffet, plenty of bedrooms to try out, water slides, movie theater, and star gazing all await us the moment we board.

I don't think I ever did anything like this as a mortal, and I'm excited to know how the other half live. Connie, of course, has done similar things, but she's never hired a private yacht for two. So bonus points to me.

And she's just as excited.

"C'mon, c'mon, c'mon . . ." She drags me up the yacht, and soon we're running around the deck, oohing and aahing over everything, from the view of the captain's cabin to the water slide curling around the side and ending up near the ocean.

"The slide descends whenever you wish, Horsemen." A tall, overly thin man with pinned-back black hair greets us. "And it is an honor to have you on board with us."

"Yes," a smaller gentleman with blonde hair and a wide grin says, "welcome. It's so exciting to have such important people join us."

The first man bows lightly and grimaces in the blonde's direction. "This is Lucy, you'll have to forgive her. She's a little excited about meeting you."

She . . .? I could have sworn . . . Oops.

I pretend like I didn't just assume someone's gender (me of all people) and smile. "It's lovely to meet you, Lucy." I bow to her.

And she giggles in that adorable way of hers. She's like a fluffy bunny. All sprinkles and rainbows. It's cute. She leans over and whispers, "Oh my god, Magic bowed to me," in the other man's ear.

I cough. "I'm half-Vampire in this form."

Lucy goes pale for a moment and then flushes a deep red. "I'm so sorry. Ohmygod. I didn't mean to offend you or anything. It's just so cool. You're like my hero. You can change forms, use both, be whoever you want at any moment of time. And I just wanted to—"

"Lucy," the other man groans, "please control yourself."

"Right." Lucy straightens and shakes her head. "Professional."

She really thinks I can be whoever I want? Like, whenever? I'm her . . . hero?

My face must have betrayed my shock, because Lucy whispers, "Not everyone hates you. Some of us think that standing up to those nasty Vampires was awesome!" Her voice ends in a squeak, but she straightens back up again and looks serious once more, side-eyeing Mr Serious next to her.

I see the headlines and I see the opinion polls, but I never really get to hear humans' points of view. Ever. It's nice to see they're not all blindly following the SC's propaganda.

"Would you like to be shown to your room for the evening?"

Connie shakes her head and grabs my hand, taking a longer-than-average perusal of my black bikini top that shows off my tattoo in all its skulled glory. Her eyes meet mine in a look I know. She wants some alone time in our room.

And this time we won't be interrupted.

"Yeah," she whispers, "definitely."

The black-haired man from before shows us to a luxury cabin with a bed that overlooks the sea in a window wall I'm jealous of. Like, I know I have a window wall of my own. But this one is curved, has an ocean view, and I want it. Can one steal a window?

"Like it, then?" Connie unpacks some of the clothes she brought for later, including the dress she plans on wearing to dinner tonight.

"It's beautiful."

I help her unpack, and soon we're hanging our evening dresses up together in the closet. They sit side-by-side, black against green. Like a couple. Like us.

Connie catches me staring and smiling. "They look good together, huh?" She wraps her arms around me from behind and rests her chin on my head, a warm presence reminding me she's part of my home. An important part of my life.

"Yeah, we do."

"I know we're on a date, but we can still do the Friday things, too. I know we've accomplished a lot this week, and I think it would be good for you to unpack it all. Emotionally speaking."

"You're probably right." But I don't want to talk about Arrie. Do I? Alright, maybe I do. Just a little. But it's our date night. I don't want to ruin it by bringing up other-man drama.

"What are you over-thinking now?"

I huff a laugh. "Am I that much of an open book?"

"Yup." She spins me around to face her. "It's all over your face." Light fingers trace the edges of my face in graceful slides of delicate fingers, and shivers run down my body. "The way your lips part and your brow furrows in concentration. You're like an emotional plasmascreen."

"Am not," I mutter under my breath.

"Are too," she whispers, lips inches away from mine. Her breath fans across them as her hands trail down my shoulders, arms, and eventually rub circles into my waist. "But I think it's beautiful. And besides, it makes my girlfriend duties easier."

"Girlfriend duties?"

"Yeah. It's part of my job to help you stay as stress free as possible, and to help you work through your emotions. The guys are rubbish at it." She looks away in thought for a moment. "Well, I guess Nine is pretty good at it, but that doesn't count."

"Eh. He mostly stays out of my relationships with the rest of the team, unless it involves Dea."

Her eyebrows waggle, and I giggle. "Sooooo . . ." She drags us onto the bed. "Spill!"

I eye her with a raised eyebrow, feigning innocence, but she shakes her bed. "I walked in on you completely naked between two very naked Nine and Dea. Soooo . . . tell me, what kinky threesome did you guys get up to?"

"Okay, okay . . ." I take a deep breath. "It started in the pool in the villa they rented for the day, but when Nine saw the fantasy floating through my mind, he showed Dea, and then we came back home to re-enact my imagination, which is surprisingly creative, apparently."

"Oh, do tell me." She grabs my hand and smiles. "C'mon, we might be a thing, but I'm still your best friend, right?"

The hint of uncertainty stabs me right in the feels, and I give in. Instantly. Damn this woman.

"Dea tied me and Nine up to the hooks on his bed, and then ordered us around, before they both . . . you know, had sex with me at the same time."

"Like, DP-ing in the same hole or one in the pussy and one in the ass?"

"You can fit two dicks inside your vagina?"

"Anyone can. It just takes patience, lots of lube, and lots of foreplay."

"Oh." I feel all weird and innocent. Which is odd considering I took two dicks not a few days ago. "That sounds . . . painful."

"Not if you do it right." She waves a hand in the air, dismissing our tangent. "So, two holes, then?"

I nod. "It was . . . amazing."

"And Dea ordered you both around?"

"Yeah, he ordered Nine to fuck me and then got impatient."

She flops onto the bed. "Wow."

Is that something she wants?

My concern must have flashed across my face, because she grabs my hand and whispers, "I'm just jealous I wasn't there to join in on the Magical fuckfest." She scrunches her nose in distaste. "I'm not sure I want something like that anymore."

"Really?"

She sighs. "I know it's hard to explain, but ever since you, everything's changed. I don't really even look at men anymore. It's just women." She shrugs. "Guess this means my sexuality's changing, huh?" She looks me in the eyes and smiles. "Don't get me wrong, I still want a threesome with you and Arrie one day. We're all so strong . . . It'll be great. And I still like men. But right now, the only person I want is you. Maybe that'll change some day, maybe I'll want to share the guys alongside you, but for now, all I desire is your legs wrapped around my face as you bury your head in that pillow over there."

A furious blush creeps up my face at her words, but I'm not embarrassed. Not with Connie. All her words do is send a thrill down my spine and a searing heat between my thighs.

She leaps from her spot on the bed and straddles my waist, pinning my hands to the soft fabric and sweeping a tongue across my closed lips. "But I'm enjoying this slow thing we're doing."

There's a look in her eyes I don't quite recognize on her, but it's all too familiar from the mirror. It's shyness. Going slow makes her shy.

I reach up and grip her bottom lip between my teeth, yanking her back to the bed with me. "I don't want slow." My hips grind into her on instinct as I take her mouth and make her mine.

Her hands wander up my body, grab the underneath of my bikini top, and move it aside. She breaks away from my kiss to travel down and then takes one of my nipples into her mouth.

Pleasure hisses through me, and I need something to grab onto, to ground me. So I slide my hands around her hips and yank them flush against mine.

Just as I'm about to pull her into another kiss, she rolls my other nipple between her fingers, and my body sparkles and aches all at the same time, like a firework about to explode.

"Connie . . ."

Our hips are a grinding dream as friction sears through me, and I know I'm close. Embarrassingly close. Our first time can't go out with me coming from just her mouth on my nipple.

But fuck, her tongue keeps doing that swirling thing in between sucking, and I can't think straight. Everything's hazy. My vision is blurring. And words aren't forming.

My back arches into her, and with a wicked smile and glee in her bright green eyes, she bites down on my nipple and pinches the other harder.

"Fuck, yes!" Tension soars through me in delicious waves and I scream her name and crash around her. "Shit."

I shoot up with a look of panic on my face. "Shit, I'm sorry. I didn't mean to finish so quickly."

Connie giggles for a moment before grabbing my face between both hands and forcing me to look her in the eyes. "There's a reason vaginas are better than penises, hon. We can go more than once." She looks me up and down. "And even if you can't, you have two forms. Might as well reap the benefits." She winks before lying beside me in a flustered heap. "Fuck, that was hot."

"So hot."

Shit. I can't just leave her unsatisfied, can I? That would be selfish. Besides, just imagining her screaming my name like that has a new fire lighting me up. I want to make her come on my tongue, I want to taste her, and I want to make her as chilled as me.

I flip her onto her back on the mattress and smile. "Your turn."

She laughs and pulls me into a sweet and gentle kiss. "We have all the time in the world for that, I promise."

"But—"

"I didn't do that just to make you return the favor. I did that because I wanted to, and because I wanted to make sure you're as satisfied as possible before the rest of our date."

"But—"

"No buts." She smiles and places a warm hand on my cheek. "Besides, I have plans for later that I want to be as horny as possible for."

"Plans, huh?"

"Oh, yeah. Big plans." She looks to my crotch and back to my face. "Huge ones."

She's talking about my cock, isn't she? Well, other me's cock. Wait. He's still me. Right? So, yeah, my cock. I think.

Chapter Twenty-Two

The Horsemen: Have They Helped or Have They Hindered?

Nothing tastes better than a mimosa under the sun with a gorgeous as fuck woman lying between your legs, head rested on your stomach, as the world drifts away.

"I think this is the most relaxed I've ever been since waking up in the house."

"Yeah?"

"Mmmhhmmm . . ." The sun beats down in harsh waves of blissful warmth that have sweat beading on my forehead and a flush creeping across my chest. "I don't have to do anything right now."

Connie lifts her head and looks at me with a smirk. "Well, nothing except me."

"You are incorrigible." I laugh, shaking my head at her antics. "I fucking love it."

"I'm not being too much or anything?" she asks, her voice muffled by the fact she buried her head back into my stomach. "You're sure?"

I lift her head to meet her eyes with mine. "You're perfect just the way you are, Conquest. Trust me." From her bright green eyes to the sexy smirk playing across her face, she's all mine. And there's no way in hell I'm ever letting her think otherwise. Using my Vampire strength, I rip her across my body and force her legs to straddle my waist before slamming my lips against her. "Mine."

Her body's pliant in my arms as she lets me lift her and wrap her legs around my waist. I flit us to the nearest wall, causing her to screech a little bit—but one look at her excited face tells me she's loving every second—and slam her into the window.

The mewling whimper that escapes her lips has the dull throb between my thighs roaring like a bonfire in July, an inferno of need I have to quench lest I go down with the flames.

Her skin smells so sweet, and I nuzzle her neck as I trail licks, nips, and kisses along her collarbone and down her cleavage. "Mmmm . . . you're so beautiful."

Her legs squeeze around my waist as her hips shift against me, trying to quench her own thirst. I snap my gaze to hers, but she squeaks and throws me off, landing in a heap on the wooden deck. Hands shaking. Breaths coming quicker than they did a few moments ago.

"Connie?" What happened? Did I scare her somehow? I snap my attention to my reflection in the window and gasp. Shit. My fangs descended without me realizing, and my eyes burn a bright red. "I'm so sorry." I quickly gain my composure with a couple of breaths and bend down to grab her hand.

She flinches and pulls away.

We were doing so well with this, but her time in those caves probably undid all of that. Crap.

"I can give you some space, if you'd like?"

"I just . . . umm . . ."

I whistle and hope someone is nearby to help.

And low and behold, Lucy rushes to our side. "Is there something I can help you with?" She notices Connie on the floor and squeaks. "Conquest!" Lucy reaches down and helps her up off the floor.

"Can you take her back to our room for me, please? I'll be there shortly."

"Of course, Magic." Lucy wraps Connie in her arms and lifts her with ease. "C'mon, Conquest. Let's lay you down for a while, hmm?"

When they are out of sight, I let the flimsy control I have on my anger slip, and the rage flies through me. "Fuck!"

The boat rocks under gentle waves as I bend the ocean to my angered will.

She was doing so well, and now we're back to square one. And it's all his fault! I killed him far too quickly. "Connie," I whimper, the anger fading out of me as I remember how defeated she looked on her knees in front of me. Like the world had broken inside of her.

She needs me.

I race to our room, where she lies under the covers shaking and crying. Alone. Shit. I shouldn't have left her like this.

Lucy comes out of the bathroom with a glass of water and an extra blanket. "She really doesn't seem okay."

"She's not." My voice is a near growl, and the boat rocks some more. "Sorry." I take a calming breath, letting a meager attempt at calm flow through me.

At least the boat stops rocking. But my hands stay clenched into fists.

I take another deep breath and let all thoughts of that monster exit my brain as I shift into my male form. My shoes shrug off and land in a pile beside the bed before I crawl under the duvet behind Connie.

"Hey, Connie, it's just me."

I'm hoping my deeper voice might keep her calm. Let her know I can't Vamp out in this form.

I curl myself around her and wrap a firm arm around her waist, settling her body against my chest and burying my head in her neck. "You don't have to be okay for me. You can just breathe if that's all you can manage."

Her sobs wreck me. "I . . . can't get his face out of my head." Her voice is barely legible, her whispers gutting everything inside of me.

My anger is more manageable in this form, though. "I know," I whisper. Keeping my voice low. Nonthreatening. "But he's dead, Connie. I killed him myself."

"I know." Her breaths calm with that fact. And after what feels like hours, her sobs stop heaving and level out to an even stream of tears instead. "But my fear didn't just die with him. I wish . . . it did."

Lucy's disappeared by now, but she left a glass of water on the side and a warm blanket at the end of the bed. Grabbing both, I sit Connie up and make her rehydrate.

"I'm sorry," she says with a sigh. "This was supposed to be a date. A happy memory." Tear tracks run down her cheeks steadily, like the sadness is leaking from her, even as her body calms. "I just need a moment, and then—"

I grab her hands and shake my head. "Don't do that. Please." My voice breaks as she looks at me with a smile. How can she be smiling right now? "I know what it's like to feel broken, Connie. And it's not going to go away just because you wish it so. So if you need to be broken today, then I'll sit with your pieces with you."

Sobs overtake her for another moment before she falls into my arms and cries her pain into my chest. And that's where we lie for the rest of the afternoon, letting Connie have a safe space away from her duties and the team and the house and the war so she can just feel.

Chapter Twenty-Three

Vampire King Has Something to Say to Supernatural
Council: 'Give Me My City Back'

I offer to call room service for dinner, but Connie says no and that we should still make our reservation.

"Are you sure?" I grab her by the shoulders. "We can stay here, chat some more." We've been chatting about how she feels, letting her vent some of that fear and frustration and guilt. "We can stay here, if that's what you need."

Her fingers find my lips and shush me into silence. "That's a nice thought, but I'm doing better now. And I want this evening, too."

"Okay." I try to smile, but I'm worried about her. What if she breaks? What if she's frightened of me again? What if—?

"Whatever you're thinking," Connie calls from the bathroom, "stop."

"How the fuck could you tell from in there?"

"You haven't moved yet, so I figured you must be doing that spiraling thing."

"Ugh. I've been trying to stop, but it's so hard." I wipe a hand down my face as I shift into my female form. "Dea says I should focus on being happy and scared in equal measure. So I've been trying to make sure the happiness counts too."

"He's right." She exits the bathroom with a face full of gentle makeup. "And I think that's an excellent strategy."

I throw some dark makeup over my eyes, conceal some of my blemishes, throw on the dress hanging on the closet door, and look over myself in the mirror.

Not bad.

The dress hugs my curves until it reaches my knees, then it fans out in a netted black tail that drapes behind me as I walk. And the plunging neckline looks outstanding, showing off both my tattoo and boobs.

Once my hair is pinned in a half-up, half-down kind of attempt, I call it a day and walk out to meet Connie's smirk.

"You look . . . like a fucking meal in that dress." She swipes a tongue over those luscious lips, and I have the sudden urge the smudge that red lipstick.

Her dress trails to the floor in a sheath design but still hugs her curves—albeit in a gentler way than mine—and the entire ensemble makes her looks innocent and gentle. Which, of course, is ridiculous. She could snap this ship in half without breaking a sweat and then still have enough energy to battle an armada single-handed.

"You look radiant, Connie. Truly."

Something in my eyes must have flicked a switch in her brain, because she runs over to me and hugs me. "Thank you." She takes a deep, shaky breath and lifts her head off mine to look at me once more. "I needed that."

She's not talking about the compliment, is she?

"Anytime, babe." I take her arm and face us toward the door. "Shall we?"

"Definitely."

The night air blesses us with its breeze as we walk down the deck, arm-in-arm, with smiles on our faces. We asked for the staff to arrange a romantic, cozy dinner for the two of us, and to go all out on the food because, well, I'm a giant food whore. So we have no idea what everything's going to look like once we get inside.

Every moment spent with Connie doesn't feel like a date. It just feels like I'm in love with my best friend, who I get to do romantic, fun, sexy, and silly things with. And this feels just like that. No nerves. No worries. Just a calm sense of home that she always brings to my heart every time she's near.

The grand doors we've been told hold our surprise are just up ahead, and as we near, two ushers dressed to the nines in suits open the doors, and we proceed to be blown away by the setting that lay before us. White and gold sashes hang from an open-air dining room, the ceiling having been opened, letting the night in. A small table sits in the center of a decked awning, flowers trailing up the tresses, and comfy seats decorating one side.

"This is . . ."

"Amazing," Connie finishes for me. "Awe-inspiring. One of the most amazing things I've ever seen."

"Think we can get a photo of something to show the guys. I want Dea and Nine to know they'll always lose to you."

She giggles and grabs my hand. "I already asked the organizers for photographs, though they were a bit taken aback that I wanted them in physical form."

"You did?"

"Yeah, they've been photographing the entire day."

"Thank you." I want to remember this. In a thousand years' time, when I won't remember how I feel in this moment, I want to be reminded. "That was a good shout."

We sit in the love seat that sits to one side of the table, and the waiter brings out water, our choice of cocktails, and some mozzarella, sundried tomatoes, and olive mix as an entrée.

And obviously, I love everything they bring out, even the things I've never eaten before; but the best part of the dinner date is that Connie gets to sit right next to me, we get to feed each other, hold hands, wrap our arms around each other, and eat all at the same time.

Clearly, whoever created this dinner knows me or they got seriously lucky. Food and cuddles are the best. No competition.

Connie's left arm is wrapped around my right as she leans against me and breathes in deeply after helping me devour the last of a massive slice of caramel apple pie that actually made me salivate just at the sight and smell of it. That dessert could have given Arrie a run for his money.

In fact, if I didn't know for a fact that Arrie would never cook for me and Connie, I'd swear this was his talent on these plates.

"Wanna take a walk?" Connie whispers in my ear. "Digest all this awesome?"

"Definitely."

We say thank you to the servers and the chefs, and then leave, both of us struggling in these dresses with all that food. But with my hand resting peacefully in hers, nothing else really matters.

"Can I ask you a question?" I say just as we reach the top deck.

"Sure. It is Friday." She smiles at me, the starlight flashing across her eyes.

"Is there something about being with the guys that makes you uncomfortable?" She snaps her gaze away from me. "It's just, a few times now, I've noticed that you typically get a little shy of uncomfortable when interacting with me around all of them at once."

"I . . ." She turns away from me. "I'm scared." Her voice is barely a whisper. "I'm scared that you'll prefer to be with them on your own. That you'll decide I'm not good enough." She giggles, but I don't think it's intended to be a funny laugh. "It's not like I have a penis."

Now it's my turn to laugh. "You think I care what body parts you have?" I spin her around to face me. "Connie, you got me off with nothing more than nipple play and a bit of grinding earlier. I don't care that you don't have a dick." In fact, I quite like that about her. "But if you'd rather it be just us when it's us, for a while, then we can."

"But I know you want us to be a big family. Like, all together and stuff. And I want to give you what you want, but I look at them and I just feel so inferior."

"I don't know if you've noticed, but I'm immortal. We have all the time in the world to be together in whatever ways we choose. But right now, I want everyone to just be comfortable and happy."

She rests her head on top of mine and sighs. "I don't know what any of us did in our long lives to deserve someone like you, but I thank God every day that you exist."

"So, do you have any limits or hard nos when it's all of us together? Not just in a sexual way, either."

She grabs my hand, and we walk along the boardwalk together, gazing up into the night. "I think I'll be fine eventually. Before the caves, I wanted nothing more than to watch you with the guys and join in. For us to all be together. But I think Antonio brought all that old fear and unconfidence back."

I've noticed. Whenever she's not looking or paying attention or doing something, she's gazing off into space and looking a little hurt. She's still a bit thin. And even though her wounds have healed, it's like she still wears those scars.

"We can work on bringing you back to your normal self, or moving forwards in whatever direction you want, together."

We stroll back to our room together, my arm slung around her waist, kinda afraid she might break if I let her go. But the moment we're back behind that door, I realize her silence wasn't concern or sadness; she was planning for this moment.

I watch her eyes go from pleasant to needy in a split second, like she had it under a tight leash until now. Her blonde hair spills around her shoulders as she smiles at me in that flirty way of hers that makes her lips part and her breaths heave and my knees weak.

"Magic . . ." She pins me to the door with gentle hands that trace tingles down my arms. "I want you to fuck me with everything you have. I want you to make me fall apart beneath you. In either form."

I nod, not able to form words in the face of the beauty asking for my virginity. Just the thought of sliding my cock into her wet heat has me heaving oxygen into my lungs as though it's vital I take every next breath to douse the fire Connie ignited.

For once, I'm not afraid. I wouldn't pick anyone else to help me explore that side of myself with.

Connie grabs my arms and pulls me away from the door to face my back to her, where she sweeps the zipper down my back and helps me step out of my dress. Her breath hitches. "I forgot you aren't wearing a bra or pants in that dress," she says on a groan. "Fuck." She rakes needy fingers over my hips and traces butterfly fingertips over my clit and between my thighs on a breathy inhale.

"Do I get to make you come this evening, too? Or are you going to deny me?" I really need to repay the favor. It's gnawing at me that it was one-sided.

She giggles while walking around to face me. "I promise you'll get to watch me come with your dick buried deep inside me." She watches my face with caution, gauging my reaction with an expectant grin. "Please?" Her eyes beg mine, creases forming across her brow as she darts a tongue out to lick her lips. "You'll do that for me, right?"

I nod, all but a slave to her words.

"Perfect." She turns her back to me and asks, "Unzip me?"

My hands slide gently down her back, grazing her soft skin like petals falling to the ground beneath their rose god, and she steps out of the dress with delicate ease before turning to face me.

I've seen her naked before, but only in passing. This time, she's inviting me to stare. Inviting me to roam my eyes over her breasts, her hardened nipples, her flushed chest and neck, and the panty line edging down her hips as she slips them off. Now she's standing before me in nothing but her heels and jewelry.

I want to say something. To breathe her in and never let her go. But I'm rooted to the spot. Gravity has taken me captive, and I'm all but a slave to its nuances as I sway on the spot and reach a hand toward her creamy skin.

One painstakingly slow heel at a time, she inches forward, her lips getting closer to mine, her body mere touches from falling into my grasp.

"Connie, I . . ."

"Yes?" Her voice is like honey, syrup glazing my mind, making words difficult to form. "Something the matter?"

"Come . . . here."

Her body flushes hot against mine, her breasts pushing against my own as our lips meet in an unhurried frenzy that lights the matches to the heat pooling at my thighs.

And I groan, unaware of how my needy hands rake down her sides as our tongues dance.

"You don't . . . need to be . . . gentle . . . with me," Connie whispers between kisses, fitting the words in with every breath she can. "I'm more . . . than willing to . . . be yours . . . tonight."

If that's what she wants, then I'm happy to oblige. Just need to keep my fangs retracted and my eyes purple.

I grip each thigh in strong handholds and lift her up, wrapping each leg around my waist, before I lave strong strokes of my tongue against her nipples, making her cry out.

She grinds against me, out of her control, and I bite down, sending a wave of screaming pleasure through her body that has her rocking against me in a frenzy. "Magic, I . . . Please fuck me."

I chuckle, thrilled by her need and more than a little heated by her demands. I throw her onto the bed and crawl between her legs, settling between her thighs like I'm the cat who got the cream. High on her lust. "This what you want?" I ask, throwing my tongue at her heat and lapping a long line up to her clit.

"Yes!" Her fingers grip the duvet in a white-knuckled grip. And she cries out again as I trail my tongue back down and thrust myself inside.

She tastes like honeyed heaven. I grip her hips and lift her up to my face, providing a better angle to reach for that sweet spot that'll be sure to make her—

"Ah, there. Right there."

A tight fist yanks my hair and pushes my head down closer to her. And just as I leave her heat to trail kisses and nips and licks up to her clit, she uses her other hand to play with her breasts and pinch at her nipples in turn.

I seal my lips around her clit and flick my tongue against her with suction.

"Fuck. Harder!"

Following her command, I suck harder and lash my tongue harsher, no longer being careful. I'm not stopping until I taste her release. With one hand still holding her up off the bed, I reach the other to her tit and roll her nipple between my fingers in demanding strokes while she handles the other.

Her cries grow as she thrashes in my grip, grinding her heat against my lips as her sex drips down my chin and she screams. "Magic, yes, I'm gonna . . ." Connie bursts into my mouth with a cry as she comes.

I ride her through, not letting up the harsh strokes of my tongue as she moans and writhes in my grip, until her cries become mewls and whimpers. Then I set her back on the bed and crawl up between her legs to plant a kiss to her cheek.

Her chest heaves in ragged breaths as she calms and returns to earth, but when I lay my head on her chest, she yanks me back up and slams her mouth against mine, licking her sweetness off my tongue and my lips.

"That was . . . so good," she mumbles.

"So fucking good," I whisper. Every part of me aches, and I itch to reach my hands between my thighs and bury them there. To switch forms and bury my cock into her dripping heat. To hear her cries of pleasure in my ear as I ram her into headboard. "So . . . amazing."

"Struggling?" Connie asks, a hint of playfulness in her voice. "Want me to help?" She reaches down and sinks two fingers into me, thrusting up in slow and gentle strokes that do nothing but fan the flames. "Or is there something else you want?"

I want her lips wrapped around my clit, my cock, setting me on fire. I want to come on her face, on her fingers, inside of her, and watch her come alive beneath me again. "I . . . yes. Make me come. Please."

The urgent pleading in my voice has her eyes glowing brighter as they meet mine in a heated gaze that tells me she'll do anything I ask right now.

Anything at all.

Connie grabs my hands and flips us, pinning me to the bed and rolling her hips into mine. Friction. Glorious friction burns through me. "I'm happy to try anything with you," she says, seriousness entering her tone. "Seriously. No need to ask permission or anything."

"Okay." Relief flows through me. I can shift at any moment, and I don't have to check with her first. She's made her want for my cock clear either way. "Thank you."

She smirks and trails kisses down my neck, across my collarbone, and laves long licks against my nipples, sending thrills down my spine and causing my back to arch.

But she's soon going lower, slow enough to kill me with anticipation and have my hips rolling on their own, seeking her mouth. Her tongue. Her lips. But when she gets to my thighs, she ignores me and keeps going. All the way until she reaches my knees and I'm groaning with impatience.

"So impatient," she giggles.

"I watched you scream my name as you rode my mouth." She nips at my groin, and I gasped. "So yeah, I'm a little past needy."

She breathes a deep breath, her tongue lapping against my skin, until she's stroking a fiery wave of pleasure from my clit to my heat, and I'm moaning her name.

"Connie, yes . . . Please." I don't even know what I'm begging for at this point.

Her eyes meet mine from between my thighs, capturing my gaze in a trap I can't look away from. She buries her tongue between my lips and taps the tip of her tongue against my clit in a rapid beat that sends tingling pulses through my body. Before she seals her lips around me and sucks hard enough to have my hips arching off the bed and my cries shouting into the air.

My mind jumps from the here and now to the fantasy of those lips around my cock, sucking me deep down her throat, and I groan as I roll against her mouth.

Magic ripples across my skin as a familiar feeling tugs me into another form. My male form.

"Shit," I cry, "I'm sorry—" I snap my gaze to Connie, who's now got her lips wrapped around the tip of my dick with a smile on her face and her brows raised in question.

Challenging me.

She takes a breath through her nose and sinks lower, burying my cock in her hot mouth as her heat surrounds me.

"Shiiiit." I groan and thrust, inching my cock deeper, wishing she'd suck like she did earlier. "Harder."

She obediently grips my dick like a vice as she buries her nose in my groin and takes me down her throat.

Fuck, that's tight.

And then she hums.

Everything around my cock vibrates, and she pulls away slightly, hands gripping my hips and pushing me back into her mouth.

I don't need any further instruction. I throw my dick down her throat in sweet thrusts while she keeps humming and sucking. "Yes, like that." Stars sweep across my vision, and I'm just about to speed up and chase my pleasure when she pulls out.

"I want to ride it," she says in a haze as she glares at my dick standing to attention. "Please?" Her lip twists between her teeth as she bites down and looks at me under those lashes.

"Yes, please. I just need to . . . come." Need laces every word, and I want nothing more than to fuck her senseless.

She climbs up my body and settles her thighs on either side of my hips as she grabs me in her hand with firm strokes while she lines us up and sinks down.

I hiss, groaning and moaning loudly as she buries me to the hilt in her tight wetness. "Oh god, that's so . . . good."

Her hips wrestle in small circles as she throws her head back and enjoys me. She pulls her hips up and throws herself back down, causing her breasts to bounce and my hands to grip them in vices.

"Play with them," she begs, her hips continuing to bounce on my dick as she squeezes me.

Bolts of need shoot across my balls like lightning, and I pinch her nipples. Gently at first, but as her moans get louder and her cries more insistent, my fingers pinch harder and twist them.

"Fuck, yes." Her face is flushed as sweat drips down her forehead. "More . . ."

I move one hand to her pussy and pinch her clit, moving my fingers in small circles as she flutters around my dick.

She's close.

She's clenching around me tighter, making her harder

than granite and my balls tighten.

"Fuck," I groan. "Yes." I grab her hips and flip us over.

Connie grabs her knees and lifts them to her chest, where I pin them. "Fuck me," she begs, "hard."

I drill into her, pounding her into the mattress as she screams my name. My fingers continue driving her orgasm closer, and soon she's gripping me like a vice, seconds away from exploding.

She holds her legs in place while I drive into her harder, fast strokes that have me nearly spilling inside her. But I want to feel her coming around my cock first.

"Come," I beg her, "please come."

I don't know how much longer I can hold on, but I don't need to worry, because as I pinch her clit harder and thrust faster, she cries out.

"Oh god, yes!"

"Yes, come for me."

Her pussy tenses around me, and pleasure shoots through my balls. But I don't stop. I pound into her while she screams, mewls, and cries, tears streaming down her face.

And a white-hot bolt of pleasure shoots through me as I shout her name. The strongest orgasm of my life flowing through me while I take it out on the amazing woman beneath me.

Catching my breath, I fall on top of her as her legs lower to the bed. "That was . . ."

"Amazing," she finishes.

And we both laugh.

Chapter Twenty-Four

FAE QUEEN SEEN WITH PRINCE PHILLIPE, HEIR TO THE
VAMPIRE THRONE

Waking up tangled up in limbs will never get old. Connie's head lies on my chest, her leg hitched up over my hip, and her lips sigh softly as I stretch awake.

"Morning," she mumbles.

"Morning." She shoots up like the sunrise and sits on top of me, grinding into my stiff cock with a smile. "Did you enjoy yesterday?"

"Uh-huh." The groan that escapes my lips sets her eyes alight, and her smile turns wicked. She goes to grab my wrists and pin them in her favorite place—above my head—but I shake my head. "I'm sorry, hon, but I have training today."

She sighs, disappointment flickering across her beautiful face. "Yeah, and I have a bunch of shit to do, too."

We both look at each other with longing, but we eventually

get up and dressed and head home, thanking Lucy and the rest of the team for a wonderful time.

Just as we land in the kitchen, something or someone glues themselves to my back and wraps their arms around my neck. Sweetieeeee!

Hey, Nine.

You're back.

I chuckle. "We are indeed." I spin around and grab him into a hug, then pull him off me.

His eyes have dark circles underneath them, are bloodshot, and his hair is falling in messy strands around his face, rather than being gelled back like usual.

"Oh my goddess, are you okay?" My hands rest on his shoulders as my brow creases in worry.

"Jees," he mumbles, "is everyone going to point out how shit I look today?" He throws an irritated glare at Dea, who's sitting comfortably at the breakfast table with a warm smile on his face, which is buried in a newspaper.

I swear he's the only person in existence to still read newspapers. The thought makes me laugh again. But then I turn back to Nine, who's looking to the floor and avoiding my eyes. "I'm sorry, Nine. I didn't mean to make you feel bad. It's just that you're usually so put together. You'd be worried about Dea if he came to breakfast in some thrown-together outfit, wouldn't you?"

"Yeah, I guess." He rubs a stressed hand over his neck. "I'm just a bit stressed from the research. It's not going as easily as I would have hoped."

Connie, Dea, and I all look at him in question, urging him to go on, but he just waves us away and wanders out the backdoor into the gardens.

"He has been like that since yesterday, Angel." Dea sighs.

"He is working himself too hard."

Guilt slices through me. I'm the one who gave him that task, and he's putting himself through the ringer just to complete it. "I hope he knows he can take his time."

Connie wraps an arm around my waist and sighs. "There are Vampires dying in New Orleans, hon. I don't think the pressure is coming from you this time."

"But he should not have to shoulder that pressure alone," Dea says through clenched teeth after slamming the newspaper down on the table. "I have tried convincing him to take a break, but he will not listen."

"Maybe we can help him with the research instead?"

"I do not think any of us are qualified enough for that."

Dea's probably right. But I wish we could do something. Anything.

"I could always force him to take a break." I shrug. "Tie him up and make him watch a movie."

Dea's eyes light up for a moment, and I know instantly where his thoughts went, but then he looks at me with a serious expression and a frown on those delicious lips. "I think this is going to be one of those times where he has to do things alone. We should just stay by his side in case he needs anything."

Reluctantly, I agree with him. Besides, this isn't about me. It's about him.

"Well," Connie announces, "I have some things to organize, people to boss about." She wraps her arms around my neck, sending tingles throughout my entire body when her lips slant and meet mine. "You have bo practise in half an hour, then you're meeting Aki for lunch and are doing some death magic practise."

I wince.

Death magic, already?

"I know you're hesitant, but it could really help."

Sighing my defeat—because she's right, as usual—I say, "Okay. But I want to travel out to talk to as many of the lower supes as possible soon."

Dea rests his hands on my shoulders, making me jump slightly, and says softly, "Then we should meet with the embassy tomorrow, after our meeting with the SC, and discuss tactics, who is going, et cetera."

"Sounds like a plan," Connie yells as she runs up the stairs and waves goodbye. "I had fun riding you! We should do it again sometime!"

Heat blossoms across my cheeks, and Dea looks to me in surprise. "So, you and Connie . . . ?"

"Uh-huh. Both forms. It was great."

"Wow, um . . ." His hands run through his hair. A nervous habit, I've noticed. "I did not expect you to get so comfortable with your male form so quickly, Angel."

"I wasn't uncomfortable with my male form. I was uncomfortable with the staring, the talking, and the freakish nature of my existence. And I'm still not okay with that." I take a deep breath. "But that shouldn't mean I can't be myself. Especially in an environment like home, where I feel safe enough to exist."

Dea's galaxy eyes explode in gold, brighter than I've ever seen before, as he sweeps me off my feet and kisses me deeply, his tongue demanding entrance into my mouth like an ancient doorknocker you can't ignore, and I give in.

"I am so glad you find comfortability here at home and with us. It is good you feel you can be yourself."

Korby jabs the edge of her bo in my direction, but I sweep my bo upward and knock it off course, so it jabs the air above my head. Making her smile.

"Nice!" She returns to her original stance a few feet away with an exhausted smile on her face. "Again."

Every muscle in my body protests. Every cell in my brain onboard to lie in a pool of sweaty exhaustion until tomorrow. But Korby's face is all determined lines and focus. And I can't let her down.

"Okay." You got this, Magic. Come on.

My feet a few inches apart, hands holding the bo staff above and below like she showed me, I root myself to the packed earth. Prepared for her attack.

But Korby is a strong Shifter, and she manages to throw me off balance nonetheless with a flurry of attacks too quick for me to process.

I lose my balance, my foot falling behind me so I don't fall on my ass.

She uses my split-second distraction to her advantage and rushes forward with a solid hit from the left, but my reflexes kick in and block.

"Good block!"

This time, I try attacking, but from the ground up in a side-stance. And yes, I manage to catch her leg and push her off balance, giving me an opening to catch her now-undefended side.

She falls to the ground in a huff and a groan, but then smiles at me—albeit with a grimace. "Well done."

I look at her with suspicion. "Did you let me have that hit?"

She shrugs. "Not really, but I have been going easy on you in general."

Oh. Well, I am just a newbie. "Care to have a go at me in

my female form?”

“Vamp speed with elemental Witch magic?” She looks to the sky for a moment. “You’re on. But you’re paying my hospital bills.”

“Deal.”

In my female form, my fitness is better, my Vampire strength makes some of the moves easier, and my general senses are heightened. I don’t use any Witch magic, though. I’ll wait till I get to fight with Arrie or Connie before I try that out.

We spend the next hour testing my strength and abilities, Korby showing me some more advanced moves, and we make others up to work best with my skills. All in all, it’s a good practise session, and the glass of cold water afterwards is some of the best liquid I’ve ever consumed.

“What’s next on your training schedule?” Korby asks from her place on the garden floor.

“Training some Witch magic with Aki.”

“Right, your twin brother?” She sounds as confused as I feel.

“Uh-huh. They separated us at birth, but we ran into each other recently. And then Nigel dropped the bomb on our shoulders.”

“And since Witches are difficult to come by for training, you’re using him?”

“Well, there are six different types of Witch magic, and most Witches can only specialize in one. But I can use all six.”

“Ahhh, I see,” she says, “so you need six different trainers in one of the hardest-to-find supernatural species. Bummer.”

“Right.” I don’t correct her. I don’t think it’s wise people know about my death magic. Or the Angel-descended Witch part of my mortal DNA Fate decided to let me keep upon my immortal death. Yippee. "So Aki's helping out for now."

"You don't sound super enthused." She sits up and looks at me with curiosity. "Not really clicking with your brother?"

"He's . . . nice enough. He was grumpy for a bit, but we chatted and realized what happened was neither of our faults, so we decided to call it even and move on. But he's just so . . . normal."

Korby laughs, her eyes catching mine afterwards. "And that's a problem?" She gestures to herself. "I'm perfectly normal, and we get along just fine."

"But he's family, y'know. I'm surrounded by weirdoes every day, and it's odd to feel connected to someone so . . . mortal."

"He's gonna die one day, and then you'll be all alone." Korby looks sad for a moment before shaking her head. "I'm sorry, that was gloomy of me."

"You're right." I lie back on the grass and watch the clouds drift by. "All of my mortal friends will die one day. But I won't be alone." Thoughts of the team and home float through me. "I'll always have them." Even Arrie's grumpiness will at least be consistent.

"I can't believe you're all together. Like, together together." She looks at me with amusement, her lip curling upward. "Does that mean you all . . ." She raises her eyebrows and makes a crude gesture with her hands. "You know . . ."

I can't help it. I crack right the fuck up. I remember when it was me sat in her shoes finding their relationships strange. Not really getting it. But I do now. It's so normal and comforting. "It's not quite the orgy you're imagining."

"Oh . . ."

"Disappointed?"

"Yeah, a little."

"Well, Nine, Dea, and I are all together like that. But my

relationship with Connie is separate."

"Oh, so it's more like you have your own harem, but two of them are into each other too." She lies back down on the grass and stares at the sky with me.

A brief moment of calm amid my training storm.

"Yeah, something like that."

"What about War?" She sighs. "Where does he fit into your harem?"

Tears prickle my eyes as a sense of loss overcomes me at the question. Where does he fit? At the moment, he's not even a friend. More just an unwilling colleague. I still haven't spoken to him yet—been a touch busy—but I want to. Maybe I'll do it after tomorrow's meeting.

"Magic?"

"Oh, sorry." I take a deep breath. "Arrie and I are just . . . friends."

Chapter Twenty-Five

Aki and I meet at my favorite café, and the owner greets me with his usual warm smile amid all that purple hair. "Welcome, Magic." He looks to Aki with a small frown before smiling. "An' . . . Aki, right?"

"That'll be me," he says with a charming smile as he offers his hand. If Aki was put off by his frown earlier, he doesn't show it. "You have a lovely place here, sir."

They've changed the wallpaper since I was last here; whereas before it was a deep red to match the deep purple chairs, now it's an ocean blue to match turquoise chairs. They even changed the décor to match the underwater feel.

"I like the new atmosphere." I walk up to the counter and place an order, then look at Aki.

"I'll let you order for me."

Okay. Sure. Cos I know him well enough order for him. I roll my eyes and order the same as me, hoping it'll be good enough.

"Yeah," the baker says, "I 'eard you were strugglin' with accessin' the water element in your Witch magic, so I thought maybe giving the right vibe somewhere you like to relax might 'elp." He looks sheepishly to the ground, but then pride smooths through his features as he lifts his head back up.

"You . . . did all of this"—I gesture to the café—"for me?"

"Indeed, Miss. Mr. Err . . . Magic." He stumbles over himself. "Sorry 'bout that."

"It's cool." I wave off his apology. "Just call me Magic."

"Right." He whisks himself into the kitchen out back, and I find us a cozy spot near the window.

"Does that not get a little . . . annoying?" Aki looks at me with tentative curiosity, as though he's unsure if he's allowed to ask about my male and female form conundrum.

A sigh breathes past my lips, and I find that I don't really know the answer. "Sometimes, I guess. It reminds me that I'm not exactly normal. But it's hard to switch to a new way of communicating with someone. It'll take time. And I need to be patient with everyone. I can see they're trying."

"Pfft. You're more patient than me." He smiles as our drinks arrive. "That's for sure."

"Remind me how you came to Sheruta again?" I laughed at his embarrassed face. "Maybe you could learn a little patience."

He looks at me with such reverence, I'm not sure how to hold his gaze. What does he even see when he looks at me like that? "I wonder which one of us is older?"

His mind works in such strange ways. "Must be what it's like to have a conversation with me," I mumble. Then shake my head. "I have no idea. Reckon Nigel will know?"

He shrugs. "Maybe. Haven't seen him in a few days."

"Wait. What?"

"Relax, sis." He looks at me with a charming smile that's supposed to put me at ease, but it doesn't. "He said he was going into work and will probably stay on Earth for a few days."

"Why the hell did no one tell me? I could have given him teleporting crystals so he could commute."

"Well, I think someone gave him one or something. Or he already had one. Because he said he'd use it if he needs to."

Must be one of the ones leftover from the mission to SC Chinese HQ. Weird to think that wasn't that long ago. Feels like months ago. But if he has one of those crystals, then he should be fine, right?

"Hey . . ." Aki grabs my hands. "He'll be all right. Promise."

"You can't promise something like that. We're at war," I whisper. "The SC are doing all kinds of weird things I don't know the motivation behind, and he's right there in the lion's den." My eyes heat with the tears brimming, but I hold them back. "And I'm leaving in a couple of days, so I won't be able to monitor him or help if he needs it."

"Wait, you're leaving?"

"Yeah," I confirm. "I'm hoping to plan a trip to some of the lower supes, to see if they'll help us." I look up to see his surprised face. "You know, even the playing field a bit."

"That's . . . pretty smart." He smirks, his lips twitching and his eyes gleaming. "Think I can come along? Or are you bringing your harem?"

"Ugh. Not you too." I huff. "I swear, everyone keeps calling the team that."

Just as he's about to take a bite out of his cake, he cracks up, laughing hard enough we get a few weird stares. "That's because it's true. They're all in love with you."

It is?

They are?

I mean, I know Nine and Dea are. We're in a good place. But the thing between Connie and I is new, and I don't even think Arrie and I are friends right now.

"Yeah, you're all so close. It's . . . weird."

"Wait. What about it is weird to you?" Frustration pours through me. "We're just there for each other. We're the only other immortal beings on the planet, and we work together all the time. We have each other's backs. And besides that, they're amazing people. They helped me when they didn't have to. They could have just kicked me out and told me to figure it out on my own, but they didn't. They—"

"Okay, okay." Aki holds his hands up in defeat. "I'm sorry. It's weird to me, but it's clear they're important to you." His smile doesn't quite touch his ears, but he tries. And he's only trying to for me.

"Okay." Taking a deep breath, I say the inevitable words of doom. "Might as well get this over with."

Twenty minutes later, we stand in a deep part of the forest, away from the popular unicorn sites and other animals. We face each other, Aki clear-headed and determined and at peace, by the looks of things, and me—in my female form, having switched a minute ago—shaking like a leaf in a hurricane.

I've been nervous before, sure. But not like this. I've pretty much spent the entire time since waking up in the house scared. But this is different. This is training me to kill. Not to harm or hone skills that could help me and others, but to train in a form of magic whose only purpose is to suck the life right out of anything I direct it at.

And we still have no idea if this magic is safe to use against another Horseman. I'm way too nervous to try that out. Plus the risk is too great.

"Our death magic is born out of survival. When we need it the most is when it's most active," Aki explains. "But we can train it to be used at will. It takes a lot of concentration, emotional control, and focus."

Emotional control. Great. Cos I excel at that.

"I saw that eye roll, Magic." He stifles a laugh and then goes back to his serious face. "What's got you worried?"

"Emotional control isn't my strongest skill, that's all." I think for a minute and then add, "And aren't emotions kinda important to Witch magic, anyway?"

"Yes. Emotional control doesn't mean taping your emotions down and being all stone-faced and emotionless. It means not letting them overtake you, being able to be sad when you're otherwise happy, and keeping them in check."

I don't see the difference, personally. That just sounds like a mediocre version of locking it all away.

"Maybe I'm not explaining myself well enough." He sighs and tries again. "It's not about controlling what you feel, but channeling it. You'll need to channel fear in order to access your death magic, but different Witches have different triggers for their elements. Some find water peaceful while others find it rageful."

"I explode into fire whenever I'm pissed off."

"Exactly!"

So I just need to channel the emotion that works best with my element. So then what does water work best with?

I've used it twice now: once when I was angry at myself for hurting Connie and again when I was working with my Fae magic.

"Focus, Magic!"

Right. I'll think about that later.

"Fear controls death magic."

"For every Witch? But didn't you just say—?"

"This is an Angel-descended Witch power, so it works a little differently. It's always fear from what I've researched."

Okay, okay. He's better at this than me, so I'll concede.

"What scares you?"

Everything.

"But not just normal fear. Intense, life-threatening fear."

"But my life can't be threatened, Aki. I'm immortal."

He scratches his head. "Oh yeah. That might pose a problem." He sits with his legs crossed on the forest floor and closes his eyes.

"What are you doing?"

"Shh. I'm concentrating."

Okaaaay.

He's so weird.

But maybe his weird will be just what I need?

"Okay," he says suddenly, making me jump, "I've got nothing."

"Nothing? Really?"

"Yup." He walks over to me. "How am I supposed to help you channel life-threatening fear if you can't even die?" He raises his hands in the air and drops them to his thighs. "How am I supposed to work with that?"

But we can die.

We just have no idea where my seal is, and we got so busy with everything else, we forgot to continue searching.

"Okay," I start, "I might have an idea, but I'll need to chat to the team first and see what they think."

Chapter Twenty-Six

Since the training session with Aki went nowhere, I find Connie and see if she's free to help me brainstorm about my seal. There are still endless corridors and doors in my library I've not explored thoroughly yet. Maybe it's in one of those?

I find Connie in her room, on the bed, surrounded by various pieces of paper. I knock on the open door. "Hey!"

She looks up, the frown on her face turning instantly into a smile. "Hey yourself." She carefully gets off the bed, trying not to move any of the paperwork, and gives me a quick hug. "What's up?"

"Nothing much. Just wondering if you have a minute. But you look busy." I gesture to the pile of papers. "What is all that?"

"Everything I could find about various lower supernaturals and where they might be. Figured I could give you some good starting points."

"You're like three million steps ahead of me all the time." I shake my head. "How do you do it?"

"With two thousand years of practise!" She drags me into her room and slams the door behind us. "Now, what did you need me for?"

"My seal."

"Shit, yeah." She rubs a frustrated hand over her face. "We totally forgot."

"It's okay. We were all busy. And I forgot too."

"Well, what reminded you?"

"Aki. He said I needed to be scared for my life in order to access my death magic, but since I can't actually die, that's gonna be hard." I take a deep breath. "Then I remembered what Nine said when I first got here. About the seals being burned and then we can die."

Connie looks at me with pensive silence for a moment. "And you trust Aki messing with your seal?"

"I . . ." Wow. Good question. "I wasn't really thinking about that. It could be any of you, instead."

She leans her head from side to side. "I don't think messing around with your seal is a good idea. Not just to access a specific type of magic, anyway."

"But Connie. I have this magic for a reason. Fate allowed me to carry it over to immortality for a reason."

"Yeaaaah, or maybe Fate didn't care and just left it there."

My hands clench into fists as frustration boils beneath the surface. "You don't know that!"

"Neither do you!" Connie takes a deep breath. "Okay, okay. There's no point arguing over this."

Speak for yourself.

"But," Connie starts, "we're both right. You do need to

explore your death magic. But I don't think playing around with your seal is the best way to do that."

"Well, how else do you expect me to fear for my life?"

"Use a memory." She looks at me like the answer's obvious, but I have no idea what she's talking about. "Use a memory of a time when your life was threatened. And then channel that emotion."

"That . . . might work."

Is everyone around here smarter than me? Or am I just a bit dumb? Eh. You can't have everything. I'm okay being a little stupid.

"Soooo, want some help with that?" I gesture to the paperwork scattered across her bed. A peace offering for yelling at her, I tell myself. But in reality, I just enjoy studying and research. All this active magic stuff is a pain in the ass. "Cos I'm pretty good with research."

"Sure. Could use a note taker."

"Then I'm your gal."

After hours of noting down various locations, scraps of information, and cultural references, Connie and I are officially done for the day. And when we meet the guys at the dining table, it's clear they're done too.

Nine's practically falling asleep, Dea looks like he's about to yell at someone if they come anywhere near him, and Arrie's bloodshot eyes and frowning face looks grumpier than usual.

I'm starting to see what Melissandre meant all those weeks ago. We're too busy and tired to manage housework for this monstrosity of a mansion.

"Any preferences?" Connie asks with a hand inches from the table.

"Sugar," Nine groans.

"Caffeine," Dea sighs.

"Meat," Arrie grumbles.

Connie looks at me, but I shrug my shoulders. "Something tasty."

Nine and Connie look to me with smirks, but it's Nine who says, I can help with that.

You are far too tired for sex right now. When was the last time you slept?

When was the last time you came to bed with us?

That was days ago! For goddess' sake. "We're all going to bed tonight. No fucking questions."

Connie raises a hand to argue, but I shush her. "Other than you. You slept like a log last night."

"It'll be a few days before I need to sleep again," she reminds us with a shrug. "One of the benefits of being me."

I point a finger at Arrie with a frown on my face. "That includes you." He opens his mouth to say something, but I interrupt. "I don't care how much you dislike it."

His face goes from tired and frustrated to genuinely angry in a blink, and everyone flinches. Well, other than Connie, who just sighs. "Who the fuck do you think you are?" He shoots to his feet with clenched fists. "You don't get to order me around." His booming voice didn't need him to shout; you could hear it from another realm.

"Watch your tone, Arrie," Dea warns.

"Sorry, I forgot you slaves seem to like taking orders." He goes to walk away from the table, trying to get past Connie, but she blocks him. "What now?" The exasperation in his voice breaks for just a second when he looks at me.

"You think you get to play asshole just because you won't man up and talk to Magic? You think we deserve your shitty moods just because you can't be a grown-ass adult?" Connie walks to the kitchen with her back to him while he just stares at her, dumbfounded.

I turn to face them, concerned about our kitchen's wellbeing for just a second. "Guys, I don't think this is the best time for—"

"I'm sick of him treating you like shit!" Connie yells. "It's all his fault in the first place."

"You think so?" Arrie asks. "You think this isn't at all on your shoulders? That all three of you haven't just become mindless slaves to one person's . . . woman's," he spits as he corrects himself, "will."

I tense in my seat at his words, my pink hair falling around my shoulders as an immediate tear falls from my eye in soundless silence.

But I'm not a woman.

Connie freezes, Dea stops drinking his tea, and Nine looks up from the table where his head was resting.

"Did you just—?" Dea starts.

"Use Magic's sex and gender against them?" Connie scoffs. "In an argument you started?" Connie's fists clench harder, her knuckles whitening and her eyes flashing with anger. "You absolute ass pig!" She grabs the nearest object to her, which happens to be a frying pan, and whacks him over the head.

A loud twang echoes across the kitchen, and we all stand in silence for a moment.

Arrie looks pissed but confused.

Dea looks like surprised.

Connie looks damn proud.

Nine looks like he's struggling not to laugh.

And I have no idea how I look, but I'm struggling to stick

to a single emotion. They're on a pinwheel right now, and the ticker hasn't decided which one to land on.

It'll probably be anger.

Yup. It's anger.

"How can you do this to me?" I scream. "I know I'm being selfish expecting you all to be okay sharing me, and I know I'm not perfect. But I at least expected a reason. A short conversation at best. Heck, even a fucking letter would have sufficed, Arrie!" I turn to face him with angry tears slashing down my face. I try to hold on to that anger, but my voice breaks as I sob. "How could you?"

His face has a red welting mark from the frying pan, which I think was swung at him with Connie's full strength because he's bleeding. But it's his eyes that catch me off guard. They don't look angry anymore. They just look sad.

And for the first time, I realize that maybe there's more going on with Arrie than just him changing his mind. That maybe that sadness isn't aimed at me.

Chapter Twenty-Seven

Is the Fae Queen Allied with the SC?

The following morning is awkward. Arrie walks to the embassy alone while the rest of us follow a few feet behind. We're supposed to meet the representatives there, and then we'll all meet Nigel, who will give us the location for the SC meeting.

We are all going. Contrary to my opinion that I should go alone so I could burn them all to the ground. That would solve all this quicker.

But no, Nine had to be the voice of reason. He said if there is someone pulling the strings behind all this, then we need to know who, otherwise they won't stop if we just destroy the Supernatural Council.

Wise words.

Annoying, but wise.

Just as we crest the hill that leads into the town center,

Nigel runs up the path, panting, sweating, and looking a bit worse for wear. He dives past Arrie, who doesn't even look at him and keeps walking, then stops in front of us. Hands on knees. "Needed . . . to . . . make it . . . in time," he pants.

"Slow down." Nine rubs circles onto his back as I stuff my hands into my jean pockets. "Catch your breath."

Nigel nudges Nine's hands away and straightens. "There's no time for that." His face is beet red. "I ran from the other side of Colorado before I remembered I could have used the crystal." He looks irritated with himself, scowling at the fact he forgot. "The date. I have the date."

We all straighten, preparing ourselves.

"Two months."

"December, then?" Nine asks.

"Exactly one year after Angel showed up?"

"A coincidence, maybe?" Connie asks with a shrug.

"Pfft." Nine looks at us. "I'm starting to believe in Fate." He laughs at himself and then turns back to Nigel. "Do you have a date?"

Nigel nods. "December 25th."

"Christmas day?" Bewilderment strikes me until I suddenly get it. "They're attacking when people are probably going to be busy with their families. Lots of species celebrate Christmas across lots of countries."

Connie laughs, but we all scowl at her, so she explains, "Christmas was a pagan tradition that was adopted by Christianity, and then it kind of spread from the western world out to the east, and now the whole damn world celebrates it." She crosses her arms across her chest.

"You'll have to forgive Connie. She knew Jesus." Nine shoves her aside and looks to me. "You need to leave. Soon. We need as much help as we can, and you're our best bet of getting it."

I nod, knowing he's right. "Then let's get this meeting over with and call the embassy to action."

"They might have more information for us, hon," Connie suggests. And when I look at her confused, she explains, "About the lower supernatural species and where they might be."

"Right."

"Wait a minute," Nine says as we walk into the embassy building a few minutes later, "the meeting's here?"

Nigel rubs a nervous thumb over his index finger. "Well, they didn't want to give away any of their meeting places, since they're not public knowledge."

"Yeah, cos that screams trustworthy." I roll my eyes. "This is gonna suck, isn't it?"

A grunt comes from the front doors, and Arrie steps out. "Can you quit complaining for one second?" His bulging arms folded over his chest, he looks like a war chief. Like a political war chief. But a yawn escapes his otherwise tempered facade.

"Did you seriously stay up all night just to do the opposite of what Sweetie suggested?" Nine asks, incredulously.

Seriously, will this guy's stubbornness know any bounds? "Arrie, can we—"

"No," he grumps before moving on and up the stairs.

We all take the elevator.

"It's okay, Sweetie." Nine wraps his arms around my waist and rests his head on my chest. "He'll come around."

"You keep saying that, and I'm sick of it," I growl. "I can't even hold an amicable working partnership, let alone friends or anything else." I shrug Nine off, but his frown stabs at me. I rub the rising pressure out of my nose. "I'm sorry. That wasn't fair of me."

"Have I ever told you how good your ass looks in your male form?" Connie asks out of nowhere.

I look in the mirror of the elevator and catch her staring at my ass while licking her lips. "You done treating me like a piece of candy, babe?"

"Nope." Her flushed gaze meets mine, and she smiles at me. "Never."

The guys chuckle at us, and just as the elevator pings to the conference floor, Connie gently kisses my temple and grabs my hand while Dea grabs the other and follows Nine out.

I know Arrie's still annoying the crap out of me, but at least my life with these three is turning out amazingly.

Okay, however, goes out the window when I meet the Supernatural Council bigwigs. They're old. They're all men. And they're staring daggers at me so sharply it's a wonder I'm still alive.

Fuck me. This is gonna suck.

Just keep your cool.

Hence my male form. No Vampire craziness here.

Well, Vampires are known for their emotional outbursts.

I know, I know. I'm the poster child of emotional outbursts. But I got this. I will keep it down and buried at the center of the Earth.

Don't forget to lock its crypt.

I shoot him an incredulous look.

What? You get cranky and irrational and flamey when you're pissed.

By the smirk on Dea's face and the laugh Connie is so obviously trying to hold in, he projected that conversation to the team.

You can all quit fucking laughing at me now. Thanks.

That was it for Connie, apparently, because she burst out laughing. Getting the entire attention of the room, including all the ambassadors and the councilors.

"Sorry." She wipes her crying eyes. "Famine likes to send jokes to us using his telepathy."

"A bit of an inopportune time for jokes, is it not?" A man with gray hair, aging features, a long beard, and an angry scowl taps his fingers restlessly on the table. "Are you ready to proceed?"

We all look at each other with worried glances, and I catch Lucien's gaze across the room. He looks worried too. In fact, all the ambassadors do.

Nine, tell everyone to say nothing about knowing the Area 50 plans. Or anything about my trip to unite the lower supe world. I'm not giving these cunts any advantages. If we can make peace, then fine, but if not, I'm done.

Okay.

No one looks our way, so it seems to have gotten through to them how important this meeting is.

The Supernatural Council is made of twelve people: three humans, three Vampires, three Fae, and three Shifters. Our council follows a similar pattern, but where they have Fae on their side, we have Witches. Humans, however, are not with us. But Nine's pretty sure humans'll be divided, anyway.

They're not known for their unity.

The Supernatural Council dominates one side of the circular table while we Horsemen take the other, and smack in the middle of the two are the ambassadors.

The same old man as before—human, I now realize—coughs into his hand to get everyone's attention and starts what's probably going to be a long-ass meeting. "Now everyone is here," he says with a sneer, as though we were late, "we can begin."

Another old man sitting next to him, who's also human, takes the first offensive maneuver of the day. "All you ambassadors, you do realize that allying yourselves with the Horsemen appears as if you are no longer allying yourselves with the Supernatural Council?"

Red, the Witch Coven's ambassador, responds, "Are you suggesting that the Horsemen are your enemy, and that allying ourselves will lose us your support?"

Straight to it then.

The red flush on the old man's face is almost worth it. Almost. "Of course not," he grinds out. "We are simply asking where your loyalties lie."

Pansy, our Shifter ambassador, looks like she's about to burst already. "Our loyalties are to our people, and always will be. That's why we choose to work alongside you both. Otherwise, how can we best serve our communities?"

Harrow looks positively amused by all this to and fro, like a bad political milkshake, but then I guess this doesn't affect him, since he's a Sheruta Vampire. "If you both worked together, this wouldn't be a problem."

We stay silent, hoping beyond all hope that they'll choose to be allies. I doubt it. But you never know.

"Of course we," another old man, Fae this time, starts, "are working alongside the Horsemen. No one suggested otherwise, Mr . . ."

He shakes his head. "We don't have last names here on Sheruta. So it's just Harrow." His inky black hair almost smiles in the sunlight filtering through the partially shaded windows. "Pleasure to meet you."

The man nods.

"Now we have that settled," Nine starts, "we wanted to ask what your plans are for helping the Vampire blood supply issue and what your thoughts are of the Fae allying themselves with the rogue Vampire faction, who have shut down New Orleans, tried to kill me, and taken one of our own hostage."

The Fae councilman from earlier blusters and stutters before finding his words. "Those are some bold accusations, Famine." He takes a deep breath. "Our queen wishes to ally herself with the new Vampire King, when he eventually takes over." He slices his hands through the air. "That is all."

Nine, is he telling the truth?

Yes.

Then she's lying to her people about the truth behind the union.

It would appear so.

"You look troubled, Magic," Prince Lucien asks. "What is the matter?" He looks at me with meaningful eyes, trying to say something.

He says that you should stand up and speak up for everyone. To stop being, and I quote, a little Horseman.

Anger flares across my mind, but I tamper it down to something resembling frustration. Okay, Magic, you can do this. "It is difficult to communicate with the councilmen when even they aren't being given truths from their own species' councils and royalties."

"Are you suggesting our queen is lying to us?" another Fae councilman asks. "That's preposterous—"

I hold up a hand to silence them. "I'm suggesting that she's telling you what you want to hear. And that not a single member of your species is strong or brave enough to stand up to her to ask otherwise." Because that's what happens in a monarchy.

He leans back in his seat, flabbergasted. "We . . . will look into your claims."

Best you're gonna get, Sweetie.

I bow my head and smile through clenched teeth. "Thank you."

A Vampire councilman turns to Lucien with a smug smile. "So where does the king sit on this matter, then."

Lucien speaks softly but clearly. "Ah, yes. Well, I have news on that front. The Vampire King announced to the Vampire Royal Council this morning that he has renounced Prince Phillipe's title and claim to the throne."

The room collectively gasps before exploding into a flurry of questions and accusations.

Nine, have you taken a look into their minds yet?

Yes. The humans have all been compelled by a powerful Vampire. They're saying what they've been told to say. Two of the Fae councilmen genuinely don't know about the Fae Queen's alignment and what they're really up to. The other, the one who's stayed quiet until now, is in line with her and waiting to see how this plays out before making a move.

What of the Vampires and Shifters?

The Vampires are shocked. All three are already on Prince Phillipe's side. We're not winning any of them over.

You're telling me we've lost seven of the twelve council members?

Yes.

Brilliant.

Chapter Twenty-Eight

DIVISION IN THE SUPERNATURAL WORLD: ARE WE AT WAR?

For the next few hours, we throw snide insults back and forth while agreeing on nothing. There's no point, anyway; over half the council are already aligned with the enemy.

But we might sway the other six, if we're lucky.

Which could be good for the future if we play our cards right. Hence why I'm still sitting here taking jibe after jibe while smiling. Like an idiot.

A beautiful idiot.

Dea made himself visible about an hour ago, so he's good, though looking a little pained. Might be because of the current conversation, though, which has just switched onto Witches.

Guess it's their turn to take a few jibes.

Nine, can you remind them to keep their cool. And I'm totally with them, I want to burn their asses to the ground, too.

Red smiles beneath what I assume is supposed to be a frown, but she scowls at the councilman telling her Witches don't need to pick a side because they don't do anything, anyway.

(Yeah, ouch.)

"So," she begins, "let me see if I've got this right. You're saying we're not allowed an opinion because we're 'unaffected' by the current goings-on in the supernatural world due to not being out in the open?"

The pretty human councilman shifts in his seat without answering. Which means yes.

"There is a coven of Witches in every country in the world, sir. And even if we practise our magic in secret, we still come into contact with other supes on the regular, including Vampires. If Vampires start hunting us again, many of our kind will be left defenseless. And that's not taking into account the war we would be starting between Witches and Fae. We rely on your peace in order to maintain ours."

Yup. It's official. I like her.

The human councilman who talked first sighs. "What is it you want from us, Horsemen, ambassadors?" He looks around the room.

Nine looks to me, then to Dea, then to the ambassadors in the room, who all nod. "Nothing now." He gets up. "Thank you for your time." And walks away.

Follow.

We all get up and walk wordlessly out of the meeting room, following Nine up the stairs and into another meeting room.

For fuck's sake. How many meetings am I going to be stuck in today?

"As many as it takes," Nine responds out loud, a slight edge to his voice. "Sorry." He winces. He wraps an arm around my shoulders and kisses me softly, gently, and with as much tender love as he usually does. "Been a long week."

Dea curls behind him and whispers, "You need to get some sleep."

"I don't have time for that." The gruff edge to his voice is marred only by the tired yawn that escapes.

Everyone takes some time to breathe, get a glass of water, and chatter amongst themselves for a ten-minute break before we reconvene.

"Well," Red starts, "that was a disaster."

"Yup." I smile. "Pretty much how I thought it would go."

Dea shrugs. "At least we can say we tried. When everyone says we started this war, we have video footage of trying."

Arrie turns his head in our direction for the first time today. "You recorded that?"

Nine nods. "Yeah."

"Good," I say, "cos I wanna watch Red verbally kicking that asshole to the curb again."

Prince Lucien laughs, and then we're all giggling at the memory. "That was awesome, little Witch."

She scowls. "What part of me is little to you, Vampire?"

He holds his hands up in defense. "Don't get your magical knickers in a twist. I call everyone that."

"Correction," Nine adds, "he calls everyone he thinks is hot that. Including Magic."

I nod, confirming.

Is that jealousy I hear in your voice, Famine?

He doesn't answer.

Red smiles and blushes lightly and then shakes her head and takes a seat near the other Witch ambassadors, including

Aki, who has remained silent today.

"You okay?" I ask him. "You've been a bit quiet."

He shrugs. "Just a little underqualified, that's all."

"No one is underqualified to speak about their own lives."

"Well, my life is defined by the fact that I have to hide my magic."

Red's eyes shoot our way, and I can only hope she thinks we're talking about Witch politics and not death magic.

Placing a comforting hand on his shoulder. "I know."

"Right," Nine calls everyone to attention, "we have some things to discuss, including what I read of everyone's minds while there and Magic's plans to leave tomorrow to unite the lower supe world."

Everyone looks to me in surprise.

But I stay silent and look to Nine, who explains what he already told me back in the meeting from hell numero uno. "The real issue," he says at the end, "is that they know we know all of that." He scowls. "They tried hard not to think about any of their plans, so I got nothing." Sighing, he slouches.

"Dude," Lucien says, "when was the last time you slept?"

Nine throws his arms up in exasperation. "I don't have the time, for fuck's sake. Will everyone just stop. I'm immortal. I'll be fine."

It's because we care.

I know. "Sorry," he apologizes. "I'm just a bit cranky."

"It is okay, Nine," Dea says, "I'll take over." He pulls him out of his seat and turns him to the couch in the corner. "Take a damn nap." Kissing the crook of his neck gently, he guides him to the couch and forces him to lie down.

Dea turns back to the table and sits down. "If I go invisible halfway through, I am sorry, but you will still be able to hear me."

"If it's uncomfortable," Harrow says, "then turn it off now. We're good."

Everyone nods, and Dea smiles. Thankful for the invisible relief, if that uncharacteristic slouch is anything to go by. And it's good to see two of my guys taking a break. They've worked so hard.

"Good," Dea says, "now Nine has updated everyone on where the councilmen were really at, we have something else to plan. Magic is leaving soon to try to get as many lower supes on our side as possible."

"But," Connie takes over, "this won't be easy. They've been largely ignored by all of us in the last few hundred, thousand years."

Everyone looks to the floor and ceiling and anywhere but us, unease spreading through the room like wildfire.

"What we need," she goes on, "is information."

"Like where the pixies are, for example," I chime in with an attempt at a smile. "Or if anyone knows of any Demons lurking about."

"Demons?" Lucien asks.

"Hey, I'll take help where I can fucking get it, little Vampire."

Lucien smirks and nods. "Fair enough."

Connie pulls out a bunch of paperwork I recognize. "We've got a few leads." They're the papers that were scattered on her bed last night. "But nothing concrete."

I wince, remembering something important. "The biggest hurdle is that I can only teleport to somewhere I've already been. Which is really fucking nowhere. So I'm gonna have to fly to a lot of these places."

On an airplane.

Ugh. Kill me now.

The world can die.

Arrie chuckles cruelly at me with a smirk on his face, and it takes some next level willpower not to wipe that shitty grin off his fucking gorgeous face. Why do I still want to jump his bones? He's being a cunt.

Focus, Magic. Focus.

"Well," Red's saying, "we Witches know where the fairies are."

Not quite pixies, but it's a good start.

"Where?" Connie asks, pen at the ready.

Red looks a little unsure, her eyes darting away from us.

"Hey," I whisper, "we're not going to cause any harm. I'm just going to ask for help. If they really don't want to, I won't force them."

Red nods, satisfied with that reassurance. "They're with the Witch Coven. But in a different part of the cavern structure."

Fuck me three ways to Sunday, I don't want to go back there. I'll probably be arrested if I even try.

Dea places a hand on my arm. "It might be a good time to make a public apology to the entire Coven. Maybe you can help them?"

"They are in need of some Fae lights," Red chimes in. "It gets awfully dark down there at night. And the witchlights are really dim."

I think I can work with that. "Thank you."

Red smiles, her red hair swaying as she brushes it back out of her way. "You're welcome."

"There's a Demon horde the Vampire Royal Council use to help with scaring newer Vampires into following the law," Prince Lucien offers with a shrug. "Could probably get you a meeting, at the least." When I look at him incredulously, he just smiles. "They don't hurt anyone, but try telling a newly turned Vampire not to drink from every human he walks past and see how much he listens." He sips his glass of water. "It's a good strategy because it works."

Well, it's better than I've managed so far.

"Okay, so fairies and a Demon horde." Taking a breath and a sip of water, I continue. "I think our best allies are going to be pixies, since they're so hunted by the Fae for their dust."

Everyone nods, seeing my point.

"But I have no idea where they are." Rubbing a hand down my face, I sigh in exasperation. "They've been seriously careful with their location."

Aki shifts uncomfortably in his seat and avoids my eyes. I throw him an accusatory glare, and he finally gives up. "They mostly live in the Amazon rainforest."

I give him a 'how do you know that' look, and he shakes his head while pointedly looking at the people in the room.

Okay, so he can't share how.

"Okay. Thank you."

Connie writes everything she can down, so hopefully we can make a plan later.

"Are you all going?" Prince Lucien asks. "Or are you going alone?"

I look at the team, but they all shake their heads. They're too busy right now. "I'm probably going to have to go alone—"

"I'm going with her," Aki interrupts, leveling his gaze my way, challenging me to say no.

Sighing, I give in. "Fine."

Now I have to make two batches of transport crystals.

CHAPTER TWENTY-NINE

NO SIGHT OF NEW ORLEANS' FREEDOM YET

My library has never looked so damn good. Can I marry books? Because I totally will if I can. The meeting lasted until dinner, with lots of people having random snippets of information we put together and ended up with an incomplete map to the lower supe world.

I have between now and Christmas to complete that map, visit all the supernaturals' homes, and convince them to join our cause. Which will probably involve me helping them first.

Oh, and I'll be doing so with my lost-lost twin brother, Aki. Sounds like a real vacation. I roll my eyes at my own internal snark and settle into a book about a hilarious cupid and her four beautiful mates.

I laugh and I cry and I choke on my own saliva more times than I care to admit for an immortal being, but by the time I'm done with book one, I'm feeling worlds better.

Who knew laughing was such mental medicine?

Literally everyone.

Nine, Dea, and Connie all round the corner of the nook I've found myself in with smiles and beauty. All lined up like this, I feel immensely lucky. They chose me. Me.

"We'll always choose you," Nine responds as he sits to my left.

Connie takes my right and wraps an arm around my shoulders. "Always."

While Dea sits on his ass in front of me, nudging my legs apart so he can sit between them. "Ah," he gasps, "I have an idea." He places his hand on the floor, and a few seconds later, a light rumbling noise alerts us that the house is creating something new.

And out of nowhere, a TV pops up in front of us.

"Want to watch a movie, Angel?"

"So long as I don't have to move."

Nine whispers into my ear, "No moving required."

We lie on the sofa together and watch two movies in a row, chatting, cuddling, laughing, and generally have a good evening before I leave for what could be a pretty long mission.

Hopefully it'll take a few weeks, and then I can come back home. But I might be gone the entire two months. That'll suck. But it is what it is.

"So," Connie starts, "Aki's going with you, huh?"

As we're walking back to my bedroom, I turn to face her question. "Yeah, I guess." I shrug.

"You are not worried about that?" Dea asks.

"Should I be?" I mean, I get he's my long-lost brother, but he's pretty nice. "Maybe it'll be a good opportunity to get to know each other a bit better."

Nine chuckles. "You really are working on being more

positive, aren't you?"

"I'm trying," I whisper, embarrassment flooding me.

Hard.

"And you're doing wonderfully, hon." Connie walks us through the door and pops into my library, then comes back with a book in hand. "I don't wanna miss our last night together, but I'm not tired yet." So she shakes a book I saw her reading a few days ago in the air.

"Sounds good."

Just as I'm snuggling between Dea and Connie, a knock sounds on my door and Arrie enters, holding a familiar flash drive in hand. "I just wanted to tell you before you leave tomorrow that I've finished analyzing all the content. Most of it's just trade, tax, meeting records, employee information, et cetera." He shrugs, his voice robotic and devoid of emotion. "Anything you need while you're gone?"

My brain frazzles. Everything in me shrivels up and dies.

He's been going through that for me this entire time?

"Err . . . Maybe give Connie and Dea a hand if they need it, and make sure everything's ready for your plans at each city." I've not looked over them. I trust him.

On the day, I'll just be one of his soldiers. And I'm totally okay with that.

He nods and turns to walk away, but at the last minute he swings his head back around. "Good luck." There's something in his eyes—he wants to say more—but I think he's holding back.

Not wanting an argument right before my first solo (ish) mission, I decide not to engage. Sometimes, letting things simmer down is the best option. That way, I can chat to him once I've processed everything and not be a snarling mess.

Smart. He's still angry at himself.

Yeah, I got that.

Nine, Connie, Dea, and I snuggle into bed, Connie reading by a low lamplight (her enhanced senses helping immeasurably), and Nine and Dea sharing both me and each other. And I fall asleep easily, happily snuggled up between my partners. My family.

Chapter Thirty

Are the SC Fit for Purpose?

Aki smiles at me early the next morning at the breakfast table, where we're both sat—alone, because no one else is up yet—eating an English breakfast.

Dea would be so proud.

"You really made ten of those crystal things?" Aki asks.

"Each."

His eyes burst wide, surprise covering his face. "Wow. That's amazing."

"One to get to Earth, two Earth-Sheruta ones, just in case, and the rest are Earth-Earth." Laying my map down on the table, I use a cup to hold each corner in place. "We're starting in North and South America, and then we'll tackle things continent by continent."

He nods. "Prince Lucien said he managed to get us a meeting with the Demon horde the Vampire Royal Council use in one week's time in the New Orleans Bayou."

"Great." That's one ticked off our list. Which I also have laid out on the table. Between all the ambassadors, we have some serious intel. "And we might be able to ask Alpha Cal if he has any further leads if we pop into Tokyo when we get to Asia."

Aki looks at me in question.

"We're pretty friendly with the Shifters. Vampires too, but they have their own issues right now."

"Yeah, Prince Lucien's been going back and forth a lot and is pretty exhausted by the looks of things."

"He should have said something." I sigh. "I would have made him some Sheruta-Earth teleporting crystals. The moron."

"He's a little prideful, that one." He stifles a giggle. "Are all Vampires so . . . emotional?"

I laugh. "Yup." Since I had to make a hundred teleporting crystals last night and this morning, I'm in my female form. "We're a little testy. I think it's a blood thing." I shrug. "Not really sure."

"Leaving without saying goodbye, Angel?" Dea walks into the kitchen in his gym gear—sweats and no top—with a smirk. "I thought I would at least get a kiss goodbye."

"Aaaand, that's my cue to leave. I'll see you outside in an hour?"

I nod, barely paying attention, my eyes fixed on Dea's swirling tattoo and his abs, his Adonis belt, and the way his galaxy eyes pierce into me without holding back. "You're . . . beautiful."

I gasp when he fazes to me and picks me up—faster than my eyes can track without warning—and wraps my legs around his waist. Resting my arms on his shoulders, I lean down to grab his lower lip between mine and bite down. Hard. Then grab his gasp with my lips and throw it right back.

"Good enough?"

He shakes his head. "Nope." He smashes my back against the nearest wall and pins me there before plunging his tongue into my mouth.

His piercings graze against my lips, and I can't help but play with them. Their cold metal a complete contrast to Dea's warm mouth.

He rolls his hips into me and I groan.

"Fuck, Dea . . ."

"Yes, Angel?"

I moan in response, and instead of letting him dominate me, I let my fangs slip and bite down on his lower lip. Taking a few sips. He does make a tasty breakfast.

Dea's knees go weak, and I nearly slip from his grasp, but he pins me to the wall again with his hips and a growl.

His whimpers spur me on, and I take deeper pulls, letting his smoky lavender taste roll over my tongue in waves of sweet nectar that blur my vision and shoot silver swirls over the backs of my eyelids.

A cough breaks the moment, and I retract my fangs and peer over Dea's shoulder to see Arrie standing uncomfortably by the backdoor. "Can I have a moment, Magic?"

"She was in the middle of breakfast, dude," Dea whines.

But rather than be annoyed, Arrie smiles for a moment. "Well, I'm interrupting."

His growly voice vibrates through me, and my hips roll against without Dea thinking. Fuck. I slip from Dea's grasp— much to my Angel of Death's amusement—and rush to Arrie.

Is he ready to chat?

He nods to the backdoor, and I follow him out.

The cool morning air hits me like a freight train, and I take a deep calming breath before sitting beside Arrie on the porch.

He opens his mouth to speak, but then he closes it with a frown. "Argh. Why is talking to you so hard?" His hands clench around his knees as his shoulders hunch.

I smile, trying to be gentle. "It's okay if you're not ready, Arrie. I'm not in a rush."

He shakes his head, frustration edging into that beautiful smile. "I'm sorry." He takes a deep breath, and it all comes rushing out. "I'm sorry for yesterday. I shouldn't have used your sex and gender against you like that. It wasn't fair. I said it because I knew it would hurt you. But it's really me I'm angry at."

"I know." He looks surprised. "You're not as mysterious as you like to think you are, Mr Tall and Grumpy."

His laugh is music to my ears. Like a light in the fog I didn't know I needed because I thought I could see just fine.

"Why are you so angry at yourself?"

He groans as he wipes a frustrated hand down his face and clenches his jaw. "Argh!" His fist punches through the chair's arm, and he winces. "Why is this so hard?"

"It's okay." I rest a hand on his shoulder. "Thank you for the apology. Maybe we can chat some more when I get back?"

He nods. "I'd . . . like that."

I get up to leave, but he grabs my hands last minute and turns me around. "Here." He hands me over a dozen vials of blood. "For your mission." His ice blue eyes pierce mine, shattering me for a brief moment. "I know I need to do more than say sorry."

I give him a questioning look, confused.

"I want to earn your forgiveness, and then maybe we can work on being friends?"

His words shoot through me like a well-placed arrow. I thought that maybe he wanted to . . . get back together. But he still just wants to be friends?

The pain's written all over my face, apparently, because Arrie looks hurt for a moment. "Magic, I . . ."

"It's okay." My voice is quiet, a brush on the wind. "I'd like that."

Chapter Thirty-One

My mind is lost to what I've dubbed "Arrie nonsense" when
I meet Aki in the front gardens, where I find him quietly
smelling the roses and letting the fairies hop from arm to arm
as they take him in.

"I'm surprised they touch you like that," I whisper.

Making him jump. "Jeez, Magic." His hand wavers over
his chest. "You scared the shit out of me."

"Sorry," I chuckle. "I'm serious, though. Usually they stay
around their nests and fly straight back into them whenever
one of us comes near them."

"Really?" Aki sounds surprised. "I've always found fairies
to be pretty social."

"Maybe you were just born lucky."

He lets out an indignant snort, disagreeing with me. And

to be honest, I disagree with myself. We were not born lucky in any sense of the word.

"Ready to go?"

He nods, grabbing the one Sheruta-Earth teleporting crystal he has on him. "Just think of the Washington monument, right?"

"That's what we agreed on." I grab my own crystal. "It should be night there at the moment."

Aki looks nervous, but after a quick breath, he smashes the crystal on the ground and disappears in a poof of smoke.

"So cliché," I mumble as I follow him.

The Washington monument glows bright white a few hundred meters from where I land, and I immediately snap my gaze around to find Aki.

"Where did he land?"

My Vampire eyesight allows me to see perfectly in the dark, and I quickly find him on the other side, sitting chill by the water. "There you are."

"Knew you'd find me, sis."

"Vampire eyesight comes in pretty handy."

It's chilly this time of year here, and I find myself needing the gloves in my backpack, so I throw them on and turn back around to Aki, who's staring at me.

He shakes his head in a huff of laughter. "Sorry, it's just a Vampire in gloves is hilarious."

"I'm also half-Witch, which means I get cold, deku."

"Ouch. Swearing in Japanese." He grabs my arm and yanks me into a hug. "I didn't even know you spoke Japanese."

I laugh, batting him on the arm. "Of course, you fucking idiot. It's my first language. I speak English because it's a common language between the team."

Though I'm pretty sure Nine can speak Japanese.

Actually, I bet most of them can. They've been around for two thousand years, for goddess' sake.

"So," he starts, "where to first?"

I grab the list and the map out of my backpack—feeling a little like a game character cliché—and see what's closest.

"Shell Beach, New Orleans."

"But the meeting isn't for another week?"

"Exactly. They're meeting us at Shell Beach, right?" He nods. "If we go there now, we can teleport back whenever we need to later."

"Riiiight. The crystals only take you to places you've already been."

"Uh-huh." I look around, wondering where the nearest airport is. "Which means we need an airport."

"Oh," Aki says, "that's this way."

The flight to Louis Armstrong New Orleans International Airport only takes an hour, but I still manage to throw up twice.

Uggh. Why didn't I make those anti-sickness charms?

The airport is only open to specific visitors, given the city-wide shutdown, but as a Horseman, I have clearance. Luckily I could persuade them into bringing an assistant with me, otherwise Aki would have had to go back home.

Alas, my powers of persuasion worked. For a change.

But the moment we step outside the airport, my relaxed demeanor changes. There's no cars, no people. Nothing. It's like a barren cityland out here.

"Wow," Aki breathes. "It's hard to believe this is New Orleans."

"Yeah."

Party central is officially asleep.

Aki taps his datachip and brings up a plasmascreen in the air, then hits maps. "Looks like Shell Beach is forty-three miles east, which'll take us fourteen hours to walk."

I snort. There's no way we're walking that far. "I can just fly us there. Probably take a couple hours."

"Can you fly two people for that long?"

I shrug. "Never tried before."

"Well, our flight to Manaus doesn't leave until this evening, so if there's anything you wanted to do while here, now's the time, right?"

"Right."

"Wonder how many shops are open at the moment?"

Aki laughs. "Shopping?"

I nod. "Yeah, Christmas is just round the corner, and I need to do some serious shopping." More December 25th preparations. "Though, we'll probably be celebrating a bit late this year."

"Maybe we should celebrate it early?" Aki hooks his arm through mine and starts our walk toward New Orleans central, though I'm pretty sure I'll have to fly us there, too. "Some people might not make it, and I just thought that maybe it would be nice to . . ."

Sighing, I agree with him. "Early might be best."

I eventually fly us to the center of New Orleans, lest we actually spend fourteen hours walking there.

"Well," I turn to Aki and say as we touch down in a park somewhere, "I could have made it, but not sure about your mortal feet."

He gasps in mock hurt. "My mortal feet can outmaneuver yours any day."

"Pfft. As if."

He punches me in the arm playfully, but he gasps when

it's like punching stone. "Chikushō!" He waves his hand in pain, then clutches it to his chest. "What are you made of?"

I shrug. "Carbon." But inside I'm laughing. Hard.

"Top tip: don't punch Arrie or Connie, either."

He looks at me with raised brows and a small smile. "But Dea and Nine are fair game?"

"Pretty much." That makes him laugh, and we both have to take a few moments to compose ourselves. "But seriously, don't punch my harem." I point a finger at him and glare daggers.

He nods. "Wasn't planning to."

Nature pulses through me, like it usually does when I'm surrounded by its beauty, but the moment we step onto the street, harrow rips through my heart.

The streets are strewn with litter, buildings are boarded up, graffiti and vandalism run rife, and the Vampires in the shadows are looking at us like we're about to be the next zombie victim.

I grab Aki's arm. "We need to get out of here."

"Huh? Why?"

Right Vampire eyesight.

"Because there are hundreds of hungry Vamps around that want to kill us and eat us. Or, more precisely, you."

I watch his throat bob up and down as his hands tremble. "It's okay. We can teleport whenever we need to, and I can fly us up."

He nods with his eyes closed and gulps. "Okay, okay."

"Psst." A hiss sounds from behind us. "Hey, over here."

I turn, dragging Aki's line of sight with me, and scan the shadows.

"By the yellow graffiti under the broken stop sign."

I swing my vision in that direction and spot an old lady

with a cane, her hands trembling and her eyes darting to the few Vampires within her vicinity.

I don't know what possesses me to go to her, but she looks like she needs help. Or at least someone to talk to. Living here must be rough.

"C'mon." I drag Aki with me, hastening our pace when we near the few Vampires looking at the old woman like she's prey. And that's when I realize she is.

She's human.

She leads us down the alleyway she has apparently come from, and then up the metal stairs on the side of the building. "We're going to the top." But her lungs heave with every step as her breath rattles.

"Here." I offer my hand, and she takes it. I walk us up the steps, not wanting to frighten her by Vampire speeding up and also not wanting to leave Aki alone. "There you go." I put her back on her feet.

She smiles at me gratefully. "You're the Horseman of Magic, right?"

I nod, not really sure if this is a good or bad direction of questioning.

"The one who created that app and the SC are talking smack about."

I laugh. "So they've started their smear campaign, have they?"

She grabs my hand and leads us to a bright rooftop garden, guarded by UV lights that make me wince as I pass them. "Sorry. They prevent regular Vampires from passing."

"S'okay." I rub the sore parts of my bare arms. "Just a little prickly." I shift into my male form, easing my time in this city. "That's better."

The old lady turns to face me and gasps. "Wow. You really

can turn into a man." She chuckles. "Bet that's complicated."

"You have no idea," I mumble.

The garden is full of humans, a couple of Fae, and even a Witch. Everyone at risk from the Vampires. Some are sunbathing in fake lights, others are clustered together in groups, while others look frightened and huddled into a corner.

"You grabbed everyone you could find and gave them a safe haven?"

She chuckles and points to an old Shifter in the corner. "We did." She takes us to meet him and wraps an arm around his waist. "Hey, Tracker."

"Hey Lu." He splutters upon seeing me, and instead of saying hi, he stutters over a few different greetings and gives up, holding out his hand. "Tr-tr-tracker." He winces. "Sorry."

I wave him off. "Don't worry about it." I gesture to Aki. "My brother, Aki."

Aki holds out a hand. "Hi. I'm a Witch, if you need any immediate assistance." He bows and smiles at me.

I elbow Aki in the ribs. What the fuck is he doing? His magic is death. He can't just go around saying he's a Witch. For goddess' sake, I'm gonna have to watch out for him, aren't I?

"What?"

"I . . ." Oh, never mind. I wave him off.

"That's so kind of you," Lu interrupts. "Our only Witch has been having a hard time keeping up with all the charms and refueling them. The poor sod's exhausted."

"Oh," I say, "I can help with that."

Aki coughs. "Me too."

Wait, what? He can? But I thought Witches only had access to one type of magic? He can do more than one?

Aki looks at me with a small headshake, and then goes to greet the Witch in question, leaving me with Lu and Tracker.

Lu offers me a seat and a drink, which I gladly accept, happy to be off my feet. (Don't tell Aki, but my feet tend to get sore too. No amount of immortality will cure that.) "So," I ask, "is there a reason you wanted to chat with me?"

Lu glances at Tracker, who shifts in his seat. "We wanted to know if there was anything you planned to do about . . . this." She gestures all around her.

New Orleans.

"We have a plan."

She claps her hands together. "Oh, thank the gods. Is there anything we can—"

"But it's going to take time to get to." I'm not sure telling them about the SC's Area 50 plans is wise, but what the hell can they do from in here. "The SC plan to shut down all the major Vampire cities. We need to defend those, and that's taking some time to plan for."

"But after?" Tracker asks, his stutter nowhere to be found now. "Afterwards, you'll help us?"

"That's the plan."

They look like hope has just hit them in the face after forgetting what it felt like. And I guess that's probably true. These people need me. And I hate that I can't do anything right now. But it's okay. I'll come back, and when I do, I'll free them all.

Chapter Thirty-Two

Thirty-Two Shifters Turn up Dead in Glasgow, Scotland as Supernatural Hate Crimes Rise

After Aki and I refuel every charm the entire group are wearing, I fly us out of there and toward Shell Beach, where we'll touch down and look around, remembering specifics so we can teleport back in a week.

But halfway through the flight, Aki's stomach grumbles, and then mine follows, and soon we're both giggling mid-air as exhaustion takes us over.

"We'll see if there's something to eat near the beach, and then we'll fly back and refuel and sleep on the plane."

"Yeah, I know. My stomach's disagreeing, but I'm all onboard for the plan."

We spend a couple hours in the air, and the hardest part of flying for that long is the concentration required. But energy wise, I seem fine to make the trip there and back again.

Eventually, when I'm worried Aki might actually fall asleep mid-air, we touch down and breathe in matching sighs of relief.

"God, I've never been so relieved to have my feet on solid ground," Aki moans.

"Feel free to fly yourself back then," I grumble.

You know, assuming we weren't going to just teleport back.

"No hate, no hate. Just glad to be able to move of my own freewill again."

I take a look around, the water lapping at my heels as I jog to drier land. "Sorry about that." Aki's ringing water out of his shoe and I'm trying hard not to laugh. "But the meeting point's over there, by the harbor." I point in that direction.

"Yup." Aki looks around, smiling at the sun setting on the wet sand and the cliffs behind us. "Think you got everything?"

"Yeah, I can teleport back here." I grab a crystal out of my backpack and smash it at my feet, thinking of the airport. And the moment I open my eyes, the doors to the airport are before me while Aki stands beside me. "There."

"Time to take a nap," he says.

"We need to board the plane first, moron."

"You're pretty crabby for an immortal being, you know."

"Next time the world's fate is on your shoulders, let me know how well you're doing."

He smirks at me. "Well, I'd certainly be doing it with more of a smile. Especially since I can teleport to anywhere I've already been, meaning I can spend the afternoon in the sun and the evening in the city and the night with whomever I choose." He winks.

Ugh. "Yeah, yeah, alright."

"I'm just saying, you should live it up a little."

"You're just like Connie and Nine."

"Maybe you should listen to your boyfriend and girlfriend." He sighs. "That's still so weird to say."

"Huh?" Why is it weird?

"It's weird that you're in a polyamorous relationship. It's just . . . odd."

"It would be odder to only be with one of them." Trust me. I roll my eyes at his inability to understand something so natural. Most people have problems with my changing sex, my lack of a set species—heck, even my tattoos get more side-eye—but most people don't have a problem with my relationship choices. "Super odd."

He shrugs his shoulders. "Whatever makes you happy. I guess you're getting more than the rest of us at least."

I choke on air for a moment before calming myself. "Yeah, I guess." Should definitely not be talking about my sex life with my brother.

Fifteen hours on a plane makes your butt sore. Or, in my case, both my butts sore. I ate and napped twice, just to be sure—much to Aki's amusement—and now I'm cranky and in desperate need of a bath. And some coffee.

Manaus, Brazil in October is warm, but it's not stifling.

"C'mon," Aki says, "I booked us a hotel while you were napping." He sniggers. "Twice."

"Yeah, yeah, I probably didn't need to do that. I was just being cautious." I shrug. "I usually just feel refreshed after a night's sleep in both forms."

"Wonder why?" He has that curious look on his face Nine often dons when pondering my insanity. "Both forms are still you, of course, so I guess you have one pool of energy."

"Which would explain why using my Witch powers so much also makes this form tired."

"Strange you can only use that energy for specific types of magic, though."

We look at each, both puzzled, and shake our heads, leaving the question be. There's a lot about my nonconformity that doesn't make sense, and I'm learning not to dwell on that.

"What hotel did you book us?"

"Nothing fancy. Just an Ibis." He points to the tall building looming in the distance. "Only have so much money."

"You idiot," I mutter. "I have enough money to finance this trip." Nine's been teaching me investment. "So don't do that again. We're not going to have to scrimp while pulling off mission impossible."

"Right." He scratches the back of his neck, embarrassment flooding his features. "I'll try to remember that."

"I'll pay you back when we get back to Sheruta." Goddess, I miss home already. Shaking my head, I focus on the hotel now looming in front of me. Its blue doors and grass-green sides made of plants are beautiful, but then lots of buildings nowadays have greenery of some form on them, to decrease CO_2 emissions in our atmosphere. "This looks like a nice hotel." Better than that shitty motel Dea made us stay in, anyway.

"We'll check in, shake off the jetlag, and then check out your lead tomorrow, okay?" Exhaustion grips at my mind, and I'm pretty sure if I don't have a shower soon, I'm going to combust.

"Sure."

Aki walks up to the receptionist, who gives us a once over—eyes lingering a second too long on my chest—and then has us register our fingerprints to the rooms' online database.

Sophisticated. "Why don't they use datachips here?"

"They do, but I sent an email explaining who you are, and

they said they'll use the old-fashioned way."

We get off the elevator and both turn right until we reach our rooms, positioned next to each other, and go our separate ways.

"See you tomorrow morning." Aki yawns. Seems he's just as tired as I am.

"Yeah, night."

We chuckle at the hilarity of saying goodnight at midday and vanish beyond our doors. The room beyond is clean, has a large window that lets in lots of light, and smells fresh. Plus, it has a large bed and a big tub.

After a long soak in the bath, ordering room service, and then taking a nap until eight pm, I'm ready to do something for a few hours before going back to bed.

But what?

I'm too far away from my library to do any research, and I don't want to use all the crystals to go home every night just because I can, Aki is sleeping, and the team are probably busy.

But I guess I should check my phone. If I even remember how to use the old contraption. It's like over a hundred years old. Seriously. Why can't we just get chips already?

Yeah, yeah, yeah, I know. The SC controls all chip data, so it won't be smart. Even if we manage to sort out this mess, it'll still be a no.

But I'm pleasantly surprised to see messages from all members of the team, even Arrie.

Connie: Hey hon! Hope you're doing okay. Remember to get me a souvenir.

Nine: If you need anything researched on the fly, let me

know. I'll happily spend time in your library while you're away. ;)

Dea: I can't wait for you to come home. I miss cuddling you and having you between me and Nine.

Arrie: Still alive?

I roll my eyes at Arrie's message, coo over Dea's, and laugh at everyone else's. Typical team. Wonder if any of them are free for one of those holocalls?

I guess Connie would be the best person to call, since she's likely the least tired. Hope she's not busy. I have no idea what time it is over there.

Pulling the device out, I enter the code I know to be Connie's and wait, watching the flashing green light spin around the top.

Please be available. Please be available.

Then the light turns green, and Connie's voice screams over the speaker. "Magic! You're okay!" She sounds out of sorts, like I've caught her at a bad time.

"Is this a bad time?"

"No, not at all. I just ran around the house and gathered all the guys. Took me a minute."

"Oh. Hey Nine, Dea . . ." Is Arrie there?

Nine screeches out of the speakers. "Sweeetie! You're okay? All alive and happy?" Only Nine would ask if I'm happy like it's a casual greeting.

"Yes, Nine. I'm fine. Just checked into a hotel in Manaus, Brazil."

"Angel, I miss you."

An indignant snort sounds over the speaker, and there's

only one person it belongs to.

"Hey, Arrie. Thanks for the blood supply."

"You supplied Magic with blood?" Connie asks. "Really?"

"How else are they gonna refuel when it's only our blood that does the trick?"

N'awww, he does care.

I think.

They don't have their holodisplay on, so I can't see them, but they're chatting, bickering, and it reminds me so much of home that my eyes mist over for a moment before I grab my emotions by the britches and haul them back into normal.

"Hey, everyone?"

They all stop talking.

"We're heading into the Amazon tomorrow to check out Aki's lead on the pixies, so I might not be able to recharge my devices for a while." Hence why I'm checking in. "But we managed to get to Shell Beach."

My silence punctures the air.

"What is it?" Dea asks. "What is wrong?"

"There are non-Vampires trapped in New Orleans."

"With a bunch of starving Vampires?" Nine asks. "Yeah, that's not good."

"There isn't enough of them to feed the Vampires, and it's like zombie town in there. I think we should send in a team to pick them up. Co-ordinate with the Vampire Royal Council."

"I'll arrange it," Connie says. "Everything's been quiet here, anyway."

"I'll help," Arrie says. "Give me something to do."

"If you're bored," Nine says, "you can always work on your groveling, since you'll need to do plenty to get between Magic's legs again."

I manage to blush, even though no one is here to witness—thank the goddess—but Connie knows me too well. "Stop blushing," she chastises. "We've all been between your legs at this point. Well," she corrects herself, "nearly all of us."

Arrie groans, and I distantly hear a door slam.

I laugh. "Stop frustrating him further. He's clearly having a hard time." I take a deep breath. "He wants to work on being . . . friends." The word slides out of my mouth like poison.

"Friends?" Connie asks. "But he—"

Someone must push her off whatever surface she was sitting on, because I hear a short scream and then an ouch as she punches the person in the arm. Probably Nine.

"Stop beating up Nine, Connie." My chest constricts as I picture them all huddled around a device just to speak to me. "He's probably still tired since he's probably still not sleeping."

Dea laughs. "You would be right about that. Though I managed to pull him into bed for a nap earlier, hence the chipper edge to his voice."

"Good. He needs to sleep."

"Stop fussing over me. I'm just as immortal as you two," Nine complains.

"Sooo," Connie asks, "how's everything going with Aki?"

"Err . . . fine, I think."

"Getting to know each other?" Dea asks.

"Yeah." Oh, Nine might know. "Nine, do you know of any Witches who can use more than one type of magic?"

"No, I don't think so. Why?"

"Because Aki can use charm magic, too."

"Really?" All three of them ask.

"Yeah. Saw it firsthand." I yank the duvet up to my chest and lay my head down. A yawn escapes me. "He helped the non-Vampires in New Orleans without batting an eyelid."

"That's weird," Nine confirms. "Maybe just ask him about it."

"Yeah . . . I guess." My eyes are starting to droop as my body slowly shuts down. "I miss you all."

"We miss you too, hon."

"Get some sleep, Sweetie."

"Have fun in the Amazon, Angel. Do not fall out of any more trees."

Nine bursts out laughing before someone turns the call off and I fall asleep.

Chapter Thirty-Three

Has the SC Created "Speciesism" and What Can we do About it?

The next morning we head to back to the airport, where we board a special helicopter I booked in advance to take us into the heart of the Amazon, away from all the usual tourist trails and things.

This will be my first helicopter ride, I think. And by the excited look on Aki's face, it's his first too.

"Do you think we'll see many cool animals?" he yells.

"Probably!" It becomes hard to talk when we lift into the air, so we stop trying to communicate.

As the world becomes smaller, I start to see the treeline up ahead, and we race toward it quicker than I expected. It's probably enhanced by Fae spells. Most of the transport industry is. But it's the beauty of the rainforest that leaves me truly speechless. The greenery goes on for miles.

After what happened in the 20th and 21st centuries, I'm surprised it's still so huge. But international laws came in to play, and large portions of the populace voted to stop cutting down the Amazon rainforest. As well as many other places. Companies were forced to look for alternatives, which then helped the job market. Prices went up, though. But it's worth it for the outcome.

Aki grabs my hand and yanks me to his side of the helicopter, where we're now low enough to see the treetops and the upper canopy without assistance. My female form could probably zoom in, but I'm in my male form. I get fewer weird looks this way, since I wasn't in this form when the video went viral.

The pilot looks nervous whenever I meet his gaze.

"There's a clearing up ahead," the pilot says through the headpiece we're now wearing. "I'm going to drop you off there, okay?"

"Yeah, that's fine."

As the helicopter places itself above the clearing, it descends, and soon we're on the ground and able to hear at regular volume again.

"That was awesome!" Aki jumps from the helicopter and lands on the flattened grass. "We're going back via helicopter, right?"

"Yup. But only because it was a two-way ticket. No one-way options."

"Hey," the pilot interrupts, "if I don't have to come back to get you, then I'm not." His gruff voice matches his stubble and wrinkled eyes. "I ain't associating myself with you." He points at me.

"Gee, thanks." I wave him off. "It's fine, we don't need your help getting back."

The relief on his face is evident, though insulting.

"I'm not some kind of monster, you know. Those Vampires I attacked were volunteers. The rogue Vampire faction are the ones working with the Fae and the SC to further divide people."

"Good." His arms crossed over his chest. "I don't want your kind anywhere near my family."

"My kind?" I take a deep breath, silencing him with a finger when he goes to interrupt. "Oh hunny, there ain't nobody in the world like me." I shift into my female form and bring a fireball to my hand, then blow it out with a strong gust of wind. I lower my fangs and think of all the tasty blood I'm missing out on by being here, and my eyes glow bright red.

"Fucking hell." The guy's face turns ashen, and he mumbles, "Freak," as he hops back into the helicopter and takes off.

"Fucking prejudiced asshole."

"There's just no persuading some people, is there?" Aki looks hurt, his eyes downcast and his lips frowning. "But maybe it might have been better not to threaten him with fire magic." He raises his eyebrows at me in question before turning away.

"Maybe," I mumble. "But he was being such a . . ."

"Bitch?"

I don't think I've ever heard Aki swear before. And the shock has me stifling a grin with one hand.

"Oh, lay off. You're as bad as Nigel. I swear sometimes." He rolls his eyes. "Speaking of Nigel, have you forgiven him yet?"

"Huh?" Oh, he's talking about keeping us a secret from each other. "Yeah, almost right away."

Aki turns to face me with another surprised look on his

face. "Really? Why?" He pauses as he looks at the bright sky. "How?"

I grab Aki's hand and drag him into the forest on the edges of the clearing, starting us down some winding tracks. "He was trying to save our lives, Aki. If he had told us about each other, do you honestly think we wouldn't have sought each other out?"

He's silent. Pensive.

"Especially when I was mortal." I take a deep breath. "I could have really used a family member." I probably wouldn't have been half as evil if I did.

"Why do you say that?"

Do I tell him? Is he going to freak out and want nothing to do with me? Will he then go the press? So far they haven't published anything about my mortal life. Yet.

"Well, I . . ." I avoid his pestering gaze. "I wasn't a good person, that's all." Sweat boils across my palms and trails down my fingertips. "Fucking hell, it's hot." I wipe more sweat from my brow.

"Yeah." Aki's breath is shallow as he wipes sweat from his brow, too. "If you wanted to talk about it . . . About your mortal life, I'm happy to listen." He smiles. "It doesn't matter what it is." He opens his mouth to say something more, but then closes it again, deciding against it.

"Thanks."

An uncomfortable silence makes the air even denser than it already was, and I'm stifling beneath it, eager to shake it off and burn it to the ground.

"So, Aki, any girlfriends or boyfriends? Married? Children? Secret lovers?" I raise my eyebrows and wink. "C'mon, dish the dirt."

"You really wanna know?"

"Uh-huh. But first, where are we going?"

He rubs the back of his neck and groans. "Unsure. But I used to do security for this guy who had direct access to pixie dust. Straight from the source, apparently. Somewhere deep in the Amazon rainforest."

"You have got to be kidding me." Does he know how big the Amazon rainforest is? I wipe a frustrated hand down my face. "At least we have supplies."

"Yup. Kinda hoping we find some evidence of them or something."

I nod. I'll figure something out. "So, dish the dirt." He's not getting away with not telling me about his life.

"I've had a few girlfriends over the years. I once had a boyfriend, too. But nothing's stuck." He shrugs. "Guess none of them were meant to be."

"What about your career? Friends? Education? Places you've visited? C'mon, Aki . . . Share! It's what siblings do."

He chuckles and then sighs. "Fine, okay." He links his arm through mine, like he so often does, and regales me with his life's story while we look for evidence of pixies.

"I grew up in the Japanese Witch Coven in Shinjuku, Tokyo. They were . . . nice. Hard at times, but loving overall. I was never very good at school. I kept getting into trouble. All I wanted to do was practise my magic, but the Coven never allowed it. Said it was too dangerous." He sighs. "So I left when I was sixteen and never looked back.

"Spent some time alone in the mountains to practise my death magic, so I didn't harm any people, and eventually got good. Really good. Now I can take life at will, give it form, and use it to attack people."

"Like a living death shadow?" Kind of reminds me of the night I died. I shudder.

"Yeah . . . You've created one before?"

I nod, not sharing the story.

"So you're powerful then." He rubs his chin in thought. "Really powerful."

"I can't do it at will or anything. It was just a spur-of-the-moment thing."

He shrugs. "Shows you can, though. We just need to tap into those powers."

"Stop turning the conversation back onto me! I want to know about you. What happened after that?"

He shrugs but looks away. "I went back to Tokyo, apologized to the Witch Coven who raised me, and got a regular job. It's been pretty normal for me since then." He coughs. "Well, until I hijacked my lost twin sister's teleporting crystal and learned I'm related to the Fifth Horseman of the Apocalypse, then became an ambassador for an important political embassy created for peace."

I laugh softly, realizing his life has been crazy over the past couple of weeks. "Yeah, sorry about that."

"Don't be. I could have left. You gave me the option."

"So, do you really think I could learn to access my death magic at will?"

Aki turns to me with a glare. "Yes." He stops us dead. "In fact, this is the perfect place to practise. We could not be farther away from other people."

"R-Right here? Right now?"

He dumps our backpacks onto the forest floor and looks at me with a smile. "Yes."

"Okay." I take a deep breath. "Connie suggested that I use a memory of a time I was threatened."

Aki bobs his head side to side. "That could work."

"Okay, let's try it." I can do this. Totally. For once, I'm not gonna fail. I bring the memory of my death to the forefront of my mind. It's honestly something I try not to think about, but today, I need to think about it. I need to let its fear flow through me. "Okay, c'mon, Magic."

The cold alleyway, the assassin's voice searing a permanent tattoo onto my brain, the fear pumping through my veins like ice. He shoots me. I flop to the ground and feel the life flare out of me like a volcano erupting its life onto the ground.

My hands tremble as my breathing hitches and something cold snakes around my hands.

"Yes!" Aki yells. "That's it! Right there!"

My eyes snap open and catch onto the dark mist swirling around my arms like poison clouds. "I did it."

"Okay," Aki says, "do you know how to get rid of it?"

I switch into my male form and smirk. "Perks of being me."

Chapter Thirty-Four

We walk for hours, well until sundown, and find no evidence of magic usage, pixie homes, or anyone else. This place is a barren forest. Empty of everything except the animals that belong here. So eventually we set up camp in a small area where we can hang hammocks from the trees to keep us off the forest floor.

It doesn't get cold at night here, so we don't bother with a large fire—just enough to cook some of our supplies with. And by supplies, I mean dried meat, canned vegetables, and oven-able potatoes that I'm pretty sure weren't okay.

Goddess, I miss Arrie's cooking.

My phone battery died sometime during the day, so I have no way to contact the team. In an emergency I can just go home, but I don't want to do that yet. I might be tired, but

I want to see this mission through.

Though, given that I only have six blood vials left, I might have to go home for a pit stop eventually.

The night is filled with noises, dark as pitch because of the canopy covering any light, and Aki's snores mean I get not a damn wink before morning lights our way again.

For fuck's sake, I'm exhausted.

I am not Connie. I need sleep.

Aki, sensing my mood, asks what the matter is, but I'm grouchy as hell and don't answer him. It's only when he looks at me with that hurt expression that I soften and apologize.

"Sorry. I slept terribly."

"Really?" He frowns. "I slept just fine."

Yeah, I know. I nearly snap at him again, but there's no point. It's not his fault. "Can you remember anything else about where we're going? Anything at all?" I really don't feel like wandering the Amazon jungle for the next week.

Honestly sounds like a vacation planned by hell itself.

"Maybe . . . I don't know."

"Even if it seems pointless, it might not be."

He nods. "Okay. Well, he said something about underground tunnels."

"Underground tunnels?" Great, now I have to find an opening to something that's supposed to be hidden. What kind of shitty luck do I have? Do I have a sign on my cosmic back saying 'please, kick me continuously'? "Entrance?"

He shakes his head.

Goddess, damn it.

There must be some way to track pixies. Something to tell if they're nearby. If I had my earth magic unlocked, I could probably sense them. But all I have is air, water, and fire. None of which helps me now.

I know a few Fae tracking spells, but I'm not sure I have the right ingredients nearby. And I'm also not sure how to track specifically for pixies.

None of my enhanced senses in either form pick up anything weirder than jungle life, so I don't think they're nearby.

I'm going to have to figure out that tracking spell.

"Magic, maybe we should head ba—"

I hold up a finger to silence him. "Shh. Thinking."

We keep walking, and my mind keeps spinning. Trying to figure out a way to do a tracking spell and tailor it to pixies. Maybe an intention rune? I do know what pixies look like. If I knew their magical signature, I could use that with a detection rune, but I don't. Lower supes are less researched, less written about.

Guess I'll have to try an intention rune.

A bit of a shot in the dark, but oh well. It's the best I've got.

"I'm going to need some teedle weed, basal flower, and Witch's brew."

"Huh?" He looks puzzled, so I explain my plan.

"Wow. You can do that?"

"Not sure, but I'm going to try."

"Okay, well I know how to make Witch's brew, so I'll do that bit."

Right. Now I just need to find the other three plants, which I'm almost certain don't grow in the Amazon. I have some ingredients in a stash Nine gave me, but I haven't rifled through them yet. He said they're the basics.

At least teedle weed is pretty basic, so he might have included that.

Yanking my backpack off my back, I lift out the white

container and flip the lid. There's more packed into here than I expected—like an herbalist's collection, they're all shoved into small bags and pots, some flowers suspended in small vials of water attached to their stems, and others are just seeds lying about.

I don't even know what they all are.

But one of the first bags I pull out is teedle weed.

"Thank the goddess for Nine."

"I've made the Witch's brew!" Aki shouts from where we settled down for lunch.

It's a brown sludge that doesn't look very appetizing, but thankfully I'm not drinking it.

"Thank you." I wave a hand at him. "I'll be right there."

Basal flowers . . . Basal flowers . . .

They're key to tracking spells, as they act like sniffer dogs, searching for their target. But is there something else I can use instead? Maybe a different plant?

What else did Nine provide?

Plants, weeds, seeds, flowers, and . . . a basal bulb. Wow. I'm surprised he had one just lying around. Here's hoping it'll work the same.

"Okay, Aki, I need you to dunk these ingredients in the Witch's brew for me."

He grabs the ingredients in my hands and places them in the sludge-filled bowl and looks to me expectantly.

Okay, now I need to draw three different runes: one for intention, one to bind the intention to the basal bulb, and one to connect the teedle weed so everything stays stable. Once that's done, I use an incantation I learned from one of my study sessions, but I recite it in Japanese. It basically forms a protective bubble around the rune and ingredients and slowly siphons my energy through, giving the magic some juice.

I pick up the bowl and watch it light up, magic sparking off it every which way. But with some reconfiguring of my intentions—an entrance to the pixie's lair—it sparks and fizzes once more before settling its light in one direction.

West.

"West it is," Aki confirms as he picks up our things and heads in that direction. "Neat spell, by the way."

"Thanks."

We follow the damn sparkling bowl for hours. My feet hurt, my arms ache, and my stomach is growling. "I need a break." The magic I'm using is exhausting, and we're nowhere near a leyline to recharge.

"Okay, but maybe stop the spell while we're resting?"

"Yeah, that's probably for the best." I stop right where I'm walking and sit on my backpack, the bowl at my feet. I stop siphoning my energy through the protective bubble and catch my breath. "Fuck . . . this . . . shit."

Aki laughs. "So, immortality does not cure all, hmm?"

"Oh, fuck off." I shove him to the floor and watch him shoot straight back up, brushing any critters and leaves and forest debris off his body. "Scared?"

He shivers. "Not a fan of bugs."

Now it's my turn to laugh. "But you're here in the Amazon with me?"

He shrugs. "Thought you might need a hand, and the others seemed busy. Besides, it's been nice getting to know you better, even if you are a grouch when you're tired and hungry."

"Who isn't?"

"Good point."

A rustling of leaves and faint footsteps my Shifter hearing can just pick up has me swiveling my head to the east.

"What's that?"

Aki guards himself, a fighting stance at the ready, and looks in the direction I'm pointing.

"Over there."

He gathers a familiar-looking ball of black magic in his joined palms and takes a deep breath. "I got this."

"We don't even know what this is," I hiss, frustration lacing my words. "It might not be an enemy."

Apparently, I spoke too soon, because something ethereal, white, glowing, and beautiful bounds toward us at the speed of light, knocking Aki to the forest floor and unconscious before I can even stand.

Large white wings shoot out of its back, and I'm floored. "An Angel?"

Chapter Thirty-Five

ANGELS AND DEMONS: EVERYTHING YOU NEED TO KNOW
ABOUT THE ANCIENT WAR

"You're an . . . Angel," I point out, shock keeping me rooted to the floor. "I didn't think you existed anymore."

She puffs out a breath and crosses her arms over her very naked torso. "Yes, well, things aren't always what they seem." Her voice is raspy and harsh, but she seems nonthreatening in her stance.

"Are you going to kill me?"

"Why bother? It's not like I can anyway, right?"

I nod. "Right." So, err . . . what now? "What are you doing here?" I gesture to the forest. "In the Amazon?"

She shrugs. "Got a good gig protecting the pixie population, and I stay out of the world's way." She eyes me up and down. "What are you doing here?"

"Looking for the pixies." I nod to Aki, who's still lying

unconscious on the floor. "With my brother."

She winces slightly. "Ah, sorry about that. But that's death magic, gifted to him by an ancient bloodline, I assume."

"Yeah, we're Angel-descended Witches. Or, at least, I was, when I was mortal." She looks at me confused for a moment. "It's complicated."

"I can only imagine." She huffs a laugh before picking Aki up and hauling him over her chest. "You Horsemen are all so . . . complicated."

She can say that again.

"You coming?" She turns to walk west.

"Where?"

"To the pixies?"

I scramble to keep up, leaving the spell behind because it's not like I need it or anyone else can use it. "You're going to help? But why?"

"Because if I don't, you'll probably kill me. And because I can't really get rid of you. You kinda rule the world."

I flinch. What did the team do to this Angel? "I have no intention of hurting anyone. Especially not an Angel. I really do come in peace." Ugh. Could I be anymore cliché?

"The Horsemen of the Apocalypse never come in peace."

"Well, this one does. Since I'm the Horseman of Magic and all, I figured maybe I should respect the magic the world already has."

She laughs under her breath. "Yeah right." She looks behind her with a scowl. "Just try to keep up."

I shift into my female form so I can keep up easier, and when she next turns around, she looks at me bewildered for a moment before shrugging and turning back around.

Wow. No questions. That's a first.

"So, where are the pixies?"

"I'd prefer not to give that information out, if that's okay. Just follow me, and I'll take you to them."

"Okay." What the hell; I only need to chat with them, anyway. "How many are there?"

"A few hundred thousand, at best."

That's it? That's so few for a whole species. The Fae really have run them into the ground, haven't they?

"Surprised?"

"A little." I walk next to her, consciously checking on Aki now and then. "I knew they'd become endangered because of the Fae hunting them for their dust, but I didn't know how bad it was."

The angel nods. "Yeah, it's pretty bad. They have to run to a new base every time someone finds them. They're exhausted." She looks pointedly at me, expecting something.

"You want me to fix it?"

"Yeah, I do." She stops walking and faces me. "This is your job. You so-called Horsemen work toward peace, but all you really do is leave the world to its own devices so long as no wars are raging. That's not peace. That's just . . . not awful." She looks me in the eye. "And now look at you. Back into the fray because of yet another war."

"For an angel, you're pretty good at sarcasm."

"I can hide the wings and stop the glowing, if I want. So I often use it to hang with regular people whenever I can." She shrugs. "Unextraordinary people are some of the best I know."

I do not miss the snide in her voice. "Okay. Ouch."

"Just do your job, and I won't maim you."

"Pfft. Come on and try, Glowy."

She laughs, her resolve cracking for just a moment. "Glowy?"

"Yeah, well, you never introduced yourself, so I've nicknamed ya Glowy. Deal with it." I look around, not noticing a reason as to why we've stopped. "My name's Magic. That's Aki. And where are the pixies?"

Please don't let this have been a wild goose chase.

She snorts. "Through the vines on your right. Keep going straight, and you'll hit a wall. State your name and your business. If they let you in, they'll hear you out." She looks to Aki. "Would you like your brother back? I can keep him safe out here if you'd prefer?"

I weigh up my options, but there's no way in hell I'm leaving Aki to this murdering angelic psychopath. "I'll take my brother back, thank you very much." I hold out my arms, and she drops him into them without a semblance of grace.

Turning around, I take a deep breath and walk through the vines, trying not to think too hard about how many creepy crawlies are living in them.

Focus, Magic. Focus.

One more deep breath, and I keep going straight, noticing that I've somehow entered a cave and that I have no light to see by. Thank the goddess for night vision.

Aki's in my arms, still unconscious, but I manage to prevent any bumps to his head on the walls, only scraping his feet a teenie bit. He may have lost a shoe somewhere back there.

Oh well, he can grab it on the way out.

The moment we can, we're teleporting the fuck outta here. I really don't like the jungle.

The wall appears in no time, and I knock. A hollow echo knocks back. "I'm here to talk to the pixie race about potentially helping them relocate to somewhere not on Earth."

Hundreds of tiny whispers flood through the cave

system, bouncing off the walls. But I can't make any of it out. Eventually, a tiny voice whispers, "Okay. You can come in."

The rock wall slides to the right, and I step through into a child's paradise. Seriously, Disney couldn't even make this shit up. Underground roots permeate the entire cave, and in every nook and cranny of them, little golden pixies have made small homes.

Pixie dust flies freely, and I find my nose itching, but I'm otherwise unaffected by it.

"Your home is beautiful."

A small pixie lands on my arm and looks me dead in the eye, his red eyes and sharp teeth looking as menacing as ever. "You are welcome here, Horseman, but only so long as you tell no one of our location."

I bow. "You have my word."

"Then you may meet Uzuki. Our leader."

"That's great. Thank you." I look to Aki and smile. "You don't happen to have somewhere safe I can leave my brother, do you? I did not trust Glowy out there." I nod back to the cave entrance.

The pixie does what I think is a smile, but he gestures to the small group of pixies who are busy making a human-sized cot for me to lay Aki on.

"Thank you," I whisper, remembering that their hearing is sensitive and you're supposed to whisper. "This is much appreciated."

After I lay Aki down, I follow the pixie with the red eyes and mean stare to a small hole in the wall at the end of the one of the cave tunnels I have to crouch to fit into.

"You must be Uzuki," I whisper, trying my best to bow in such small confines. "Thank you so much for meeting me."

A larger-than-average pixie, just slightly larger than male-me's forearm, steps out of the darkness and lights up the crevice like a fairylight, a short and stuffy smile on his face. "It's a pleasure, Horseman of Magic." He gets straight to the point. "I hear you want to help us?"

"Yes. I can offer you safe passage to Sheruta, our homeland. It's separate from Earth. You won't be hunted there."

"And in return for such generosity? I assume you want our allegiance in the upcoming war with the Fae, SC, and rogue Vampire faction?"

"You're awfully up to date for a pixie," I huff.

"We need to be. It's how we stay alive down here."

"Fair. I'm so sorry my fellow Horsemen haven't helped you sooner. But I'm here now, and I want to help, allegiance or not." I can't leave them like this, cowering for their lives. I'm sure we can find somewhere for them to call their own on Sheruta. "If you'll let me, of course."

"We have no room for pride in these troubled times."

"I guess not."

"Do you have a plan on how to transport us to your . . . realm?"

A plan. Right. Since I came up with the relocation offer on the fly, no, I don't. But they don't know that. I can't create portals, I don't have enough crystals, so they'll have to get to the main portal. But that'll be dangerous.

"Yeah, yeah I do." I look around. "You don't happen to have a plasma energy socket anywhere around, do you?" I hold up my dead holocaller in an eager smile.

Uzuki nods to the pixie who led me here with a smile. "Show Magic where she can plug that thing in and make her plans. We're with her." He turns to the few pixies around him and yells, "Tell everyone to get ready to fly out. We're moving tonight."

Pixies charge forth, getting ready, making plans, and something else blooms in the caverns that wasn't present when I entered. Hope.

Chapter Thirty-Six

Once my holophone is charged up enough, I dial the only person I trust to escort hundreds of thousands of pixies from Brazil to Colorado safely.

"Arrie?"

His gruff hello tells me it's the middle of the night there.

"Sorry, is it late?"

He grumbles something, then yawns. "Three am, but it's okay." His holodisplay looks tired, but he's awake, and that's all I need. "What do you need?"

"You."

His smile lights up the call. "Really?"

"Yup. Hundreds of pixies, and there's only one way to transport them to Sheruta. So I need a pixie escort I can trust."

He sighs. "You want me to babysit a species for you?"

The pixie from earlier huffed. "We do not need babysitting, War." His arms cross over his chest.

"Arrie, stop being an ass. I'm trying to do politics over here."

"Right, sorry. But you did wake me up."

"Yeaaah, sorry about that. I don't really understand how the time difference works across realms."

"Do yourself a favor," he replies, "and do not ask for an explanation from Nine."

I giggle, glad we're at the joking phase of our new . . . friendship. "Duly noted." I sigh. "Look, I know it's late, but how quickly can you get here?"

"I can be in Manaus in a few moments. But I'll need an escort to where you are."

"Yeaaah, even I don't know where I am."

"You don't know where you . . . Then how am I supposed to find you?"

"We'll have to meet you near Manaus somewhere."

The pixie chimes in, "We can get to River Negro through these tunnels. It comes out somewhere near Santa Maria."

"I can meet you there," Arrie grumbles. "I'll leave now." He ends the call, and I wince.

"I feel awful for waking him up."

"Well, he's a friendly one."

"Yeah, sorry about him. He's a bit of a grumpy gill. But he's the best fighter we have. If anyone can escort you to Colorado safely, it's him."

"If you say so." He hops back onto my arm as we make our way back to Uzuki to relay the plan. "So," I finalize, "if we can get to Santa Maria safely, then Arrie will take you the rest of the way."

A bright glowing light I recognize and shiver at lights up the back of me, and I turn with an uneasy smile. "Glowy, hi."

"Magic." She nods her head at me. "You're really escorting them out of here?"

"Yup." I look smugly at her. "And Arrie is escorting them from Santa Maria to Colorado, where the main portal to Sheruta is."

She looks troubled, and she spins on her heels and storms away. Well, she tries. She's a bit tall for the cave system.

"Is she okay?"

The pixie on my arm hums and laughs. "I don't think she's particularly keen to reacquaint herself with the person who destroyed most of her kind."

Right, the ancient war. The Horsemen killed most of the Demons and Angels so they'd stop preying on the other supernaturals. Seems a bit drastic, if you ask me. But then, I wasn't there.

I didn't exist yet.

Jesus Christ, my lovers are old. Talk about an age-gap romance. Oh well, age gaps are pretty on-trend right now, anyway.

I shake that thought from my head. Focus, Magic, focus. Now is not the time.

"Magic!" a familiar voice calls from the nearby tunnel.

"I'm down here, Aki. Come hear my plan."

He bounds toward my voice with a smile. "You found the pixies!"

"Well, we found the angel guarding the pixies, and then she beat me up—a lot—and eventually gave in and took me straight here."

"Ah." He gestures to my female body, which has sustained no damage, with a question. "You don't look beaten up . . ."

"You should see my male body. I ran out of Fae magic, and since we're nowhere near a leyline"—probably one reason the pixies settled here—"I'm exhausted." More than exhausted, actually, but it's not important right now.

"So, what's the plan?"

I tell Aki the plan, and he seems to approve, though he's a little worried about my exhaustion, which is apparently obvious to see.

"Maybe take a break?"

"No time for that. We need to meet Arrie in Santa Maria as soon as possible." I sigh, looking at the large number of pixies that have to travel a few miles. "I wish I could scout ahead and find Arrie and bring him back to the tunnel entrance on that side, but I can't leave them undefended."

That brilliant white glowing light is back, and this time, it comes with a pissed-off angel. "They are not undefended. Nor will they ever be. Nor do they need the Horseman of War to help them relocate." Her arms are crossed over her chest as she huffs at me and spits Arrie's name.

"Well, I wanted to be sure. Nothing wrong with a little backup." She looks like she disagrees with that statement, but I don't give her the chance to argue. "Fine," I say in place of whatever foul thing was about to come out of her mouth, "you and Aki can lead the pixies out. I'll scout ahead, make sure it's safe, and find Arrie so we don't have to wait around in an unsafe location."

She nods sternly and turns her back to me, her white glow diminishing ever so slightly because I can now look at her without getting eyestrain.

Getting her to work with Arrie is going to be a pain in the ass, isn't it?

Chapter Thirty-Seven

New Blood Supply Route Running Everywhere but New
Orleans

Three lefts, two rights, another left, and I should be a few
meters from the Santa Maria entrance. Apparently. So Uzuki
says. But for all I know, he's led me on a wild goose chase for
shits and giggles.

And believe me, these tunnels are not made for regular
sized people. If I wasn't so drained in my male form, I would
shift into a cat or something to make this easier. But alas, no
can do.

I'm just about to turn the last left when I come to an
abrupt halt. There's a river up ahead that's rushing faster
than I can probably swim, even as a Vampire, but the exit is
on the other side. I can see daylight throbbing through the
small cat flap-like hole.

"Shit."

There's no room between the river and cave tunnel ceiling
for me to fly, so I'm going to have to swim through.

If I die doing this, I'm so blaming Arrie.

It isn't really his fault, but I'm blaming him, anyway. He
fucking deserves it.

The water is cold enough to make me scream when I dip
my feet in, and shock holds my body hostage for a moment.
Fuck. I won't make it across this without turning into an icicle.

And either way, Aki and the angel won't make it across.
The pixies can probably fit in the gap between the water and
ceiling, so they'll be fine. But I do rather need my brother
alive. And I guess I need the stupid angel, too.

An idea flicks to mind, but I doubt myself. I've only done this once before, and not on this level. But it was a similar situation. I was puzzled. I needed a solution. Bonus: no Fae magic needed.

I scuttle away from the water's edge, place a hand on the ground, and feel for the water's energy. Just like with the air. After a few frustrating moments, I find it, but it's like catching flies with your bare hands. It's so slippery.

"C'mon, Magic . . ."

Just when I'm about to scream from frustration, I catch the water's energy and give it a good yank.

The river stops still.

Good. Now, what happens when I pull the energy apart?

The river slowly separates and forms a path along the riverbed.

Wow. This is like some Moses shit right here.

I can't keep it like this though, so I'm going to have to come back once I've found Arrie—who really should have given me a better meeting place.

Santa Maria is a municipality, not a city. A fact that becomes clear the moment I step out of the hole and into a park surrounded by a city.

"A city?" I grumble, "For fuck's sake."

"Gonna grumble the entire time, Killer?" Arrie says from somewhere behind me.

I jump out of my skin, screeching loud enough to wake the neighborhood. "Jesus fucking Christ, asshole!" I throw a fireball his way, but he just dodges, and I quickly put it out before it burns the grass. "What the fuck were you thinking?"

He laughs.

Arrie actually laughs.

And the sound delights me so much a tear trickles down

my face as I stand there dumbfounded before my senses return. I run at Arrie, wrap my arms around his neck, and bury my nose in the crook of his neck, his pine needle scent washing through me. But then everything he's said and done rushes at me, and I jump away. "Sorry."

But damn it's good to have a member of the team by my side once more. Even if only momentarily.

"It's . . . okay." He sounds surprised, like he doesn't know what to do with me now. Which is probably how he feels, actually. "Where are they?"

I point behind me, to the hole in the base of a tree. "Through there. I'll need to help them cross the river below."

He walks to the hole, and watching him trying to fit through it is comical. Seriously, a seven-foot, made-of-muscle moron trying to squeeze through a hole that comes to my knee in height and is barely wider than me.

"Come on, big guy, you can do it."

He grumbles something under his breath. But after some wiggling and repositioning, he manages to fit through the hole and disappears beyond. "Wow. It's tiny in here," he echoes from below.

"Yeah," I say as I crouch through after him. "It really fucking is." I sit next to him on the other side, the river racing in front of us. "They're a few miles away."

"Sure." He leans against the dirt wall behind him, ducking his head.

Now there's nothing to do but wait. Alone. With Arrie. In silence, because anyone can hear us up top.

Great.

The need to break the silence with any sort of sound pinwheels through me, spinning and spinning and spinning until it fires out of control and sparks fly through my mind in the form of thoughts no one should really be thinking.

"Magic?" Arrie whispers. "I . . ." He hesitates. "I'm sorry."

I shrug and avoid his icy stare, full of expectations I'm not willing to fulfill. "It's—"

"Don't say it." He shakes his head. "It's not okay, Killer."

The familiar use of my old nickname whispered from his lips makes me shudder, and I can't hold back the tilt my lips curl into when they attempt to smile. "No, it's not." I finally lift my gaze from the floor and pierce his eyes with everything he's made me feel over the last few weeks: pain, confusion, frustration, anger, guilt, embarrassment . . .

The mask Arrie usually wears—the stone face he never sheds—melts like ice in the desert. His eyes water, tears threatening to spill over the edges, as a pained grimace slices through his face like a knife. And I watch as frustration ebbs and flows through him in equal measure.

Eventually, he swipes the tears away.

"You can talk to me, you know," I whisper.

He looks wide-eyed at me in surprise.

"I know there's more going on than just wanting to be friends." In truth, I don't think he wants to just be friends, but I don't mention that now. "I know there's something you're not saying. I won't force it out of you, though I'm sure I'd get great satisfaction from trying. But you can tell me, if you want."

I dodge his gaze again, but he forces my chin up and my gaze back to his with a harsh yet gentle finger. His eyes flit to my lips with a needy breath and wide eyes.

I lick my lips, my throat dry and my voice vanishing.

"I'm not . . . ready."

To tell me the truth or to kiss me?

Both?

"Maybe one day," he whispers as he leans forward and rests his forehead against mine. "One day . . ." More tears track down his face, but this time, he lets them be. A groan escapes his voice when he opens his lips next, but instead of pulling away and replacing his stone mask, his lips brush mine in the gentlest of touches that shoot sparks through me.

"Hey," I whisper, "we're immortal. We literally have all the time in the world."

He chuckles at that, and a sound of fluttering wings and an annoying female voice barking orders breaks the moment.

Just as they round the corner, the angel in the lead, Arrie swears under his breath in Norse. He grabs my wrist and yanks me into his arms. "What the fuck is she doing here?"

"Oh, so you're familiar?" He gives me an incredulous look. "Well, Glowy has been guarding the pixies, so you're helping her transport them safely."

"No I am fucking not." His arms curl across his chest as he stares daggers at me.

"Listen, asshole." I jab a finger into chest. "I do not have time for your attitude. It'll only be for a few hours." I do my best at begging him with my eyes.

And eventually—though it takes longer than I'm going to admit—he sighs and scrapes a hand through that luscious white hair. "Fine. But only because you asked."

I give myself a mental fist bump and crouch to the floor a few feet from the water's edge and repeat the same Moses shit from earlier.

I hear Arrie gasping in awe behind me, and I think another fist bump is in order. Maybe two. Who knows? I am on a roll tonight.

The angel leads the charge but stops dead in front of Arrie, and for a moment, I'm worried I'll have to break them up.

Somehow. But she just glares at him and moves on, shoving him out of the way. The pixies follow her, and when we get to the end of the line, Aki is bringing up the rear.

"Hey, Magic." He smiles weakly at me, and it's clear he's exhausted.

"Hey." I clap him on the shoulder. "Don't worry," I whisper, "we're gonna rest up in a hotel soon. Preferably somewhere on a leyline."

"I'll look up a leyline map and grab a hotel for us."

I eye him gratefully. "Use this." I throw the payment chip at him after digging it out of my backpack's front pocket. "No more paying for shit."

Chapter Thirty-Eight

The SC Quoted Saying 'Humans Come First'

It takes some doing to prepare Arrie for flight; I have to make him a flight charm—well, I make six, just to be safe—before sending them on their way. They didn't seem happy to be working together, but hopefully it'll be alright.

We also gave the pixies the go ahead to set up anywhere they want in Sheruta, so long as they work alongside the Sheruta Council. Which we assured them is nothing like the Supernatural Council.

"Hope they'll be alright," I whisper as we hop onto a train toward the nearest city on a leyline.

"I'm sure they will be." He places a gentle hand on my shoulder as he rests his head on the train window. "We should rest. It'll take a couple of hours to get there."

We agreed to take a couple of days to recuperate and replenish, and then we're heading to the Witches in South

Africa. I shudder at the thought. I don't wanna play their dumb game. Not again.

We're there to find the fairies. Nothing else.

I stay awake through the night so Aki can sleep, and we eventually arrive at our hotel just as dawn breaks and I'm about to collapse from exhaustion.

"Go rest up." He practically shoves me through my hotel room door before heading off to his own down the hallway.

The bed beckons me home, and I flop down and lose myself in the soft sheets, the cool, crisp pillows, the snuggly duvet, and the blackout option I blink the windows to. I have just enough sense to shift into my male form before falling asleep.

Now I can recharge mostly in my sleep.

Yay for sleep mode.

A banging on my door wakes me up somewhere in the future, and I grumble to my feet and sweep it open with a growl. "What do you want?"

"Err . . . Magic?" Aki asks. "I've been trying to get in here all day!"

"Huh?"

He laughs as he barges in. "You've been asleep for eighteen hours!"

"Whaaa?" I flick the window back to normal and blink in the harsh daylight blazing into my retinas. I hiss and dim them to a more appropriate level.

"You must be starving? Wanna get dinner downstairs in the hotel restaurant?"

I nod, sleep still clouding my brain. "Shower. Food." I say each with a finger count, forcing the order of importance.

"Okay. I'll meet you down there. It's on floor five."

"Mmmhmmm." I zombie walk to the bathroom, where I mechanically step into the shower and wash two bodies, get out and dry two bodies, pee twice, and then clothe, style, and present two bodies. "This shit takes way too long," I mumble as the process wakes me up and my stomach forces me out of the door.

Turns out it's nearly sunset. And as I shove a forkful of whatever Aki ordered for me, I formulate a new plan. "We should leave as soon as possible." I sigh. "Not that I want to."

Aki looks at me in question. "They really hate you that much?"

I grimace. "I kinda air-blasted the air Witch last time I was there, got me, Dea, and Nine arrested, and then had to be rescued by Connie and Arrie, who killed a few of their soldiers in the process." I do not mention it's Arrie, specifically, who killed them. He suffers enough without my twin brother thinking he's evil.

Ugh. No, Magic. He hasn't suffered enough yet.

I'm gonna make him grovel hard enough he'll beg to be let up off his knees.

Aki winces. "That's . . . not so great."

I shake my head. "But they agreed to the embassy idea, so they can't completely hate us." A few more bites of what I later realize are tacos, and my male stomach is full. "They didn't try to kill me, at least." I shrug as I change into my female form, ready to fill up stomach number two.

"So, are you planning on making up with them?"

"I'll try, but I doubt it'll work." I meet Aki's purple eyes with a questioning gaze. "What's your relationship with them like?"

I didn't really see him having a friendly relationship with them back on Sheruta, but they didn't ignore him. They were civil.

"We're . . . friendly, I guess." He shrugs. "They don't really know me that well." Finishing his last bite, he coughs and stares at me. "What? I tried to stay off everybody's radar."

Makes sense. He wouldn't want anyone knowing about our death magic. Or our Angel-descended Witch magic. That could be a disaster.

"Okay, well, we need to leave. South Africa is five hours ahead of us right now, so it's getting late there."

We finish up dinner, gather our backpacks, check out of the hotel, and find an empty alley to teleport to South African from. A rush of fresh air, the scent of soil and trees, and the taste of open plains greet me, forcing a smile from my otherwise grim lips.

"Have you considered that maybe they'll be more receptive to your male form?"

Errr . . . "Right, yeah, probably." I shift forms, and while the beauty of my surroundings still brings me peace, it's different somehow. "Huh." It no longer feels like I'm breathing in the earth; it's just a pretty background.

Must be a Witch thing.

"Come on." Aki grabs my arm and yanks me down the side path that leads to the same entrance we used not a few months ago.

Déjà vu blares warning sirens through my mind, but I ignore them. It'll be okay. I can do this.

Just as we pass the waterfall and enter the cave beyond, something moves in the dark. I can sense it.

"Aki!" I yell. "Look out!"

A Witch storms toward us and grabs Aki by the scruff of the neck and lifts him off the ground. "You are not welcome here, Horseman of Magic."

"Oh, so you'll let Arrie back." I roll my eyes, hands on my cocked hip. "But I'm the problem."

"Arrie's magic is a plague, even to himself. We know this." He steps into the light, and I recognize him from before. The one with scars covering most of his face. "You caused the problem."

"Yeah, well, I cause a lot of problems, so you'll have to get to the back of the queue and wait your turn to air your grievances."

The male Witch stands in silence, waiting for my next move.

I sigh. "Look, I don't really want to be here either, but in case you haven't noticed, we have a war on our hands. A war that'll affect you lot, eventually."

"We're not even here for you," Aki chimes in. "We're here to visit the fairies."

The man's eyes widen. "How did you . . .?"

Aki tries to shrug, but he doesn't succeed. Instead, he ends up flopping like a fish on a hook out of water (I would have laughed if the situation didn't demand my focus). "Discovered them once when I was a child after I'd walked off when visiting with Nigel."

"You know Nigel?" the man asked, his shoulders relaxing.

I look to Aki, who nods his approval, and says, "He's our godfather."

"Our?" His face scrunches in confusion. "You two are related?"

"We're twins."

The man drops Aki to the dusty floor immediately and stands there, silently heaving slow breaths. "You're Asuka and Kame's children . . ."

Chapter Thirty-Nine

Pixies Seen Flying to Colorado in the Thousands

Both Aki and I stare in disbelief at the man.

"You knew our parents?" I ask.

The man nods. "We knew where all the Angel-descended Witches were." He sighs and runs a hand down his face. "We didn't know there were any left." He spins on his heals and stalks off. "Follow!"

We stay on his heel, keeping up, though I occasionally have to tug Aki along as he falls behind. The snail. And as we enter the central cave, the witchlights creating a soft glow every few meters, I'm reminded of how much I really do love it here.

"Come along," the Witch says. "I'm taking you to the seer Witch."

"Err . . . why?" What the fuck can she do to help right now?

"Because she knows all."

"That's not really how seer magic works, but sure," I mumble.

We continue following him, Aki still struggling to keep up with the large man's pace, until we eventually come to a small home on the corner of the large cave. It's covered in leaves, flowers, and even has a small tree growing next to it.

"Please," he says, "stay here until called upon." He walks up the short garden path and knocks on the door.

We all wait with bated breath as she answers the door, a nightgown donning her body as a robe is wrapped around her shoulders. "What could you possibly want at this hour, Maxus?"

She sounds exhausted, and when two topless older men step up behind her, I realize why. We have interrupted something. Oops.

"I apologize, ma'am, but I have learned of some crucial information I think you'll be interested in." He gestures to us.

I give a little wave, hoping she'll remain as kind as she usually is to me. "Sorry for interrupting your night." I bow. "We're here to—"

"They're here for something unrelated, but it's important, so I thought . . ."

She sighs and stands aside, her men following suit. "Come on in then."

We all shuffle inside the small home. Witchlights hover at various intervals, illuminating the cluttered features, the dust-gathering items shoved onto every nearby surface as though they hold some sort of significance to the seer Witch.

"Make yourselves at home," she says. "We'll just be a moment." She and the two men trot off—probably to get dressed—and I resist the urge to use my Vampire hearing to listen to their conversation.

She has two men. Are they all together, like me and the team?

Aki and I sit on the few stools dotted around the room that are shaped into various animals. I sit on an elephant, while Aki takes the monkey. Maxus remains standing. A scowl upon his scarred face.

When she comes back, the men aren't with her, but she carries a pot of tea and four cups. Placing everything on the table, she pours out four cups of what smells like peppermint tea and sits on the couch, sighing after her first sip. "Help yourself." She gestures to the filled cups.

We all grab one, except Maxus, who clears his throat.

He opens his mouth then closes it again, opens, closes. It goes on like that at clunky intervals for a few minutes until the seer Witch says, "Just spit it out, Maxus."

"They're Angel-descended Witches. Ma'am." He lowers his gaze from her accusing eyes and fixes them firmly on the floor.

She rolls her eyes—a right sassy grandma, this one—and says, "Well, of course they are." She looks at me, then at Aki, and smiles. "I've known what you two are for quite some time. I left you alone because I figured if you needed someone or the Coven, you'd come to us."

Maxus stares at her in horror. "But, Ma'am, surely you should have said something—"

"There was nothing I should have done, Maxus. I do not share every piece of seer knowledge with the Coven, as you well know." They share a pointed look. "Besides, the Coven Council already knew. Nigel informed them."

"Wait," Aki interrupts, "Nigel told you?"

She nods. "You were there during that visit, I believe. The

same visit that encourages your visit today."

Aki's eyes widen, understanding dawning behind his features. Filling in the gaps in our shared splotchy past. "I see." His voice threatens to break, his eyes closed.

I reach out and grab his hand. "It's okay. Nigel was just doing his best."

The seer Witch looks to our joined hands and smiles. "It's so lovely to see you both together again. Nigel informed us so we were kept in the loop, but he made sure to explain that he wanted you left alone. Which the Coven Council thought was for the best."

"They could have killed entire covens!" Maxus shouted, his frustration finally boiling over into anger. "They were just children with an enormous power, left in the hands of random coven families—"

She stands to her feet and scowls at him, a finger pointed at him in anger. "You think we didn't monitor them? That we left them unattended? Do you have no trust in your Coven Council, Maxus? We are, after all, the reason you are alive."

Maxus' face shines guilt through the night's witchlight. "Right. Of course, Amalie. I am sorry." He turns to face us, his scowl softening and a gentle smile returning. "Amalie will be able to answer your questions." He leaves, clicking the door shut behind him.

"Now," Amalie says, "what is it you came to talk about? I assume it's important if you are here, Horseman." She raises her eyebrows in my direction while drinking her tea. "After all, you did cause quite the turmoil when you were here last."

"I . . ." I take a deep breath. "I am so sorry." I bow deeply. "I should not have lost my temper, and I should not have caused any harm to your people."

"Yes, we lost seven Witches at the hands of the Horsemen

of War that night. Many of their families are not fans of yours."

"I understand." I don't know what else to say. Will she kick us out before we've had a chance to—?

"But, that being said, you are an important person, and I will hear you out nonetheless." She looks to me, puts her cup of tea down, and adorns what I think might be her business face. "What can we do for you, Horseman of Magic?"

Hearing my title from the mouth of such an important person sends shivers down my spine. "The fairies."

"Ah, I see. You're hoping to get lower supernaturals on your side."

I nod. "Hopefully."

Aki steps in. "And I know they're here. Safe."

"Please," I say, "we mean them no harm. I won't even speak of this to the other Horsemen, if that's your wish." Though, there would be no hiding it from Nine, but I leave that piece of information out. Not like he would say anything, anyway. "Please."

Amalie's eyes glaze over a pale white as she gasps and grips the couch in a white-knuckled grip. But it's over quickly, and when she returns, she looks at me with a gentle smile. "I see you have moved the pixies to Sheruta? That is a good plan. I approve."

"Was that a . . .?" Aki asks.

"A vision, yes. The seer gets all kinds of visions. That one was just a snapshot." She raises an eyebrow. "And an Angel? Color me impressed."

"Well, she just looks after the pixies. Not sure if I'd count her as on our side."

"Don't discount her just yet." She winks at me, and I take that as a sign to mean our angel might come aboard if we give her time. "Well," she starts, "I need to consult the rest of the Coven Council, I'm afraid. This is not a decision I can make alone."

I wince. "Is that really . . . necessary?" The fire Witch is not my friend.

She laughs, a booming cackle that makes me flinch and then smile. "Relax. They do not hate you quite as much as they pretend. We Witches are on the precipice of drastic change, and they will have to adapt whether they like or not."

"Change?" Aki asks. "What kind of change?"

She winks and touches her nose.

Then, she gets up and grabs a glowing blue crystal on the side and sets it on the coffee table next to her tea. "The Coven Council, please."

The blue crystal glows a fan of plasma into the air, and before I know it, the rest of the Coven Council Witches' faces float in the glowy plasma air.

"Is that a . . ."

"It's a recent gift from the Fae Queen, actually," Amalie says. "You like?"

I don't say anything. A recent gift from the Fae Queen? That means they're trying to recruit the Witches. Shit. I don't want to go to war with two pillar communities. Shifters and Vampires versus Witches and Fae (plus the rogue Vampire faction). The results would be devastating.

Amalie grabs my attention and waves a hand in the air, as if to say don't worry. She turns to face the other Witches with an apologetic smile. "I am sorry for waking you all."

A series of grumbles follows.

The fire Witch scowls. "We are too old for this rubbish, Amalie."

Indeed.

Amalie smiles. "I know. But we have the Horseman of Magic and Aki here with me, and they have a small request of us."

"You expect us to personally help that cretin after what they did to our Witches?" She scowls—again.

Seriously, does this Witch know any other facial expression? Like, smile a bit, you know. Eesh.

"Yes, I am aware of Magic's . . . past." She throws me a pointed look. And I get the idea she knows everything. "But they're here to speak to the fairies. Ask them to join our side, probably in exchange for some kind of help with something they need, but we have their word they'll leave them be and not spill their location to anyone."

"Yes, but I'm going to need more assurance than that," the water Witch says. "While pixie dust stimulates a magical high, fairy dust temporarily boosts someone's magic power. We keep them safe for a reason."

"I know, sister," Amalie chimes in.

Are they really sisters? Wow. They look nothing alike.

"But," she continues, "this could be useful to the war, and we've all agreed that we can't just sit this one out. If you remember."

A few of the Witches bristle—fire and water mostly—but the rest nod, agreeing with Amalie.

"So, can I lead them there without committing treason?" Amalie manages to sound both sincere and sarcastic at the same time, and I realize that I might genuinely love her. Like a granny I never knew I needed.

A series of yeses follow, and I can only assume that means they're voting in our favor. What I don't understand is why.

Chapter Forty

HORSEMAN OF MAGIC SPOTTED IN MANAUS, BRAZIL. WHAT
ARE THEY UP TO?

An hour later, after Amalie said goodbye to her husbands—I know, I'm shocked too—we're heading down a series of cavernous passageways that are more winding than the pixie tunnels.

"Remind me not to get lost in here."

Amalie laughs. "You cannot get lost when in the earth, Horseman. You have all the Witch powers, do you not?"

"Yeeeeeah." I look sheepishly to the ground. "But I've only managed air, fire, water, and charm so far."

"No premonitions, then?" Aki asks.

I shake my head, no.

"They'll come," Amalie reassures.

"If you say so."

"I do."

She leads us down a final tunnel before coming to a clearing in the distance that glows a brighter shade of gold than the sun.

Fairy dust. So much fairy dust.

"Wow," Aki breathes. "That's insane."

"I thought you've been here before?" I ask.

"Well, yeah." He hesitates. "But I was young, and I only got a glimpse before I ran away." After a questioning look from Amalie, he answers with, "What? The Coven Council used to scare me as a child."

Amalie chuckles, and I laugh, too. "We don't hurt children." She places a firm hand on our shoulders. "I think you should go alone from here. I'll wait to guide you back."

"Thank you." I hope my honesty and sincerity shine through, because she's been a real help in a situation that could have ended vastly different. "You're a great Witch."

She pats my cheek. "I know, dear." Then she takes a seat on the floor and opens a plasmascreen from her pocket.

I grab Aki by the sleeve—he's still staring at Amalie—and drag us down the tunnel toward the glowing light.

Toward the fairies.

I've never seen a fairy on Earth before. They're so rare, some people regard them as myth. Decades before I was born, they went into hiding because people were using their dust for their own gain: boosting magic during wartime, greedy corporations gaining even more money, etc. But no one really knew where they went, just that they all vanished one day. Almost overnight.

The only reason I even know much about them is because we have fairy nests in the gardens at home, back on Sheruta. Otherwise, they'd be a complete mystery to me. Alongside everyone else.

The clearing is covered in specks of fairy dust, like glowing gold flakes waving through the air, and I take a moment to really appreciate what I'm about to do. There's nothing I can offer these fairies—they already live good lives thanks to the Witches—but we need them either way.

"They're never going to help us," I mumble.

"What makes you say that?" Aki asks.

"Someone is asking for help to win a war, Aki. After they went into hiding to avoid being used in such ways. It's disrespectful."

"Well, we're desperate." He wraps an arm through mine and pulls us forward into the clearing. "So let's go."

The bright smile he flashes my way makes me glad I brought Aki along. He's encouraging. Kinda like a ball of positive helpfulness.

Fairies are asleep in little nests that spiral up from the ground in spires of flower vines—various flowers growing on top—and with each exhale of their little breaths, fairy dust trickles into the air, adding to the cloud of it suffocating the atmosphere.

It's so cute. I might die of cuteness overload. Is that a thing? It's definitely a thing.

Aki chuckles. "Nothing is cuter than this."

Just as I take another step, twenty or so fairies whizz toward us, all armed with various weapons just bigger than their six-inch frames. Similar to pixies, they have wings that help them fly—though the myths say that they don't need them to levitate—but unlike pixies, fairies are gold in color and similar to the children's book version.

The one at the front with small horns and a green dress flies close to my face while the rest whisper amongst each other. "Horseman of Magic," a tiny voice whispers. "What is it you want?"

Seems my identity has become known even amongst the depths of society. Great. "I . . ." I look at Aki, not knowing what to say. "I apologize for disturbing you, but I would like to speak to whomever your leader is, please. If that's not too much trouble?"

The fairy's face scrunches as her grip tightens on her staff. "Our queen is resting."

"Then I'm happy to wait until she wakes."

A regular-volumed voice echoes across the cavern. "That will not be necessary." A four-foot fairy, as golden and glowing as the rest, glides forward, heading straight for us. "I am happy to speak with her now."

The twenty or so fairies who stood vigil fly to the edges of the cavern, allowing her to pass.

And when she reaches a spot not two feet from where Aki and I are standing, she stops with a cautionary smile and her hand in the air.

The whispers cease.

"Please, will you join me?" She gestures, with a wide open arm, toward the cavern that lies before us. "It would be an honor to host one of the Horsemen. Our kind has not done so in quite some time."

We follow her around the maze of vines and into a small cottage at the center, where the dust is thickest. "You've met the other Horsemen before?"

She chuckles. "No, not personally. But my mother, the previous fairy queen, did. She was most fond of Conquest. Rumor has it they partied for days."

Yeah, that sounds like Connie.

"But that was a long time ago. Much has changed."

"You're in hiding, for one. And the world is at war, for

another."

The door unlocks with a wave of the queen's hand, and her childlike form floats through the doorway lined with salt and mushrooms.

After ducking low enough to pass through, Aki and I settle ourselves in the clean, open-plan lounge. Everything is lined with a fine layer of fairy dust, but other than that, there's not a thing out of place or even a speck of dirt to be seen. And with a plasmascreen hovering in the air, one of Nine's new holophones on the table, and various pieces of modern tech lying around, the fairy queen is more than up to date on the modernity of the world.

The queen coughs to grab my attention, and I snap my head in her direction. "Can I get either of you a drink?"

"I'd love a glass of water, if you don't mind," Aki says.

She looks at me, but I shake my head.

After a few beats of silence I'm not quite sure how to fill, she comes back with two glasses and places them on the stone coasters. "I assume," she begins, "you're here to ask for the fairies' help in the war."

It's not a question, but I feel the need to answer the silence nonetheless. "Yes, your majesty."

She waves a hand through the air. "Please, spare me the title. I have enough of that already. You may call me Seraphina, if you like."

"Seraphina, I . . ." I sigh. What the hell is the point? "I assume you know all the horrible things happening to the supernatural community, given the amount of technology in this room alone?"

"I do."

"Then," Aki interrupts, "you must know how vital your help would be?" He shoots me an apology with his eyes, but I shake my head. I don't mind. "With your help, the Horsemen can stop the rogue Vampire faction and the Fae and return the world to normal. To peace."

"Whose peace?" she asks. "Your peace? The human's peace? A Horseman's idea of peace is leaving the communities to squabble and pillage as they please. Is that the peace you'll be returning us to?"

"It'll be our peace, and no. I've already set up the embassy, and I'm happy to offer three representative seats per species, regardless of their standing in the supernatural world."

This clearly catches her by surprise, because her long lashes widen and her mouth forms an O before she can stop herself. She regains composure quickly. "I was not expecting that offer, I must say."

"The Fae and the rogue Vampire faction have all but infiltrated the SC, and they plan to bring down every main Vampire city on Christmas Day." I look to her pleadingly, hoping that'll shake some moral sense into her. "We're going to stop them, with or without your help. But we'll lose many fewer lives with you on our side."

She stands abruptly, her dress flowing around her ankles. "I'm sorry, but we cannot help you."

"Please," Aki pleads, "is there nothing we can offer to change your mind?"

Her eyes meet mine in a battle of wills, our opposing forces leaving me breathless and gasping for air.

"I'm sorry," she says finally, tears lining her eyes. "We lost millions of our kind to the outside wars before my mother took us to shelter with the Witches. I cannot let my people be used to fight other people's war. It would be an act of betrayal. And there's nothing you could give that would remove its sting." She gestures to the door. "If you would please leave."

Chapter Forty-One

Is Anyone Out There Aiming for Peace?

"Well," Aki says in the hotel restaurant a few hours later, "that was a disaster."

"It went pretty much how I expected it to go."

"Really?" His surprised tone catches me off guard, like he really expected to get the fairy's help.

"Yup." The glass of cold water reaching my lips sends a pleasant chill down my spine. "It's not like their troubles happened all that long ago, Aki. I dislike the Witches outdated political moves because it's been centuries since their plight. But it was only a few decades ago the fairies were all but wiped out after having their dust harnessed for war." I take a few bites of the melktert in front of me. "Tell me, would you go against your people's wishes like that, just at the behest of a random person you don't even know?"

Maybe it would have been better had I brought all

the Horsemen along with me. But then Arrie wouldn't be planning the war strategy and moving forces, Connie wouldn't be keeping everyone in line, Dea wouldn't be running the embassy, and Nine wouldn't be working on a blood supplement. This is the best way.

It was a good choice.

If I keep telling myself that, I might just believe it.

It's only been a week, but I miss them—even Arrie's assholery. And whenever I think about them, my chest hurts. There's so much I want to do with them: cuddle, watch more movies, sunbathe in the garden, beat Arrie to a pulp, research with Nine, learn how to get another tattoo . . .

One day, I'll be free enough to settle down. But for now, I might have to fight to get there.

"Hey, Magic? You okay?"

Aki's looking at me with a worried lip and a furrowed brow, that cute little wrinkle making me wince with guilt.

"Yeah, sorry. Just thinking . . ."

"About the team, right?"

"How . . .?"

He smiles. "You get this glowy sort of dazed look in your eye. It's totally gross." He grabs another glass of water before rejoining me at the table. "Guess it's time to go back to New Orleans and meet the Demons, right?"

"Yup." The silly straw I'm using with my smoothie slips from my mouth, and mango juice goes everywhere, making us both laugh. "Oops."

A server hands me some towels, and I use them to pat myself dry while she cleans the table.

"We'll leave in the morning," I say to Aki once the server has left. "Get a good night's sleep, because I've never met a Demon before and I'm not sure how this'll go." He looks nervous, but I rest my hand on top of his. "We'll be fine. I promise."

The room is small, but it has a bed, a shower, and room service, so I'm happy. Aki's next door. For now, I have a call to make.

"Call Famine," I instruct the holophone.

It glows deep green for a few seconds. I wonder if he'll pick up or if he's asleep, but then Nine's face comes into view. "Sweetie!"

"Nine," I whisper, relief washing through me. "It's good to see you."

His glowing blue brows furrow in concern. "You okay?"

I shrug. "Politics is tedious. And I miss you all." Ugh. I'm so pathetic. I've become one of those girls. Guys. People. Definitely people.

I can't make too many details of Nine's face out, but he looks tired. Or maybe I'm just expecting him to look tired. "Are you okay? You look a bit . . ."

"Tired? Yeah, that's 'cos I am. But we've made fantastic progress on the blood supplement. We might be able to move into the trial phase soon."

"Wait. You did it? Really?" A smile looms across my face and his, and when he nods, I squeal. "That's fantastic! I'm so proud!"

Aki knocks on the thin wall separating our room in annoyance.

"Oops."

At Nine's questioning look, I explain, "Thin walls in this hotel."

"So," he starts, "how far have you got?"

"Is everyone else there?"

He holds up a finger, telling me to wait, and then nods. "Now we're all here."

Everyone says hi in turn, and hearing their voices soothes an on-edge part of me that feels like a long-held breath.

"Well, we didn't get the fairies on board, but I'm not surprised. They were lovely, though. Amazing species. Have you seen their nests? They're sooooo cute."

"Hon, never call a fairy cute to their face. They hate it," Connie said from somewhere in the background.

"Their little staff sticks really hurt when there's lots of them," Arrie chimes in. "Trust me."

Everyone chuckles, including me, and just the thought of Arrie getting beaten up by a bunch of six-inch fairies with pointy sticks is hilarious. Goddess, I've missed them.

Nine falls to the side with an oof, and Connie comes into view. "How's everything going with you and Aki?"

"It's . . . going great, actually. We've gotten to know each other more. But I still have so many questions." A thought flickers across my mind. "Have any of you heard from Nigel?"

"He's here at the house. Once he got the date for us, he quit and ran here as quickly as possible." She smiles. "He's safe."

Goddess, my godfather is living with my boyfriends and girlfriend. Alone. Without me. Kuso. What if they share embarrassing stories? What if Nigel grills them all father-style? What if the team gets annoyed with him?

"Stop spiraling!"

"Come on, Angel, we talked about this. Stop focusing on the anxiety. The more you focus on it, the worse it will be."

I nod. "I know, I know. And I've done so well on this mission. But you're living with my godfather. Without me." I snort a laugh. "Forgive me if I'm a little nervous."

"Relax," Nine says, clearly having recovered from Connie's shove. "He's been hanging out, training with Arrie a little and helping Dea with the embassy stuff."

"He's training with Arrie!? Are you insane? He's mortal!"

"I can hold back, Killer. Unless you've forgotten the weak-ass punches I threw at you when you first started training?" I can hear the smirk. "I can always remind you, if you like?"

Connie smiles at us, satisfied we've found some more common ground. Even if it's only as friends. Just the reminder sends a slash of pain through me, and my smile falters.

"I hope I didn't wake any of you."

She waves a hand. "Nah. It's midmorning here."

"Oh good. Arrie, did the pixies travel okay?"

Connie moves aside to make room for Arrie, who just about fits in the frame, though his shoulder cuts off. "Yeah. They're all settled in the northern part of the island, far away from other people."

"That's probably for the best. They don't trust easily."

"They seem to have no problem trusting an Angel," he grumbles.

"Ah, Glowy. How she's doing?"

"Still a grumpy asshole."

Look what pot is calling the kettle black.

I hold my tongue. Now is no time for an argument.

Arrie smiles and chuckles, and my heart flips, beating double time. Fuck. I'm in love with my . . . friend. That realization sends pangs of loneliness through me, as though three people aren't enough.

I'm such a whore. Can I not just be happy with three?

Dea's face fills the holoscreen, and one look into the blue-glowing version of his galaxy eyes, and I know I'm being stupid. It's not about the number. It's about the people. It's not that I want or need four—three is quite the handful as it is—it's that I need Arrie. And that need has nothing to do with my current relationship with Dea, Nine, and Connie.

"You doing okay, Angel?" The sincerity in his voice shakes me out of my head. "Really?"

I wiggle my head from side to side, unsure. "I'm . . . not doing awfully. But I . . ." I sigh. "I'm a little confused."

"About what?" I don't immediately answer, and he frowns. "Come on, you might as well tell us. Bottling it all up will not help."

"He's right, hon. You can always chat with us."

"The world needs me, but the only thing I care about is my own desires and needs. Doesn't that make me a little selfish?"

"Just normal," Dea says. "You think political leaders, kings and queens, MPs, and doctors do not worry about themselves all the time? That they are not still capable of worrying about both themselves and others simultaneously? We are all only a part of nature."

"And nature," Nine chimes in, "is pretty selfish."

"But you don't all have existential crises every other day? You're all so calm. You never need to chat or talk things through. It's just me. I'm so . . . needy." Ugh. And here I am, being needy about being needy. Shoot me now. This is an awful conversation.

Connie giggles, the echo making me want to hug and punch her at the same time. "We're a lot older than you. Like, a lot. But even so, I needed you to take care of me on our date, didn't I? I needed saving. I needed to chat about"—she gestures to the surrounding guys—"this."

"You did?" Dea asks. "Really?"

She nods, shyness overtaking my usually confident

girlfriend. "It's dumb, but my relationship with Magic feels so . . . personal. It's not something I want to share on an emotional level." Her blonde hair waves as she looks to the floor.

"It's not stupid," I say. "It's okay to do things separately. Together. Or a bit of both. And it's okay to change your mind."

"And," Dea says with a hand on her shoulder, "it is okay to be uncertain."

"I'm not uncertain about my feelings for Magic. And I'm okay sharing. Really. It's just a little . . . overwhelming." She groans in frustration. "This is so unlike me."

"What is it that's making you uneasy?" Arrie places a hand on her shoulder, and she flinches.

"I'm not uneasy. Just feeling a little selfish. I want all of your time, hon. But I can't have it."

I wish I could jump through the holoscreen and wrap my arms around her. She's suffering. And I'm not there. I'd teleport back, but I don't want to leave Aki here alone. "You're still our badass Horseman of Conquest," I reaffirm. "Ain't nothing gonna change that. And I'll spend as much time with you as you need."

"Soooo," Nine says, "what was that I heard about your male form, Sweetie?" I can hear his eyebrows raising and his eyes darting to us both.

Connie's tears dry up with giggles, and she eventually bursts out laughing, holding her sides and trying to splutter an apology. "I'm . . . sorry." She gasps for air.

People do weird things in times of pain. I spiral out of control and forget to breathe, so who am I to judge?

"Well, we were . . . you know—"

"Fucking," Connie helpfully explains. "We were having

sex, and I was about to give Magic the best orgasm she'll ever have in female form by someone's tongue, but then she burst into male form, and yes her dick just magically poofed into my mouth, and then we just continued." She shrugs.

Goddess, it's like a dagger to the soul. Like being grated against the flow—it doesn't fit anymore. I don't fit anymore.

I shrink. Connie didn't mean it. Connie didn't mean it. Connie didn't mean it. But tears threaten to burst forth nonetheless, and I can't help it as they rupture their banks and gush down my cheeks.

"Shit," Arrie swears. "Connie!" His rumbly voice takes on that angry, quiet, bitter quality it does when he's mad at me. "What were you thinking?"

"Quick," Nine says, "has anyone ever been to that hotel before? Maybe one of us can teleport there."

"I can just fly or faze," Dea chimes in.

Connie, meanwhile, freezes on her perch that is Dea's knee, her face a mixture of shock and hurt. "I'm so sorry," she whispers, her voice barely audible over the guys' panic. "I wasn't thinking, I . . ." Her eyes drop to the floor.

I'm pretty sure she's crying. Again.

Damn, we're a mess this evening.

I wipe my face and catch my breath. "This is ridiculous."

Everyone stops talking and returns to me.

"It's okay. I don't mind."

"Don't do that," Connie says. "I know you mind. We all know. We've tried to avoid using pronouns at all to avoid the issue, but it's hard. And we don't want to force you to do anything before you're ready."

"And," Nine says, "we don't want to make you take a new pronoun or anything, but it might be something to think about."

"A new . . . pronoun?" I haven't really thought about it. I guess I've stopped using my female form as default. I don't even really think about it anymore, I just exist in either form, regardless. "But what would I use?"

Connie shrugs. "No idea. But maybe have a think about it. If you like the idea, we can all brainstorm together, if you like?"

A smile widens across my face. "I'd like that. A lot."

"What about they?" Dea asks. "That's pretty popular, at least."

"In Chinese, we use tā for both men and women," Nine points out. "I think that's pretty cool."

"In Japanese, our language is tailored to who we are. So we can speak in a very feminine way or a very masculine way," I explain. "What pronouns we use not only depend on the gender of the person speaking but also on the social context of the situation and the social standing of the person we are communicating with."

"That sounds complicated," Arrie grumbles.

"A lot of it is something you just grow up with. It's normal." I shrug.

"So maybe not something linguistic, in that sense," Nine says. "Hmmm . . . we'll have a think about it. I'm sure we'll come up with something."

"Right." I shake my head. "It's not really something I'm focusing on right now. We're heading to the meeting with the Demons tomorrow. We headed to the meeting spot earlier in the week, so we can just teleport there."

"Good," Dea says. "Be careful."

"Don't worry. I'll kick their asses if I have to."

"Demons are known tricksters," Nine explains, "so make sure not to get played by them. Be specific about what you want from them. Include all exceptions and all inclusions you need, otherwise they will use that against you in the future."

"Demons are tricky assholes. Noted."

"And Magic," Connie says, her voice gentle and soft, "I am really sorry." She opens her mouth to say something else, but she must decide against it because she closes her mouth and smiles. "Be careful."

"And remember we love you, Angel."

"I love you all too."

I end the call, feeling lighter and more at ease than I have in days.

Chapter Forty-Two

New Orleans isn't as calm as South Africa. Not by a long shot. And I'm missing the scenery almost as soon as we get there. Though my female form seems a little more achy—must be a Witch thing.

"So, do we have a plan?" Aki asks after he teleports beside me moments later. "I feel like we should have a plan for Demons."

"You're probably right, but I know as little about Demons as possible. They like to make deals, and the wording is vital. Nine says they like to play tricks on people."

"You plan to make a deal with Demons?"

"If it gets them on our side? Yes."

Aki mutters something under his breath, but without my Vampire hearing, I can't make it out. Which is probably a good thing. "I can't believe we're about to do this."

"So fighting an Angel is okay, dealing with Witches that probably want me dead is fine, but dealing with Demons is where you draw the line?"

"It sounds ridiculous when you put it like that," he mumbles.

"That's because it kinda is."

"Hey!" He punches me in the arm, but it does nothing but make him wince. Shifter strength and whatnot. "Wow, really, nothing?"

I shrug. "Sorry." I return my attention to the morning sky and take a deep breath. "We're due to take a boat from Shell Beach in half an hour."

"Right. Demons."

The boat arrives on time, and we take the quick trip to Demon central in the middle of the Bayou. We have teleporting crystals, weapons, and my ability to fly us the hell out of there if anything goes wrong. We'll be fine.

I hope.

"Magic?" Aki asks out of the blue. "What's your favorite color?"

"Orange. Yours?"

"White."

"That's . . . cool." Weird. That's weird. I just don't have the heart to tell my long-lost twin I find his favorite color strange.

"I know, it's odd. But it's like a blank canvas. I can make anything from white."

"Okay, I can understand that." I look at the sky once more and just breathe. "Orange reminds me of both the sunrise and sunset. Makes me feel all gooey."

"Gooey? That's what you're going with?"

"You know, when you're all melting on the inside because life has reminded you that it's beautiful after spending so long in the darkness. Gooey."

"Sometimes I like the darkness," he whispers, his voice a deep timber I don't think I've heard before. "It's like a familiar dream."

My hand rests on his shoulder, a hopefully comforting presence. "You're not alone anymore, Aki."

He looks at me like I've burst some kind of depression bubble like a reverent goddess. "You're a great sister. I'm glad we finally got to meet and spend some time together."

"Me too." I grab him into a hug and squeeze. Gently. "Okay, okay, my turn. What's your favorite thing to read? You do read, don't you?"

He shrugs. "Sometimes. When I do, I tend to stick to mysteries, thrillers, things with a little bit of darkness and a little bit of hope. Plus some action."

"You're pretty emotionally open, you know that?"

"Is that a bad thing?" The worry in his eyes that he might have disappointed me shoots straight to the heart.

"No, no, no. Not at all. Just an observation. I kinda like it."

"Really?"

I nod. "Uh-huh. It's refreshing. Most people stay closed off until you really know them, and even then, they only come out of their social shell when you prod them to. Otherwise they keep the emotions expected of them."

"You're not wrong. Okay, okay, my go." He flaps his hands in excitement a little. "Who was your first boyfriend/ girlfriend? And how did it end?"

"Err . . . I might have to get back to you on that one. My

mortal memories are pretty new, and while they're all there, it's like a file I have to flit through to find the right thing."

"Okay, then I'll go first." He takes a deep breath. "He was this really emo dude in high school. The kid at the back who's all quiet and moody but is actually really interesting and smart." He looks into the distance all wistful and gross like. "We had a summer fling end of senior year, but it ended when we both went off to college. I cried for three days when he left." He laughs, embarrassment coloring him pink. "Kinda cliché and ridiculous, huh?"

"Aren't most first loves?" My first relationship . . . "I'm pretty sure it was this asshole in tenth grade. He was Fae, but I didn't really understand that then. He tried to use this spell that would make me sleep with him, but it backfired and just made me irrationally pissed off at him for a week. I tripped him up in the hallways, punched him in the face—twice—and stuffed his locker full of expanding foam."

Our laughs echo in the Bayou's stillness, but the tears leaking from my eyes are loud as they spill off my jaw and onto my hands.

"That's . . . such a better . . . story," Aki says between heaveful breaths. "I feel sorry for that guy. Pissing you off is not a good idea."

"I wasn't a Horseman then, remember. So I wasn't nearly as badass."

"Right." He looks at me with confusion. "Because you're technically dead. And immortal."

"Yup. Difficult pill to swallow, huh?"

"A little."

The captain shouts, "We're here!"

And Aki and I disembark and wait by the port for the Demons to show us to their . . . lair?

Chapter Forty-Three

What would a Demon lair look like? Would it be all dark and mysterious? Full of blood and the bones of their enemies? Yeah, somehow I doubt they live like they do in books. I've been pretty surprised by the species I've met so far, and this isn't going to be any different, is it?

Aki shifts from foot to foot beside me, hands clenching his sleeves and teeth chewing his bottom lip.

"Hey," I say, and he jumps a little, "we're gonna be fine. Promise."

He nods. Takes a deep breath, and then he grabs my hand and shoots me an apologetic look. "Sorry. Nerves."

His hand squeezes mine, and I squeeze back.

"Well, we can always teleport right out if something goes wrong. This isn't a video game. There's no no-teleporting zones. And Aki?" I look at him. "I'm immortal and much stronger than you, so please don't come rescue me and get yourself killed. Okay?"

"Right. Yeah." He looks away, his gaze dotting everywhere but at me. "So, there's no way to kill a Horseman? Like, at all?"

Everything in me freezes. Shit. Do I tell him? "Well, that's not strictly true. But it doesn't matter." I wave his question off. "It'd be fucking impossible to pull off." Especially given we still don't know where my seal is. It still hasn't turned up.

"Oh, okay." He looks disappointed.

And damn it. It really undoes me. "I'll tell you about it when we're back on Sheruta, alright?"

His smile brightens the fog we've found ourselves in, and I breathe an easy breath. I switch to my female form and use my Vampire vision to penetrate the thick low-hanging cloud, hoping for a sign. Anything. Red eyes glow in the distance, sitting atop bulky, mismatched forms I can't quite make out.

They must be farther away than we thought.

"Alright," I yell, "you can come out! We're not gonna hurt you."

A chorus of high-pitched giggles echo around the trees.

What are they, hyena Demons?

"Seriously, high-pitched giggles? Really?"

"What would you have suggested, Magic?" a deep, barely there voice sounds not seven feet from where we are. "A bunch of hisses? Demon whispers?"

Aki leans in close. "What's a Demon whisper?"

I shrug. Beats me.

"A Demon whisper, young Witch, is a spell unique to Demons that allows us to temporarily take control of another." He looks to me and adds, "Not that it works on Horsemen."

Relief sweeps through me.

Aki, on the other hand, tenses further. I didn't know that was even possible. But I still have hold of his hand, so I squeeze in reassurance, trying to remind him we can leave whenever we want. His shoulders drop. Minutely.

The Demon in front of us steps out of the fog, and I get my first look at an actual Demon. Bright green horns, skin as black as night, curling nails that have green tips, and a surprisingly beautiful face. You know, in an evil, Hades-decorated-this-guy kinda way. "My name," he says, his voice a more regular timber, "is Verity. Welcome to what we Demons call home."

I bow low. "Thank you for allowing us to visit." I look up at Aki, who is still staring at the Demon, eyes wide, and I cough. "Bow," I hiss.

He shakes himself out of his stupor and bows.

"Now we have the pleasantries out of the way," the Demon says, "we can retire to the mansion."

"Mansion?"

He leads us through dense fog and even denser trees, past winding bushes and creatures I don't know the name of, until we reach a fork in the road marked by an old-fashioned signpost you see in cartoons. Only the words marked on this sign post comprise letters I've never seen.

"Demon language?" I ask the Demon leading us.

"One of them, yes." At my questioning gaze, he explains, "we Demons once roamed Earth in the thousands. Millions, probably. We had many species across many lands, and therefore, we had many languages." He points to the signpost. "That one is Liggish. One of the many languages of the ancients. It's what we use in spells to help guard and protect our home." He waves his hand in the air. "And we also use it for signposts."

Aki's ears perk up, his eyes inquisitive. "Demons can perform spells?"

"Of course." A smile splits the Demon's face in two. "We were the original spellcasters."

"Is it like Fae magic?" I ask, all but forgetting my surroundings and that I'm talking to an actual Demon. "Ingredients, runes, and castings to make the magical essence that fuels their magic—fueled in turn by the leylines?"

"So you're a geek, too, hm? Just like that teammate of yours. Famine, wasn't it?"

As if he—it, they, something else?—doesn't know who Famine is. My eyes roll of their own accord. "Yes, Famine and I are . . . similar in that regard."

"A pair of geeks." The Demon giggles in that high-pitched way Demons seem to do, apparently. "How quaint."

The sarcasm is not lost on me.

This is gonna be a long day, isn't it?

Goddess, help me.

After a few more minutes, the fog clears, and a loamy mansion covered in moss and made of great cracked stones looms in front of us. Dim yellow lights illuminate the dense foliage every few meters, lighting up the cracks in the masonry and the deep green plants, shrubs, and bushes that make up the floor.

"Are they witchlights?" Aki asks, taking the words right out of my mouth.

The Demon turns to us and smiles. "Of course. They were kind enough to lend us their magic after The Great Purge." Venom drips from his lips at the reminder of their torturous past.

I've read about The Great Purge—when the team purged

the Earth of most Demons and Angels, leaving small pockets left to lie in the rubble of their kind. The history books make it out to be all heroic, that the Horsemen were simply getting rid of evil. But I know better. They were ridding the world of creatures that preyed upon humans. The species and few Demons and Angels left behind were the ones causing no, or minimal, harm.

But to those Demons left behind, it must have seemed like a slaughter. When I asked Nine about it, he said they tried to negotiate and make peace, but no one was interested, bar a few.

I'm not sure where I stand on the issue, but it's supposedly where the Horsemen got the name Horsemen of the Apocalypse.

They're two thousand years old. I guess I can't expect them to always have made wonderful choices or to have been good people. Just like me, they grew into who they are today.

Despite the dark and gloomy outside, the mansion he leads us into is light, airy, and somehow welcoming. Looks like I was right. Demons don't pander to fictional stereotypes. The large open windows with fake landscapes and lighting brighten the entrance foyer, where white marble floors meet white marble walls. Trees, flowers, and other natural pieces of the Bayou trickle in now and then, but it's otherwise a whole different world from the outside.

"This place is incredible!" I exclaim, awe painting my every breath.

Aki can't stop looking at everything, running up to various plants and pieces of artwork to get a good look. Like a kid in a candy store.

I grab his arm and drag him down the hallway the Demon just turned onto. "C'mon."

"Oh, right." He drags behind me, his gaze catching on another one of the sculptures wrapped in vines. "But everything is so . . . pretty."

"Well, we might be here for a day or two, if they let us, so you'll have time to explore." I yank on his arm again. "But right now we're losing our Demon guide, and I don't want to get lost in a Demon mansion in the middle of the Bayou." I grind my teeth and clench my free fist.

"You make a good point." Aki reins in his amazement and walks beside me, only occasionally getting lost in the flowers and needing a gentle nudge. "But there's something about this place . . ."

"I know."

He's right. It's almost reverent. Like a goddess's home or some shit.

"Mr Demon!" I shout, trying to catch up with a slow as fuck Aki at my heels.

Just as we turn another corner, we run smack into a black back that smells like sulfur. "Mr Demon?" he asks, surprise etching his tone. "I don't think anyone's called me Mr Demon before."

I don't know if I've insulted, upset, or pleased him. It's kinda hard to tell. But he spins on his heels to face me, and the grin shooting from ear to ear answers my question. Seems he likes the moniker.

"We don't deal in things as corruptible as names here, darlin'." The smirk on his lips glints off the small dagger piercing his left ear. "But you can call me Sir anytime you like."

Aki coughs, stirring the air.

I flinch away from the Demon, who I am not calling Sir, and say, "If you don't mind leading the way, we really need to speak to your leader or king or . . ."

"Lord," he answers. "Our Demon Lord."

Chapter Forty-Four

The SC Locked Down Magic's Mortal Past. Why?

The Demon Lord, if you can really call him that, lounges across the throne, legs swinging over the armrest, some kind of handheld game console getting beaten under quick, punchy fingers while he laughs. "Ha! Suck it, Yoshi!" He looks up, meets my gaze with surprise, and jumps to his feet with a clearing of the throat. "Horseman of Magic!"

His four-foot stature barely reaches my chest, with red, yellow, and orange coloring firing along his black skin in waves. But it's the lack of scruff and mature bone structure that shocks me into a silence I don't know how to break.

The Demon Lord is a child?

I shoot a questioning look to the Demon who escorted us, who now leans against the wall near the door, cleaning lint from his claws.

He just smiles at me.

Swinging back around to the Demon Lord, I raise my hand in offer. He might be a child, but he's still of importance. Best be polite.

Aki bows low, staying quiet.

Thank goddess.

The Demon Lord edges forward, his eyes never leaving mine. "I've seen what you can do, so please forgive me my unease at being in your presence."

"I promise not to harm you, my lord." I look at Aki, who smiles softly. "I'm not really the type, anyway."

His eyebrows raise. "Really?" He presses the datachip in his wrist and brings up the datascreen, quickly types and presses a series of buttons, then swipes it around to face me. "Then how do you explain this?"

The this in question is the viral video of me attacking the Vampires in New Orleans a few weeks ago.

Remind me again why no one said anything about that plan? Not even a hint of forewarning. The fuckers.

"I was not really harming them. They volunteered to fake fight to draw out the rogue Vampire faction that harmed one of our own."

"Ah." His eyes grow understanding beneath the bright white irises. "A coup. Interesting." He skips back to his throne and smiles at me. "In that case, welcome to our home, Magic. I may call you Magic, yes?"

"Of course." I gesture to Aki. "And this is my brother, Aki."

"Brother?" He looks as confused as I felt when I found out. "Really?"

"Twin brother, actually. But he's mortal."

"So . . . he's your twin brother you left behind when you died and became the Fifth Horseman?"

"That about sums it up, yeah."

His faces relaxes into a stony expression, his back rigid on the throne. "What is it you have come to see us for?"

"Well"—I scratch the back of my neck—"we're trying to gain as much support as possible from the lower supernatural communities. And we thought that maybe—"

The Demon Lord laughs. A high-pitched screech that makes my hair stand on end and my hackles rise. He wipes his eyes and looks back up at me. "I'm sorry, but for a moment I thought you asked for our help."

"She did," Aki confirms. "The Fae are—"

The child holds up a hand. "I don't discuss politics without my advisors present. I'm just a child."

"A very well-spoken child." I was beginning to believe he's not as young as he seems, but I was wrong. "You seem almost old in nature, but inside a childlike body."

"I get that a lot. Thank you." He sighs, his face relaxing once again into that of a casual acquaintance. "My father, the previous Demon Lord, passed away six months ago. He had been the Demon Lord since The Great Purge, so it's caused some . . . teething issues."

Wow. His father was the Demon Lord for over a thousand years? Damn. These Demons can grow old.

"I see." A thought occurs to me. Out of the blue. "Well, maybe helping us can restore some of that broken peace. A show of strength, if you will."

He raises his hand, but I interrupt halfway.

"All I ask is that you hear us out. If you don't want to participate, we won't make you. We'll leave in peace."

"Oh, very well. But you'll have to wait until my advisors get here. They understand political complexities better than I."

"Thank you." I bow low once more, hoping to catch his good side. If he has one. "It's been an honor being in your presence."

While we wait for the Demon Lord and his advisors to be ready, we're shown on a grand tour of the mansion by the first Demon we met. Verity. Or Mr Poison, as I've donned him in my head.

"And here we have the old pits, where we fight for societal standings, when making deals, and just for the hell of it." He laughs at a smaller Demon fighting in one of the pits with a large boulder of a Demon. "He tries to defeat Borl every day. One day he'll learn." He shakes his head.

The pits are a series of underground hollows made of stone, surrounded by crude stone seats leading up all sides, like an amphitheater.

"People watch these fights?" Aki asks.

"Of course. The betting fields are ripe for the taking, if you know who's been doing better in training." He winks at Aki. "Fortunes have been made here."

Aki looks disgusted, but thankfully for us both, he keeps his opinions to himself. That doesn't stop him from frowning at the Demon's back, however.

"So, how does one make a deal with a Demon?"

He stops in his tracks and spins to face me. "That's your plan? Bargain us into helping you? A bold move."

"Assuming you won't just help us outright, then yes. Hopefully." Looking back to the pits. "And I might know just how to do that."

"You think so, Magic?" His green-tipped claws tip my head up his towering frame. "Ever fought a Demon before?"

"Ever fought a Horseman of the Apocalypse before?"

Pain lances across his eyes, a memory rising to the surface if his far-off gaze has anything to say about it, but he shakes himself out and returns to the tour.

The lower levels of the mansion are older, more crude in their design that resembles the Bayou outside of the walls. But the farther up you go, the more grand the marbling, the more prestigious the Demons walking around the halls, and the grander the décor is. Demon hierarchy seems similar to the human hierarchy. Crude, perhaps, but at least it's something I'm familiar with.

We are just about to settle down to watch a movie in one of their theaters when a white-skinned being with large wings rushes into the room, heading straight for us.

I grab a dagger on instinct, prepared to fight with my second angel.

"Stand down, Magic," the Demon says. "It's just Sayal. He's here to carry a message for the Demon Lord." He looks at Sayal and smiles. "Word?"

"Yes, sir. They are ready for you both." He doesn't meet my gaze, but since I'm still holding a dagger in my hand, I don't blame him. "Maybe don't threaten the council, if you want them to cooperate." He looks to the floor. "Just a thought."

Right.

Chapter Forty-Five

Back in the throne room, the Demon Lord sits in his usual seat, but this time he's surrounded by six older Demons—all clearly adults—who are spread out on either side of the throne.

The Demon Lord stands and clears his throat. "Thank you for allowing me time to gather my advisors. It is appreciated."

A Demon to his left—black-skinned with swirling gold patterns covering his body and gold-tipped horns adorning his head—clears his throat and shoots the young Demon Lord a withering look.

"Right." He sits back down. "You wanted the chance to be heard out. Well, here it is." He gestures the room. "Speak."

"Of course, my lord." I clear my throat and take a deep breath. "As you may or may not know, the Fae have been gathering their armies. They have joined with a rogue Vampire faction—not affiliated with the Vampire Royal Council—and are now threatening not just us, but the general Vampire population. They have the Supernatural Council under their thumbs, and they are doing everything in their power to suppress the general supernatural communities."

A few gasps litter the room, but the advisors remain stoic. The Demon Lord looks interested and concerned, but without the help of his council, I'm powerless here.

"They shut down New Orleans, and now they're planning to shut down the other main Vampire cities. They'll do this on Christmas Day morning."

"Turned Vampires cannot go out in the sun," one advisor clarifies. "But outside of New Orleans, there aren't many born Vampires." He smirks. "It's an excellent strategy."

"Indeed. You can see our concern."

"Of course," the Demon Lord says. "But why do Vampire politics matter to us?"

"They've been attacking the Shifters and Witches as well. Not to mention what they've been doing to the pixies for centuries. We believe they're trying to take over. A new Vampire-Fae rule. To do with the humans as they please. And they're starting with subduing the current Vampire system. They'll then likely move on to the Shifters and humans. It's unclear how they'll attack the rest of the populations, including the Witches, but they will eventually."

Everyone holds their breath.

No one speaks. No one moves.

And I think I may have stunned the Demons into silence.

The Demon Lord looks forlornly at the stone floor, a sadness on his face. "It will change everything if they succeed, won't it?"

The advisor who scorned him before answers, "Yes, my lord. But whether or not that will be in our favor is yet to be determined. If we allied ourselves with the Fae, we could join their new world."

This is what I was afraid of.

We offer nothing as an incentive. And not every species will do things out of the goodness of their hearts.

"We're prepared to make a deal," I offer. "Something you want or need that we can provide in exchange for your help." I smile, hoping to seem confident. "The morale you gain from appearing strong is just a freebie."

An old frail Demon with graying colors looks alarmed at me, his eyebrows raising toward his horns. "You are prepared to make a deal with the Demon Lord?"

"I know the risks." I think. "But they cannot be worse than letting the Fae, humans, and rogue Vampire faction take over."

The Demon Lord strides forward, his eyes glowing a fiery red as a deep, menacing smiles takes over his features. "Then what is it you offer me in return for our help, Horseman of Magic?"

"Best make it a good offer," one advisor says.

Think, Magic, think. What do they want? What do they need?

I look around, taking in their mansion in the middle of nowhere, and something clicks in my brain. "Support. The Horsemen will officially support you and whatever choices you make to further your species and help you grow. If you want to be an outed species and join the embassy, you can. If you want to stay hidden, we'll help protect your home with our own magic. Whatever your choice, if you help us, and so long as you do not cause any grievous harm to another species, we will help you."

"Really?" the Demon Lord asks, astonishment floundering across his face. "That's . . . quite an offer. But how can we trust you?"

Aki, silently stood beside me until now, steps forward. "I'll fight you for it. In the pits. You win, we'll walk away and never bother you again. I win, you take the deal and join our forces."

Laughter skitters across the room, bouncing off the marble walls, filling the flowers and vines with raucous hope. But it fills me with dread.

"Aki," I hiss. "What are you thinking?"

"Of saving the Vampires."

The pits fill with Demons, a few angels, and the advisors within the hour. Word spreads fast down here, it seems. The Demon Lord is behind the left pit door, while Aki and I are standing behind the right pit door. Both open into the largest pit in the mansion.

"Aki, you can't kill him. And you must fight fair." I sigh, rubbing a hand through my short blonde hair. "You mustn't lose control of your death magic. We'll create more enemies that way."

"No shit, sis." Aki's bubbly exterior has vanished, and out of the ashes stands a stony expression, serious eyes, and pursed lips. "All I need to do is fight him in hand-to-hand combat, and we'll have the Demons on our side."

"But I should be fighting him!" It would have been easy with all the magic at my disposal. "This is ridiculous."

He places a firm hand on my shoulder and smiles. "I'll be okay. I'm a pretty good fighter."

"You are?"

"Yup." He's dressed in shorts that dangle to his knees and nothing else. "This should be a piece of cake. He's just a kid."

Yeah, something tells me that this will not be that simple. He might be a child, but he's still the Demon Lord.

The door opens, and our escort pokes his head through the door with a smirk. "It's time."

"Our first contestant is Aki, Witch, and brother of the Fifth Horseman of Magic."

Aki jogs into the pit, and I find a seat near the front.

"Aaaaand, fighting our guest today is none other than our very own Demon Lord, Lord Seraphety!"

His name is Lord Seraphety?

Verity whispers, "It's a placeholder name. Not his real one. Names are powerful things to us Demons. Knowing them can allow us to control you. So we withhold them to everyone bar those we truly trust."

Oh.

He struts into the pit, naked from the waist up, like Aki, and the fiery coloring on his horns and skin glowing brightly.

"The rules are simple," the announcer yells. "Hand-to-hand combat until someone draws first blood. No serious injuries or death here today, since the opponents are people of import. All forms of non-active magic are allowed, including mind control, telepathy, boosting charms, and things of the like."

Both Aki and Lord Seraphety circle each other as the announcer counts down.

"Five . . . Four . . . Three . . . Two . . . One!"

Lord Seraphety lunges at Aki quicker than I thought possible. And when Aki dodges and rolls to the left just as quickly, I change into my female form so I can follow. Aki swings a low punch, but Lord Seraphety blocks with a solid arm, absorbing the hit.

"Scared to take a hit, my lord?" Aki taunts. "Not very Demon-like of you."

He hisses at Aki, his eyes glowing brighter, and then charges. Horns first.

Aki's eyes widen, and just as those horns are centimeters from his gutting him, he jumps back, landing on two solid feet.

The Demons surrounding us boo and hiss. Disappointed.

"He nearly had him then," our escort shouts. "C'mon, he's just a silly Witch!"

I snort-laugh. If only they knew.

Luckily for everyone, Aki is holding back.

I do not want to be carrying his carcass back to Sheruta after he accidentally kills the lord of Demons. That'll be sure to get them to join the Fae.

Drums line the fence, all manned by Demons, and they pick up a single, thrumming beat when Aki recenters and aims for a throat punch.

It lands!

"Yes!"

The Demon Lord coughs and splutters for a split second, but he regains composure quicker than expected. Frustration ebbs. And he throws that anger out of him with a curved charge that catches Aki in the middle with the curve of his horns.

Aki flies across the pit and lands in a heap not far from me.

"Aki!" I Vampire speed to the fence, throwing the drummers out of my way, worry clouding my senses. "You okay?"

Aki stands, shoots a smile my way, and turns back to the

fight. "Yeah." He's not bleeding yet.

How can a child throw a grown man so far across a room like that? Demon or not, that's insane.

Sitting back in my seat, confusion must rain clear across my face, because our escort whispers in my ear, "Impressed, huh?"

"How is he so strong?"

"Demons have Vampire-like strength."

Well, fuck. "Perfect."

"I know, right?"

"Sarcasm not a thing with Demons?"

He shrugs. "I choose to ignore such a stupid form of communication. Other Demons might engage. Idiots."

Aki lands a punch to Lord Seraphety's face, but he retaliates by throwing a rapid succession of knee strikes to Aki's gut.

Aki sputters and coughs, then throws himself out of the way with a spin. But he's off balance.

And Lord Seraphety notices. He takes advantage by charging, horns first, in Aki's direction.

This is it. It's over.

We've lost.

Aki reaches into his short's pocket and yanks out something small and black he smashes on the ground. Black smoke engulfs him seconds before those horns would have reached him.

A Witch charm!

When the smoke passes, Aki's a few feet off the ground, and Lord Seraphety charges into nothing, losing his footing and landing on his hands and knees.

Aki kicks him in the ass, sending him flying into the pit's wall.

The drums stop.

The announcer rings out, "First blood!"

The Demon Lord stands up and wipes his nose clean, a smear of blood on his hand, and I smile.

"Yes!" I stand up with a scream and punch a fist into the air. "Ha!"

"Alright, settle down," our escort says.

And that's when I look around and see everyone sitting in silence.

Chapter Forty-Six

New Orleans Still Locked Down: When Will the
Vampires be Free?

"A few bruises and scrapes, one broken rib, and a mild concussion," the doctor says. "You got off easy." She places her equipment back into their case and stalks off.

Leaving Aki with me.

He goes to stand up and stretch, but he winces and places a hand to his broken rib.

I grab a cup from the side and prick my finger with a single fang, dropping a small pool of blood into the bottom. Just a few drops. Nothing substantial. "There." I shove it under his nose.

His nose wrinkles in disgust.

I pull the cup back. "Fine. Deal with the broken rib yourself." And shrug.

He scowls at me but yanks the cup from my fingers and

downs it in one. "There. Good as . . ." He wobbles on his feet and places a steadying hand on the nightstand. "Uwa."

"Here." I help him sit back down. "How are you feeling?"

"Lightheaded. But strong." He twists one way, then the other, and then opens his eyes and smiles up at me. "Thank you. That's . . . amazing!"

"Yeah." I scratch the back of my neck. "Figured it out when Connie needed me." The memory sends a deep chill through my body. Seeing her like that . . . A mess of fear and depression. It was harrowing.

But she's getting better. Slowly. And one day she'll be okay with someone other than me touching her.

"Some real uses there."

"Huh?"

"For the war, I mean."

"Oh, right." I guess he's right. I could produce a bunch of blood pouches or test tubes or tablets or bubbles or something to each team for emergencies. "Probably couldn't produce enough for the whole army though."

"But enough to arm the higher-ups with a few cases in case they need them?"

I nod. "Certainly." Might get Nine on that when we return. Speaking of which . . . "I'm running out of blood. We'll have to return home soon."

Aki frowns. "Can you not just stay in male form?"

I shake my head. "Magical weakness affects all of me, regardless of my form. I can stay in male form without getting overly malnourished, but I'll be angry and annoyed and grouchy and generally a pain in the ass."

"Right." He places a smiling hand on my shoulder. "We kinda need you friendly when dealing with all these supes."

"Yup."

The doors to the infirmary burst open, and our escort Demon barges through and marches toward us. "So, you're both doing okay, then?" He looks us up and down. "Good. The Demon Lord will see you now."

"Huh?" Aki asks.

"For your deal." His eyebrows raise, and he chuckles at Aki's surprised face. "Yes, it wasn't just for the bro points of fighting the Demon Lord. Which you would have lost had he been fully aged and trained."

Aki chuckles, places a hand on the Demon's shoulder, and walks ahead of us, out of the infirmary. "I have no doubts about that."

If I ever see another throne room in my time, feel free to just off me. I swear, these fucking supes and their superiority complexes. Though, is ruling the world as a Horseman really any different?

Damn, Magic, way to ask yourself the complex questions while staring at the Demon Lord.

"Our deal." The Demon Lord hands me a piece of paper ripped from an office-style notepaper and a pen. "Read, negotiate, and sign." He doesn't look at me when he talks.

"Are you really upset you were beaten?"

He shrugs and sinks back onto his throne, reminding me this Demon Lord is still a child.

"C'mon, you have loads of training to go. Think of all the strength you'll gain as you grow up."

He sighs. "Doesn't matter."

Before looking at the business in my hand, I walk up to the throne and kneel to I can look up at him and meet his gaze. "Hey, listen to me." I rest a hand on his knee. "Training's hard work. I was useless at magic a few months ago. I didn't know how to unlock my Witch abilities, I didn't know how to control my blood lust, I didn't know how to craft a Fae spell, and I certainly didn't know how to shift between forms or into an animal."

He meets my gaze, tears shining in his eyes. Unshed. "Really?"

"Uh-huh." I grip his hand and squeeze. "And, if you like, I'd be happy to donate some time to your training." I wince, thinking of my already insane list of things to do. "Maybe after I've dealt with the war. Sorry."

He waves a hand through the air, dismissing my apology. "I'd love to take training sessions from you or any of the Horsemen."

His advisors at the back of the room gasp and murmur.

But the Demon Lord is having none of it. He stands on top of his throne and turns his back to me, facing them. "I know they decimated our kind, but they had their reasons. The Great Purge was before my time. I can only lead our people into the future based on what we have now. Not what we had then." He shuffles back into his seat, then mumbles, "Always wanted to say that to those old crones."

I chuckle to myself and take an in-depth look at the words on the notepad in my hand. It all seems pretty standard to me. But I wish I had Nine here. He would know what seems fishy and what seems okay.

"So," I start, "you help us during the war, and we support you in whatever non-murderous endeavor you decide to take your species on in the future."

"That about sums it up, yes." He beams at me. "And I think I want to take our species out of the closet." Shocked gasps echo around the room. "So few know we exist, and there are many of us who wish to live in the outside world.

I'm trapping my people here due to a centuries-old fear that isn't founded anymore."

"We'd be delighted to help with that."

"But maybe after things have settled back down."

Laughter flows from my mouth. "Yeah, that'll probably be best."

"Are there any other species you've gained help from?"

I look at him in surprise, his logic impressing me.

"I assume we're not the only lesser supernatural species to grace your presence in the last few weeks. The pixies were moved to Sheruta a few days ago. I assume that was your doing?"

"Yes. We thought it best to save them, regardless of their potential help." I take a deep breath. "But the fairies refused."

He stares into the distance, thoughtful, for a moment. "Well, as my first act of assistance, I want to advise you to take a trip to Switzerland. There are rumors flooding the Demon world that there might be a family of phoenixes living around the Jura Mountains."

My interest peaks, ears metaphorically flipping his way. "Phoenixes, really?"

"Indeed."

But I've never been to Switzerland.

Fuck, damn it.

I'm gonna have to fly.

CHAPTER FORTY-SEVEN

THE FIVE HORSEMEN: NOTHING BEATS FAMILY

We stayed with the Demons for another night, I gave the Demon Lord a few drops of Vampire blood to heal his battle wounds as a show of good faith, and Aki drank more alcohol than I thought possible by any living being.

We leave the next morning, Aki moaning and groaning beside me as we walk around the airport, picking up food from the few stalls open.

"Ugh," Aki groans for the hundredth time, "I don't think I can do it." He looks at the bacon roll in his hand with a slightly green tinge to his face. "It's like it's mocking me." His voice pitches higher, I assume, into his bacon voice. "Eat me, you're hungry." His voice pitches lower—into his stomach voice. "No, don't eat me, or I'll throw up what little contents I have all over the airport floor."

I can't help it, I laugh. His current pain is hilarious.

He scowls my way. "What's your problem?"

My laughter doesn't cease, but I manage to get a sentence out in between heaving gasps. "You shouldn't have drunk so much. You knew we were leaving in the morning."

"Why can't you heal me?!"

I shrug. "I can't heal a hangover, just injuries." I bite into my bacon roll and groan. Goddess, this shit is fantastic. "You're on your own."

"So much for sisterly love." He groans again as his head hits the table. "I shouldn't have had those last five shots."

"Five? Last?" I act shocked. "Just how much did you have to drink last night?"

"More than I've drunk in my entire life combined, and enough to drag that sexy Demon escort to bed." He smiles beneath his arm, I can feel it. "In fact, that might be worth this hangover." He raises his head and smiles, a wistful look brushing across his face. "Yeah, definitely worth it."

"Ew, ew, ew . . ." I bat my hands in the air. "I don't want to hear about my brother's sex life."

He swivels to face me. "But he was soooo good. Seriously, more than once, he got me off—"

I throw my hand over his mouth to shut him up. "Seriously, ew."

"Just because you're not getting any doesn't mean I can't have fun on our trip." He grins up at me, then winces and holds his stomach. "Besides, I bet your sex life is wild. Three— four?—partners? Orgy alert!"

"Oh my goddess, shut up," I hiss between clenched teeth. "Don't shout my sex life to the world . . ."

"Why? Trust me, you're getting more and better than the rest of us."

How has my life arrived at this moment?

"Because," I begin, then trail off. "Just because."

"Oh, what's that?" He cups his ear. "It's because you're a giant prude?"

I punch him—lightly—on the arm.

He flinches. "Hey! I'm ill!"

"It's self-inflicted, you giant douche canoe."

"Hey, I'm not a do—"

"Flight 201 now boarding," the lady over the tannoy echoes. "That's Flight 201 now boarding."

I grab Aki's hand and yank him behind me. "Come on, moron. And don't be sick on me on the plane."

The flight is long, Aki's sick a lot—but thankfully in the toilet—and I'm left to my own devices while he suffers. You know what that means? Reading time!

I load up my reading app on the plasmascreen, and there's a notification in the corner. A gift. Someone gifted me a digital book. Clicking on the icon and loading up the gift, I gasp. "Someone bought me a lot of books."

There's a note attached: To Killer, Some inspiration for your romance world. Love, Arrie.

He's gifted me one hundred romance books. And upon closer inspection, I realize they're all poly. Every. Single. One.

Rereading the note, my eyes can't look away from the signature. Love, Arrie. Is this some sort of an apology?

The first on the list is Not Quite Human by Kaye Draper, with another note from Arrie attached: Start here. So I dig in. And after several hours of wonder at reading a character similar to me, and many breaks to check on Aki, we land in Zurich Airport, Switzerland.

"I'm telling you, Aki," I say as we're clearing security, "Sam is just like me!" Then I think about it for a moment. "Well, maybe not exactly the same. I mean, I switch between man and woman while Sam is both always, but it's just . . . fuzzy."

"Fuzzy?" Aki asks as we're collecting our bags. "In what way?"

"Do you know what it's like to look in the mirror and never see yourself? No matter how hard you try, there's always a stranger staring back at you?" I wrap my arms around myself and try not to fall apart on the inside. "It's like not being able to recognize your own shadow. But seeing reflections like yours, even fictional ones, reminds you that maybe you're not as much of a stranger to yourself as you once thought." I smile, tears brimming. "So yeah, fuzzy."

Aki looks at me with a serious, deep, affectionate expression on his face, his eyes soaring into my soul and his heart beating alongside mine. He places firm hands on my shoulders and stops us walking. "Listen to me, sister. Just because your beauty isn't something you see on everyone else doesn't mean it isn't worth looking at, admiring, and being inspired by."

The brimming tears swim past their dam and pour over the edges in rivulets of warm pain spinning out of my body like a puppeteer emptying my vat of hurt and pouring it on the ground.

"Right." I sniff and enter his offering arms. "Thank you." My voice is barely a whisper, but being close enough to hug means I don't need to be brave enough to speak any louder.

He pulls away. "Now, shall we go find ourselves some phoenixes?"

"Yup." I wipe my face and compose myself before we exit the airport.

"How much do you know about phoenixes?" Aki asks as we grab a cab from the terminal and pay an exorbitant fee for the driver to take us to the Jura Mountains. Well, the nearest starting point, anyway. "I didn't even know they existed. I thought they were just legends, you know."

"Mmmm . . . It's kinda hard to know what's real and what's not when most of the supernatural community is still in hiding. Some things really are just legends, like dragons. But some things apparently exist."

"Like phoenixes?"

"Like phoenixes. But no, I've not ever met one. But I did know they existed. Nine mentioned their healing abilities once."

"They really have healing powers? That's rare. Even for the supernatural."

I nod. "Yeah, born Vampires have that power in their blood if offered, and some Witch charms have basic healing powers, but that's about it. I don't even really know what phoenix's healing abilities are like, if I'm honest. I didn't ask."

The truth is that we got a little distracted making out.

Oops.

But I'm not about to say that to my brother.

Not that he'd have a problem talking about my sex life.

Such a weirdo.

He seems to be in a better mood, less hungover, and more chatty now, so he takes the opportunity to pick up where we left off. "So, what's your earliest memory?"

Not the question I thought he would ask.

"Umm . . . Mom buying me one of those Hello Panda candy things. She took me took the park while we waited for Dad to finish work. We just . . . played. Nothing really grand. But I remember her beautiful smile as she pushed me high on the swing."

"Oh." Aki look at me with wonder and hurt in his eyes. "What were they like, Mom and Dad?"

"I don't have too many memories of them. I was pretty

young when they passed. But the ones I do have always make me feel loved. They were kind-hearted. Good people. Dad used to do a cookout in the courtyard of our apartment building every month. He'd invite every neighbor in the building, and everyone would bring something, and we'd all eat, dance, play, and chat. He was always seeking the comfort of others—just being around them and absorbing their energy."

"They sound . . . wonderful."

"What were the Witches like in Japan? The ones who raised you?"

Aki shrugs. "I was raised by these two sisters who shared a house. They were . . . kind enough, I guess." He looks at my imploring eyes and sighs. "We just never clicked. They wanted me to just not use my magic, but I couldn't. It's . . . a part of me."

I nod. Understanding completely. "I can't not use that magic either. It just pops up when I'm in danger or seriously upset." Like when I tried to kill Arrie, for example. But I refrain from bringing that up. "My magic is like the air I breathe. I couldn't imagine giving it up."

I'm in my male form at the moment, given that my female form gets recognized too much, but the driver snort-laughs and tries to cover it up with a cough.

I side-eye him, doing my best to tell him to shut up without actually having to tell him.

He drops his eyes from the rearview mirror and refocuses on the road.

"Right," Aki agrees. "When I asked if they could just give up using theirs, it caused a huge argument and I left."

"How old were you?"

"Sixteen."

"I wish I knew you existed. I wish I were there to help."

He grabs my hand and squeezes. "I know. Me too."

Chapter Forty-Eight

The Five Horsemen Use Teleporting Crystals, Made by Magic, to Get Around Faster

The driver gets us to a small town not far from the Jura Mountains. I can see their huge mass looming in the distance—spanning 22,686 km² across more than just Switzerland.

"How in the world are we supposed to find phoenixes in there?" Aki asks the question on the precipice of my mind.

"I have no idea." I sigh, frustration gnawing. "I might need some help." I look to Aki. "We should teleport back to Sheruta so I can do some research with Nine. I'm running out of blood, anyway."

He nods. "Okay. Good plan."

Now we're in spitting distance of the Jura Mountains, we can teleport back whenever we need. So we grab our crystals, smash them at our feet, and think of home. And in fewer seconds than I can count, I'm standing in the kitchen with a mass of black feathers surrounding my entire body as harsh, demanding lips encompass mine.

Dea.

Some kisses are sweet, some remind you that you're loved, but some are all-consuming infernos; teeth, lips, groans, and hands all coming together in a wind tunnel of love and passion. That's what Dea's angel form is. A tornado of passion.

My mind turns that hazy shade of dizzy whenever I'm near his angel form, but I ignore it and rake my hands up his golden torso, meeting his kiss with equal amounts of force as I trace the outlines of his swirling tattoo and run gentle fingers across his lips before tugging on his piercings.

"I've missed you, Angel." His voice skitters across my skin, leaving a fiery path of goosebumps in its wake.

"Yeah," a rowdy voice echoes from somewhere on the other side of Dea's wings, "so have we, ass pig, so move out of my way!"

Dea spins around to face her and growls, his muscles tensing, his fists glowing red. "Mine."

"Dea," Nine's gentle voice pierces the tension, "come on, bro. Pull your mind back together." His hands run the length of Dea's jaw as their lips press together. But unlike the fiery volcano of our kiss, theirs is gentle—a lapping wave caressing the shore.

I run my hands up Dea's back, trying to soothe us both with some skin-on-skin contact. "We can snuggle later, if you like."

"Like this?" he asks, need and desire shooting through his voice.

A quiet chuckle escapes my lips. "I bet your wings'll make a great blanket."

Dea takes a deep breath and shudders at my hand

wandering down the space between his wings. But after a few long seconds, his form shimmers and he changes back to himself. "I'm sorry," he pants, out of breath.

"Don't be," I reassure. "No harm done."

Connie huffs and pushes Nine and Dea out of the way, lifts me into her arms, where I wrap my legs around her waist, and peppers kisses up and down my neck. Shoving me to the nearest wall—which just so happens to be the fridge—her hands are free to roam my curves, my ass, and slip up my tank top . . .

A coughing sound echoes from the doorway, and Aki looks at me with an embarrassed smirk and a raised eyebrow.

"Err . . . right."

Connie puts me down, and I straighten my clothes out.

Hey, Nine. I missed you.

I missed you too, Sweetie.

Goddess, the silky soft voice inside my head is something I seriously missed. I never want to go without his voice in my head again.

No one loves my telepathy more than you, he chuckles.

Yeah, well, it has its uses.

I throw a sexy image of Dea in his birthday suit up in my mind and watch him close his eyes and smile. I wink in his direction and then clear my throat before addressing the room. "We're actually not done yet, but we've hit a bit of a knowledge gap. And I'm out of blood." Not to mention I'm thirsty as fuck for fresh blood. The chilled stuff Arrie provided is fine, but it's stale as shit.

"What knowledge gap?" Nine asks.

Arrie's still at the kitchen table, but he lifts his head from the newspaper and smiles at me.

Progress!

I spin back to Nine. "Phoenixes in the Jura Mountains, Switzerland."

His eyebrows shoot to his hairline. "Phoenixes? They exist?"

Aki finally enters the kitchen. "The Demon Lord seemed to think so. He's the one who gave us the tip."

"Ohhh," Connie says, "how'd the Demons go?"

"Good question." I face Aki with an accusatory glare. "Wanna answer that, Aki?"

His gaze shoots to the floor as a red flush blushes his features. "Well, I kinda maybe challenged the Demon Lord to a fight, won, then . . . slept with a first ranking Demon." He mumbles the last part, but I'm sure they all pick it up.

Heck, Connie has super hearing.

Aki was loud and proud with me, but with the rest of the team, he's all shy and whimpering. Why is that?

Maybe he's a little intimidated by us?

Is that what's in his mind?

Actually, I can't read his mind. Never have been able to. It's a bit like the shield you sometimes throw up when you don't want me hearing something.

Oh. That's a bit strange. Maybe it's an Angel-descended Witch thing?

Maybe.

Connie, Dea, and Arrie are all stifling giggles, but it's Connie who asks him, "Ohhh, sleeping with a Demon." She wraps an arm through his. "How was it?"

He looks at her with raised eyebrows, then smiles and delves into more detail than a sister ever wants to hear.

I shove hands over my ears. "La la la. Not listeniiiing!"

Connie drags him away, out of the kitchen, and I shift into my male form so I can't hear them anymore.

Galaxy eyes pierce me with a scolding gaze, and I remember how attracted to me Dea is in this form.

"Hey Dea," I whisper. "Hey Nine." I turn to the kitchen table to say hi to Arrie, but he's not there anymore. "Hey . . . Oh." Probably doesn't want all this PDA, anyway.

At the first sign of disappointment, Nine and Dea wrap their arms around me. Silent companionship. Love. I don't need anything else. Especially not someone who doesn't love me back.

"We're in the testing phase of an early prototype of the blood supplement, so I have a few days free," Nine offers. "I'm sure Connie's planning how to get away from management duties for the night, too."

"How about," Dea starts, "a night under the stars, a bonfire, some smores, drinks, laughter?"

"That sounds perfect." I hesitate, frustration bubbling to the surface. "I need to top up my blood supplies while I'm here and do some research into the Jura Mountains. Maybe something will pop up that hints to the phoenixes' location." I grab something from my bag. "Oh, and here's the deal I made with the Demons." I hand the contract over to Dea.

"I will give it a once over, but I am sure you did a splendid job, Angel."

"If you and Aki need some help, I'd be more than happy to spend some time in the library with you." Nine smirks. "We've yet to christen the stacks, after all."

"Nine," I groan. "We can't fuck in the library with my brother there. That's weird."

"Fair shout," he agrees. "I'll have to find another little slice of time to slide into your schedule."

Goddess, I've missed his bad puns.

"Glad I can be of service."

"I, too, can help, if you need it." Dea's arm wraps tighter around my waist as he grips my hip and places a soft kiss to my hairline. "We're all at your disposal."

"Okay, then let's grab Connie and Aki and make it a team effort!"

The scent of old books, new books, and stacks upon stacks of my own collection works better than any massage known to man. My shoulders unclench, days of travel wash away, and I breathe a deep breath of familiar, homely air. "Goddess, I've missed this place."

"I have missed seeing you in it, Angel."

"Yeah," Connie says from a nearby corner, "it's weird being here without you in it."

We round the corner, and I watch as Connie and Aki natter on a multi-colored couch, each of them curled up in either corner.

Aki smiles at me, big and bold. "Connie here was just telling me of your immortal journey so far. Seems it's been quite a ride."

I stare at Connie and point a finger her way. "No telling him the juicy bits! He might be your guys' friend, but he's my brother, and that's weird." And I don't trust her not to brag.

She salutes me, all serious-like. "Yes, sir." Before we both spill into giggles.

They both get up and walk over, my soldiers standing in a row, and Aki says, "What do you need from us?"

"Information. Phoenixes in the Jura Mountains, anything odd about the Jura Mountains, legends from French and Swiss mythology, etc."

"I'm going to start with the geography," Nine announces. "Maybe something'll bounce out at me." He wanders off, his face that gentle smile he gets when he's puzzling something out.

"And I'm going to look into mythology." Aki wanders off.

"I will join you," Dea says, "but I am sorry if you cannot see me."

Aki shrugs before they turn a corner. "S'okay."

Connie wraps an arm around my waist and smirks. "Guess that just leaves us, hon." She wraps both arms around my neck and snuggles her chin into my chest, inhaling deeply. "God, I've missed you."

Hands settling on her lower back and pulling her flush against me, I whisper, "I've missed you too." A sweet kiss to her head has her looking up at me with a twinkle in her eye and promises of things to come tonight. "I promise we'll spend time together this evening. Though, you're gonna have to share." I shrug. "Sorry."

"That's okay. You're worth sharing."

"C'mon," I say as I grab her hand, "guess we should get to my desk and ask my Seeing Stone."

A short walk around plenty of corners brings us to my desk, where papers are scattered everywhere, the flash drive rests next to my plasmascreen, and tucked away in my drawer lies the Seeing Stone.

This Seeing Stone works like a magical book finder. I just think the things I want to know the answers to, and poof, books appear on my desk that hold the answers. Today, I need answers regarding phoenixes in the Jura Mountains. Or just phoenixes in general. Either works for me.

Thud, thud, thud, thud . . .

A small mountain of books lands on my desk one by one, causing Connie and I to share a look.

"It's gonna be a long day, isn't it?"

She shrugs. "At least you got here in the morning."

"Guess there's that."

Chapter Forty-Nine

Shifter Alpha, Cal Brealia, on Rise in Supe Hate Crimes: "It is International Terroism Speared by a Lack of Governmental Cohesion"

Five hours later, our three teams have all rejoined back at my desk, where Connie and I have been scouring the books—to little avail. Dea, Nine, and Aki have had some success, but not much.

"So, to recap"—I run a frustrated hand through my blonde hair—"our only lead is the Jura Mountains Region National Park, which hasn't been open to tourists in over two hundred years and is managed by a shell company whose real identity is wrapped up tighter than a virgin's asshole?"

Nine finds my joke funny, as does Connie, but Aki and Dea seem a little put off by the imagery. Which is rich coming from Dea, the guy who loves fucking Nine and me in the ass.

"Yeah," Nine says as he wipes the laughter from his eyes,

"that about sums it up."

"Well," Aki chimes in, "that does narrow it down. 1,650 km^2 of space, rather than 22,686 km^2."

He has a point.

"If it comes to it, I can probably fly around that area and use my Vampire vision, but it hurt like a bitch last time."

"Well," Nine says, "according to history, there used to be border towns at the entrance that allowed admission, so maybe start there. It sounds to me like the phoenixes might be running their own community. But they'd need outside help for that."

"Right." Dea strokes comforting circles around my wrist. "And if they are keeping things this locked down, it seems only a natural jump there might be more species there than just phoenixes."

Aki's eyes widen. "You think they're running a commune or rescue center for lower supes?"

"We've seen weirder things in our time, kid," Connie answers. "This one even makes sense."

"Yeah," I say, "the lower supe world has been being exploited long before the pillar communities came out of the closet, so it makes sense they'd help each other out and create a safe haven."

"Maybe the humans there originally were helping?" Aki suggests. "Maybe they parted ways for a reason."

Dea and Nine share a look, and Nine explains, "They probably parted ways when we outed the supernatural world to humans. I imagine the lower supes wanted complete safety from humans."

"I wish we knew of all the supernaturals that exist," Dea says, "that way we will not leave so many out when we make a decision that affects them."

"You did the best you could." I rest a comforting hand on his shoulder and squeeze. "You can't work with what you don't have."

"It is our job to help everyone, Angel. But the more of the lower supernatural world you uncover, the less helpful I realize we have been." With creased brows and dull eyes, he storms off to some other—probably quieter—part of the library.

"Is he going to be okay?" Aki asks, worry ruining his usually smiling face.

Nine looks at him with a weak, reassuring smile. "Before Magic, Dea was in charge. Now they kinda co-lead, but everything was on his shoulders before."

Understanding dawns on Aki's face. "He feels guilty?"

He's surprised by that? "We're living, feeling beings, you know. Ones with a fair number of responsibilities resting on our shoulders. Of course he feels guilty. What the fuck did you expect? For us to be robots?" I storm off to find Dea, shifting into my female form so I can scent him out easier.

Just follow the smoky lavender scent.

When I see Dea on the floor, his head in his hands, I push my frustration at Aki away and wrap my arms around Dea's neck. "Heeey, it's okay."

"No, it is not," he grumbles. "The Demons we left alive hate us for good reason and have been living in isolation, the pixies are all but decimated because we did nothing to help, the fairies will not help us because we did not help them when they needed us, and now there might be a whole population of ragtag speecies we had no idea existed, all of whom have suffered and found their way to a safe haven we did not provide." His fists curl tighter, his knuckles whitening, and a growl escapes his lips. Only, it turns into a sob halfway through. "I should have done better."

"There are hundreds of species out there, Dea." I settle in front of him and force his chin up. "You have done amazingly without any guidance or help trying to lead a world that refuses to be anything more than broken pieces that refuse to glue back together." My hands rest on his wet cheeks, and I try for a smile. "You are an amazing person, Death, and I love you."

More tears spill, but a smile breaks out. "I love you, too, Angel."

"Where's my declaration of love?" Nine asks from a few meters away.

I didn't even know he was there.

Dea grabs his hand and yanks him down to where we're sitting and envelops him in a group hug. Looking him straight in the face with vulnerable eyes that are barely glowing and a weak smile, he whispers. "I love you, Famine. Do not forget it."

Nine's confident facade cracks as he rests his forehead to Dea's. "I love you, too. And I'm so sorry for not telling you sooner and letting us go so long apart—"

"Shhh . . ." Dea presses a finger to his lips. "There is no need for that."

Nine kisses Dea's finger, leans forward, and looks at us both. "Kiss me."

We both press our lips to his at the same time, our tongues tangling in an awkward, messy kiss that's somehow perfect. But with Dea's tears and Nine's cautionary vulnerability, I'm left feeling everything they're feeling, like an empathetic vat of emotions has just poured itself over me.

Connie's standing awkwardly off to the side, like she doesn't quite know what to do, so I break away and drag her to the floor with us, inviting her to bathe in the vat of gooey emotions.

Hey, there's plenty to go around.

She lays her head in my lap while Nine does the same on Dea's lap, and we bask in the simple act of being together after a long week apart.

"Where's Aki?" I ask, worried about abandoning him after snapping like that.

"Somewhere around the library," Connie answers. "Probably giving us all a moment alone."

I cringe. "I should apologize, huh?"

Nine chuckles. "Yeah, probably. But I like that you stand up for us." He grabs my hand. "It's very sweet."

"Pfft. I'm not sweet."

Connie laughs. "Yeah, you are."

And if she weren't in my lap, I'd punch her in the arm. Bitch.

Careful, she'll probably eat you for breakfast.

I can only hope.

Nine laughs in my head, and then out loud, and when Dea and Connie look at him in confusion, he repeats the conversation.

"Does sound like a good breakfast, to be fair," she confirms.

My cheeks burn hot, embarrassment flooding through me.

"Oh, come on," Connie says, "you've slept with all three of us. You can't possibly be embarrassed right now."

Apparently, though, I can. Which is weird because she's right. But oh well, whatever.

"Angel, do not make me prove you should not be embarrassed by us or yourself." He raises his brows, and his eyes glow brighter, some of that gold coloring brightening my smile.

If it makes him smile like that, I'll do whatever he wants.

Chapter Fifty

The Ancient Horseman War: Everything You Need to Know

Something smells amazing in the kitchen! Tomato-y, lemon-y, and fantastic. "What is that smell?" I wander my way into the kitchen in search of answers.

Arrie's standing at the stove in his frilly apron with a frying pan in hand that he's tossing cherry tomatoes in. "Tomato and garlic bruschetta, butternut squash risotto, and lemon tart with homemade cherry compote."

"Marry me." There's nothing I won't do to have a cook like this in my life forever. "You're amazing."

He laughs and the sound lights me up. "You're easy to please."

"Only when they want to be," Dea chimes in from the kitchen table.

They . . .

That doesn't sound too bad.

Maybe.

Realizing I'm standing in the kitchen doorway, gazing into thin air, I readjust my mind and shake myself toward the table. "Has anyone seen Aki? I tried to find him to apologize, but he's vanished."

"He left hours ago, Angel. Said something about giving us some privacy. Nigel's staying at his place, too. He left here a few days ago."

"Right." Guilt rocks through me. "I shouldn't have snapped."

"You are not perfect, Angel. Nor should you have to be."

Nine and Connie walk into the kitchen, both groaning at the smell of Arrie's cooking.

"Damn, you who tryna impress?" Nine asks, a smirk on his face. "I'm sure they'll love it."

"Get off," Arrie grumbles. "If you all settle down, I'll feed you." We all shut up, Nine takes his seat next to me, and Arrie laughs. Again. "It's like I've offered a bunch of toddlers an ice cream if they give me five minutes of peace."

"Puhlease . . ." I roll my eyes behind his back. "Your food is much better than ice cream."

"Especially the kind you give children," Nine agrees.

Arrie ignores our jaunting and serves the first course, placing my plate down with a smile.

You two seem friendlier?

Right. Friendlier.

I throw the conversation I had with Arrie while waiting for the pixies his way.

Nine just looks at me with a deep sadness. I'm sorry.

It's okay. I have to respect his decision. If he isn't ready, he isn't ready. There's nothing I can do about that. I just wish he would tell me why.

Maybe one day he will.

Here's to hoping that day is tomorrow. Or yesterday.

Give him time.

It's really all I can do.

"Soooo," I say to the group, trying to run away from that conversation, "what have I missed?"

"Well," Connie starts, "Arrie and Dea have been coordinating efforts to combine our forces for the upcoming defense of the five Vampire cities. The Vampire King is immensely grateful for everything we've been doing. Nine has been drowning in tests, science, and other nerd stuff, but he's pretty close to a workable blood substitute. Oh, and the pixies have taken the north forest as their own. The Sherutan residents welcomed them with open arms and are helping them set up home."

"Okay. That sounds great." They're doing better than me. "We should expect Demons soon, so you're probably going to need to prepare for that."

Connie nods. "Yeah. Since Demons prefer darker environments close to nature, we've been coordinating efforts with the Witches and Vampires here in Sheruta to brainstorm the best place to create a base for them."

"I assume Glowy is with the pixies?" I raise an eyebrow at Arrie.

He nods. "Wants nothing to do with us."

"Glowy?" Dea asks. He's been unusually quiet today.

I wonder what's bothering him?

"The Angel," Arrie confirms. "Magic didn't even try to fight her, so I assume you're a bit salty?" He looks at me.

I snarl. "I am not salty."

Connie and Nine chuckle at my obvious saltiness.

"Alright, I'm a little salty. But I was tired, nowhere near a leyline, and in the middle of the Amazon fucking jungle. I'm sure I'd have put her on her ass in any other environment."

"I didn't even know Angels still existed," Nine says. "Well, I assumed there were some still around, but I didn't realize we'd come across one."

"There are more with the Demons," I add. "I spoke to one, but there were some in the crowd watching Aki and the Demon Lord fight." I shrug. "You didn't kill them all, so of course they're still around. It's a small world."

"Getting smaller by the day," Dea mumbles.

The second and third courses are just as fantastic as the first, and with Arrie in his element, everyone is full, happy, and content.

"What does everyone want to do this evening?" I ask. "I promised Dea we'd cuddle, but other than that, is anyone free to hang out?" I know Connie, Dea, and Nine are. But is Arrie? I look to him. "Arrie?"

He shrugs. "Sure." But he doesn't look happy.

"You don't have to, if you'd prefer to do something else."

He sighs and meets my gaze. "I was going to leave you alone to spend time with your . . ." He looks at the others. "Partners. But if you want me there, I can hang out."

"I want you happy."

His gaze pierces mine, and the sad little smile on his face breaks some deep part of me.

Suddenly, I know exactly what to get Arrie for Christmas. And it'll for sure make him happy. Yay. That's two ideas down. Just two to go. Then everyone else.

Fire crackles into the night sky, setting the stars aflame and our faces alight. Connie's roasting smores with Nine while

Dea lies in my lap, wings spread wide beneath us, and Arrie's chatting with Dea about a new car he wants.

"Will that engine not be a bit . . . loud?"

Arrie chuckles. "Dude, you're missing the point."

"Probably." He laughs. "I have never understood the point of cars and engines. Horses work well enough."

"Sure," Arrie counters, "if you want to get to your destination by the end of the year."

"I'm with Arrie on this one," I chime in. "Horses are slow. Cars can go up to three hundred mph nowadays."

Dea groans. "You young people are always trying to get places quickly. If you slow down, you might have less to moan and bitch about."

"Hey, who you callin' old?" Arrie asks.

Connie gasps. "He swore!" She grabs Nine's shirt sleeve and points to us. "Dea swore!"

"Outside of the bedroom?" Nine asks, acting shocked, as though he doesn't hear him swear every other night. "Well I never."

"Oh, lay off," Dea grumbles. "I am allowed to express myself."

I run soothing hands down his shoulders and brush his wings, and he shivers and sighs like he's been doing all night. Leaning down, I whisper, "I love you in both forms."

He leans his head back and reaches my lips, brushing them with the lightest of touches it feels like a feather blowing across them.

"Alrrriiiight!" Connie bounds over to us, carrying three bottles of tequila. "Who wants tequila shots?"

We all groan, but I laugh and ask the house for shot glasses. Five shot glasses pop onto the grass. One for each of us. Everyone grabs one, and Connie makes us wish we all didn't agree to her idea of a bonfire.

Twenty-three tequila shots are far too many, even for a Horseman. As evidenced by the fact Arrie is wobbling around with his head thrown back in laughter at Dea, who just dropped me out of the fucking sky.

My head hurts. I think I broke my ass. And if I don't get to a toilet soon, I'm gonna pee myself. "Need to pee! Need to pee! Need to pee!" I wobble to the toilet in the gym, not using Vampire speed or shifting, because both of those things seem like a bad idea given I can't walk in a straight line. We don't need another drunk flying incident.

Pretty sure my dick misses the bowl multiple times, and a realization hits me. Men don't poop when they pee. They might pee when they poop, but since they're standing up when they pee, they still have to control their bowels.

Wow. What a world.

So I sit down to poop.

And then stumble back out to the party, where Nine and Dea are making out by the fire, Nine grinding into Dea with drunken fervor; Connie is shouting at the stars for shining too brightly, and Arrie is picking a fight with the bonfire.

Connie downs another shot and trips over the log, falling into the edge of the flames. "Ahhh!" she shrieks. "Shit!"

Everyone stops what they're doing and worries over to Connie.

She's writhing on the grass, but her burn is already healing. "Someone just make it stop . . ." The sobbing comes next, and I know I need to get her to bed.

"You know," I say as I wrap my arms around her body, "it's usually you helping me."

"Well, it's my turn to be a mess for a change."

"Here"—Arrie offers his arms—"I'll take her. Stay and

enjoy the night."

I hand her over and watch him stumble through the kitchen door, hoping they'll be okay.

"I'm sure Arrie will get her to her bed, Angel." Dea wraps an arm around my waist and leans on me, tucking his wing behind my back. "But if you like, you can go check on her. We'll be okay."

"It's okay. She's probably passed out now, anyway. I'll crawl in next to her later."

Nine tucks himself under Dea's wing and wraps an arm around my chest. "She'll like that."

"Join me when I do?"

"Of course."

Always.

Chapter Fifty-One

OUTPOURING OF HUMAN LOVE AND SUPPORT FOR HORSEMEN AND SUPERNATURAL IN INTERNATIONAL PROTESTS ALL OVER THE WORLD

Connie grumbles into my ear the next morning as Nine presses his backside into my dick and Dea lies on top of us all, wings still out. He stayed in his angel form all night? I don't think I've ever seen him do that.

Nine's sleepy voice echoes in my head. I don't think he has. But he's been itchy since you left. His angel form's been popping out all over the place. He's been struggling.

He's been struggling that much? Why didn't anyone tell me?

He didn't want us to. He wanted you to be able to be independent.

You've been helping him feel loved, right? In my place?

He chuckles inside my head. Of course. But there's only

so much I can do to soothe an angel mating bond.

I need to spend some time with my angel when we get back. I'm hoping I won't be gone for more than a few days this time, anyway.

Connie groans again.

And I flip around to face her. "Hey, beautiful." I press a gentle kiss to her forehead, careful to give her space first thing in the morning. "You doing okay?"

"Mmmmm." She wraps an arm around my waist and snuggles into my neck. "Better now."

Dea shuffles on top of us, and we all groan.

"Bro, get off," Nine complains. "You're crushing me."

Dea rolls and weasels his way between me and Nine so he can grab me and yank me on top of him.

Connie and Nine rearrange themselves on top of Dea's wings, and now everyone is staring at my topless body, roaming their eyes over what little muscle I have.

You're hot. Don't be unconfident.

Thanks.

Dea offers me his wrist with a smile. "Breakfast?"

"Or you can drink from me instead, if you like?" Nine offers, holding his wrist out.

Connie stays silent, but I'll never force or expect her to feed me. Besides, I have three other . . . Two. I have two other partners for that.

I look at Connie, who smiles at me and takes a deep breath. "I'll be okay. Go ahead."

I shift into my female form and grab both their offered wrists, bend their hands back, sink one fang into each man, and drink from both at the same time. The rush of euphoric pleasure shoots across my body, and I instinctively grind down onto Dea's rapidly hardening cock.

The last time I was in this form, I was showering before slipping into Connie's bed, so I'm naked, and Dea's angel form makes it uncomfortable to wear clothes, so he's in nothing but his pants.

Connie gasps a little, and I feel her breathing rapidly and her heart throwing itself around, but she cautiously approaches and rests a hand on my face.

Nine and Dea are groaning beneath me, with Nine struggling to stop his hips thrusting into the air. But the moment I touch his cock through his pajama pants, that small amount of control snaps, and he meets my palm.

Still drinking from the guys, I look to Connie, my eyes blazing red and my face one that likely haunts her dreams.

But she doesn't seem scared anymore—the lust in her eyes pins my hand on Nine's cock and the way I'm riding Dea's in a haze I recognize from our time together. "Keep going."

I slow down my feeding because I don't want to take too much, but I'm not ready to lose the connection.

Connie straddles Dea's legs behind me and presses her breasts to my back in scorching heat that travels all the way through me. Her hand travels over my waist and down, meeting the wet heat below that's dripping onto Dea's pants. "God, you feel delicious, hon."

Nine's eyes snap open and focus on Connie's hands as she delves a finger into me and causes me to snap my jaw around their wrists harder as a moan escapes me.

I'm getting a little dizzy, Sweetie.

I let go of their wrists, but I still need them. Need what only they can offer.

As if sensing where my mind is at, they don't hesitate in shucking their clothes off.

Connie steals me to herself for a while, adding two, then

three fingers and riding me into her soft mattress as my hips grind into her palm. Her kisses petal across my collarbone and up my neck, where she nips and sucks to the rhythm of her hand.

Dea's wings encompass us both when he returns to the bed, his dick on full show in front of me as I wet my lips.

"Wait," Nine says, "Dea, are you going to be okay sharing Magic in that form?"

I meet his eyes, questioning him, and he shrugs.

"I do not know for sure, but I am not feeling any murderous intentions right now. You are all making my angel happy, therefore you can all stay."

"Good," I say, "then get over here." I open my mouth and stick my tongue out flat against my chin.

"I think she wants your dick, bro."

"You do not say." Dea crawls over to me and teases my tastebuds with the tip, a smirk falling on his face when he looks into my eyes.

Connie crawls down my body, peppering kisses on her journey, and scores one swipe of her tongue up my heat, causing me to buck into her mouth and cry out.

"Don't stop," I moan.

Dea fills my mouth slowly with a single crawling thrust. "Yes, Angel."

I swirl my tongue around the head and encourage him to thrust, to use me and leave me in a puddle beneath him.

Connie thrusts two fingers back into me, and I cry out around Dea's dick. Curling them up and sucking my clit into that talented mouth of hers has me arching off the bed and crying her name.

Nine comes around to my side, avoiding Dea's wings, and leans his head to my chest before taking one of my nipples into his mouth.

Together, they're wrecking me in the best way. And I try to hold on, I really do, but they push me over the edge pretty quickly, and soon I'm screaming their names into Dea's dick and begging for more.

I remove Dea's cock and throw myself at Connie, pinning her to the bed with a flash of Vampire speed I know frightens her a little bit. But she calms when I nibble my way up her thighs and swirl my tongue through her wetness.

"Magic . . ." She grips tight fingers into my hair, pushing my head closer. Her head throws back onto the mattress as a rush of breath leaves her.

"They look so hot," Nine says. But Dea must shut him up, because he moans and loses his words.

The next thing I know, someone is entering me from behind and pushing me farther into Connie's pussy.

"You're so tight," Nine praises as he pounds me harder and then cries out. "Yes, Dea!"

Lifting my head to see what they're doing, Dea's wings are flapping in the air as he thrusts into Nine and controls all our actions from behind.

Connie whines beneath me, so I return my attention back to her and add a finger to the mix, hoping to feel her explode around me. "Yes, yes . . ."

Dea groans and slaps something hard—Nine's ass I assume, because he cries out and pushes into me faster, riding his pleasure through me. "I cannot hold back any . . ." Dea trails off as he explodes.

Goddess, this is the hottest way to start my day.

But right now, I want the beautiful goddess beneath me writhing in as much pleasure as possible, so I add two more fingers and suckle at her clit. Hard. Nipping gently here and there.

Her hand grips the sheets as she arches off the bed and cries out, spasming around my fingers and panting, out of breath.

Nine grabs my waist and yanks me around to face him, then throws his lips against mine in a passionate frenzy that has me riding his lap.

Use me.

He leans back on his hands and throws his head back.

I grab on tight to his shoulders and squeeze his dick and grind my clit against him.

Harder.

I follow his instructions and ride him harder, slamming down on his lap and lavishing the skin-on-skin sounds we're making. My body tightens, and I know I'm getting close.

Bite me.

When I hesitate, he yells, "Now, please!"

My fangs snap down and latch onto his exposed neck, sinking in deep. Blood rushes down my throat and I clench around Nine's cock as another orgasm rockets through me like I'm on fire.

But the scream that leaves Nine's mouth is one of pure pleasure, echoing through both the air and my mind. "Magic . . ." he moans as he comes down and caresses my sweaty body.

"That was . . ." Connie starts.

"Seriously attractive to watch."

"Fucking hot," she corrects.

Nine flops onto the bed in a haze, panting, drawing in desperate gulps of air.

"Are you okay?" I ask, making sure I didn't break him or something.

I'm . . . Fuck, that was the best orgasm of my life. You all need to try that. Trust me. He chuckles out loud. Oops, sorry Arrie.

He must have sent that to everyone, not just us three.

The kitchen is filled with breakfast food and the table is filled with family: Connie, Arrie, Dea, Nine, Aki, and Nigel. And I'm filled with smiles and rainbows. No surprises there then.

Arrie hands me a batch of vials filled with blood. "Here." And tries to smiles at me, but it's weak.

I smile in way of a thank you, then turn to Nigel. "So," I say, "you handed in your notice?"

"Yeah." He scratches his head, embarrassed. "The moment I found out the Area 50 date, I couldn't do it anymore. For years, I pretended to myself that I was doing the right thing, but I wasn't." He looks to the table. "I still can't believe the Supernatural Council are our enemies."

"I know," Aki says. "It's crazy."

"When we helped create them," Dea says, looking just as embarrassed as Nigel, "we thought we were doing the right thing. Uniting the pillar communities."

Nine strokes his hand on the table. "We were."

Aki looks at Dea, who's visible while we eat, seriousness lacing his stare. "You can't be held accountable for the actions of others, no matter how godlike you might be."

Dea sighs. "I know."

The defeat in his voice laces my mind, and I just know he doesn't believe a word Aki is saying.

Looking back to the rest of the table, I stuff more food into my mouth. "We shouldn't be gone long. We teleported here from near the Jura Mountains, so we're teleporting back and scouting the area until we find the phoenixes."

"So, a couple days, tops?" Aki asks.

"Uh-huh."

"Why?" Connie asks him. "Got something better to be doing?"

His face flushes. "Well, I kinda have a date on Saturday."

My head snaps up. "With who?" Moreover, when over the last week or so did he have time to arrange a fucking date?

"Verity." He avoids my eyes.

"Oh, him."

"I can steal one of those teleporting crystals, right?"

I wave my hand in the air. "Sure. I'll make you a batch of each type."

His smile stretches from ear to ear.

"In fact, I might just start making them in batches and leaving them in baskets outside my bedroom door. Free for anyone who needs them." That'll save me from fulfilling everyone's orders.

"Good plan," Connie says. "I'll ask the house to set something up. Hopefully. If it listens to me."

Nine and Arrie laugh.

"Am I missing something?"

Nine answers, "She asked for a ballroom a few hundred years ago, full of gold décor and other specific design features that took the house a little time to complete, and it's been a little stroppy with her ever since."

Laughter colors my voice. "Well, if you can't get her to cooperate, I'll do it when I get back."

"Her?" Arrie asks.

I shrug. "Feels right."

Arrie doesn't answer, just goes back to his breakfast plate.

"How do you plan to scout that large an area?" Connie asks. "It's kinda a big mountain range."

"I'm gonna fly around and look. Probably as an eagle. Maybe a falcon. Whichever's fastest."

"Peregrine Falcon," Nine answers. "Should be flying around 200 mph."

"Cool." Aki grabs a final piece of fried toast and tops it with strawberries. "That should make things quicker."

"It's possible they've got a spelled barrier, though. Who knows what kind of creatures are there if they really do have a sanctuary," Nine warns. "Might be worth going a little slower and feel for any spellwork."

"Noted." I swallow my mouthful. "And we're gonna start near the old villages and towns, see if they still have an entrance to the National Park."

"Need practise shifting into a falcon?" Nigel asks.

No, but I'll humor him. "Sure."

We go outside, and Nigel instructs me to stand feet apart. Ready. "Something every Shifter shares is the unique way in which we shift. It can be slow, but it's possible to be quick if you practise." He scowls. "And you don't put nearly enough practise into your shifting."

"That's because it's so natural to me."

"Just because you're talented, kid, doesn't mean you away with practising that talent."

Great. More training.

"Whatever complaint you just threw at me in your head, save it. This is important."

Damn. The man knows me. "Okay. Show me what you got, old man."

Chapter Fifty-Two

Protests Turn Violent in a Frenzy of Blood and Fear:
Are the SC to Blame?

It's late evening in the Jura Mountains, but as I shift into my practised falcon, I realize that it's not an issue because falcons have fantastic night vision. I squawk at Aki, hoping to convey that everything is working out, and then take off.

He'll be fine.

Right?

Right.

The mountains span out in the distance below me, and I head in the direction the map on Aki's datachip outlined.

Rock. Rock. And more rock. What a surprise?

This is like the Andes Mountains all over again.

But, after about an hour of flying, I feel something. Something like a spell, but not quite. In fact, I don't think I've felt anything like it before. Maybe it's some kind of magic from a species I've not come across yet?

Hmm. Maybe.

But I have a bad feeling.

Something about this spell feels wrong.

I swoop down to get a better feel for the spell, but I'm stopped by a barrier. What the fuck? Who puts a barrier up this high? How rude.

Right. I take a deep breath. I need to fly around this thing and find its entrance.

After another half hour of flying, I come across some ruins to an old village and an end to the barrier spell. Upon landing, I shift back into human form and read the glowing sign swinging in the mountain wind: WELCOME TO HURRO VILLAGE.

Bits of old rock jut out of the ground in vague, house-like shapes every few meters, moss growing up the sides and infiltrating the cracks like its own personal battlefield. And it's winning. At the end of the village, the barrier spell stands, barring me entry. At first, I think it's a Fae barrier, like the one my trainer in Sheruta uses for the forest Fae, but upon closer inspection, I can't detect any leyline magic. Whatever energy is making this spell, it isn't what the Fae or Witches use. This is something new.

Excitement runs through me, bordering around my curiosity like an old friend, as I run my hand up and down the invisible barrier. I poke and I prod, but nothing changes. It doesn't budge.

"Damn." I'm impressed.

Even the grumpy Fae who refuses to give me her name would have a hard time dealing with this. Or she might not be able to at all, actually. Fae seem endlessly impressive, as though they can do anything. But that's not true. They can only use the energy they store from leylines.

If we could figure this out, or gain favor from whomever uses this magic, we might turn the tides of this war.

Magical energy reaches me from the other side. Not massive amounts, just slight tremors, like shaky breaths, pass through the barrier and surround me. Someone's there.

"Hi! My name is Magic. I'm the Fifth Horseman." I take a deep breath. "I know you've created a safe haven here, and I know you want it to be secret. I promise, no one outside of the Horsemen's primary team knows of your existence. If at all possible, I'd love an audience with your leader." I bow low, keeping my hands shown. "I am sorry for trespassing."

More magical energy surrounds me. It's not threatening, just examining, but given it doesn't feel like any magical energy I've ever felt, I don't have the power to push it away. And that leaves me feeling uneasy.

I'm too used to being the strongest in a room.

A blue-glowing light outlines a door shape in the barrier, and a beautiful lady stands there, a long-flowing skirt a bright ocean green that matches her hair and eyes blows in the breeze. "Magic." She bows her head slightly. "You are welcome to Hurro, but please do not use your magic offensively while you're staying."

I bow my head. "You have my word."

She turns and leaves, expecting me to follow, no doubt.

With no small amount of trepidation, I step through the door and gasp. Wonder fills me. There are creatures everywhere, some of whom I've never seen before, and they're all interacting as though they get along. There are also creatures I do know about: pixies, some fairies, lots of Witches, and even a few Fae. None of them explain the barrier, though.

The lady stands next to me, allowing me to take everything in with a smile on her face. "Beautiful, isn't it?"

Tears threaten to leak from my eyes, but I brush them away. "It's everything the world is supposed to be."

"And more." She places a gentle hand on my shoulder and guides me forward. "Come on. I'll show you to the people who act as leaders. But we don't really have leaders like other communities. It's more of a population-run community."

"That sounds nice."

We walk through fields, past houses of all shapes and sizes, through groups of children playing in the grass, past couples and groups of friends chatting, and I'm pretty sure my mouth is still hanging open.

"How many people live here?"

"Twelve thousand across the entire park, but only a few hundred here at the entrance. Mostly it's the children and families of those of us who guard the barrier."

That makes sense. The National Park is an enormous area. They wouldn't want to commute if they couldn't travel quick.

Looking back at my guide and her unusual coloring, I'm struck by how odd her species identity is. She seems similar to a Shifter, but she's not. It's probably rude to ask, so I keep my trap shut for a change.

See. I'm learning.

"They're just through that door." She points to a stone building that reminds me of a hunting lodge, but more modern. "Heads up. They don't like guests."

Great.

The massive double doors open as I walk up the steps, and standing in them is a man as large as Arrie, with a frown just as grumpy, and hair just as long, sitting at his shoulders.

In fact, I'd say this is his brother or son if I didn't know better. And the similarity has me instantly backing up a step.

He chuckles, a deep, boorish laugh that isn't at all like Arrie's. "Don't worry, Horseman. I'm not going to fight someone as strong as you. I value my life."

I ascend the final few steps and smile. "Wise choice."

"Please"—he gestures to the doorway—"come on in. We were all just having some food. Join us."

"I've eaten recently, but I'd like to join nonetheless."

We enter the modest-sized room, and again, I'm kinda impressed with how this place looks. "This is not what I expected." Plasma screens line the walls, showing news from all corners of the world, while banks of computers line the far wall, work benches litter the space, and bright open art décor and shiny wooden accents decorate the walls. Various people work at the various stations, some of whose species I recognize, some I don't.

"What were you expecting?" he asks. "Cozy fireplaces and bearskin rugs?"

Yeah, actually. "Something like that."

"We like to monitor outcasts and people who might need our help." He gestures to the room. "This is how we do that."

"You help people who need you?"

He nods. "As best we can."

"That's . . . amazing."

"I'm glad you approve." He guides us to a room off to the side, where a large round table sits with food dotted around and two smiling, cheerful faces adorning the seats. "Everyone, this is Magic."

Their eyes widen, coughs splutter, and faces drop their smiles.

"I'm not sure why he's here. But I'm sure there's a good

reason."

An older woman scowls at me and points. "If you're here to draft us into your war, then you can leave. We want no part in any of the communities you claim to protect."

"Please," the large man from before says as he gestures to one of many empty chairs, "sit."

I take a seat away from the others, who are sitting at the other end of the table. "Thank you for allowing me to join you. I promise not to discuss your location outside of the Horsemen team. I understand the necessity of your discretion."

"We thank you for that," a young gentleman with brown hair and honey-colored eyes says. "My name is Eldry." He points to the large man and says, "This is Reetus." He then points to the scowling old lady from before and says, "And this is Wendy. You'll have to excuse her impoliteness."

I bow my head in each of their directions and grab a glass of water from the center of the table. "Before I begin, I was wondering if you could have someone fetch my brother from the eastern side of the mountains? I may have left him there as I searched for your location in falcon form."

Reetus howls with laughter. "The poor fella is probably freezing his butt off. I'll get Treelus to fetch him. He'll be here within the hour."

Within the hour? Just how fast can Treelus fly?

"We have a chopper," Eldry explains. Clearly, the confusion was written all over my face. "It's pretty fast."

"So now we have that out of the way," the old woman spits, "what is it you've come to ask of us, Horseman."

"Please, Mama," Eldry says, "be more polite. Magic is just here to help their people." He smiles at me.

"Thank you. And yes, I'm here to ask for your help. But

I'm not naïve. I know you will not want to risk your people or the community you've worked hard to create. So I won't ask that of you." I'm not really sure where to start, so I guess the beginning will have to do. "The Fae have teamed up with a rogue Vampire faction the Vampires don't agree with, and they have the SC under their control. With that in mind, we created the embassy. Currently standing, it has representation for Vampires, Shifters, Witches, pixies, and Demons. We're happy to add any species, no matter how small their population."

Both men smile, but the old lady sticks to her scowl.

"We're trying to unite as many species as possible so we can usher in a new world. Yes, there's going to be fighting involved. It would be naïve of us to try otherwise. Peace treaties are off the table since all the enemy wants is to rule the world, kill humans whenever they want, and generally be a bunch of lawless assholes."

"Sounds very like the Fae Queen," the old lady agrees. "Same old, same old."

"What if that wasn't the case? What if we could make a difference? What if we could reform the Supernatural Council to care for every species, create laws that protect, not restrict?"

"A pipe dream. You are young." She frowns, but she relaxes somewhat. "Many have tried before you, and all have failed."

"They didn't have the Horsemen." I sigh, frustration bubbling. "Look, I don't mean to be rude or egotistical, but I was quite literally created for this purpose. That's how Horsemen work. We're plucked from the recently dead and reborn with a purpose whenever the world needs us."

"Is it true the original four purged the world of Demons

and Angels to protect the supernatural and human world?" Eldry asks.

"Yes. Though we are trying to make peace with the few Angel and Demon populations left."

All three look impressed; even Wendy seems unable to prevent her satisfied smirk.

"So what is your plan?" Wendy asks.

"We have a short-term goal and a long-term goal," I begin. "To start with, we would like to protect the Vampire population from the SC's Area 50 plans. They're going to shut down all the main Vampire cities. If we want to stay united, then we have to protect our vulnerable. And they are indeed vulnerable during the day on Christmas Day."

"Not a bad strategy," Reetus says. "Not condoning, but it is a good strategy. While New Orleans might have a high population of born Vampires, the rest of the Vampire cities do not. And made Vampires cannot protect themselves during the day. So they rely on other species. But Christmas Day is celebrated by most species across many countries, so they'll be busy and ill prepared."

"Yup." I cross my arms over my chest. "It's a bloody good plan. The only hole? They have no idea we know."

Reetus's booming laugh penetrates the air. "Aww, c'mon, Mama! This would be the best action I've seen in years."

Wendy scowls at her son and whacks him across the head. "Always with the fighting!"

I smile at them, pleased that out of all the places I've visited and species I've interacted with, these seem like a family. "How about this: those who want to join our cause may, but it's not necessary. And there are plenty of non-fighting roles. Any help toward peace will be useful."

Wendy looks to her sons and sighs. "Fine. But only because

these two have been begging me to get involved and help for the last few weeks."

Eldry stands with a smile. "It's our job to help the lost and lonely, and right now, the supernatural world is lost and lonely." He kisses his Mama on the head and heads over to me with a handout.

I shake it with a smile. "It's good to have help come so easily."

"Child?" Wendy asks. "I won't force my people to get involved, and this space we have here in the Jura Mountains is to remain a secret and not used in your war in any way. Do I make myself clear?"

"Perfectly." I offer my head. "Thank you for your help."

She shakes my hand with a small smile—the first I've seen—and asks, "What are your long-term plans?"

"Peace."

She shakes her head. "All these young people aiming for the same thing, you'd think they'd align."

Looking out the window at the community surrounding me, I take a deep breath and smile. "I have so many questions."

Eldry places a hand on my shoulder and smiles down at me. "I bet you do. When your brother arrives, I'll be happy to answer them."

His tan skin contrasts the moonlight sky out the window, and it strikes me how much this man reminds me of Nine. The easy-going playfulness, the way the light bounces off his skin . . .

Goddess, I miss them all.

I need more than a single night with my boyfriends . . . girlfriend . . . partners? Life buddies. Yup. Definitely life buddies.

Chapter Fifty-Three

Hate Crime Death Toll in the Thousands

Aki and I stay in a guest house at the entrance village that night, and we're both out like lights despite the time difference. Something about being here utterly drains me.

"Morning, sleepyhead," Aki grumbles at me sometime in the morning. "C'mon, get up." He kicks my bed from his across the small room.

"Alright, alright." I yawn and stretch and blink in the morning sunlight. "I'm up."

"Good, 'cos the big burly guy was just here, and he dropped breakfast off."

Ohhh, breakfast.

I sit up and sniff the air, immediately waking up.

"It's just toast," Aki says, his smile widening.

"Yeah, but it's food. And I'm hungry." In fact, both forms are hungry right now, but I'm gonna focus on male me first.

"Ooh, and there's honey."

An hour later, when we're fed, showered, watered, and clothed, we arrive at the same house as yesterday to meet with Eldry, who is going to show us around and answer all my questions.

"Magic!" He gleams. "Aki!" He opens his arms wide and brings us both in for a hug. "Magic, you're in your female form today? How wonderful."

"Oh, yeah." Just how I feel today, but sure, let's roll with the compliments. They feel nice. "I can see best this way. Vampire vision."

"Cool." He steps into a small truck with plasma windows you can completely see through or choose to make opaque. "Hop in."

Aki and I sit in the back, gazing out the window.

"We don't do this very often," Eldry says, "usually only when a new resident arrives. But you're a bit special, so we're making an exception."

"I'm sorry," I say, "I don't mean to make your people feel like zoo animals."

He looks at me in the rearview mirror and smiles. "It's okay. They're going to be a bit of a spectacle today, anyway. News of your arrival has spread far. Mama sent out a message that anyone who wishes to assist in your cause may do so and are to meet us at the entrance village this evening at eight pm."

"Oh, that's so thoughtful of you."

"Nah, it's nothing." He drives us up a rocky path and over the hilltop, the sunrise lighting the distance. "Truthfully, Reetus and I 'av wanted to intervene for some time. Or at least to do something. You know? But Mama was against it." He shrugs and sighs, the weight of having done nothing sitting on his shoulders. "I think she was worried we wouldn't make it out alive, but with you and the Horsemen here, with the makings of an army, she feels a little more hopeful."

"She didn't look hopeful," I mumble.

Eldry bursts into laughter, shaking his head. "She's a grumbler, for sure."

Wonder if she and Arrie are related?

"Oh my god!" Aki shouts. "Look at that!" He points out the window to a field on our left in the distance. "Are they . . . unicorns?"

A gasp escapes my lips as I grip the edge of my seat and look to where he's pointing. And lo-and-behold, before my very eyes are unicorns on Earth. "You have a unicorn pack? Here on Earth? But Nine told me they were hunted to extinction."

Eldry looks at me, confused.

"Famine saved a small pack and relocated them to Sheruta. We have a large herd in the rainbow forest outside my bedroom window."

He blinks at me. "There're more of them?" He blinks some more. "That's . . . Wow."

"I think, Eldry," Aki says, "you'll like Sheruta and the Horsemen very much."

He chuckles. "Well, Reetus is already dying to go toe-to-toe with your Horseman of War. Says he wants to fight the strongest being to ever live."

"Pfft." I'm stronger. "Good luck to him."

Aki chimes in, "Aren't you technically stronger than Arrie?"

"Eh. It depends what you're measuring. I'm more versatile. I have lots of abilities and strengths, whereas the other Horsemen only have a select few. But Arrie's strength is unparalleled." I shrug. "I don't really know. I've never arm-wrestled the guy."

"Sounds like a fun afternoon," Eldry says. "Maybe you should run a carnival one weekend and put on some events. Would let the world see who you are more, too."

"That's . . . Not half bad an idea, Eldry." Surprise laces my voice.

He acts mock hurt. "Hey, I'm more than a pretty face, you know. I do run this place."

"With help," I counter.

He smiles. "With help."

"So," I say, preparing to start asking my questions. "We actually came to look for phoenixes. Demons told us they were here."

Eldry laughs. "Those fuckers."

"Huh?" Aki asks, leaning forward. "What?"

"They're forbidden from talking about this place. They helped us form it, actually."

"So they gave us a false tip leading us to the Jura Mountains so we'd find you?"

"Well, we do have phoenixes. They're intelligent and might listen, but they're like unicorns. They can't communicate with us using language."

"Ah, I see."

I fidget in my seat as we continue on our drive, passing all kinds of non-communicating species on our way.

"Go on, ask me all your burning questions. I promise you won't offend."

And before I can put my mind into coherent thoughts, my questions flood from my mouth like a landslide. "What makes the barrier? What kind of magic is that? The woman who met me at the barrier, who is she? What kinds of species are there here? When did you form? Why are you in hiding? Why did you not ask the Horsemen for help? Sheruta is safer than this barrier, regardless of how cool the magic is. What are you and your brother?" I look sheepishly to the car floor. "Err . . . sorry."

Aki and Eldry both laugh at me, but Eldry shakes his head. "It's okay. No apologies necessary. I'm actually surprised you kept all that locked away until now. Usually new residents list an endless stream of questions for days until they're left to process them."

"How do new residents come here?"

"We have agents who usually go out and save them, then return them to their new home. They have a choice, of course. If they want to stay out in the normal world, we usually help find them a temporary place and monitor them until things settle down. Sometimes they don't have a choice, like if a hunter is looking for them."

I wince.

The world still doesn't know about that. I've not even told Aki. It's going to come out soon, I can feel it on the edges of the upcoming disaster.

"Who are the agents?" Aki asks, as intrigued as me.

"Volunteers usually. Ones who have benefitted from our system and society who want to give back. We don't really have an economy here. Though we do have some money for outside of our little world."

"Wait, there's no money?" I ask. "How does that work?"

"Well, I guess we do have some basic form of an economy, but no. We don't have money here. Every household participates in this society in one way or another. And we work together to make resources that are shared amongst everyone." He looks at me in the rearview mirror and smiles.

"It only works because our society is so small. You could never change the outside world's economy into something like that."

"No"—I shake my head—"I imagine not."

Aki looks out the window at the mountain next to us, awe leaking from his eyes. "Cool though."

I grab Aki's hand and squeeze, hoping his lack of chirp isn't because of me yesterday. "I'm sorry about yesterday."

Aki shakes his hand. "Don't bother. It's okay. I totally get it. You were right. I was being insensitive. I'm sorry." He smiles at me, but it's clear his heart isn't in it. He squeezes my hand back nonetheless, though.

"Err . . ." Eldry starts, "I have a question, if I may?"

I nod, telling him to go ahead.

"How are you related? Like, how does a Horseman have a brother."

"Twin brother, actually." I smile at his surprise. "I was born mortal, Eldry. Aki is my mortal brother. I died and was reborn a Horseman."

"Oh . . . oh." His tone changes halfway when he realizes I'll outlive him by thousands of years.

"It's okay," Aki says. "Magic has a great immortal family. She'll be just fine." The calm exuding his voice and the smile that accompanies it warms me.

"I'm glad you like them."

He scratches his head and leans toward me. "Yeah, sorry about the judgey asshole I was before. I just didn't . . . get it."

"It's cool." I shrug. "Many people don't get it."

"Hey," Eldry interrupts, "we're coming up to the first community I think you'll want to meet."

We reach a clearing in a valley surrounded by mountains on all sides, and in the center of the valley is a massive lake with bright-haired people playing, chatting, living.

"Welcome, Magic and Aki, to the mermaid community."

"Mermaids are real?" I squeal. "Really?"

Eldry laughs in my face. "Yeah. Not all of our communities are species-specific, but some who have specific requirements are."

"Like mermaids," Aki confirms. "Makes sense."

A familiar smiling face walks our way, her hand waving in the air, blue-green scales trailing up her arm and covering her shoulder.

"It's you," I exclaim. "You're a mermaid?"

She finds my surprise hilarious, her placid face from yesterday one of amusement today. "Yeah, guilty. Name's Lilly. Come on, meet some of my friends." She grabs our hands and drags us near the water.

Aki looks concerned. "You're not going to turn out to be those evil mermaids like in Peter Pan, are you?"

I shrug. "I can hold my breath indefinitely."

"I can't!"

"Sucks to be you."

Lilly looks at me with such reverence, I stand still for a moment. "You can really hold your breath indefinitely?"

"Yup. Vampire trait."

She looks at me, confused.

"Oh, I'm part Witch, part Vampire in this form."

"This form?"

Clearly, she doesn't keep up with the news. Oh well, I don't mind. "Yeah." I switch into my male form and smirk at her shriek. "I'm part Shifter, part Fae in this form." Then I switch back.

"You're . . . all," she gasps. "Now I understand."

"Kinda my shtick. Male, female. All species. Attracted to all genders. And . . ." I trail off, the words getting caught in my throat. "Nevermind."

She smiles gently at me. "I saw the notice on the board this morning." She nods to a plasmascreen floating in the air a little way from the lake. "You're looking for help to win your war. That's why you're here."

"Yes," Aki says, "but we're looking for more than just fighters. Healers, strategists, scholars, communication experts . . . Any skill that might be of use to us. Lives don't need to be put at risk in order to do the right thing."

"You know, Aki," I say as I look to him, "you're good at this whole talking thing."

"They're just words. It's not too hard."

Sure. Says the guy finding wording easy.

"Anyway," I say, "if there's anything we can offer in exchange, we're willing to help."

"Just you?" she asks. "Or all of the Horsemen?"

"All of us."

"So, the Horseman of War could come and . . . help?" Her eyes dart to the floor as a blush creeps along her pale skin.

She's interested in Arrie? But he's my . . . friend. He's your friend, Magic. And she's pretty hot. "I'm sure I can find something for him to do. Shirtless, of course."

Lilly's eyes light up as she shifts on the spot. "Wow . . ." She shakes her head. "Seriously, though, we could use his help. Or maybe you'd be a better option?"

"What is it you need from us?"

"Well, we've complained to the owners of the park many times, but no one can seem to defeat it." She walks us to the other side of the lake, where no mermaids are running around and the brush grows wild and free. "Down there is a naga." She points to the murky lake water—dark and mysterious compared to the mountain freshness of their side. "It kills us every time we swim too close, but it's taking more and more space, shutting us out of our own waters. Soon, we'll have to move. But this is the only lake large enough in the park."

They'll have to leave their sanctuary.

"The oceans are too dirty for our kind nowadays. And humans kill us on sight."

"So you want Arrie or me to kill this thing?"

"Just how big is it?" Aki asks, worry filtering through his tone.

"No one knows. We've never seen its whole body before."

"Any of us Horsemen could probably help, but I can send Arrie if you'd all like to ogle him at the same time?" The suggestion in my tone is a little bitter, but I try my best to hide it.

"I was just joking before. This is a serious problem for us. Whoever you think is best will do."

"I'll consult with the team and get back to you. I'm sure we can help, even without your help in the war."

"Really?" The worry in her eyes shoots straight through me.

"Yes. This is something we should have been helping with all along."

She waves a dismissive hand through the air and laughs. "The Horsemen aren't meant to help every little supernatural out with every issue. They're made to balance out the magical world."

"But we should be able to—"

"She's right," Aki interrupts. "You can't just help everyone. That isn't feasible. And you'll wear yourself out trying. Isn't that why you created that help board app to begin with? So you could rally the world to help each other."

I breathe deep, the mountain air scorching my lungs. "Yeah, you're right." I scan my surroundings, taking the view in. "But they can't use that app here. But I bet we could set up a local version, just for the park!"

"Really?" Lilly asks. "You can do that?"

"Well, I'm surprised they haven't already, but yeah, probably."

"They're more interested in keeping everyone safe and saving people from the outside world. They care, but that's their main mission. We're left to our own devices around here."

"You sound like maybe that's something you'd like to change?" Aki asks, curiosity dripping from every word.

"Perhaps. I'm just glad they saved my pod when they did. We would have died had they not protected us from those hunters."

Eldry hangs back by the car the entire time, but eventually we head back, both of us smiling the entire time. "So," Eldry says, "how did you like the mermaids?"

"They were amazing!" I clear my throat, trying to return to some semblance of professionalism. "But they're having problems with a naga. I can send a member of my team to them to have it removed, if that's okay with you?"

"You could kill a naga?"

"Well, I've never tried. And besides, I need to continue on, making friends and getting as much help as we can. But I'm sure War or Conquest could manage it just fine."

"Yeah, sure." He smiles, gratitude filling his face. "Send any of them over. I'll make sure we let them in."

"Thank you." I bow my head.

Chapter Fifty-Four

Eldry takes us to see all kinds of communities—from mixed villages to species-specific environments, like forests, treetops, underground cave systems, and large mountainous caverns. Every community welcomes us with open arms and are curious about my male-female shifting abilities and what I am. Meeting so many people in such a short space of time is tiring, but it's magical to watch how the communities integrate and communicate and work together. There's no politics, no arguing, no 'they only get along with them and not with them', no ancient wars and social nonsense . . . They're just people making the best of their home.

"Up that mountain," Eldry says a few hours before the sun is due to set, "is cave. You'll find the phoenixes there." He switches off the engine and stares intently at me. "But listen, Magic, the phoenixes aren't here because we rescued them. They've lived here for thousands of years. This is their home. Please be respectful. We do not want to make enemies of them."

"How many of them are there?" Aki asks.

"Thousands."

"I don't know much about phoenixes," I admit. "They're rumored to have healing abilities greater than Vampire blood, though."

Eldry shrugs, not knowing the answer. "We don't see them a lot. They tend to stick to the skies. Flying Shifters avoid them, say they give them 'fuck off or die' vibes."

I turn to Aki and smiles. "Ready to meet some phoenixes?"

"Why not."

"Good luck," Eldry says as I exit the car and shut the door. "I'll wait here for you."

I gather air around us both and lift us off the ground.

"Whoa," Aki exclaims. "I forgot how weird this feels." He waves his arms around, trying to balance himself in the air.

Not that he needs to.

"I've got you. Promise." I grip his hand and squeeze. "Up we go." I shoot us up fast enough that my hair whips behind me and Aki's ears tip red.

It takes a few minutes, but we eventually reach the pinnacle and both breathe a sigh of relief, our hands still squeezing onto each other's. In front of us is a large hole in the rock side, a dark cavern hollowing it out, going farther than even my Vampire vision will allow me to see.

Aki is the first to step onto the rock's ledge, settling his feet down with trepidation, worry clear in his eyes. "It seems . . . safe."

I settle myself onto the ledge, feet just tiptoeing onto the rock. My entire body is tense, locked up and ready to spring at the first sign of danger. Something about this place scares me. Puts me on edge.

"Do you feel that magic?" Aki asks as he grips my hand again.

"Yeah." It screams danger. And it's denser than anything I've felt before—even Dea's angel form. "You should stay here."

"Not a chance."

"But you're shaking." I squeeze his hand, trying to comfort my clearly frightened brother. "You don't have to do anything that scares you."

"But you're scared too."

And he's right, of course. I am scared. "But this is my job. And I can't die."

"And you're my sister I lived without my entire life. I'll be damned if I don't stand by your side now." His brows furrow in concentration, his stance ready for anything.

He's serious.

"Okay."

And we step into the cave.

Chapter Fifty-Five

The farther we walk, the darker it gets, but I don't notice at first. Until Aki stops and groans. "I can't see a thing."

"Oh, right." I light a flame in my palm, doing my best to control it. "There we go."

"That's better."

The flame flickers off the walls, bounces around the dark, and lights up the previously shadowy space. I imagine a movie moment, where my flame flickers onto some kind of monster, and judging by Aki's stance and gaze, so does he, but there's nothing in the darkness.

Nothing yet.

The path winds a bit, but it's nothing compared to the pixie tunnels, so I manage to keep track of where we've been in my mind.

"If there are thousands of them, then why haven't we

come across any yet?" Aki asks.

"I have no idea."

Maybe this place will lead to somewhere special, like the Witches. Or maybe it'll lead to our deaths. I don't feel like regrowing limbs to bury my twin brother today. No thanks. But I keep moving forward. Keep hoping to spot a glimpse of a phoenix.

"Shhh," Aki hisses. "Do you hear that?"

Something rushing in the background pounds against my ears. Something that sounds a lot like . . .

I run, eager to see it for myself. But I stop when I reach the vertical tunnel running from the top of the mountain and down the center. And everywhere I look are thousands of bright gold birds set aflame.

"Wings."

Covering every square inch of the walls, phoenixes rest, glowing fiery reds and oranges and blues all the way up and as far down as I can see.

"Wow," Aki breathes.

"This is . . ."

In all our travels, I've never seen anything this magnificent. Nine'll freak out when he visits.

Before I can fully process everything, Aki dives off the edge, screaming, "Catch me!"

"Aki, no!" I dive after him, fear running through me. What if I don't catch him in time? "Wait!"

I push myself down the tunnel's hole quicker, using many bursts of air to increase my speed, and soon I've caught up with my idiot brother and grabbed his hand. "Are you fucking insane? Kutabare. You cunt bucket."

He snorts and laughs as I descend us the last few feet till we reach the floor. "Oh, your face was priceless!"

"What were you thinking?" My voice edges into a shriek as I grab him by the arms and yank him into me. Squeezing tight. I push him away again and look him up and down. He looks fine. A little wind-brushed, but otherwise fine. So I punch him on the arm. "What the fuck were you thinking?"

"Ouch!" He rubs his arm, flustered as he's had to take a step back. "What the hell?"

"You jump into a seamingly endless pit of phoenixes we know nothing about, and you're the one who's shocked?"

"Okay, okay." He holds his hands up in defense. "Not my finest moment. But I was excited and—"

A gust of foul-smelling wind howls over us, and the phoenixes this far down all hop off their rocks and fly up. Away. Silence follows.

Aki's eyes widen in shock, and I grab him toward me, gripping his sleeve tight. "Don't move."

There's something powerful near us, but I can't see it. Not even with my Vampire eyesight.

"What's going on?" he whispers in my ear.

"Shh!" I move in front of Aki and face the direction the power is coming from. "Don't move."

"Yeah, okay. Got it. You're great and I'm not," he mumbles.

"Seriously," I hiss between my teeth, "now is not the time."

A tumbling earthquake sound rumbles toward us, and we go still as statues. The ground shakes beneath our feet as we do our best not to completely freak out and run away. But something roots me to the spot.

Whatever is coming, I need to face it.

Out of the shadows, a clawed foot double the size of me pierces the rock in front of us, sending shards shooting in every direction. Then another lands several meters away.

I shield us with a wind barrier, the shards of rocks bouncing off it.

A snout leans toward us, entering the light, and before my judgement gets the better of me, a scream rips from my throat.

"Is that a . . ." Aki goes to ask, the words dying in his throat, "a dragon?"

Chapter Fifty-Six

Claw-tipped wings tuck onto its back, the lack of space in this mountain preventing it from flying, and its bright yellow eyes pierce my gaze, sending shivers down my spine.

"Aki, go!" I shove him farther behind me, signaling him to leave. "Leave now!"

"I'm not going anywhere." He steps up beside me and yanks two daggers off his waist, letting his death magic suffuse around them in waves of black mist. "I can help."

I smile at him, hoping it won't be the last time I get to do so for a while. Not really sure what happens to my body if it gets shredded by a dragon. "Alright, but don't die."

"Wasn't planning on it."

The dragon hovering over us roars, and the air vibrates hard enough to loosen shingle from the rock tunnel above.

With rocks raining down on us, a dragon leering over our lives, I arm myself with fireballs in each palm and spread my feet apart, keeping my balance. "You really wanna do this, dragon?"

It roars again, letting loose more shingle.

"I guess so," Aki confirms. He charges the dragon's foot, screaming the entire way.

I match him, Vampire sprinting to the other foot.

I throw the fire in my hands at the dragon's underbelly on my way, but they bounce right off. Okay. Lesson learned: dragons are impervious to fire attacks.

A deep whimper escapes its throat as it cradles its other foot underneath its body.

And Aki cheers and whoops.

"What did you do?"

"Cut off one of its claws!"

Hmm. Not a bad strategy. If it can't walk well, and it can't fly, then it can't really move to attack us.

"Keep going! Injure it until it can't move."

Aki nods, then dives into the dragon's underbelly and beneath its line of sight, dodging out of the way of its swipes and roars.

For a mortal, he's a pretty good fighter.

His death magic is doing damage, but it's not outright killing the creature. Briefly, I wonder why. Then I remember I'm being attacked by a mythical monster and shake my head. Get it together, Magic. Now is seriously not the time.

If we can just keep damaging it in small ways, we can wear it down long enough to land a serious blow.

Aki must do some damage somewhere because the beast roars and whines, rearing its head and stomping its feet to the floor.

I just manage to roll out of the way in time.

Goddess, this thing is strong. It's left indents in the floor where it stomped.

Rushing air around my body, I fly up to its head, careful to avoid its jaw, and land on its head. It tries to buck me off, but I'm careful. Gripping one of the many talons. Hard.

The dragon thrashes its head, and my body tries its best to fly off, but I hold steadfast.

I have a few knives on me, but not as many as usual. This was a diplomatic adventure, I didn't want to look dangerous. What a shit decision. Apparently, you never know when you might run into a dragon.

My knives don't even pierce its hide. "Dammit!"

"What's wrong?"

"Nothing I try is doing any damage. Its skin is too thick, and it's immune to fire."

Aki sounds out of breath, but he responds, "Use your death magic!"

That sounds like a terrible idea.

I shift form and change tactics. Maybe some of my Fae spells might be useful—when we get back, I'm going to study some more attack spells before we actually have to fight any Fae.

The dragon roars, and spittles of fire launch from its mouth.

I freeze.

So the myths are true. They can breathe fire.

Aki screams from somewhere, his voice sounding pained.

I rush to look around. "You okay?"

"Yeeaah . . ." He doesn't sound okay.

But I don't have time for that right now. He's alive. And that is some kind of miracle.

Using my magic reserves, I create some basic runes to start an entrapment spell. The incantation rushes from my lips, and I watch as a green glowing ball surrounds the dragon. I hop off and rush toward Aki, who's running away from the spell.

"How you doin'?" he asks.

"Eh."

The green glowing ball surrounds the dragon, but it rears its head and I know it's not going to hold.

"The spell isn't strong enough." I wring my hands and try to move my brain faster. C'mon, Magic, think.

Shifting into the largest bear I can think of, I wait until the dragon crashes its head into the spell and watch it crack and splinter. One more crash and it falls, crumbling to the ground.

Its eyes track its surroundings and lock onto us with a growl deep in its throat.

Before it can do any damage to us, I charge at the foot Aki injured earlier and let loose a roar of my own. I swipe at its foot, hoping to do something. But my claws barely do anything against this beast.

"Use your death magic!"

Goddess, he's right.

Sighing, I shift back to male, then back to female, and steady myself on the floor underneath the beast that is seriously ruining my . . . What day even is it? Well, it's ruining my fucking day. That's for sure.

I channel my emotions—frustration at this stupid dragon, loneliness at missing the team, and pain at Arrie wanting to just be friends. That familiar cold, achy tremble surrounds my hands, and I look down to see the same black mist I always see.

Panic trembles through me.

The mist grows, and I don't know what to do with it.

"Calm yourself!" Aki shouts from somewhere near me. "If you panic, it'll consume everything around you."

Calm. I can be calm.

I channel the usual empty calm I use when doing yoga, and the emotions numb as the mist stops roiling and sits on my arms. Ready to use.

"Now tell it what you want it to do."

Tell it what to do? So it's a living entity? Or something similar?

Eh, I'll ask Aki later.

I move out from under the dragon and face it, its maw dripping with fiery saliva and its teeth—all larger than me—glinting in what little light is filtering down the tunnel above us.

At my command, the mist moves, grows, and shapes itself around me, like a puppet in my control. It grows four legs with monstrous claws attached, two wings it pins to its back, and a monstrous set of teeth.

The dragon's eyes widen as it takes it in, and then it roars, frustrated. And then it does something weird. Unexpected. It submits. With its nose on the ground and tail wrapped around its back legs, it whines and growls. Reminding me that it might be submitting, but it isn't happy about it.

"Wow!" Aki shouts from somewhere behind me. "That was amazing!"

The mist is still surrounding me, still in its dragon form. I'm kinda afraid to put it away. But I'm growing tired.

"Yeah . . ." I cough and splutter, my body aching. "Now what?"

"Err . . ."

The dragon glows bright gold, a sun in the bottom of this

pit. Its snout shrinks on its head as its feet also shrink and its body decreases to the size of a small iguana.

I take a deep breath and let the death magic go, returning to my previous level of awesome. Though not feeling too awesome right now.

"Death wizards . . ." A small, high-pitched voice echoes. "What do you want with me?"

I look to the dragon, small and cowering on the rock floor. "Are you speaking to me?"

"To you both, as it happens." I think it sighs, but it sounds more like a balloon deflating. "Are you going to kill me?"

Kill it? "No. You're the last of your kind, aren't you?"

"Indeed."

"Then definitely not," I confirm.

"Then what on Earth are you doing down here?"

"Good question." I stare daggers at Aki. "Wanna answer that?"

He shifts on the spot as he pierces his gaze to the floor.

The dragon laughs, a high-pitched child's giggle that has me struggling to hold back my own laugh. "I see. You should have just said something."

"Would you have let us go if I did?"

"Maybe." He looks up the hole. "What are you doing here at the park in the first place, wizards?"

"Wizards?" Aki asks.

At the same time, I answer his question. "Gaining as many followers as possible for the war."

"War? What have those Demons done now?"

Aki, ever the silent partner when I'm talking to a dragon— fair, to be honest—stands beside me and grabs my arm. "I'm not sure telling all our secrets to a dragon is a good idea. Who knows what side he's on." He flicks his gaze at the dragon.

"You are a he, right?"

"Yes, young wizard, I am a male dragon. If I were a female, you two would not still be standing."

"So," I ask, "female dragons are stronger than the males?"

"Yes." He walks up to us and looks up at me. "Female dragons protect egg clutches, so they have to be. We males just like to fly around and look good."

I bend down and lay my hand flat on the floor.

He walks up and settles himself on my palm. "Well, we used to."

"What happened?" Aki asks. The tremble in his voice matches the one in my heart. Whatever happened to the dragons, it's going to be awful, isn't it? "I can't imagine anything strong enough to wipe out all dragons."

"Meteor."

"Oh," we say at the same time.

"It killed many of us instantly, but many more were left in a barren world, fending for themselves as they slowly starved to death. It was not a preferable way to die."

"I'm so sorry," I say, because I am. But the smile on my face probably says otherwise. "Sorry," I say again, "I just can't believe I'm talking to an actual dragon."

Aki points a thumb at me. "If you understood how many dragon books Magic here reads, you'll understand how much of a miracle it is they're not jumping up and down in squealing delight."

"As if you're not equally amazed!" I shift into my male form and smile at the dragon in my palm, who's looking at me like I'm amazing. "I have a shirt pocket in this form." I offer the small dragon my pocket and explain, "This way, other people won't know you exist."

"Ah. Yes. That is probably for the best." He looks to me

with a question in his gaze. "Am I coming with you?"

I wave a hand around the cave. "Unless you'd like to continue living here, where you can't even fly?"

"Not particularly, no."

"Then you may come with us to our realm, and you can fly, make a home somewhere, and be free."

"Realm?" he asks from my pocket.

"It's . . . separate from Earth."

"How?"

I look to Aki, who shrugs. "I have no idea. But Nine might be able to answer your question. Actually, he's going to completely freak out when he meets you."

"Who is . . . Nine?"

Aki laughs. "Her boyfriend. Well, one of them?"

"Ah, so humans take multiple partners. I see."

"Well," I say. "Umm . . . Sometimes."

"My twin here is a little special," Aki says, and he shoots me a look I instantly want to wipe off his face.

"Yeah, well, you try bringing peace to this world. See how many boyfriends you need then."

Aki holds a finger up. "Let's not forget the girlfriend."

"Girlfriend?" the dragon asks. "That does not make sense to me."

"Well, love doesn't always make sense. You love who you love, you know." I shrug, trying to brush it off.

"I sense I have upset you in some way. I apologize. I have not seen humans in hundreds of years. But you are right. Whom we fall in love with is of little consequence. So long as they make you happy."

Chapter Fifty-Seven

SC vs Horsemen: Are We Safe?

Eldry waits for us at the bottom of the mountain, and on our way down, the dragon—named Lo—tells us the phoenixes protect him. They usually don't let people travel down the hole, but they must have sensed something important or valuable in us and let us pass. We inform him about the park's current use, and it seems to please him.

"You are still alive, I see," Eldry says.

Lo flies out of my pocket and faces Eldry. "You are the leader of this . . . community?"

"Err . . ." To Eldry's credit, he composes himself pretty quickly and smiles. "I am one of three of us, yes. But we're a population-run community here. My mother, brother, and I just make sure everyone's needs and desires are met and run our outreach program."

"Outreach program?"

"They help lost and wayward supernaturals," Aki answers. "It's soooo cool."

Eldry smiles at him. "I'm glad you think so. Come on, we should get back. Mama's making a feast to see you off."

"Or celebrating that we're leaving," I mumble.

Eldry just looks at me with a smile in his eyes, suggesting I may be right.

Back at the entrance village, and after Reetus and Wendy have gotten over the shock of dragons existing and have asked their million and one questions to the poor dragon, we settle down and eat great food. Even Lo eats some steaks and char-grilled fish.

"So," Aki looks to me, "I made a list of all the residents' requests that we may be able to help with. I figured Connie would be the best person to send it to?"

I nod, shock filtering through me. "Err . . . Yeah."

"Cool." He fiddles with with some buttons on his datachip's screen. "All done."

Wendy frowns at Aki, and I realize that we probably should have cleared that first. I clear my throat and prepare for a verbal bashing. "Err . . . Lots of your residents are having problems you and they don't seem to be able to fix. Like the naga issue with the mermaids? So I sent a list to our team's manager, and she'll designate some of our time to helping your residents."

Wendy looks at us, calculating, before she forces a smile. "It pains me to know there are things we can't do for our people, but it pleases me that we have help."

I think that was a thank you?

"I still can't believe we've lived near a dragon this whole time and didn't know it," Reetus says. "Bloody crazy."

"Yes, well," Lo says, "I was trying to stay hidden."

"Is there a reason for that?" I ask, curiosity getting the better of me.

Lo crawls across the table and settles against my hand. "Humans have not been kind to the few of us who survived the meteor. I thought it best to hide for a while. But I fear time may have gotten the best of me." He stretches and flicks his tail into my palm. "I did not know quite how long had passed." His eyes slowly close as he yawns and falls peacefully asleep.

"We're taking him with us, don't worry."

Wendy blinks in surprise but looks secretly relieved.

"Even if he doesn't help us, he deserves freedom. He can have that on Sheruta. Hopefully."

"Hopefully?" Aki asks.

"Well, I've never brought a dragon home before. I don't really know what the residents will think. But they're usually kind people who like to provide homes to the magical." I look up at our hosts. "A bit like you guys, actually."

"We'll let any of the Horsemen through our border, but if they make trouble, I'll kick 'em out!" Wendy exclaims, fist in the air.

"They'll be respectful." I hope. "Oh, I forgot to ask a question. Where does your magical barrier come from? Who made it? What it is?"

Eldry looks at me with a curious smile. "I was waiting for you to ask that." He clears his throat and stands. "Follow me."

He leads me and Aki outside to a pillar that stands in the center of the village. "There are four of these at different locations around the park."

I run my hands along the wood, around the outlines of the runes etched into the surface, and smile. "Is this full of everyone's magical essence?"

"Yup." His arms across his chest, he smirks some more. "Everyone who agrees to live here has to agree to mark their magical signature on all four of them before settling. Then a Fae spell takes those and uses them to create the barrier."

"But I didn't detect a Fae spell?"

Aki looks like he doesn't even know what we're talking about, but he listens and smiles, anyway.

"It's hidden in a unique type of magic created by one of our founders. They were a special type of Witch using some kind of Angel magic."

Aki snaps his attention to me. "You don't think?"

"Maybe. Not sure I'd know it if I felt it."

Eldry looks puzzled. "What's going on?"

Aki raises one of his blades and activates his death magic. "This kind of magic?"

Eldry takes an instinctive step back. "Yeah, that's the one." His eyes widen as he looks at us both. "How can you . . . .?"

Aki looks to me and nods, and then I turn to face Eldry. "Because we were born Angel-descended Witches. Just like our parents." I shrug, not really sure what this means. "If you ever need to fix the barrier for whatever reason, at least you know who to call."

Aki and I find that funny, but Eldry seems stunned. Rooted to the spot. "This isn't . . . possible. They all died out. I . . . ."

Aki looks to the floor, a longing on his face I don't often see. "Our parents died when we were four. Hunters."

Eldry's face screws up in anger, and he spits on the floor. "Nasty people."

Aki agrees, but I take a step back, not knowing what to say or what part of the conversation to glob onto. How do you tell your brother you worked for the organization that killed your parents? I have to tell him.

But maybe not right now.

"We should probably get going," I say, breaking up their hate-fest. "It's late, and we have plans to make."

Eldry nods and shakes Aki's hand. "It was nice to meet you. I'll send you any sign-ups we have."

"Thank you. It's been a pleasure meeting you and your people. You have a wonderful community." I bow low and then grab my teleporting crystal and freeze. "Wait. Can I teleport with a dragon?"

Aki raises his brows at me. "He's tiny. It'll be fine."

"Just because he's shrunk his size doesn't mean his power has also shrunk. He's still the monster we fought."

"Maybe take him through the main portal?"

"I don't want to turn the last dragon into magical ether particles, so yeah, the main portal it is. And we'll have to fly there." I whine, bitch, and moan, but in the end, I know it's for the best.

"Well," Eldry pipes in, "we have a jet you can use."

"Good. Because I don't know how to get a dragon through customs."

Chapter Fifty-Eight

Is Immortality Possible for Regular Mortals?

Placing Lo on one of the wooden seats in our Colorado portal, I cross my fingers and hope I'm not about to kill him.

"You should learn to relax, Magic," Lo says, smiling with all his teeth out. He's currently the size of a small dog, and the grin looks somewhat creepy. "You might give yourself a . . . What are they called? Those wars of the heart?"

"A heart attack?" Aki suggest.

"Yes! A heart attack."

I sigh. "I'm immortal, Lo. I can't die from a heart attack.

"Well, then maybe your heart could just spasm forever. I hear they are quite painful." He curls up on the chair and rests his head on his front claws. "Please activate the portal."

I relax into my seat, watch Aki do the same, and have one last second to panic before the whirling and hurling begins. When it stops and we're safely in Sheruta, I try my best not to vomit everywhere.

"For an all-powerful immortal being, who can add dragon tamer to their list, you have quite the weak constitution," Lo comments.

"Are you going to point out all my flaws or just the ones you find personally amusing?"

"All right, all right. Do not get your underthings knotted."

Aki snickers. "That would be panties in a twist."

"Oh, pfft." The dragon hops off the chair, walks toward me, and shrinks. "You humans have such a complicated language."

"This is just one of those languages, too," Aki informs. "Humans have a total of 6,500 languages across the globe."

Lo hops into my hand, and I tuck him into my breast pocket. "How on earth do you all communicate?"

"Badly." I pat my pocket and smirk. Nine is gonna freak. "Now hold still, I want to impress my boyfriend with our new pet dragon."

A heat envelops my nipple, and I look down to see my breast pocket on fire and a hole in my shirt.

"I am not tame enough to be a pet," Lo scowls, that high-pitched voice contradicting his powerful nature. "Do not suggest so again. You are my friend."

"Okay, okay." I hold my hands up in defense. "I want to impress my boyfriend with my new dragon friend."

"Better."

I transfer him to my trouser pocket and stalk as quickly as I can through town. I do not want to lose my trousers in public. And my female form is wearing a stupid long top and leggings so has no pockets to hide my new friend in.

Aki struggles to keep up, but he manages.

As I get within headshot, I mentally yell, Hey, Nine. Can

you bring everyone out to the garden if they're in? I have a surpriiiiiise. Don't peek!

Hey Sweetie. If you don't want me to peek, then shut me out or think of different things.

Dea's massive cock.

Dea's massive cock.

Dea's massive cock.

Dea's massive cock.

I keep repeating that in my head, filling my mind with the rather pleasant image, as I get us into a large clearing in the garden and let Lo out.

He settles amongst the grass, almost invisible to the average eye.

The team rush out, all standing in a line before me.

"Wait right there!" I step in front of Lo and smile. "I present to you the last dragon!" I gesture behind me, where Lo is increasing his size and returning to normal.

The team stares at Lo with varying degrees of shock, but Nine is by far the most surprised.

"Wait a second . . . Dragons are real?"

"Yes," Lo says, his deep, booming voice penetrating the air. "We are indeed real."

Connie steps forward, inching toward Lo. "But you're the last of your kind?"

"I am not certain, but I have not seen another dragon in hundreds of years."

"So, Nine asks, "you live forever? Or are you just really old?"

Lo puffs smoke out of his snout and snarls. "Since dragons do not age, we cannot be what you humans refer to as old. But we do indeed live until someone or something kills us."

"So, you're born this size," Nine asks.

"We are born in our smaller forms, but we can shift to this size straight away. We also do not mature with age. We learn things as we go, but we can speak, fly, and converse from birth."

"Wow." Nine's jaw is still open, the shock still registered on his face. "You're free to make a home here on Sheruta wherever you like. If you'd like to see a map, I can show you where other species are."

"That would be most appreciated, thank you."

"My name is Famine."

"Ah. One of Magic's boyfriends."

My face heats slightly, but the team just look at me with adoration on their faces. Even Arrie.

"Where, then, is this girlfriend you spoke of?" Lo asks.

Connie giggles. "That would be me." She raises her hands. "We're all a little new in this relationship, so it's strange hearing someone talk about me being Magic's girlfriend."

"So you two"—his head shifts to Dea and Arrie—"must be her other boyfriends, then. It is nice to meet you."

"Oh, err . . ." I try to get Lo's attention. "Just Dea." I point to my sexy angel. "Arrie and I are . . . just friends." My voice comes out as a pained whisper, even though I try to make it sound normal and strong. Damn it. I don't want to look weak in front of him.

Lo shrinks to the size of a donkey and looks me in the eye. "Why would that be? Would it not be easier to romantically involved with the entire team?"

Arrie turns and walks away, clearly not wanting to deal with this conversation.

Connie rests a gentle hand on my shoulder. "It's complicated. How about I show you around our house and unload all the gossip?"

Lo shrinks further, fitting into the palm of Connie's hand. "I would like that."

"Con," Nine says, "if you bring him into Dea's study when you're done, I'll have an updated map for you both to look at."

"Kay." And they're off, making fast friends as usual.

"Guess that leaves you two to update me, huh?"

"Actually," Nine interrupts, "that leaves Dea. I need to do that map, and I'm in the middle of analyzing the trial data." The bags under his eyes suddenly look darker, and his tired skin and droopy eyes reminds me that he's been pushing himself.

"Okay." I wrap my arms around his waist and pull him to me. "But I want a cuddle later."

"Consider it a promise." He leans up and kisses me before kissing Dea on the cheek and returning to his nerd hole.

"Just us, then?" I look at Aki and Dea.

"I'm gonna chill out in your library for a bit," Aki says. "That okay?" He turns to leave without hearing my answer, the asshole. "I'll be gone by dinner, though!"

"Alright!"

Dea wraps a tight arm around my waist and smiles. "Just us, Angel."

The nickname sends shivers down my spine and forces a grin onto my face. "Perfect."

He pulls me along the beautiful garden path, and we walk in silence for a while, just soaking up each other's presence. "I will update you if you update me?"

"Deal." And so I explain about the details of the last two days, including our epic battle with a dragon and all the species we met along the way. Dea seems surprised by some but not others. For example, the team already knew mermaids exist—

they've just never gone looking for the solitary creatures. "That about sums it up."

We've reached the shinto shrine, so we walk up the hill and sit, breathing in the beauty of the fairytale gardens we call our own.

"Beautiful, is it not?" Dea's eyes are closed as he breathes deeply. "But I confess, it has been lonely without you here."

"I'm sorry I had to go. Next time, maybe we can go together, like the good old days?"

Dea chuckles, his light laughter pulling my eyes to his. "I would like that." He opens them and locks gazes with me, the world fading away. "I did not know two people could come to mean so much to me. I cannot even imagine my life without you in it."

Tears prickle my eyes as I grab his hands.

He sweeps a piece of short blonde hair from my eyes and smiles. "It is okay to cry."

"I know, but I'd much rather kiss you instead."

"That I can help with." He leans in and brushes his soft lips against mine. Barely a whisper. "I love you." Before he delves his tongue past my lips and tangles it with mine, a war I will always willingly lose, and it's like I can feel his soul sighing in relief.

Passion is like a fiery red blaze beneath my skin, an itch I have to scratch, but this isn't like that. This reminds me of the ocean, lapping and rolling along the earth like it knows it belongs. It will always belong. And when it meets at the shore, those frothy tears spill over the edge because they both know they'll have to say goodbye for a while, but they'll always be there. A meeting of two suns.

And that's what kissing Dea is like in this moment. A meeting of two suns.

Breathless and unsteady, I pull back and lean on my elbows as I lie back on the stone. "I love you too."

He lies next to me and grabs my hand as we watch the clouds drift by. "The embassy is running smoothly. We are all moving supplies, gathering armies, running some extra training for those who have not fought a Fae or Vampire before. Arrie has been the busiest of us with the strategy preparations. Especially since there are five cities to defend. Each one has its own strategy given the layout of the city and location of the Vampires, et cetera."

"So he's not wallowing in self-pity anymore?"

"Not while he is kept busy, no."

"That's good."

"You are too kind for us, Angel." He rubs a thumb in circles over my hand. "He does not deserve your kindness."

"He's in pain. I'm not sure why, and I don't know how it relates to me, but I see it in his eyes. He's in burning agony and is keeping it all in."

Dea says nothing, practically confirming my theory. "Connie has been managing us and helping me with the embassy, though I think she is now going through your list of help requests from Jura Mountains Region National Park. Nine and the other scientists are all working diligently on the blood substitute, and he hopes we will have a working blood tablet by the time we have taken back New Orleans."

I shoot up. "Really?" My eyes widen in surprise as my heart beats like a drum in my chest.

"He is very good at what he does." Dea drags me back down and nestles me in his arms on the grass. "Just let me hold you." His voice rumbles halfway through, the tone changing slightly, so I know he's changed into his angel form.

Since we realized our Angel magics have mated, Dea's

been clingier, needing more hugs and reassurances; but it's not affected my relationship with the others. Huh. So much for all those possessive fated mates stories. They're apparently a load of bullshit.

"What are you thinking?" he whispers in my ear.

"That all those fated mates stories are a load of possessive bullshit."

He laughs. "It would seem so. I could never cause you pain by holding you back. The thought hurts my soul."

"Are all angels such drama queens? Glowy is insanely dramatic, too."

"I am just expressive of myself," he grumbles.

"Uh-huh. Keep telling yourself that."

"Come on. We have something for you." Dea yanks me to my feet and guides me inside the kitchen, where a giant sign hangs from the doorway: VE'S HOME!

Connie, Arrie, and Nine are all standing underneath it, smiling at me with love and adoration in their eyes—even Arrie.

"Ve?"

Nine looks at me with a smile. "It's a neopronoun. It's also a neutrally charged particle in chemistry, which I thought you'd like. You add a plus or a minus sign to make it positively or negatively charged."

"Oooooh, Nine." I wrap my arms around his neck. "Thank you so much. I love it."

"Actually, Sweetie. As much as I love taking credit and gaining boyfriend brownie points, this one was all Arrie."

Connie chuckles at my surprised face.

But when I turn to Arrie, the look of uncertain embarrassment floods me with something bubbly I'm trying my best to ignore. But I ultimately fail. I run at him and wrap my arms around his neck, bury my head into his shoulder, and whisper, "Thank you."

He wraps unsure arms around my back and hugs me close, breathing me in, letting himself have just one moment.

"C'mon, c'mon, c'mon," Connie jibes. "There's something else."

I untangle myself from Arrie and look at Connie. "What else?"

She grabs my hand and drags me down the hallway, up the stairs, and into my library, where she stops in front of a table.

Looking at that table makes me gasp. Because sat upon it is something we no one could find until now. My seal.

Aki runs around the corner. "Huh? Where's the fire? I heard running and gasping." He stops, slightly out of breath, beside me and stares at the scroll. "What's that manky old thing?"

"That," Nine says, having just joined us, "is a Horseman seal."

"And, and, and," Connie starts, "I have found the perfect place to store not just yours, but everyone's." She guides us around the corner and through a door I've not seen before. But the magic on the lock is powerful enough I might have to puzzle it out later. "I've already placed ours in here."

"I don't get it," Aki says. "What's a Horseman seal?"

I look to the team, who all nod their consent. "A Horseman seal is what binds our magic to us and keeps us alive. We couldn't find mine until now. It just never turned up with me."

Aki's eyes widen a fraction as he looks at the seal in my hands. "That . . . thing is keeping you alive?"

I nod. "If you burn it, my immortality will burn with it." I place it onto the table inside the room and lock the door, fiddling with the mechanism for a moment before I give up and promise to get to it later.

I'm tired.

Chapter Fifty-Nine

The next month is spent training with Aki, Korby, and the mean Fae lady who still won't tell me her damn name. Meanwhile, Arrie, Dea, and Connie help collaborate our allies via the embassy and give embassy positions and Sherutan homes to all the lower supes we recruited; Nine runs more tests and trials for his new blood substitute, though he refuses to let me test it, saying that it won't work for a Horseman, anyway; and Lo can't find a place that's right for him, so he stays with me in the library. With a strict 'No Fire' rule, of course.

Everything is running smoothly, but with two days before the Area 50 plans, everyone is a little tense.

"C'mon," Connie whines, "it's Christmas Eve tomorrow. We should celebrate!"

"Con," Arrie grumbles. "We're going to war in two days.

Now is not the time."

"That's why it's the perfect time. Besides, I got you all presents." Her eyes find mine at the breakfast table and beg and plead.

And goddess damn it, I cave. "Fine!" I throw my hands up in the air. "We can have Christmas Day on Christmas Eve and exchange presents. I also have bought everyone gifts, so . . ."

"You have?" Connie asks, the excitement clearly written all over her face.

"Yup."

"Eeeekkk!"

Dea smiles. "As have I."

"What?" Arrie grumbles. "No one told me we were doing gifts this year!"

"Do you not usually?" I ask the table.

Nine shakes his head. "We predate Christmas, Sweetie."

"Riiiight. Sometimes I forget how old you all are. You're all so . . . modern."

"Well," Dea says, "it would be awfully cliché of us to stay in our old tongues and attitudes. Of course we have evolved and grown over the centuries. That is normal."

"As normal as being immortal gods can be," I joke. "Sooo . . . how are we celebrating?"

"Errr . . ." Nine stumbles.

Dea looks like he might combust if he has to talk to one more person—bless him, all that talking with the embassy people while only having two hours of visibility a day.

Arrie doesn't even bother weighing in.

Connie, on the other hand, is practically vibrating in her seat. "Can I? Can I? Can I?" She bounces on her seat.

We all laugh at her. Even Lo chuckles from his seat next

to Arrie, currently curled up on the chair the size of a Terrier dog. "I have not celebrated Christmas before."

Mwuhahahaha . . . I even have a gift for the dragon.

"Ohhhh . . ." Connie squeals. "We should open it up for anyone fighting for us. Like an open invitation to have a small Christmas celebration."

Arrie looks at her, confused. "You know we have armies in the thousands, right?"

She waves her hand at him, dismissing his concern. "Most will have their own plans, anyway. I bet the only ones to turn up will be the ones without loved ones and some of the higher-ups."

"It's a nice gesture," I suggest. "We are asking a lot of these people. Some of them have stayed in the shadows for years, and they're risking exposure for us." I furrow my brows and grab Connie's hand. "But I don't have thousands of gifts."

She snickered. "I don't expect everyone to exchange gifts. Just to chill and celebrate life before we ask them all to put theirs on the line."

"I think it is a swell idea," Dea says. "But I cannot stay visible all day." He looks uncomfortably to the floor.

I side-eye Nine with a smirk.

He's going to love it.

I know.

He's going to cry in public.

Would it be the world's best gift if it didn't?

Guess not.

Maybe we can wrap it with a pack of tissues.

Nine snorts his coffee by accident, and everyone looks at him strange. "It's nothing."

"I've actually missed that," Arrie grumbles. "Watching you both have internal conversations and laughing like children."

Everyone stares at him like he's grown a second head. Arrie? Being openly emotional?

"Wow. We really are going to war."

Arrie throws a strawberry at me. "Shut up."

I deflect with a small air shield, and it flies back at him and bursts on his head.

He wipes a finger through the splat of red on his forehead while everyone laughs, but he just smiles and shrugs as he wipes it off.

"You wanna organize, Connie? Or are you busy?" I ask her.

Dea chimes in, "Do you require help?"

"Yes, no, and yes," she answers in order. "All available hands on deck!"

Arrie groans, but Dea and I smile.

"I'm leaving the rest of the production to the rest of the team. I'm needed here at the moment," Nine explains. "It's just production paperwork, government approval nonsense, and stuff to deal with. But even without government approval, we'll find a way to distribute."

"Right, because why would the SC approve something that contradicts what they're trying to do?" I mock ask, then groan. I look to Connie. "Still no word as to that last interview?"

She shakes her head. "It's been over a month now."

"I know. I'm worried."

"I bet they're waiting on the outcome of Area 50," Nine suggests. "That way they'll have more information on where countries and the humans sit."

"Or they're waiting on us," I suggest. "See what we'll do in response, not knowing we already know their plans. Or maybe they do know that we know . . ."

"Nigel did not suggest that they knew," Dea says. "I feel he would have picked up on something."

"You're probably right." I shake my head. "I just have a bad feeling about something."

Connie claps her hands. "From this point on, we are celebrating. No shop talk at Christmas." She points to Nine. "Invite anyone and everyone you want, ensure to include all ambassadors and their families, Aki, Nigel, and some of our friends from around the kingdom."

"Yes, sir." Nine salutes her.

"Dea," Connie says as she points to him next, "you're on decoration duty. Find some space in the house where we can host my great plan. Plan for a few hundred."

He nods, but he looks confused. "You have not told us of your great plan yet, Con."

"Oh, right." She clears her throat and smiles at us. "We should have a chill-out party! You know, where we all watch movies, put on some music, open presents, eat food, and just relax before the big fight."

"So, nothing high maintenance, then?" I look into Connie's bright green eyes and plead with her to say no. That her idea is low maintenance enough I can get away with wearing my pajamas.

"No," she sighs, "nothing high maintenance." She looks like that's a big disappointment to her—her forlorn eyes shooting straight to my soul.

"Maybe our next date can be something extravagant?" I offer. "Something dramatic."

"Ohhhh, I'd like that. I still have to beat those two's snorkeling date yet." She thumbs Dea and Nine, who smirk at her.

"Yeah, well, we need to beat sex on a boat and stargazing,"

Nine offers, "so I guess we can call it even."

Arrie huffs. "If you really want a good date, you should come out with me. I'd beat any of these losers." He looks at me with a smirk, then realizes he's flirting and snaps his gaze away.

I sigh, hope lingering in a whisper. "I'd like that." Friends can go out on dates, right? You know, like meeting for coffee or getting lost in a giant bookstore . . . (Yeah, keep telling yourself that applies here.)

"One of my gifts involves me making something here at the house, at the very back of the garden, near the open fields. So no one go that way when the house rumbles. No one!"

They all agree, and by the time breakfast is finished, Connie is ordering everyone around—Dea to the great ballroom, Nine to his study to contact everyone we know, Arrie to town and Earth to buy presents—but she orders me to my library with her.

"We," she says, "are going to come up with an epic plan for the whole event." She bounces in her seat on the rainbow couch she first sat on when we came in here for the very first time.

That seems so long ago now.

"Well . . ." I sit next to her and wrap a short arm around her shoulders as I try to sit taller. But I get frustrated and switch forms, utilizing my taller male form. "Do you have any ideas?"

"I figured everyone is going to want the morning to themselves, so I was hoping you could have the house do a breakfast in every room?"

"I've never tried," I admit. "But I could probably pull that off. We're asking a lot of the house over the next couple of days . . ." Let's hope she doesn't hate me as much as she hates

Connie. Apparently. Though I don't know how anyone could possibly hate Connie. "Does that mean we're preparing guest rooms today?"

"Yes. After this. And we'll drag Arrie and the house staff in to help."

"Aki and Nigel are in their apartments in town, so they might be able to help too."

"Yes!" She nestles against my side, a pad of paper and a pen in hand. "Then we'll let everyone celebrate with their own family and friends in the guest suites for a while. Besides, that gives us some morning time." She winks at me, and I instantly blush. She shoots up all of a sudden and asks, "Is he serious?"

"Huh?"

She shakes her head at me. "Nine says Arrie wants to cater Christmas dinner for all the guests."

"All of them? But that's . . . insane."

"Yeah." She sighs. "I bet he wants something to do to keep himself busy. He's not good with people."

"No shit." I roll my eyes. "But if that's what he wants, I'm sure we can lend a hand if he needs it. I can cook toast and pizza."

Connie laughs, and she smiles at me before nestling back into my side. "Okay, okay. Then we'll all gather for Christmas lunch, music, et cetera."

"Are we doing presents for the guests?"

"Maybe we can grab something last minute? Like a small gift bag from us all in their rooms to open in the morning. Not everyone will have gifts, after all." She jots everything down on paper, putting ticks next to some and circles next to others.

I leave her to her system.

"Then I figured we can all hang out and watch Christmas

movies in the cinema room. Assuming it's big enough. I won't really know until Nine's finished." She looks frustrated by that, a wrinkle in her perfect brow.

"Hey." I turn to her and smile, running a thumb through the wrinkle, straightening it out. "No need to be stressed. This is a last-minute plan, and the house is handling most of it, anyway."

She takes a breath. "I know. It's a little more work than I thought it would be." She giggles. "Like always."

Chapter Sixty

We spend all morning and afternoon doing up the guest suites—the ones we created temporarily for Aki and Nigel, but also some of the older wings we don't use anymore. Nine and Arrie both join us when they're done with their respective tasks.

"So," Nine says, "everyone wants to come. Even the Vampire King, his family, most of the Witch Coven, and some of the Shifters, including Alpha Cal."

"What?" Connie shrieks. "I didn't expect any of the bigwigs to come. That's . . . awesome."

"Nine?" I ask as I'm making a bed. "Did you invite my Fae trainer?"

"Yup." He tucks the sheet's corners in and smiles up at

me. "I knew you'd want her here. You like her, even if you won't admit it to yourself."

"She's done a great deal for me over the last couple of months. I know all kinds of attack spells, and I've even mastered water magic in my Witch form thanks to her."

He smiles at me as we put the finishing pillows on the bed.

So far, we've managed 104 rooms with the staff's help. But we're about done and ready to send them home to celebrate Christmas with their families.

We all meet up at the end of the hallway and look exhausted.

Melisandre frowns at us. "Are you sure you do not need any more help?" Her brow furrows. "We can stay if you need us?"

I chuckle. "Don't be ridiculous. Go home and enjoy the holiday." Someone should. "We're done here, anyway. Only a couple of small things left to do."

The guests are due in a few hours, come nightfall.

"Okay, Magic." She bows lightly, though she doesn't have to. "And thank you for speaking to Death about my back. He healed me up good as new." She beams at me.

My heart flutters. "It was my pleasure." I'm so glad Dea spoke to her and helped.

She grabs the dozen staff behind her and signs them out for the day, all of them with relief and smiles on their faces.

"I had no idea we had so many staff members."

Nine chuckles. "We have a lot of money, so we wanted to give back a little. So we employ as many as reasonably possible. I think we have twenty staff members in total."

"Yeah," Connie chimes in. "We even have some chefs on standby to use if we ever need to." She turns to Arrie and scowls. "Do you need them for your stupid plans tomorrow?"

He runs a hand through his hair with a grumpy smile on his face. "It's just been a while since I've been able to cook for a crowd, and I wanted to give it a shot. Sorry."

"It's far too many—"

"Connie," I interrupt, "it's okay. We can help if he needs it. But there's nothing wrong with stretching your muscles every now and then." I punch Arrie in the arm. "Besides, it might take a few weeks to regrow these gorgeous arms if he loses them."

"Pfft." He grumbles under his breath. "It's been some time since I've lost a body part in battle. I'll be fine." He smirks, his beautiful face lighting up my insides. "You should be the one worried. You've never been in battle before. Be careful not to lose your big head."

My hands clench. "I do not have a big head!" Right? (Are there any exercises to shrink one's head?) Magic, concentrate, he was just joking.

He shakes his head. "You are too easy to tease." He turns to leave and walks away, but just before he turns the corner, he turns back around and smiles. "Well, are you coming with me to help Dea, or have you all forgotten him?"

Connie, Nine, and I run after him.

The great hall is looking unrecognizable from when I was last in it—the announcement ball. Holly garlands decorate the walls, the largest Christmas tree I've ever seen sits decorated in the corner, and five rows of tables divide the center of the room. And in the corner is Dea, with his golden skin and black wings, flying at the top of the Christmas tree to put the angel on top.

I snicker.

"Yes, yes," Dea shouts from across the room, "I know it is funny."

"Funny?" Nine asks. "Bro, it's hilarious."

"Fuck off," Dea swears.

And we all fake gasp.

"Oh, bugger off if you are not going to be of use. I am exhausted."

"I'm not surprised," Connie says. "I was not expecting you to have gotten this far. How did you manage all this?"

"Well, I did most of this in my angel form so I could fly around and do things quickly." He floats to the floor and turns around.

I switch forms, lift myself into the air using air Witch magic, and fly over to him.

He wraps his arms around me tight and takes a deep breath. "You smell like cherries." He sighs.

"It's my shampoo." He smells like smoky lavender, and I inhale his scent like an addict, never getting enough of his amazing this man smells. "You smell like smoky lavender."

"Lavender?" he asks, bemusement in his voice.

"Yeah." I take another deep breath. "It's the first thing I remember smelling when I woke up here, and it's always obsessed me."

Dea stretches an arm out, and Nine enters our cuddle, squeezing himself between us and stealing all the room with a wicked grin on his face. Nothing I love more than being between you two.

I can practically hear his wink.

"You are terrible," Dea whispers.

"Alright!" Connie shouts from across the room. "Cuddle time's over. Get back to work!"

We all turn around and salute her. "Yes, sir."

She scowls and throws a plate at us. "Fuck off!"

By the time our guests start to arrive, we're drained, exhausted, and utterly defeated by Connie's drill sergeant orders. We smile at them, make friendly conversation, and show them to their rooms.

"Here." I show the seer Witch and her two husbands. "I picked a room at the top of the house with a balcony, and you're close to the forest and gardens out here, so I'm hoping it's peaceful." The room itself is also nature-based.

"This is lovely, dear. Thank you." She settles onto the couch by the window and smiles as she takes in her surroundings. "I have to ask, but why did you invite everyone over for Christmas?"

I hold my hands up in surrender. "Not my idea. Just following my girlfriend's orders."

The men chuckle as they open the luggage and start to unpack. "We know that feeling."

"We just thought it would be nice to invite all our friends and family from around the supernatural community to celebrate with us. It might be the last time some of us see each other."

Her smiles turns solemn and she nods. "You are right, young Horseman." She looks me up and down with a laugh in her throat. "Though, you look like you need to nap for the next ten days, child."

"I feel like it." I sigh. "Connie thought this plan up this morning over the breakfast table."

The men choke with gasps. "You prepared all these rooms and got everything ready in under a day?"

"Yeah, but we do have staff who helped. Though, we've sent them home for the holidays now." I watch them all settle down and chat for a bit, staying to lend a hand if needed. "Breakfast will be brought to you in the morning, and feel free to lie in, spend time together, open presents, or whatever you would like to do. The house and grounds are yours for the next few days to explore. You may come across a few locked doors, but if the rooms are open, you're free to go in. I recommend taking a stroll through the rainbow forest. Lunch will be at one pm in the great hall tomorrow. And there's a full itinerary on the boudoir there." I point to where we left printed itineraries and information about the house and grounds. "If you'll excuse me, I have more guests to greet."

They thank me and settle down for the evening.

I greet Lucien, the Vampire King, some Shifters (including Korby), some of the pixies, and a few people I've never met in person before.

Nine, Arrie, Connié, Aki, Nigel, and Lo all also greet our guests and show them to their rooms. Everyone gasps at Lo, but no one is too surprised we own a dragon. Go figure. Dea sits it out, not wanting to be more energyless after using his visibility up. But by the time we're done and everyone is settled in for the night or exploring the house and grounds, we all head to my library and plonk ourselves down on the various couches.

"That was . . ." Nine sighs.

"Exhausting," Arrie finishes for him.

"Yeah, but did you see everyone's faces?" I ask. "They all loved the invitation and being here in general. Prince Lucien even asked if there was a way to do this every year."

"Maybe once every five years," Dea suggests.

Everyone laughs.

"What did you all want to do this evening?" Connie asks. "I hear the Witches are having a bonfire in the garden and some of the Vampires are watching movies in the cinema room."

"We should probably mingle," I suggest, "spend time with our friends. Isn't that the point of Christmas?"

Arrie stands and stretches. "Well, I'm going to start some early prep for the food. Got lots of vegetables to chop."

"Maybe it'll go faster if you use your axe," I say as he leaves the room.

I tune in my Vampire hearing and listen to him laugh as he exits my bedroom. Ahhh, that laugh. I'll never tire of it.

"You two seem friendly?" Connie asks, that suggestive tone she always uses when she wants information. The gossip kind.

I shrug. "He wants to be friends. I guess that involves being friends?"

Nine sighs. "I hate this." He groans and runs a hand through his hair. "I hate knowing you both and your desires and wants and not being able to do anything about it." His chest heaves, as though talking about this is painful by this point. "Especially Arrie. I want to knock some sense into that moron."

Connie groans, too. "I know. He's being an idiot."

I don't really follow their conversation, since I don't know Arrie as well as I know the others. But maybe one day that'll change. I found some time earlier to make Arrie's Christmas present at the end of the garden, and then I covered the entrance with a bow. I hope none of our guests think to use it. I did put up a sign.

"Where's Lo?"

"I think one of the Shifters wanted to fly with him, so he's out mingling with the guests," Dea says, wrapping his arm around Nine's shoulders.

"That'll be good for him. He's going to enjoy all this company after being alone for so long." I lay my head in

Nine's lap, and Connie sits on the floor below me, her head by my belly as I stroke soft fingers through her luscious hair. "I'm glad we made more allies."

"Me too," Dea says. "It will help in the long run, but I also think it might help bring the world a little closer together."

"No shop talk," Connie says through a yawn. "I said . . . no shop talk."

"Okay, we're sorry." I run my hand back down her head and smile at her half-asleep eyes.

Chapter Sixty-One

The next morning, Connie wakes first and bounces on my bed to wake us all up.

Dea groans, Nine complains, and I just smile, realizing that the rest of my life is going to be like this. It's going to be this perfect. Full of my favorite people in the world, all making concessions for each other so we can be happy and live our lives to the fullest.

"Presents! Breakfast!" Connie shouts. "It's Christmas Eve . . . Or our Christmas Day!"

Right. Breakfast. Let's get that out of the way first.

I step out of bed, wearing pajama shorts and a vest tee, my long pink hair flying around my face as I wipe the sleep from my eyes. With one hand on the wall, leaning to keep me in place, I ask the house for breakfast to be sent to every guest room, and ours, and for it to be a nice fancy spread.

Look, I know you've been worked ragged over the last couple of days, and I'm sorry. But we're going to war tomorrow, and this might be the last day we see some of these people. Help us make it one to remember?

The house is silent for a while, and then a series of intermittent grumbles follows, echoing around the house, followed by one of our very own on a silver cart at the end of the bed.

"There. Breakfast for our 123 guests."

Nine, Dea, and Connie blink at me, shock surprising them still. "Wow," Connie says, "I didn't think the house would listen."

"Yeah," Nine says, "the house never fulfills any request that large for me."

I shrug. "She must just like me."

"Or you're just full of magic," Connie suggests.

Nine looks at her like she's grown a second head.

"What?" she asks. "Magic is the Horseman of Magic. It makes sense."

"Yeah, I just didn't think of that before." Nine scratches his head. "What's happening to me?" He gestures to me. "First Magic helps fix the Armen's Gap." Then he points to Connie. "Now Con comes up with a good theory for why the house likes Magic." He sighs. "How come I didn't think of these things?"

He looks genuinely hurt and perplexed, so I sit in front of him, wrap my arms around his middle, and squeeze. "You're overworked. And you can't be expected to do all the thinking. You're just one person."

"Yeah, yeah . . . I know." He rests his weary head on my shoulder. "I'm just a bit tired."

A heavy knock sounds on the door, and Arrie pops his head round the corner. "Can I come in?"

I nod. "Of course. It's present time!" I squeal as I pop into my wardrobe and grab everyone's gifts. "I wrapped them all ages ago, and I've never been so excited."

Arrie pops his pile down on the end of the bed, his sleep tee riding up and showing off those delicious abs. "Does everyone have theirs? Because there's a giant pile outside your door."

Dea gets out of bed and fazes, but he's back in under thirty seconds with a heaving pile of gifts that he places next to mine and Arrie's at the end of the bed. "There."

"Guess it's just us, then?" Connie asks.

Nine nods and gets out of bed. "We'll be back in a minute."

They both leave to grab their presents, leaving Dea, Arrie, and I in my bedroom alone.

"Guess we should bring the other gifts in," I say. "Wonder who they're from?" We pile the gifts around my bed and smile. "That's ridiculous."

"You have stayed in your pajamas?" Dea asks, a smirk on his face.

"Figured you all would be." Arrie sits in the rocking chair by the fire, which he starts up. "Besides, I don't really want to get dressed on Christmas Day."

"When did you finally get to bed last night?" I sit on the stool beside him, warming my hands by the growing flames. "You didn't stay up too late, did you?"

He shakes his head. "Nah. But I did manage to chop all the vegetables." My gasping surprise takes him a moment to process, but when he does, he smiles. "I am a professional chef, you know."

"Yeah, yeah, yeah . . . No need to brag."

I'm back, Nine says. He places his presents on the growing pile, which is now looking a little silly.

Connie walks in moments later, her over-the-top pile taller than her head, and wobbles through the door. "Err . . . A little help?"

Dea laughs at her but grabs some of the gifts and unburies her face so she can see where she's going. "Just how many presents did you buy Magic?"

She blushes and tries to act cool. "A few."

Arrie snorts. "It's like you emptied out a mall."

"So what if I did? My partner deserves the best!"

Arrie surrenders, hands in the air, metaphorical white flag waving above his head.

We all sit on the various chairs, couches, and comfy spaces around the room, smiles on our faces.

"It's been so long since we've done this," Connie says, wonder filling her voice. "Why did we stop?"

"Because we had no one meaningful to buy gifts for," Nine answers while looking at me. "Besides, Magic is excited for Christmas."

"Of course I am!" I clear my throat, the admission on the tip of my tongue. "I had a few friends and Nigel, but I didn't really have a close-nit family before. This is kinda a first for me."

"Well, now I feel like an asspig for not arranging something more spectacular." Connie grabs a gift from the top of the pile and hands it to Arrie. "Here, asshole."

He reads the tag on top and smirks. "You tagged it 'To The Asshole'?" He scowls at Connie, but he's wearing a smile that shows he's not being serious. The oaf. He rattles the box that's just a little bigger than his hand and frowns. Unwrapping the paper, he smiles and looks at Connie with a little bit of pride. "How did you find some of this?"

Looking over to his hands, he's holding some kind of coffee, but the label's foreign so I can't read it. "What is it?"

Arrie holds it up and explains, "About 150 years ago, there was this small brand of coffee I loved, but they went out of business after twenty years. It was a shame."

Connie shrugs, pride filling her. "A woman never shares." She smiles at Arrie. "But I did find ten more boxes on my journey. They're in my room whenever you want them. But I'm pretty sure they're the last in existence, so you know, use them wisely and all that advice shit."

"Any you wish to open first, Angel?" Dea offers the entire pile my way.

But I'm at a loss. "Err . . . Maybe whoever is the recipient of that big box over there, toward the back?"

Arrie snickers. "Big boxes do it for you, huh?"

"Shut up." I whack him on the head, but he ducks out of the way.

Dea hands me the giant box.

"Ohhh," Connie squeals. "That one's from me. It's actually part of a set of gifts." She rummages through the pile and pulls out all of the relevant gifts from the matching set. "Here."

They tower by my feet. "Connie . . . You don't think this is a little much?"

"Pssh. Don't be stupid."

Box after box, gift after gift, I unwrap all her presents and am surprised each time. She's bought me an entire wardrobe. Hundreds of items of clothes, shoes, and accessories. Both male and female. "Connie, this is . . . insane."

"I knooow!" She's wiggling in her seat, excitement

coursing through her.

"My gifts do not in any way rival this," I admit. Because they really don't.

The guys laugh, all of them looking at me with fondness—even Arrie.

Dea explains, "Everybody feels that way when receiving a gift from Con."

"Yeah," she says, "it's fine."

"If you say so."

We spend about an hour getting through random gifts from all our random friends around the world, including a bright pink dildo from Prince Lucien with a tag that says: IF THEY WON'T DO IT, THEN THIS WILL.

"I can't believe my first dildo is a gift from a Vampire Prince. One who I am not in a relationship with." A fit of giggles overcomes my good sense for a moment. "Okay, okay. I'm good." Phew. I grab my gifts for Connie and Nine off the small pile and hand them to them. "Here."

Connie rips hers open with gusto and then huffs when she has to open the unmarked box within. And when she finally gets at it, she smiles. "Hair growth serum?"

"Well," I look to the floor, "I feel kinda guilty that I had to cut your beautiful hair, so think of it as an apology. But there's more."

She dives back in and pulls out the tickets to Pour Moi, a new pop group she loves, and smiles. "I love these girls!"

"I know. I hear you listening to them when you're working."

"Yay! Now we have another date, right?"

"If that's what you want, but you can take anyone."

She nods. "Then I'll take you." She brings out the last gift, a felt box, and looks at it inquisitively. "What's this?" She opens it and gasps. "It's beautiful . . ." A silver and bronze dagger appears in her hand, carved with the goddess of Amaterasu-Ōmikami, the Japanese goddess of the sun. "I love it."

What girl doesn't love a knife as a Christmas present?

Nine, meanwhile, is opening his with more care while watching Connie open hers. He looks down and then back up at me confused. "It's a pad of paper?"

I chuckle. "It's a magical pad of paper. You talk and it writes it down in note form on the paper for you."

"That's super cool, Sweetie. Where did you find it?"

"You're kinda hard to buy for, you know. And goddess did I try to find something a little more unique. But I was struggling, so I went to a fancy tech company's website and bought a new piece of cool tech I thought you'd like." I shrug. "It's not the best gift in the world, but there are more—"

Nine flies at me, and we go sprawling onto the floor. "Thank you." There are tears in his eyes, and his cheeks can't stop smiling. "I always know what people are going to get me. This is the first time I've received a surprise gift, since you're the only person in the world who can block me out."

"Other than Aki."

"Right. Other than Aki." He sniffles and helps me to my feet. "Thank you. I love it." He opens the rest of his gifts— geeky pun t-shirts, the strongest coffee in the world, and a few other smaller things—and thanks me. "Should we give Dea's to him now?"

"Yes. Because we're going outside for Arrie's." Arrie looks at me with surprise, but I ignore him, focusing my attention on my boyfriend. I pull a small box out of my nightstand drawer and hand it carefully to Dea. "Here. It's from us both."

Dea looks at our serious faces and then back at the wrapped box. He carefully unwraps the layers of paper and flips open the box. "It is a charm bracelet . . .? It is lovely."

Nine snickers while I giggle. "No, you idiot," Nine scolds, "it's a Witch charm bracelet. Those charm beads are filled with visibility magic. You should be able to stay visible with it on for forty-eight hours."

"And we have a spare because you'll need to recharge them, so you can rotate . . ."

Tears leak down Dea's face. "How . . .? Why . . .?"

Nine smiles and grabs his hand. "Because we saw how much you were struggling. And because we love you."

"Damn it," Connie curses, "they gave the best present."

Everyone laughs, even Dea.

Connie scowls at us. "Next year, though, it's on."

"Bring it on, Conquest."

Arrie stands and grabs a gift from what's left of the pile. "Before we leave to see my outdoors gift, we should give you the rest of ours." He picks up a small box and hands it over. "Here."

He got me a gift?

I unwrap it and marvel at its beauty. In my hand sits a carved dragon statue, similar to the Fae doors all those months ago. Its wings are made of trellised roses while its body is made of vines. All carved out of some kind of rainbow wood.

"Arrie, it's beautiful." I looked up at him. "You made this?" But I thought he only did his shopping yesterday? Oh. He shopped for them yesterday, but he had a plan for me all along.

"You're welcome."

Nine and Dea hand over their gifts, and I open them, kinda giddy and excited but still in wonder over Arrie making me a gift weeks in advance. Before we even planned anything for the holiday.

The box in my hands opens, and laying inside is a book older than any I've ever seen.

"Here, Angel." Dea hands me a translational bookscreen. "This will help."

I place the screen over and wonder. DRAGON LORE: MYTHS, MAGICKS, AND MAYHEMS.

"It is the oldest book on dragon mythology and lore in existence. I bought it from a museum."

"Of course you did." I snicker. "I love it. Thank you." I'm going to need one of those fancy glass case thingies, aren't I?

Nine hands me a small gift first, soft and pliable. When I open it and look confused, Nine explains, "Unfold it."

So I unfold the piece of fabric and realize it's my very own nerd pun t-shirt. But this one says ERROR 404: GENDER NOT FOUND.

Nine's second gift is a box taller than me, but I manage to open it with a bit of spinning around and flexibility. The wooden box itself is a gift, with its intricate design of runes and other magical symbols. But when I open it, the world falls away. "Is this . . .?" My own bo staff.

Yep.

There's a large black crystal at the top, with various other multi-colored charms and crystals imbedded into the wood on the top third. In the center are runes littering the entire middle third, while the bottom third is blank except for a single rune. Fire proof.

"It should work well with your magic and shift with you. It should be flame proof and not erode after many water attacks. And the bottom third should be shiftable when you gain your Earth abilities. When you shift into an animal, it should shift with you into a small bead that should be easy to carry on this bracelet." He hands me a charm bracelet like

Dea's. "This can mold to any size and should shift with you into any animal."

"Wow." I gape at the magnificence of it. "You really thought of everything."

"I have no idea how it'll hold against your death magic, so no, not quite everything."

"We can test it later." I look to Arrie. "Ready?"

Chapter Sixty-Two

RUMORS REGARDING AN EXCLUSIVE EARLY CHRISTMAS
CELEBRATION WITH THE HORSEMEN: EVERYTHING WE KNOW

Arrie's face is priceless.

Perfect.

Gorgeous.

Damn it, I'm getting distracted again.

"You made a racetrack?" He gestures to the loops and twists of road in front of us that used to be nothing but fields.

"With a new Axterix car." I cross my arms over my chest and puff with pride. I've stumped him.

"Wow," Connie says. "The house really does love you."

"Well." I look to the floor, avoiding everyone's eyes. "Since Arrie struggles to communicate with me, I thought that maybe we'd talk more often if we were driving."

Arrie sucks in a breath. "That . . . is . . . Umm . . ."

Nine chimes in with, "Thank you. He's trying to say thank

you."

"Oh, I see." I jump at Arrie and wrap my arms around his shoulders. "You're welcome."

"Also, that is a seriously hot car," Connie says from where the car is parked. "Did you ask the house for it or actually buy it."

"I can't afford a car like that! I asked the house for it."

Arrie rests his hands on my shoulders and leans down. "I'm happy to drive you anywhere, Magic. Anytime."

Suddenly, a dragon as large as our house flies over my head and lands behind me, chuffing away.

"Hi, Lo." I pet his knee (which is as high as I can reach when he's this size) and smile. "Happy Christmas!"

Lo shrinks to the size of a large Labrador and growls in jest. "Happy Christmas."

"I have your gift for you in my room, if you want it?"

"You bought me a gift?" he asks, surprise lacing his voice.

"Of course we bought you gifts." Connie rubs her knuckles along his head. "You're our friend, aren't you?"

"Well, yes, but—"

"So then we bought you gifts."

"But I did not purchase such gifts for you to experience."

I chuckle and shake my head. "You don't give a gift in order to receive one. And besides, we knew you didn't. You can't exactly wander to Earth and buy one."

Sheruta has grown used to a flying dragon, and some have even been brave enough to come close when he lands somewhere public, but Lo still hasn't met any of the residents. He's a little wary.

"Arrie? Do you not have a hundred people to feed in a few hours?"

His face drops, his eyes widening in the closest to fear I've ever seen. "Shit, shit, shit!" He sprints off to the kitchen and leaves us be. "Happy Christmas!"

"I guess we should go and see our friends, then?" Dea asks, a hand on my shoulder.

"Yes. I have more presents to gift people." I grab Connie's hand, and Dea grabs Nine's, and with Lo beside us, we travel around the house and greet everyone, wish them a Happy Christmas, and provide some of our closest friends with gifts, such as my Fae trainer, Korby, and Prince Lucien.

Our last stop are the rooms Aki and Nigel are staying in for the night. I'm more than a little nervous about gifting my brother a Christmas present for the first time.

You'll be fine, I promise. If it makes you feel better, he's just as nervous.

Will he like my gift?

Yes, of course.

Good. Then I'll be okay.

I knock on the door and shout, "Happy Christmas!"

"Just a minute!" Aki shouts back. He shuffles around a second, and there's another voice in the room that he tells to be quiet, before he answers the door a crack. "Can you wait for me in Nigel's room down the hall?"

I try to be embarrassed for him, but I'm not. It's hilarious. "Sure. I'll just go visit our godfather while you finish with your Christmas hookup," I snicker.

"Says the person with three partners." He shuts the door and then laughs from beyond, probably forgetting about my Vampire hearing.

"C'mon." Connie drags us down the hall a little ways to Nigel's room. "Let's wait for him here."

"Happy Christmas!"

Nigel answers the door, his hair mussed, a pair of pajamas

on, and sleep in his eyes.

"Sorry we woke you. We can come back later." I turn to leave, but Nigel grabs my arm and yanks me inside.

"Don't be silly, kid. I just drunk a little too much alcohol at the bonfire last night. Even for a Shifter."

Connie and Nine snicker as we all lounge in the sitting area.

"Where's Aki?" he asks.

Connie and Nine snicker some more.

"Indisposed," Dea explains.

Nigel rolls his eyes. "Was it that Demon he was with last night?"

"Demon?" I ask. "The same Demon from before?"

"They seemed to know each other."

"D'you think it's gonna be serious?" The idea of Aki with a Demon chills me slightly. Who knows the kind of trickery they'll pull over him.

Nigel shrugs. "Never seen him with a boyfriend before, but who knows."

"Wait," Nine says, "never?"

Nigel shakes his head, no. And smiles. "He's always been a bit private. It must be genetic because I had the same problem with you." His gaze sears me. "But you seem to have grown into yourself now you're immortal."

I offer Nigel my gift. "Here. I bought this for you."

"You got me a gift?" Surprise leeches from his eyes, those swirling grays a mixture of emotions I struggle to read. "You didn't need to do that." He pets Lo on the head, who, as I've learned, is more than content to watch and listen and learn.

"You're my godfather, I wanted to get you a gift."

He smiles as he pulls me into a hug. "As it turns out, I got you and Aki gifts too."

Ohhh . . . He did?

The door flings open and Aki stumbles through, still rushing to do up his shirt buttons. "I'm here. I'm here." He shoots me an embarrassed look. "Sorry."

"Don't be. You're allowed to enjoy yourself." I gesture to the empty seat next to us. "Come. Sit. Nigel is about to give us gifts."

"Oooooo." He laughs and rushes into the brown leather lounge chair. "What'd he get us?"

"No clue."

Nigel's booming laughter fills the room while Nine, Connie, and Dea watch with endearment filling their eyes. "Well, if you kids would sit still for five minutes, I might get around to giving them to you."

We all break into a fit of giggles, Aki and I lapping up the father-like attention like a pair of starved cats. We settle into our seats further and zip our lips.

"That's better." He reaches to the armoire beside the bed and grabs the two wrapped presents resting on top. "It's not much, but I hope it'll . . . help." His eyes turn serious, his lips in a straight line, and his gaze piercing ours in equal measure.

Aki and I grab the gifts from his hands—one each—and slowly tear into them as tension fills the air.

As I pull the last of the paper away, my eyes fall onto a picture frame that has tears brimming in my eyes and Aki's mouth falling open. "Is this . . .?"

"From the day you were both born," Nigel confirms. "I thought you both might like to have a copy."

The photo in the picture shows a young Mom and Dad sitting on a white hospital bed, smiling like their world wasn't about to fall from under them. Aki and I are wrapped in bundles in their arms, both of us crying.

"I'm sorry it's not much, but—"

I rugby tackle Nigel to the bed and wrap my arms around his neck, sobs leaving me. "It's perfect." I sniff, trying to not look too ridiculous. "Thank you."

Aki helps Nigel up, and they embrace, whispering words I ignore and tune out, giving them their moment.

Instead, I turn to my team and smile.

Connie pats her legs, asking me to sit on her lap, and I do so, letting her wrap her soft, strong arms around me and bury her nose in my hair. "Seems Nigel won the best gift title this year."

Nigel unwraps our gifts next, then Lo opens my chocolate coin maker and laughs, and Aki steals the show by squealing at the top of his lungs when he opens my charm bracelet gift. Now he can use all kinds of Witch magic and not be limited by only using death magic.

"C'mon," Nine says as he drags me to my feet. "We should help Arrie. He's stressing."

Connie stands and laughs. "Let's hope we have a kitchen left by the end of the day."

Chapter Sixty-Three

Tensions Rise as Hate Crimes Soar Across the Globe: Thousands Dead and more Injured

The rest of the day blows by in a breeze: we help Arrie finish the dinner, with Dea and I using our speed abilities to quicken the pace (you'd be surprised how fast you can whisk as a Vampire); we serve everything with the help of some of the other Vampires, including Prince Lucien and the king, who are more than happy to lend a hand; the Fae and air Witches move the plates up and down tables to help guests pile their plates with everything they want; and everyone gets along.

I'm just resisting the urge to pop a button when Korby smirks at me from across the table and throws a pea in my face. "Think fast!"

"Ah!" I don't manage to put up an air shield in time, and the pea lands on my forehead. "Hey!"

My Fae trainer shakes her head in disapproval and returns

to her plate.

So I flick a pea at her and snicker.

But boy do I regret that decision.

She stares daggers at me and growls low in her throat. When she picks up a roast potato with her spoon and aims it my way, she smirks.

It flies across to me, but I duck and it keeps flying, until it misses and lands on the seer's head.

"Shit," my trainer swears.

"Crap," I say.

"Fuck," Korby cusses.

We all stare at the seer, apologies on our faces, but she bursts into laughter with the rest of the table.

Relief floods through me.

It's already slightly tense with Vampires and Witches in the same room, but with them helpfully ignoring each other and generally paying no attention, everything's been running smoothly.

Arrie scowls at us from a table over, his ice blue eyes stabbing mine across the distance.

He says no food fights with his food.

Fine, okay.

Arrie turns back to the guests near him, reuniting with our divide and conquer plan for this seating arrangement.

But I might throw a piece of cake at him later. Just for the laughs. Could you imagine the look on his face?

Don't rile the beast, Sweetie.

If I wanna poke the bear, I'll goddess damn poke it. After all, it's a pretty hot bear.

Nine laughs in my head. You're on your own, then.

Pfft. Fine.

I'm still gonna throw cake at him.

It really wouldn't be Christmas without the best gift.

"So," I turn to ask my Fae trainer the question burning a hole in my brain, "you joining the fight tomorrow?"

A few heads turn our way, including Prince Lucien and the Vampire King. Seems I'm not the only one wondering if this beast of a Fae will help us. Not that she hasn't already helped us, of course, by training me.

"Yes."

She says no more on the matter, but the wide eyes and gasps that echo from those who were listening in confuse me. Why is everyone so shocked that my Fae trainer is helping?

"Who are you?"

She sighs and places her silverware onto the table in exasperation. "I thought I told you not to ask that."

"Yes, but everyone else seems to——"

Prince Lucien leans over and smirks. "C'mon, Tally, put the poor little Horseman out of her misery."

She scowls at him, baring her teeth. "Magic prefers ve or they/their. Show some respect. Ve's about to save your entire species tomorrow."

My jaw drops, shock coursing through me.

Did she just . . . defend my pronouns?

I look her way, my eyes watering and blinking hard. "I . . . Thank you." I bow my head. "Tally."

Another sigh leaves her. "Great. Now ve knows my name. Now I can't ignore you when you're pestering me."

"Pfft. As if you could ignore me in the first place."

A few whispered words leave her mouth, and the wine in my glass flows out and lands in a heap in my lap.

"Hey!"

Everyone around me snickers.

Alright. Now it's on.

The water in the pitcher shakes, vibrating on the wooden table like a rattle. Threatening.

She looks at it with genuine concern in her eye. "No . . . wait."

The water streams out in a vortex and heads toward Tally, stopping just before her eyes. I let go of my hold.

But nothing happens.

It doesn't splash.

Tally remains dry. She smirks at me. "You really think I can't deflect some water?" Her hand is raised in the air, a glowing rune on her thumb alight with magic. "I thought I trained you better than that."

"Pfft." I return to my dinner, leaving my water fight firmly in the past. Besides, Arrie is right, this food took ages to make. I don't wanna ruin it. "Fine. You win."

Hours later, the sun has set, witchlights set the room aglow, and we've moved the tables out and replaced them with sofas. Everyone lounges, chats, meets new people, and tries their best to forget about what's coming tomorrow. The armies are all ready to go, having been moved the old-fashioned way, but we're all leaving by teleporting crystal in the morning. So until then, we might as well enjoy life.

After all, some of us might not have much life left.

"So, you're really fighting with us tomorrow? Against the SC?" Aki asks Nigel, both of whom are sitting next to me. "Seriously?"

"Yup." He looks proud, finally being able to take a stand. "I sure am."

"Magic," Aki asks, "have you seen Nigel fight in his panther form? It's amazing!"

I laugh, fully aware how awesome our godfather is. "Yup.

Unfortunately so." I look to Nine, remembering his lifeless body and the hatred I have for the rogue Vampire faction. "He's pretty impressive."

Stop worrying about things we can't change. I'll be fine.

I know.

"He's huge!" Aki says, arms wide, a sloshing drink in one hand. "Like the largest pussy cat I've ever seen."

Nigel laughs, a red flush covering his cheeks. "Yeah, yeah. Alright."

Lo flies over and lands on the side table, facing Nigel. "You are a cat?"

"Yeah, a panther to be exact."

"Oh, I thought Aki was referring to one of those small cats."

Nigel scowls at Lo. "You thought I was a housecat?" Arms cross over his chest as a huff leaves his throat. "Really?"

"Well, it would be adorable."

"I am ferocious," Nigel snarls.

"Okay," I intervene, "you're all awesome. But please don't fight a dragon. Aki and I nearly died doing that once. Not really willing to repeat."

Lo turns to face me. "You cannot die."

I shrug. "Being torn into a million pieces by a dragon's talon . . . death. Don't really see the difference."

Arrie pats a large hand on my thigh. "You would come back."

I take a deep breath and look around the room.

He's right.

No matter what happens tomorrow, I'll heal. But they won't. They're risking it all for us.

Dea stands behind me, his visibility bracelet glowing faintly on his wrist, a beaming smile on his face. "Do not worry, Angel. We will make sure your loved ones stay safe."

I look to Lo, Nigel, and Aki, and concern rapids through me, my heart racing in my chest. How much protection can we give them when we'll be busy fighting an army? Not much.

"Hey," Aki says, punching my arm, "we can take care of ourselves. We don't need you." He gestures to Lo. "And don't worry about him. I doubt anyone could take out a dragon."

"While I thank you for your enthusiasm, I am not infallible. I am capable of being killed." He looks to me, warmth in his eyes. "But do not worry your pretty head over it, Magic. I doubt any modern-day army is strong enough to achieve such a feat."

"If you say so, Lo." But I can't stop my hands from clenching the edges of my sleeves. "If you say so."

Chapter Sixty-Four

The night ends too quickly. One minute I'm trying to persuade Prince Lucien to challenge his father to tippy cup, the next I'm waking up alone in a cold room with panic racing through me.

We decided to sleep alone last night so we all got as good a night's sleep as possible and Arrie didn't feel left out.

A knock sounds on my door.

"Come in." I jump out of bed and head to my bathroom.

"Hey, hon," Connie says from the bathroom doorway. "How are you holding up?"

I shrug, removing my pajamas. Then I shift into my male form and remove yesterday's clothes. "I'm okay, I guess. Just a bit nervous."

She snorts her disbelief. "Yeah, right. A bit?" She walks up to me and wraps her arms around my neck. "You're terrified, and you're wondering if we'll all make it out alive." She lays the gentlest kiss upon my lips as a hand rakes through my hair. A promise of more to come. "It's okay to be scared. War is scary. But we'll be fine. And by the end of the next few days, the Vampire cities will be protected and they'll have New Orleans back."

Her confidence seeps through, and my panic subsides.

I'm nervous still, but I can do this.

"Now go shower and get ready. Quickly. Arrie is like a drill sergeant downstairs already."

"Ugh."

Connie giggles and leaves.

Once I've showered twice and geared up into the combat armor Nine bought for me, strapping various weapons to both forms, charms, spell beads, and runes lighting me up like a magical Christmas tree. I look ridiculous, but I'm the best protected and prepared I could ever be.

My staff leans against my nightstand, and I grab it and toss it around a bit. I had the chance to ask Nine about some of the runes and charms imbedded into it yesterday, and I'm pretty excited to put them to the test. I let go of the staff and shift into my male form, then grab it again. I practise that once or twice until I get the hang of it.

And boom, I'm good to go.

Downstairs is a veritable army of important people geared up in various armors and holding all kinds of weapons, everyone looking forlorn, wary, and like they would rather be doing anything else.

"Magic!" Aki runs at me and wraps his arms around me. "You okay?"

"Yeah, I'm just a bit—"

"Magic!" Arrie yells from across the garden. "Where have you been?" His angry face shoots straight through me, clenching in fear. "Get over here!"

"Sorry, I have to go and—"

"Now!"

I Vampire sprint to Arrie, arms crossed over my chest. "There. Happy now."

He holds a glass out to me with a twirly straw. "Drink up."

The pine wood scent of Arrie courses through me as I quickly down the glass and hand it back to him.

"Get in line."

I turn around and join Connie and the guys, all of us facing Arrie.

"Okay," he says, "now we're all here, I have a few announcements to make. First, all Vampires across the entire army have blood vials on them for healing. If you are injured then find a Vampire, or if you're a Vampire and see someone injured, please help them."

Mine are strapped to my male vest.

"Each Horseman will be in charge of a specific city's army, and they know the strategy they need to take. I will be in charge of the entire operation, and I will be leading the defense of New York. Conquest will be taking charge of Shang Hai. Magic will be taking charge of Dhaka. Death will be leading Delhi and Famine will be leading Cairo."

I already know the details of the plan for Dhaka, but Arrie didn't bother teaching us the strategy of each other's cities. We shouldn't need to know. I have Korby and a regiment of Shifters, Prince Lucien and an army of born Vampires and older turned Vampires, some pixies, Demons, and a Witch named Vicky and a small unit of Witches to use as support.

Not all of the Witches can use offensive magic, so we've used them in cities where they're needed most. But with the largest Shifter army of the entire operation, we don't need as many.

Aki is with Nine's unit while Nigel is with Dea's unit.

Arrie says I'll be less distracted this way.

Connie called dibs on the dragon.

"You know where your teams will be placed and the general strategy for your area," Arrie continues. "Follow orders, stay safe, and do your best." He looks to the Vampires in our garden and nods. "There is no plan B here. There are no plans to pull back if things go wrong. We can't fail."

The Vampire King steps forward and smiles at us. "Thank you for your assistance in this matter. We will all forever be in your debt. I know there are those of you here today who disagree with helping Vampires, and I know we have a famously awry background with Witches. But I cannot thank you enough for putting that aside." He turns serious, his eyes piercing Lucien's. "Vampires, if any of you see Prince Phillipe, kill him on sight."

A few gasps filter through the air, and Prince Lucien looks to the ground as sadness fills his eyes for a moment. Then worry and confusion. But he quickly composes himself and meets his father's steely gaze.

Tally stands to my left, silent and tense, anxiety radiating off her like a tidal wave. Her fists clench into bundles beside her, her eyes darting around the group of people like we're supposed to be her enemies.

"Hey"—I place a warming hand on her shoulder—"everything's gonna be okay." My voice is barely a whisper, but the hard edge her shoulders lose tells me she heard.

Her fists unclench, and she grabs my hand and squeezes gently. She turns to face me. "Magic, I'm actually not who—"

"Alright," Arrie says, taking back control of the tittering whispers and chattering echoing around. "We'll each be in different time zones, but the SC have planned it so that each city will be attacked during daylight hours at the exact time around the world. That means the turned Vampires under one hundred years old cannot leave their buildings. This means our plans revolve solely around defense.

"The New York team with me will need to wait until sunrise before we see any action. But the Dhaka team with Magic have the opposite problem. You'll run out of daylight within the hour. I'm uncertain how the SC will react to that. But it's likely they'll be the largest force we face today. They'll want to get it over with as quickly as possible."

So Arrie placed "greatest warrior" in charge of that area. His words, not mine. I still think it should be Arrie.

But there's no time for that now.

This is the plan. I trust Arrie's battle strategy.

I have to.

Chapter Sixty-Five

Who Will the New Vampire Heir Be?

I don't say goodbye. I don't have to. I'll see everyone I love first thing tomorrow. Prince Lucien, Korby, Verity, and I teleport to Dhaka, Prince Lucien leading the way (he's the only one who's been there before) and landing us in the center of a sordid room that smells of blood and sex.

"I apologize," Lucien cringes, "but it's one of the only places I've spent any amount of time in. I don't come here often." He leads us out of the Vampire lounge and onto the streets. "Our troops should be waiting just outside the border of the city—opposite to where we think the SC's troops will be waiting."

Nigel really came through with the info we need. He had their entire locational plans for all five cities. Mix that with the information on the thumb drive, and hey presto, you have a battle plan.

Arrie gave me strict instructions I must follow.

"Okay. We have two hours until the SC are due to attack, then one hour until we run out of daylight. Most of the Vampires in this city live in the same area, and we asked the local Vampire governors to discretely move all outlying Vampires to that location. This gives us a focal point."

"But not everyone will have followed, right?" Korby asks. "I mean, people don't like taking orders."

"Right," I confirm. "Which means we need street teams scouring Dhaka to confirm where the rest of the Vampires are to protect as many as possible." I turn to face Korby. "This is your job. Shifters can scent out Vampires from hundreds of miles away. Take the fastest few hundred and send them out in teams. When you know where one is, leave two-person teams as guards, then highlight them on the map on your datachip." That'll send the info straight to my plasmascreen. And in the next hour or so, we'll have a real-time locational map of every Vampire in the city.

Korby runs in the direction of our armies to follow orders, leaving just me and Lucien.

"What's next?" he asks.

The serious set of his face jars me into reality. "We need to move. Bring the remainder of our army to Baridhara and the surrounding areas."

He sprints at full Vampire speed in the same direction as Korby, retrieving the rest of our army. Meanwhile, I head to Baridhara, the center of Dhaka's supernatural district. The surrounding areas are also part of the supernatural district, but Arrie wants us to use a central strategy, spiraling out from the middle, therefore protecting the center as much as possible.

Plus, it's where all the city's important people are.

If I wanna get something done, I'm probably going to need them.

I sprint at full speed, getting there in ten minutes. And I'm floored by the busy beauty of this city. There are so many people, but it all seems to work in a continuous flow that has a kind of rhythmic pattern to it I can't help but admire. Like a well-oiled machine with smiling, happy cogs.

Of course, there are fewer people about on Christmas Day. Which doesn't make any sense considering the main religion here is Islam. But Nine said that Christmas is a public holiday still, with many people getting into the spirit, even if they don't follow all its religious traditions. Plus, there are Christians here in Bangladesh.

Either way, most of the city are celebrating in their own ways, with the young Vampires locked down for another—I check my plasmacreen's clock—two and a half hours.

Prince Lucien grinds to a halt on the street beside me, a little out of breath. "They're on their way."

"Okay." I bring up the defense positioning map Arrie made on the plasmascreen and start walking Lucien through who needs to go where, dividing out the Witches, Vampires, pixies, and Demons we have. "I'll need to walk Vicky through this as well. Send her my way if you see her?"

"Will do, little Horseman."

By the time Lucien has most of the army in the desired defense positions, Korby starts pinging me various locations on the map from around Dhaka, outlining where the Vampires are.

We're not sure what the SC are going to do with them, but we don't trust them not to round up the ones they can find. Especially if those Vampires can't fight back. We need to keep all of them safe.

Not a single one dies today.

Vicky runs up to me, exhaustion already setting across her features. "Magic, I've got the report for the number of enemy magic users. Over two thousand. Easy."

Shit.

A Shifter flies above me, his crow squawking before he shifts and lands next to me. "Four thousand soldiers, sir. Err . . . ma'am. Err . . ."

"Okay. Thank you." So we have four thousand soldiers heading our way, half of whom are magic users. Fae probably. We have an army of two thousand in total: 1,235 Shifters, 154 Witches, 38 Demons, 296 pixies, and 277 Vampire. I turn to face Vicky and the crow Shifter. "Shifter, go help Korby's team highlighting straggling Vampires."

He shifts and flies away, and soon he's out of sight.

I turn to Vicky and walk her through the defense positions, where we're using the Witches we have. "You're mostly defensive, so we want you in strategic positions around the perimeter of the central district. Any offensive magic users can join our teams."

She nods and turns, jogging away at a steady pace.

Looking to the sky, the sun is getting low on the horizon, so I air lift myself up, above the buildings, and sit on the highest skyscraper I can find. In a neat circle surrounding the central district is a series of glowing yellow dots marking our soldiers' positions.

Good.

Now I know where to place the barrier.

I shift into my male form and breathe in the fresh air. Okay, Magic, you can do this. I raise shaking hands and mutter a complicated incantation while drawing runes that link together to form a mini dome, and I watch as a light purple dome sparks from the floor up, growing, eeking forward, and eventually meets in the center a few meters above my head.

By this point, concerned citizens that aren't trapped by daylight have started noticing our activities, and the soldiers are doing their best to inform everyone to return to their homes and please remain cautious.

I asked Arrie if we were going to evacuate the cities, but he said that would help the SC and the Fae, not inhibit them. They want the Vampire hubs gone. So we need to protect them. However, by now the local government should have sent an update to everyone in the city with instructions to remain indoors. Good ol' datachips.

All we can do is hope we don't start a mass panic.

The dome won't stand against that many Fae, but it'll buy us some time. It won't let anyone in or out, regardless of species, other than me, so unfortunately, we can't let any Vampires who might seek a safe haven in either. Korby's on her own out there.

I hope she'll be okay.

I shift to a crow, securing my bo staff in its charm form around my wrist, and fly to the ground and land beside Lucien.

"Not long now," he huffs. "They're coming."

Shifting into man then woman, I hear what he does.

The soldiers are moving.

Chapter Sixty-Six

The Five Horsemen: Likes and Dislikes

As I stand at the edge of the dome, listening to the soldiers' feet marching this way, I wonder how the other cities are doing. I bet Arrie's still waiting for sunrise, but Connie, Nine, and Dea are probably mid-fight right now. I hope none of them get hurt. And goddess, I hope Aki and Nigel are okay. They're the most vulnerable of my loved ones. I wish they stayed home.

But Aki was right. He's a good fighter. His use of death magic is far superior to mine. The Vampires need him.

Lucien and Vicky stand on either side of me, behind the dome, both stoic and silent, trying not to drown under the tension.

Just as I'm wondering what's taking the enemy so long, the first set of feet crest the horizon, and hundreds of Fae follow, a firm line set across all their faces.

Our soldiers outside the dome tense. A few Witches call balls of flame into their hands, Vampires prepare themselves to attack with their fangs descending, and the Shifters shift into their various forms.

I step through the spell, ready to join.

The leader of the enemy's army stops the procession, a snarl on his lips. "Seems we have encountered the same problem at every city we planned to attack."

I make my way to the front of our army and stand silently. I have no interest in talking.

Clicking on his datachip, he scowls and turns to his men. "We have been ordered to take the city under our control by any means necessary." He looks back at me, words on his lips, but instead, he raises an arm, hand splayed out, and closes his fist.

A few hundred Fae charge at us, spells hurling our way, while a line of long-range attacks rain down.

I shift to my female form and produce an air shield wide enough to cover the whole army.

The magical arrows and spells bounce off.

Fae swords clash with bear claws as jaws snap necks and lightning bolts shock bodies dead.

I keep the air shield in place and hurl fire bolts at the surrounding Fae. One catches an unsuspecting Fae in the face, but the other is dodged.

A scream rips from my left, and one our Vampires falls, clutching the side of their face.

I grab her by the scruff and shove a pricked finger into her mouth. "There."

She recovers and returns to fighting.

The battle wages around us, the sounds of death and fighting overwhelming my sense. But if I shift form, my air shield will come down.

Shit.

I don't have a choice.

I shift forms and watch the shield fall.

But I shift into a falcon and shoot to the long-range spell-casters, then shift in front of them and throw a magic-disabling spell at one half while trapping the rest in a magical barrier that'll feed off the magic around it.

Ripping my staff out of its charm bracelet, I slam the base into the ground and activate one of the runes.

The long-range spellcasters howl in pain as they cripple to the ground. "What is it doing?" many of them yell. Heads thrown back, bodies twitching on the ground, I leave them a pained mess.

Crack.

My head snaps around. "Shit. My dome!"

Cracks run up the side as it splinters into a thousand pieces.

I knew it wouldn't last forever, but I thought it would buy us more time than this. Fuck. I run back through the fighting army, dodging various attacks and healing a few people along the way, and I sprint through the breaking barrier.

Lucien and Vicky meet me, alongside Verity.

"Prepare our first and second lines of defense. We can't let them cut through us."

They spin on their heels and charge to their second-in-commands, all of whom follow the same actions. A few seconds later, lines upon lines of soldiers form rings around our perimeter—ten deep.

"When the dome falls, fall back!" I order the remaining soldiers still on the frontlines. "Fall to your commanders and follow their orders."

My plasmascreen pings, and I quickly glance to see several of the lights marking our Vampires blinking out.

Shit. They're dying out there.

One large crack pierces the dome's structure, and then it all falls apart, sprinkling ether dust into the wind. The soldiers fall back. The Fae and Vampire army facing us pause while I check how many we lost.

Too many.

But they don't pause for long; instead, they charge forward, meeting our swords with theirs. Some magiguns shoot off, incapacitating any supe in its snare.

I shift into my female form and stand with my soldiers. I whip my staff around to clonk a Fae in the head, then catch another in the stomach, preventing them from hurling whatever spells they were about to throw our way.

"Thanks," one of the soldiers says.

But I don't have time to turn and face him. A Vampire rushes me, so I send a tunnel flame to burn him alive, catching the two Fae behind him, and watch all three bubble and burn alive too quickly to even allow them to scream.

Suddenly, I'm surrounded by twenty or more enemies, and they're all looking at me like I'm an ant they need to crush under their boot.

Fuck that.

Using the water charm on my staff, I create a stream large enough to drown an elephant, and I send it hurtling along their faces like a whip.

"Shit. She's strong!"

I stamp my foot and send a barrel of flames at him, then spin on my feet and shift, hurling a bursting spell at the three on my left. Shifting back, I let the rain blood land on my tongue before racing along a line of six Vampires and ripping their throats out.

The enemies fall quicker than they can attack.

There are people everywhere, littering the distance for as far as even my Vampire eyesight can see. Shit. I need to get above everyone so I can see how we're doing. A bird's eye view.

I fly up, manipulating the air around me, and look around to see—

I'm yanked back to the ground. Hard. My head bouncing on the concrete. "Fuck!" My hand comes away from my head red and wet. I get my feet under me, wobble a bit, and—

Someone knocks me to the ground, straddling my waist, and my staff gets knocked aside. Raising his fist, he swings it down, fangs blaring, with a hiss. "Die, freak!"

I buck him off, twist his body around with my legs, and pin him to the floor. Thank fuck for all that training with Arrie. "Not today." I whip my head to his neck and drain him dry, his thrashing body slowly going pliant and limp.

The air around me shifts, and soon I'm flying high above the action, taking in how many of our men and women are alive vs theirs. The first ten lines of defense have been shattered, with many of them still fighting. But the last ten lines are standing strong. No one is getting through them.

Looking in the distance, though, where the other half of their army sits, waiting.

At this rate, we won't make it through this battle alive.

I need to do something big that'll wipe out a lot of soldiers at once without hurting our own forces. But what? I've spent the last month studying tactics, Fae spells, battle strategy, mastering my bo staff and Fae magic, helping Arrie with the five-city strategy, and trying to help Connie relay all the information to our allies. But at the end of the day, it all comes down to what happens when things go wrong.

It all comes down to what happens now.

I don't want to lose all our forces just to keep one city alive and pumping—how will we keep it defended once we've won if we have no one to defend it with?

I see Lucien surrounded by eight Fae by the river, one misstep from falling in, so I swoop down to help, throwing daggers at six of their heads while throwing a fireball at the other two.

"Thanks." The relief on his face is palpable. "What do you need?"

"Have everyone turn on their yellow lights."

He looks at me quizzically but sends the command out through his datachip. "There you go." He switches his on, too.

"Good." I slip down the river bank and wade in.

"What are you doing?"

"Saving our soldiers." Treading one foot carefully above the water's surface, I lift myself up and walk across the water. "And hopefully ending this battle's first half before we lose any more lives," I mutter to myself.

I get to the center and rise into the air, hair splaying out in the wind whipping around me, my breathing ragged after all the fighting and magic usage.

I've never lifted this much water before, but I'll be goddess damned if I don't manage it now. I have an audience, after all.

Hands raised with three charms and two runes glowing on my staff, enhancing my magic, the river water rises, swirling into a tornado beneath my feet. Straining, sweating, and panting, my limbs shake as my whole body aches and groans. We'll rest after we've won this battle. Promise. But for now, I need you to work with me.

A few of the soldiers near the river stop fighting, staring in awe, some of the Witches are cheering, chanting, and clapping, and the world around me stops.

Air. I need air.

I line the streets with a strong line of air to keep the water from touching the houses, then provide an air pocket for each yellow dot to keep them safe.

With a swish of my hands, I hurl the water over the battlefield, drowning the soldiers in a tidal wave. Screams pierce the air as bodies crush against the concrete walls, drown in trapped underwater areas, or simply get washed away with the tide. After five minutes of swishing the water around a giant loop on the streets, I pull it back into the river and look back at the results.

It's a mess. I've completely destroyed the city, save for the houses that I protected—and really, that was only because they have people inside. But trees are gone, debris from the river and streets litter the concrete, roads have been upturned, parks and areas of grass have been decimated. We're probably gonna get complaints about this, aren't we?

Fuck it.

That's a problem for tomorrow's me.

Right now, we have the other half of the army in the distance and something pinging on my plasmascreen. I yank it out and watch a bunch of lights huddle together in a cluster with next to none outside of it. Korby must have consolidated them to one area, worried they couldn't keep them safe on their own. Smart bunny.

I drop to the floor to catch my breath.

Lucien runs to my side with a smile larger than the Eiffel Tower. "That was amazing!" His arms widen and encompass me into a hug, where he tries to squeeze the life right out of me. You know, assuming he could.

"Thank you. If you could please . . . let me go."

"Oh, right." He drops me. "Sorry. Got a bit carried away." He offers me his wrist. "Here, if you need it."

"Err . . . . thanks, but I'm fine." Prefer my team's blood, and I don't want that level of awkward.

"I'm good. Besides"—I shift into my male form—"I still have plenty of energy in this form."

"Good," Vicky says as she joins us, "because the other two thousand soldiers are coming our way."

Chapter Sixty-Seven

"Resume the original defense positions," I order. "I want as many tight concentric rings around this area as possible." I turn to Vicky. "Take all the Witches and go to this location." I point to where Korby is on the map. "Help them."

She nods and runs off to collect the Witches.

"Lucien!" I spin to face him. "How are the Vampires doing?"

He looks uncertain. "They're tired and hungry, Magic. And they don't understand how to win this war."

"Neither do I." I look him straight in the eyes. "But Arrie does. And I trust him."

He takes a deep breath. "Then so do I." Lucien turns to his men and barks orders, sending them in the right direction.

Arrie said this would be the best strategy for them. Splitting their army into sections to see what lies ahead and test the waters. This next battle is going to be harder. And we have fewer men, less energy, and my female form is exhausted.

Switching back to my female form, I drink a few vials of blood Arrie prepared for me earlier and perk up a little. What I really need is sleep, but that'll have to wait. For now, the blood and my staff will have to do.

I fly up to a building not too far from ground level to get a better vantage point. I don't have the experience to really fight on the floor with spellwork, it seems, so I'll do it from above. Where I can see everyone.

The army march from the east, but it seems to not be all of them, simply half of what's left. So this will be the second wave, not the final wave. Balls. Now we'll have to last another battle before finally being near the end.

Looking down to the ground, I spot a commander near me. "Hey, Commander!"

He looks up at me with a smile. "Yes, Magic?"

"They're dragging this out, hoping to tire us. There'll be more waves of enemies in the future. We need to go easy, conserve energy. So tell Lucien to hold half our forces back. For now, have them check on the houses, the human governors, and see if everyone is okay."

"Yes, Magic." He salutes and strides away.

Arrie said this might happen. He also said if we only use half our forces, then we still have the other half for later when things get tiring. I hope he's right.

A wolf Shifter runs up to my building, shifts, and shouts, "Two minutes, Magic."

"Noted."

It's the moment of calm before the storm—the break in the chaos I don't know what to do with. It's the only one I'll get. How do I best use it to my advantage?

Aha.

I fly up to the large skyscraper from earlier and repeat my barrier spell. It didn't do a lot last time, but it did stagger the enemy's forces, giving us time to weed out the long-range soldiers and frontline heavy hitters. Maybe I can repeat that.

Plus, I'll be able to see their layout that way. It'll be naïve of me to assume that they'll use the same layout and strategy. I need to figure that out before I can adapt.

With the barrier spell forming the same purple dome from earlier, the first line of soldiers are stationed in front of it, all of them twitchy and nervous, their hearts pounding. But I'll stand with them.

I fly over to the front line, through the barrier, and land in front of them, meeting many of their gazes. "You soldiers holding up okay?"

They stand straight and salute. In silence. Like the trained soldiers they are.

"Good. Cos they're coming, and it's only half of what they've got over there. There's a good chance they could overwhelm us."

"We'll never give up!" a soldier shouts from somewhere down the procession line. "We'll die if that's what it takes."

Cheers shoot through the line of soldiers, pride lifting their frowns into smiles.

Silence hushing the air, stagnating our exhaustion and tempering our rage. We'll win. We'll win this because we have to.

Chapter Sixty-Eight

Horsemen vs Supernatural Council, Fae, and Prince Phillipe

Destruction rains around me, Vampires and Fae clashing in random flurries of fury so violent I can't make out the soldiers' uniforms well enough to tell enemy from foe. But none of it matters. This wave of enemies are stronger spellcasters. So the spells hurtling at us are causing damage—sometimes even lives.

I spin my staff and whack a Vampire over the head, then send a whip of water slashing through three Fae and a fireball barreling into five Vampires.

Shifting into my male form, I hurl a series of attack spells at anyone not in our uniform I can make out, sending each one to the ground. A few daggers later, and I'm putting my staff away and shifting into a panther.

Slashing claws across their faces is so satisfying. Better

than hurling spells. The blood teasing my nostrils, even in this form, but I ignore the urge to shift and feed and use the rage it causes to fuel my shifting. Falcon—brown bear—horse—beetle—fly—wolf. I shift in and out of various forms, letting me weave through the clashing armies and cause damage where it'll hurt the most.

A fellow soldier's moaning on the ground, not quite dead. So I shift back into man, then woman, and prick my finger and shove it into their mouth.

Once their breath is back and they've healed and recovered, I help them up and toss them back into the fray.

There's no time for conversations on the battlefield. Everything moves faster than you can follow, and your only goal is to keep alive while downing as many enemies as possible. There's no time to think about the kill, mull over the ethics. It's kill or be killed out here. And I'd like to not regrow any limbs today.

"Magic!" someone shouts from in the distance.

I spin around and notice the barrier cracking, almost depleted. "Shit."

I shift into a falcon and fly back to ready our next line of defense.

Lucien meets me, evidently having been the one to call my name earlier. "Magic, they're getting slaughtered out there."

"I know." I meet his steely gaze. "That was the plan. Take as many of them down with them."

"That's . . ." He looks at a loss for words.

"That's war, prince. Arrie gave us many strategies to use depending on the situation. This was one of them. I won't hesitate here. Everyone with us today is prepared to die if that's what it takes."

He takes a deep breath and looks at the chaos behind

what's left of the barrier. Then he looks back to his commanders and shouts, "Ready yourselves!"

The barrier finally fails against the Fae's attacks, and the next two lines of defense surge forward, joining the fray.

Lucien and I follow, Vampire sprinting to the center.

A few of the enemy at the rear stop fighting, our soldiers breaking with them, looking outwards as if confused.

"What's going on?" I storm through the crowd of soldiers, barging my way through. And when I get there, I stand stock still.

In front of me is a giant crowd of Dhaka's human population, facing with their backs to us. Because in front of them is the rest of the Fae army. And they all have arrows, guns, and spells aimed at the innocent lives bravely guarding us.

I run up to them and scream at them to run. "Please! You must leave!" They won't be safe here. They'll get hurt. Nothing will stand in the Fae's way. Whatever Prince Phillipe offered the Fae Queen, she wants it badly enough to murder entire populations, sway the SC to her side, and capture whole cities under her command. Whatever her end game is, it won't end with their deaths.

"Please! You'll get hurt!"

An elderly woman turns to face me with a smile. "We cannot stand by while you fight for us." Her accent is thick, but her English is nearly perfect.

"But this isn't your fight," I implore, trying to get her to see reason.

"They threaten the safety of our residents. Just because we are human does not mean the Vampires are not a part of us." She turns back around and walks to the front of the human crowd, arms raised in the air. A metaphorical white flag.

A Fae with a stupid orange hat on his head, white feather

poking out, steps forward, magigun trained on the old lady. "You will step aside or you will die. We are following the Supernatural Council's orders."

Gasps and cries erupt from the human population—in the mob and those watching. Seems many people are seeing the truth for the first time.

"Step aside," he repeats.

None of them move.

"Please return to your homes, where you are safe," I encourage. "We can handle it from here."

Again, none of them move.

It doesn't matter what I say, does it? They're determined to play their part. Nine was right. Humans are unpredictable.

A loud crackle shoots through the air, and the old woman falls to the floor.

For a moment, the world stands still and the crowd are silent. But it only lasts a moment. It starts with a few shouts, then an ungodly scream as a young woman rushes forward and tries to shake the old woman awake. Her screams pierce the air, rumbling through everyone's fear and contempt. Shaking the earth to quake.

The Fae ready themselves, the Vampires among them descending their fangs. They're going to attack.

Without thinking, I shift into a falcon and fly into the air, zoom to the front of the crowd, and land with a thud. Quicker than I've ever managed, I shift into my female form and instinctively create a barrier of fiery water behind me. "Not a chance."

The leader snarls, his stupid feather hat bustling in the mild wind. "You will protect them? But not your own army?"

"My trained army volunteered to help defend the Vampire population from having their homes ripped from them.

These are innocent people. They don't deserve to die by your ungodly hands."

Nothing is breaking through this barrier.

There's not a Fae spell strong enough.

Chapter Sixty-Nine

HUMAN GOVERNORS CALL FOR PEACE AS THEY'RE CAUGHT IN THE MIDDLE OF A MAGICAL WAR

The sounds of battle rage behind me while I handle the standoff in front of me. I'm not backing down.

Turning back around, I walk through my barrier and face the humans. "Please, I need you to return home."

Some of the people turn on a flickering light on their datachip—translators—and soon I'm facing dozens of flickering blue lights and eager eyes.

"I'm not willing to risk innocent casualties. I will protect this city. I promise. I wasn't there for New Orleans, but I'm here for this."

Some of them seem pacified, but none move.

"If you want to help, then record them, upload the videos, tell everyone what's happening. Tell the world the SC, the Fae, and a rogue group of Vampires are creating war. And it's humans that'll be caught in between." As fucking usual.

The group slowly dissipates, but they don't return to their houses; they stand on the sidelines, away from any fighting, all with their datachips set to record.

This could turn the tide of the war.

I remove my barrier and face the Fae in front of me. They're a thousand strong, and my army is busy dealing with the thousand or so behind me. It's me versus an army of Fae.

Great.

I open my staff from its bracelet and whack it on the ground, hard, then shoot of a few lightning spells as fast as I possibly can. Kinda want to catch them off guard.

Shifting, I hurl water at one half, fire at the other, and then fly into the air before soaring back down and tearing open a few necks.

All before they realize the fight has begun.

But when I land on the concrete, a thousand Fae shoot all kinds of spells at me, and dodging them is a bit like what I would imagine playing dodgeball with Connie and Arrie would be like. Like hide and seek in a minefield.

Block, counter, block, water shield, fire spray. Then I shift and quake the ground after cracking it with a pretty powerful group spell, and I watch a few Vampires and Fae fall through the crack. So I seal it back up.

Yup. I'm that kinda bitch today.

(Don't judge me, I'm fucking tired.)

They're edging closer, and one gets within arm's reach.

I yank the woman's hair and toss her away, drinking in those delicious screams as she hurtles into the distance.

I look around me, noticing the hundreds of enemies left for me to deal with and feeling the exhaustion burn my insides. This is taking too damn long. I shift into a fly and buzz my way above the horde of enemies, taking in the sheer ferocity we've dealt to this city.

Lucien and my army are still fighting, but no one looks overwhelmed. I can't see Korby and Vicky anywhere, and I don't have time to check my plasmascreen, so I just have to pray and hope they're okay. But below me is a writhing mass of shit I need to deal with.

In the distance, it's clear.

So this is the last of them.

Good.

I shift into my female form and call up a wave of fire, hold it as long as I can, then shift back and enhance it with Fae magic. It sprays to the ground, melting the skin of anyone it touches. I quickly put up a water barrier around the edges of the road, keeping the onlookers safe.

They gawk, they gasp, they take a step back. But they record everything like I've given them a mission they're willing to risk their lives over.

Returning my attention back, I look at what's left—the stragglers that might put up a fight. But when I lock onto the few twitching bodies, the few crawling Fae, I feel a sense of dread and guilt. I did that to them. To their entire people.

They were only following orders.

My feet touch the ground and I sigh, knowing I'll have nightmares about this for weeks. Months. Maybe years. But in the moment, the only thing I can do is help a few of the leftover bodies recover and let them go.

I bend down to deliver some blood to three people who missed most of the blast by hiding under an already dead body. "You can go."

They don't ask questions or talk shit. They run the moment they can away from this hellhole.

And I do that for every living body I come across, allowing those who are left to be unharmed. They don't need to die to accomplish my goal. Looking back at Lucien's success, we've already won.

The humans cheer, the soldiers chant, and in the distance, if I focus, I can hear Lucien barking orders over how to deal with the wounded, setting up a teleporting system back to the house, where a team are waiting to deal with injuries.

"Please," I say to the humans watching, "go home and wait for news. The city's governors should be ready to act and help as soon as possible."

A few translators blink at me, but otherwise they leave and go about their business, cheer on their faces that their city and its residents are protected.

I sprint to Lucien and meet him mid-order.

"No, we need all our functional soldiers here to protect the city. We'll need to reinforce our stance as much as possible."

The tired soldiers that are still standing groan and heave back to their positions, distaste and frustration ebbing at their frowns.

"Hey, little Horseman." He hugs me. "Guess you're not so little anymore, huh?" He looks around him with a sigh, the chaos grimacing. "Did you ever think to just take out the army yourself?"

I shrug. "Dea dismissed the idea pretty early on. He said that it wouldn't make political sense for us to just step in without uniting other supes. It would just look like we're fighting the SC or the Fae and everyone else is collateral."

"Yeah, I guess it wouldn't have gone as well." He wraps an arm around my shoulders. "Besides, we should be fighting our own wars. Thank you." He looks at me with sincerity in his blue eyes. "Seriously. We couldn't have done this without you.”

“You’re welcome.”

Wonder how the others are doing?

Connie’s probably won by now, but Arrie might take a little longer considering the SC were going to wait until sunrise. But what about Nine and Dea?

Lucien laughs at me, snapping me out of my worry. “Go.”

“What?”

“Go on. Go check on your boyfriends and girlfriend. I can handle the cleanup.”

“You sure?”

He shoves me. “Go!”

“Okay, okay. I’m going.” I turn to shift, but then I turn back around at the last minute. “You need to check on Vicky and Korby.” I hand him the plasmascreen. “This is where they are.” I then shift into my male form and grab an Earth-Earth crystal from my one of my outfit’s many pockets, then I pause. “Shit. I don’t really know the other cities.” Pretty sure I’ve been to New York before, but that’s the one location I was going to leave until last, since Arrie will need another few hours.

A soldier with blonde hair and green eyes standing near me says, “I’ve been to Cairo before, if you need a guide. Th-that’s how these crystal thingies work, right?”

I smile. “Perfect.” Grabbing him by the scruff, I drag him to me and wrap an arm around his shoulders. “Get your Earth-Earth teleporting crystal out, smash it on the ground, and think of Cairo.”

“Right.” He follows my instructions, and I make sure to smash my crystal in time with his. The next thing I know, we’re standing on a different street, in a different country, and he’s wobbling beside me. “Whooooa.”

"Here." I stabilize him a little and hand him another crystal from my pocket. "Use this to get back. Same technique."

He nods. "I'll need a minute, but you go on." He leans against a concrete wall to catch his breath. "I'll be fine."

I shift into my female form and listen for anything that sounds like a battle, but it's silent. There're no significant sounds coming from anywhere. Just general life stuff. That's weird. I fly up and over the buildings, hoping to spot something, and after flying for ten minutes at top speed, I notice a large group of people in the center of the city. None move, but there's a few bodies shouting in the middle of a large ring.

This does not look good.

I fly down and gasp. It's the team. They're all here.

I land behind them, and Connie, Dea, and Arrie all turn to me with equal looks of guilt, horror, and pity running across their faces.

"What's going on?" I ask. "Why are you all here? Where's Nine?"

Don't come any closer, Sweetie. I've got this.

Wait what?

Connie grabs me by the shoulders and meets my wandering gaze. "Did you know?"

Arrie stands next to her, a familiar scowl on his face. "Are you working with him?"

Dea fazes behind me and rips me away from them. "Of course ve's not. Look at their face!" He spins me around. "Erm . . . Something has happened. It is Aki . . . He is—"

I push him away and sprint past Arrie and Connie. "Where's Aki? Where's my brother?"

"Ahhh, there's my little sister," Aki's voice echoes my way.

I smile, walking toward it, until I notice him.

He's wearing all black, his death magic pouring from

every surface, swirling around him. A menacing smile rips across his face at the sight of me.

"Stay right there!" Nine shouts from where he's standing in front of Aki, guns raised.

"Nine, what are you doing?"

Aki laughs, a high-pitched wail that grates on my ears. "As clueless as usual." He sighs at my confused face and holds up a scroll of ancient paper I've seen before. It's a Horseman seal. "He's trying to stop me. But it's futile."

"What are you . . .? I don't understand."

Behind Aki stands a small number of Fae and Vampires, including the Fae Queen and Prince Phillipe, who smile at him with adoration. But it's Aki himself that breaks me. He's looking at me like I'm an enemy—someone he needs to crush beneath his boot.

"Oh, sister," he coos. "I've spent a long two months with you, and I'll admit, I thought it would be harder to fool you than it was. I slipped up sometimes, but you never once suspected. Not even when I forgot to steal another teleporting crystal from your stash after returning to your home to plant your seal in your library."

It can't be . . .

He couldn't . . .

Could he?

"I don't . . . understand."

"Stop!" Nine screams. "This has nothing to do with Magic."

Aki scowls at him. "It has everything to do with her! It should have been me!" He rips his gaze back to mine, tutting at the tears streaming down my face. "But you went and died around the same time. The sister I didn't know I fucking had." He laughs. "And you are . . . so weak. If I had your powers,

I wouldn't waste them on whoring myself out to the rest of the Horsemen, having panic attacks because 'oh no, poor me, I now have a penis.'" Aki wipes pretend tears away. "No! I'd use them to bring balance back to this forsaken world."

Arrie, now. Get him while he's talking.

No! I . . .

Magic, he's been running this show from day one. It's why I can't read his thoughts. It's why he went on the supe collection mission. He is holding your seal. If we don't fix this, you'll die.

But I . . .

"Did you really not see this coming?" Aki asks. "Wow, I must be more convincing than I thought. You didn't really believe all that spiel about just being yourself, did you?" He laughs at me, head thrown back. "Wow. I was just talking out of my ass."

Before I can even process what's happening, Aki brings a fireball to life using a charm on the bracelet I got him for Christmas. "Great gift, by the way. Thank you." And brings it to the parchment.

"Noooo!" Dea screams as he fazes forward and grabs the scroll right out of his hand.

Well, he nearly does.

Aki rushes back and flinches out of the way in time. "Nu-uh-uh." He smirks down at Dea's growling form. "We mustn't touch what doesn't belong to us."

"That's mine!" I scream, finally able to find my voice. "It belongs to me!"

"Well, you know what they say. Finders keepers, losers weepers." He chants the rhyme as though he stole my favorite toy, not the thing keeping me immortal. His laughs pierces the air.

Our army behind us is frozen, probably holding still on Nine's orders. But it seems they won their battle and Aki stepped into the limelight last minute.

I still can't believe it.

"Ohhhh, I wonder what the fierce Four Horsemen will do now I've got their whore's life on the line." He lights up his hand once again and raises it to the scroll.

Connie and Arrie rush in front of me, Connie with her bow and arrow, Arrie with his dual battle axes.

"Not a chance," Nine breathes through clenched teeth.

All four of them are standing in a line in front of me, protecting me with everything they have. But they can't. Not from this.

"Aki, please," I beg, "we can talk about this."

"Oh, I'm done talking to you. Listening to you whine and bitch about your perfect fucking life with your perfect harem and perfect world." He spits on the ground. "You're a terrible Horseman of the Apocalypse."

Aki raises the flame to the scroll.

Connie shoots arrow after arrow, Arrie throws a battleaxe at him, and Nine shoots, but they all bounce off the air shield he raises from his charm bracelet.

The scroll catches light, and Aki laughs as he drops it to the floor and watches it burn to nothing but ash. "Well, now all I have to do is kill you." He meets my gaze, murderous intent lingering in his eyes. "Shouldn't be too hard."

Arrie rushes me and carries me over his shoulders. "You need to leave. Now." He throws me into an alleyway with a dead-end. A defensible position. "Use your crystal to go back home."

"I . . ."

"Now!" Dea screams as he flies down from the roof.

Right. I shift forms and fumble through my pockets, looking for my crystal with shaking hands. Right.

Connie and Nine rush into the alley and stand in front of Arrie, weapons drawn.

You won't die here.

I finally manage to wrap my fingers around the right crystal and yank it out of my pocket.

But an explosion powers through the alley, and then everything slows down. Dea rushes me, eyes wide, and brushes his wings over us, as he tackles me to the ground. Silence ensues.

"Niiiiiine!" Connie screams. "Nine! Wait, no!"

Realization hits me, and I shove Dea off of me and race to the front of the alley. "Nine?"

My gorgeous red-haired Horseman of Famine is fading, his body crumbling into the wind. Dying.

"Famine!" Dea roars as he flies to him, struggling with his wings that have their feathers burnt to a crisp. "Nine . . ." The sob that leaves his throat is the last straw.

I grab Nine's face as both his arms have crumpled, leaving nothing but a limbless love of my life standing in an alleyway with shock plastered on his face. "Nine, no. You can't die." My lips slam to his, begging him to not leave.

"Nine, dammit, you ass pig. Don't you dare fucking die on me!"

But he fades and crumples until the last thing left—his lips—follow him.

I crumble to the floor, the life drained out of me, my heart pounding with a need to do something. Anything. But the only thing I can manage is a half scream, half sob that racks my body. "Niiiiine!"

The End (for now)

Author Ramblings

Breathe! Do not throw your kindle. Breathe.

I'll give you a minute.

Still there?

Good.

I'm so sorry for that cliffhanger. It just had to be done, you know? But don't worry, book four is not too far away. So you won't be waiting long.

Thank you so much for sticking with Magic's journey this far. I know ve can be a pain in the ass with the mental spiralling and not really knowing what they want, but I love that ve gets so much support from you all. That the world can be loving and understanding (despite the social media comment sections proving otherwise) really warms my heart.

This book nearly killed me to write. It took so long, and for that I apologise. I had a full mental health relapse during the process of this book (the first in my adult life), and I was genuinely concerned for a minute there. But I managed to not only pull through, but to finish writing this book and get Magic to an even better point in their life. I think there was something about knowing that ending that I just really didn't want to get to. It kept me up at night. I cried for a solid two hours after writing that last paragraph, and I swear to you all, I won't be killing off a love interest again any time soon. Holy mother of boobies, that shit is hard! I don't know how murdering authorial psychopaths do it.

Thank you all for sticking with me, for waiting so patiently, and for leaving reviews and posting about my books online. It all helps keep this series going and keep me feeling loved and blessed that I found the perfect readership for me.

Stay tuned for more Magical updates in my reader group:

Kilmari's Keep